Charlaine Harris
Presents

MALICE DOMESTIC 12:
MYSTERY MOST
HISTORICAL

D132017Ʒ

MALICE DOMESTIC ANTHOLOGY SERIES

Elizabeth Peters Presents *Malice Domestic 1*

Mary Higgins Clark Presents *Malice Domestic 2*

Nancy Pickard Presents *Malice Domestic 3*

Carolyn G. Hart Presents *Malice Domestic 4*

Phyllis A. Whitney Presents *Malice Domestic 5*

Anne Perry Presents *Malice Domestic 6*

Sharyn McCrumb Presents *Malice Domestic 7*

Margaret Maron Presents *Malice Domestic 8*

Joan Hess Presents *Malice Domestic 9*

Nevada Barr Presents *Malice Domestic 10*

Katherine Hall Page Presents *Malice Domestic 11: Murder Most Conventional*

Charlaine Harris Presents *Malice Domestic 12: Mystery Most Historical*

Charlaine Harris
Presents

MALICE DOMESTIC 12: MYSTERY MOST HISTORICAL

An Anthology

Edited by
Verena Rose, Shawn Reilly Simmons
and Rita Owen

Copyright © 2017 by Malice Domestic, Ltd.
Original stories copyrighted by their
individual authors.

Published by Wildside Press LLC
www.wildsidepress.com

Dedicated to the late
Ruth Sickafus,
who will remain forever in our hearts.

ACKNOWLEDGEMENTS

The editors would like to thank John Betancourt and Carla Coupe at Wildside Press for their constant and unwavering support to Malice Domestic and these editors. We also thank Judy Barrett of Judy Barrett Graphics, Alexandria, VA, and illustrator Deane Nettles for their delightful graphics.

Nancy Gordon in New Jersey has been generous in her unfailing dedication to the excellence of proofreading of this Anthology and Malice Domestic's annual convention materials.

The editors would also like to express their special thanks to the selection committee—Martin Edwards, Kathy Lynn Emerson, and Art Taylor. As a result of their hard work and dedication to excellence, we present for your reading enjoyment *Malice Domestic 12: Mystery Most Historical.*

TABLE OF CONTENTS

All stories are original to this Anthology

Dedication v
Acknowledgements vi

CHARLAINE HARRIS PRESENTS ix
MYSTERY MOST HISTORICAL
The Blackness Before Me, *by Mindy Quigley* 1
Honest John Finds a Way, *by Michael Dell* 13
Spirited Death, *by Carole Nelson Douglas* 23
Home Front Homicide, *by Liz Milliron* 37
The Unseen Opponent, *by P. A. De Voe* 51
The Black Hand, *by Peter W. J. Hayes* 63
The Trial of Madame Pelletier, *by Susanna Calkins* 77
Eating Crow, *by Carla Coupe* 91
Mr. Nakamura's Garden, *by Valerie O. Patterson* 103
A Butler is Born, *by Catriona McPherson* 115
Night and Fog, *by Marcia Talley* 125
The Seven, *by Elaine Viets* 135
The Lady's Maid Vanishes, *by Susan Daly* 149
You Always Hurt the One You Love, *by Shawn Reilly
    Simmons* 163
The Hand of an Angry God, *by K. B. Inglee* 167
The Cottage, *by Charles Todd* 177
The Measured Chest, *by Mark Thielman* 189
He Done Her Wrong, *by Kathryn O'Sullivan* 203
The Corpse Candle, *by Martin Edwards* 215
Death on the Dueling Grounds, *by Verena Rose* 227
The Barter, *by Su Kopil* 237
Mistress Threadneedle's Quest, *by Kathy Lynn Emerson* 249
A One-Pipe Problem, *by John Gregory Betancourt* 257
The Killing Game, *by Victoria Thompson* 269
The Tredegar Murders, *by Vivian Lawry* 283
Summons for a Dead Girl, *by K. B. Owen* 297
The Velvet Slippers, *by Keenan Powell* 311
The Tragic Death of Mrs. Edna Fogg, *by Edith Maxwell* 323
Crim Con, *by Nancy Herriman* 335
Strong Enough, *by Georgia Ruth* 349

AUTHOR BIOGRAPHIES 363

PREFACE

CHARLAINE HARRIS PRESENTS

Murder is a crime as old as Cain, and the detective who tries to find the guilty culprit is no new phenomenon. This year, the *Malice Domestic 12* anthology is chock full of death and destruction, taking place in times ranging from Puritan Massachusetts to the post-WWII era, and geographically from Buffalo to Wales, and beyond.

Though I'm not a writer who sets books in the past, I'm a reader of historical novels and short stories. Editing this anthology was one of the big pluses to the Lifetime Achievement Award. I got to read about pre-Civil War Washington, Prohibition-era Pittsburgh, mid-nineteenth century France, and turn-of-the-century Johannesburg . . . to mention only a few of the times and places in which these talented writers chose to set their stories of scheming and mayhem.

A Quaker, a con woman, a plumber, and a Chinese judge prove that detecting can be done by anyone astute enough to reason and patient enough to investigate a crime thoroughly.

And those characters, times, and locations are only a sampling of the sleuths – or victims – of these marvelous tales.

Though not every story features a detective solving a crime, there is always a crime at the center of the story. After all, that's what we enjoy.

Will the guilty be punished and the innocent go free? The best answer is, "Not always." After all, most people are guilty of *something* . . . and innocence can be a debatable state.

Enjoy these wonderful stories as much as I did. There's something to please everyone.

Charlaine Harris

MYSTERY MOST HISTORICAL

THE BLACKNESS BEFORE ME

by Mindy Quigley

*In this epistolary account, a young woman
sails to Johannesburg to act as a governess,
hoping to find the husband of her dreams. Her dream
becomes more of a nightmare . . .*

4 September 1889
My Dearest Susannah,

You cannot imagine my elation at receiving your letter when we docked at Cape Town. The familiar hand and warm words comforted me almost as much as did setting my feet firmly upon dry land for the first time in twenty-two long days. I feared more than once that the ship's name, *Waterloo*, was all too apt, and that this voyage would see my own decisive end. Indeed, from the Bay of Biscay nearly until we reached the Equatorial Crossing, our passage was dogged by uncommonly foul weather, and as roiling seas buffeted the ship, I could take nothing but a few dry biscuits and small sips of a brandy tonic Mr. Barnhill, a kind fellow passenger who hails from Timperley, provided. I know you will be wondering if Mr. B might be the "Knight in Shining Armour" I am so ardently hoping I should meet in Africa. Alas, I fear not! Mr. B is over fifty, with a set of white whiskers and a countenance that makes Prime Minister Gladstone's grim expression seem quite cheery by comparison. Moreover he, too, has come to the far reaches of the Empire to better his lot, having lost his share of a hauling business when the Bedford Colliery disaster—you will remember it, the explosion of firedamp that left so many unfortunate widows and orphans—left him nearly destitute.

I shall continue to pray most earnestly that My Good Sir Knight awaits me yet in Johannesburg, for my only hope to establish a household of my own is to make, as you have, a good match. I could not hope to find someone to equal your Mr. Hicks if I had stayed in England, as women of no fortune, no family, and unremarkable looks are in ready supply there. I haven't even any friends save you. I know you shall not like me saying so, as you, kind Susannah, are ever thinking I am fairer and cleverer than I am, but the truth of the thing is that Johannesburg, still with so very few white women compared with the number of eligible men, is my best hope. This year, I shall be thirty-one, and if I have not found a husband by then, I am sure I shall be rendered with the knackering horses and made into book binding and shoe leather!

One of my shipboard companions, Miss Pitt, a fellow governess also travelling under care of the Female Middle-Class Emigration Society, urged me to return to England at once, for, according to her, I should find only "uncivilised natives and even more uncivilised Whites" in the colonies, seeking nothing but easy riches and their own pleasure. She further stated that rumours of the abundance of prosperous gentlemen in want of wives are only that—rumours.

This was her second passage to Africa, having returned to England for three months in the company of one of her young charges who has begun school at Harrow. I admit myself somewhat shaken by Miss Pitt's admonitions. The prospect of traveling to the ends of the Empire and finding only empty promises . . . Well, I must hope that Miss Pitt's foul temper and goitre have something to do with her lack of success in finding a husband, and that my own prospects will prove better.

Post time is 4.30 pm, so I shall conclude and write more once I am settled in Jo-burg, as it is here known.

Thankful for your prayers,
Your fondest friend,
Althea Pym

***

28 December 1889
My Dearest Susannah,

Thank you for your letter and for the Christmas parcel. Fripperies like silk ribbon are so very hard to come by that one would think we were living on the face of the moon rather than in this leafy corner of Jo-burg. Strange to have such hot weather on Christmas Day, but then I suppose it is practically the height of summer here.

Work continues to consume nearly every hour of my waking day. You may recall the dire admonitions of Miss Pitt, whom I encountered on the passage. There is, I fear, some truth in her words. The city on the whole is positively raw—dusty, half-built, and some quarters full of lawless establishments selling "rotgut" liquor. On payday, the state of some of the miners—black, white, Afrikaner, mulatto, and Cape Coloured all spilling into the street like some ungodly stew—is beyond description. We must hope that over time as family life takes hold, the character of the place will become more settled.

I cleave almost entirely to Parktown, which is ruled with necessary strictness by the so-called "Randlords"—the mine owners who are even wealthier than my own employers. Parktown is quite the island of civilisation in a sea of African lawlessness.

As to the work itself, you will recall I was told I would have two small boys to look after and educate and "modest household chores." You will also recall my recounting to you the emigration agent's promise that an English governess should live like the very Queen here, with servants of her own, so much in demand are we. Alas, in that regard, he was mistaken. To the housekeeper, Mrs. Turner, "modest household chores" encompass tidying the nursery, washing and mending my own and the children's clothes, and even occasionally serving at table on the rare circumstance the Reeds should host a dinner. I have thought about complaining to Mrs. Reed, but she is so often ill that I am loathe to trouble her with tales of the housekeeper's despotism. Mr. Reed is a largely absent figure, being much involved in the business of the mine. He stays away for weeks on end and locks himself in his study when he is home with only the houseboys entering or leaving, and so is more ghost than man. Even if I could muster the courage to approach this aloof figure, Mrs. Turner would no doubt learn of it, as she seems almost Argus-like in her keen awareness of the comings and goings of the household.

Still, Masters Thom and Nathaniel are dear little puddings, and ever so affectionate. Indeed, they fuss over me so, and tell me every hour how they love me. It is all so very dear and amusing. Both have professed their desire to marry me, so I shall have my choice—the eldest of these most ardent suitors shall be seven next month. If only I could find a genuine suitor so enamoured of me!

Even despite the hard labour, I am grateful that my lot is better than poor Gussie's. Gussie is the dear little Cornish girl who came to the Reeds from the Cape a few months ago, just before my own arrival. She was hired as a chambermaid, but Mrs. Reed grew ill shortly after her arrival, and she now does the work of a nursemaid as well as a maid-of-all-work. Despite Gussie's fortitude and obvious desire to make herself useful, Mrs. Turner has been most brutal with her, treating her little better than the legion of black "houseboys," young men, really, who form the basis of the household staff. I believe I told you in my last letter of the marvelous names these boys have—Soldier, Othello, Jupiter, and... Marvel. A truly "marvelous" name! It beggars belief what names some of these boys are given. Only the other day, I encountered one serving the Van Onselens who was called Kettle.

In an English household, I would hardly speak to a

chambermaid, especially one so young and simple as dear Gussie. She will be sixteen next July, but she is really quite a child, with a freckled nose and large, round eyes—trusting as a cow's. Here we are very much thrown into each other's society, being the only white help other than Mrs. Turner. Alas, there is little chance of forming a bond with Mrs. Turner who eyes all of us—even the Reeds—as if we were muck clinging to her shoe.

Give my affection to Mr. Hicks and little Susie.

Yours in true friendship,

Althea Pym

***

27 February 1890

Dearest Susannah,

I am sorry to hear of the flooding in Yorkshire, and glad that no one was killed and that you are safe and well, despite the general hardship. I can picture your sweet ministrations to those in Mr. Hicks's congregation who have had their farms and livelihoods destroyed. Someone with your tender heart is perfectly suited to the life of a minister's wife.

I'm afraid that the news from here is no better, and is indeed worse. After months of middling but persistent illness, and despite the almost constant ministrations of various physicians, Mrs. Reed died one week ago today. Thom and Nathaniel are as forlorn as you might expect, but have soldiered on like the brave little chaps they are. I share in their grief for my pretty, delicate mistress, though Mrs. Reed has been ill nearly the whole time I've been here, so I cannot say I knew her well.

With the death of Mrs. Reed, the work seems to have multiplied, and the household is in disarray. Mr. Reed has remained ensconced in his study of late with a bottle of port and his favourite of the houseboys, Marvel, attending to his needs. Mrs. Turner stomps around issuing orders like Lord Nelson. I would admit only to you, my dearest friend, that we all despise her. Her latest draconian pronouncement is that Gussie and I must no longer be friends, and she has privately admonished me to "remember my station."

Gussie and I are determined to thwart her. Though Gussie can scarcely read and write, she and I pass notes to one another like schoolgirls with an over-strict headmistress. She draws the most amusing caricatures of Mrs. Turner as a fire-breathing dragon and the like. I hope you will not think less of me for being so childish and uncharitable. If only you could see how Mrs. Turner treats us, and how somber the character of the whole household has become, you may at least begin to understand why we afford ourselves the luxury of undertaking these small, ungenerous acts.

I will do what I know you would have me do—hold to my prayers and hope to improve my character, even if I cannot improve Mrs. Turner's.

Yours sincerely,
Althea Pym

***

5 May 1890
Rand Daily Mail

TWO CHARGED IN HOUSEKEEPER'S MURDER SCANDAL IN PARKTOWN

At the Pretoria District Police Court yesterday, before presiding Judge Mr. Arthur Bainbridge, Mguni 'Marvel' Cebekhulu, 19, houseboy, and Althea Pym, 31, governess, were remanded and charged with being concerned in causing the death of Mrs. Letitia Turner, née Runyon, 45, housekeeper of Land's End House, Jubilee Road, Parktown. The two are further accused of conspiracy to cause such death. Mr. Evans, solicitor, defended the prisoners.

Mr. O. Cobb, solicitor for the prosecution, said the capital charge with punishment of death by hanging would be preferred by the police, for whom he appeared. He summarized the circumstances of the case—the discovery of the woman's bloodied body concealed in some bedclothes upon a hand-cart, the profession of innocence made by the prisoners, the subsequent discovery of a valuable comb and brush set belonging to Mrs. Turner and other evidence in possession of Miss Pym.

The post-mortem examination showed that laudanum had been administered to the victim some time before the attack, allowing the assailants to gain access to her chamber unchallenged. Laudanum was discovered mixed into a bottle of eau de toilette in Miss Pym's room.

Several witnesses were called to testify to the circumstances of the murder and the character of the prisoners and the deceased. Miss Augusta 'Gussie' Japps, 15, housemaid, averred that she and the accused governess had been on terms of friendship, but that she was wholly ignorant of any plans to harm Mrs. Turner. She was asked to examine evidence—a series of notes from Miss Pym found in her possession—stating Miss Pym's extreme dislike for the deceased. Miss Japps, weeping piteous tears, acknowledged that these notes had been given to her by the accused prisoner and that Miss Pym had on many occasions expressed her enmity toward the deceased.

Mr. Virgil Reed, mine engineering supervisor and householder, confessed himself stunned at the betrayal by Marvel, who had been a promising servant. He further averred that Miss Pym had been recommended to him by Hull & Co. Emigration Agents, as having excellent references. He expressed his horror that these two characters were concealed in his home and that Miss Pym should have been entrusted with the care of his two young sons.

Mrs. Reginald Van Onselen, who resides in Coleridge House, abutting the rear of Land's End House, testified that she had seen through the garden windows Miss Pym and the houseboy known as Marvel closeted together in intimate conversation in the rear parlour of Land's End House for several evenings leading up to the murder.

Miss Pym pleaded with the magistrates that the incriminating possessions were gifts to her from members of the household and that she had not known their nature or origin. Miss Pym and the houseboy claimed that they were victims of an elaborate plot to cover affairs too scandalous to print herein. At four o'clock, Mr. Bainbridge and the magistrates adjourned the case until the morning.

***

28 July 1890
Eastern Star

Mr. Virgil Reed of Land's End House, Jubilee Road, Parktown, was yesterday united in marriage with Miss Augusta Japps, 16, by the Reverend Charles Wright.

***

15 February 1936
Dear Mrs. Hicks,

I hope you will forgive the unusual circumstance of my writing to you.

My brother, Mr. Nathaniel Reed, our half-sister Miss Gertrude Reed, and I recently discovered a number of letters, addressed to you but unsealed, among our deceased stepmother's personal effects. We, of course, have not read them, and are unsure what they contain, but you will note that the return addressee is the notorious murderess Althea Pym who caused such sorrow in our household. We have been quite unsure how to proceed, not wishing to cause you distress should these letters be unwelcome and not wishing to delve too deeply into how or why our stepmother became possessed of them. Our father died shortly after our sister was born, and our stepmother would have been the only living soul who could have shed light on these extraordinary matters. My brother and I came to school in England after our father's death, and have resided here since, seeing our stepmother only rarely.

We, however, learned through mutual friends that you knew Althea Pym before the utter corruption of her character, and that you and the late Reverend George Hicks were most aggrieved by her trial and subsequent execution. Therefore, we trust we made the right decision in forwarding these letters to their intended recipient, even so long after they were meant to have been sent. Burn the letters, or do what you will, as we feel it only fitting that the choice should lie with you.

Yours sincerely,
Mr. Thomas Reed, Esq.
Chichester, England

***

2 April 1890
My Dear Susannah,

Thank you for your letter. I cannot say I looked forward to my birthday with quite the same enthusiasm as your kind wishes might entreat me to. Such is the unfortunate state of affairs for an unmarried woman that each birthday is met with dread and hoped to be passed in silence! Lest you think me overly maudlin, however, I will tell you of the fuss that was made over me this year upon my birthday. I had let slip to Gussie, in a rare moment when Mrs. Turner could not observe us, that it was to be my birthday, and how I was dreading the approach of another year added to my age and another step further from my goal of marriage. Gussie kindly assured me that prosperous husbands could still be found, and that one only had to devote oneself to the work of finding one. She also made certain Masters Thom and Nathaniel made a special day of it for me, though the household is still in mourning for Mrs. Reed.

The boys gave me a bottle of eau de toillete. I assume this was on behalf of Mr. Reed, perhaps intended for Mrs. Reed before her passing, though the boys claim it came "from the fairies" who left it in their nursery with a note instructing them to give it to me! So I suppose it is the boys and "the fairies" I must thank.

Sweet little Gussie surreptitiously gave me a small ivory comb and brush set. I confessed myself quite shocked at the present, knowing well that her meagre wages could never stretch to affording such a treasure. She said that the set had been her mother's and begged that I do her the honour of accepting it, as I had been like a sister or even a mother to her. The girl is so very dear, beaming her dimpled smile and with such tears in her eyes that eventually I was prevailed upon to cease my protestations and accept the gift.

Mrs. Turner reprimanded Gussie once again about paying too much attention to Marvel. Because his grandfather was an Afrikaner, he enjoys some special privileges compared with the other blacks, and Gussie treats him almost as an equal. I am sure you observe as I do that even my friendship with Gussie speaks to the discomfiting confusion of social status one finds here in Joburg. Judge my surprise, for example, at meeting one of the principal men of business here on the Rand, and discovering he was none other than an ex-publican whose establishment I used to occasionally walk past when I worked for Lady Greene!

Such bewildering reversals of fortune, coupled with the presence of Russians, continentals of all stripes, and the ubiquitous blacks, cannot help but create disorder. Furthermore, Mrs. Turner has entreated Gussie to maintain more distance between herself and Mr. Reed. I must confess that in these particulars, and though I am loathe to admit it, I am inclined to agree with Mrs. Turner. Intermingling of whites of different classes is one thing, but it is quite another thing altogether to form unnatural friendships between the races. And with regard to Mr. Reed, who is still fresh in his grief for his dead wife, many a housemaid has met her destruction in that way. Alas, I fear Gussie is too naïve for this rough country and may not hearken to advice on any account.

I have nearly missed the post, but Gussie has offered to run this down to the gate.

Grateful for your prayers and your continuing friendship,

Althea Pym

***

8 April 1890
Dearest Susannah,

I am truly sorry to have worried you. Far from ceasing our correspondence, I have continued to write to you most faithfully and haven't the foggiest idea why my letters have not reached your hands of late. It is most distressing to think that our intimate personal correspondence has gone astray, and I will enquire at the Postmasters Office to see if something is amiss with the train or the mail boat. I am heartily glad you were able to get assurances from the emigration agent as to my well-being. If this continues, though I dread the journey, I may have to ask Mr. Reed for leave to go into town so I can send you a telegraph to reassure you that I am indeed safe and well.

I do hope this letter will reach you, as I long to tell you that I have taken on a new charge—the houseboy, Marvel. You will not credit it, but I tell you it is the truth. Mr. Reed has asked that I teach Marvel his letters and numbers and encourage him in the learning of rudimentary arithmetic. Mr. Reed believes the boy is clever and that, with some tuition, he may become more able to help with the running of the household. Mr. Reed is unnaturally fond of the boy and seems to look upon him as a prized thoroughbred.

Marvel is undoubtedly clever, but Mrs. Turner strongly cautioned me against taking the charge. She begged me to consider what it would mean to teach a raw native, so fresh from the veld and from his tribal ways, and to be asked to sit in front of him of an evening, with him in the very desk occupied by little Master Nathaniel during the daytime hours. Marvel is called a "boy," but of course he is practically a man—with sinewy dark limbs and far taller than I. Mrs. Turner intimated that she is convinced that Mr. Reed has utterly taken leave of his senses in contriving this scheme. I suspect she thinks me unequal to the task.

There was a most dreadful row between myself, Mrs. Turner, and Mr. Reed. I was sure I or Mrs. Turner were to be dismissed or forced to quit. However, sweet Gussie struck upon quite the Solomon's compromise and prevailed upon us to enact it.

Gussie pleaded that this project was our Christian duty, rather like the brave missionaries who have gone into the bush in the remote parts of the Empire to bring His Holy Word to light these dark places. When she said this, I thought of you, dear Susannah, and how you and Mr. Hicks have beseeched your flock to support such work to root out the bottomless superstitions and barbaric customs of which these benighted tribesmen are possessed. Mrs. Turner cast an icy glare upon us and retreated, sulking, to her room.

The arrangement is thus: I am to be paid double wages for the next month as I take charge of Marvel on a trial basis, plus a £1 bonus at the end if I succeed in teaching Marvel to do simple sums and subtractions. Mr. Reed has allowed us the use of the back parlour on the main floor, as he did apparently see some sense in Mrs. Turner's entreaty that I not be ensconced with Marvel in my little nursery schoolroom upstairs. The back parlour is the only room in the house that is in full view of the Van Onselen's house and garden. Mrs. Van Onselen is a notorious busybody, so I'm sure I shall be quite safe under her watchful gaze. I cannot imagine the gossip she will spread about Mr. Reed's fanciful project, but that is no concern of mine. I am satisfied that I have done what was asked of me as a Christian and struck a good bargain in the doing.

For his part, Marvel also seemed rather wary of the whole business, unused, I suppose, to being made to sit indoors and lorded over by a woman. Here, too, Gussie's innocent charms prevailed. I told you before that Gussie sometimes seemed overly familiar with the houseboys, and with Marvel in particular. Well, it's obvious that the small attentions she has paid to him have made him quite favourably disposed to answer her requests. He is rather like a dog who can be summoned with the slightest twitch of his master's eyebrow.

After this agreement was settled and peace restored, Mrs. Turner caught my arm as I passed her on the stair. She whispered that I was a fool whose eyes were closed to the blackness before me. I replied that I was quite aware of the colour of my charge and had only agreed to the arrangement on a trial basis, ensuring that Mr. Reed would make the experiment worth my while. It appeared that she would say more, but Master Thom called to me from the nursery, and I hastened to him.

I will write more soon, and let you know how I get on.

Your affectionate friend,
Althea Pym

***

12 April 1890
Dearest Susannah,

I am so shocked, I hardly know what to think, or indeed if my brain is even capable of forming thoughts. Early this morning, I heard moans coming from Mr. Reed's bedchamber, and hastened to the door to see if he had perhaps taken ill. I discovered Gussie emerging from the room, her hair and clothes disordered. Scandalous though this was, it is an old story, played out far too often even across our own country. What is more appalling, though, is that Marvel was ensconced with her and Mr. Reed, emerging in an even more shocking state of undress! I am almost sick with the telling of these horrors and I fear I will scandalize you with these revelations. I am sorry. I know not where to turn. Desperate as I am, I flew even to the side of Mrs. Turner, hoping for her counsel as to how to disentangle myself from this Sodom and Gomorrah. For her part, she was already packing her trunk, having discovered these abominations a few weeks prior and secured a new post in Rhodesia. She advised that I do the same, which I will endeavour to do with the utmost haste. I see now that she has been trying for some time to warn me.

I do fear for the boys, and have half-thought of spiriting them away with me, but I must fly far from Jo-burg, where Mr. Reed will no doubt poison the locality with calumny about me to hide his own shame. I have hired a coach to bear me to the rail station this afternoon. I know not what will become of me except that I cannot stay in this den of iniquity a moment longer. I should not be at all surprised if I see the lot of them dangling from the gallows.

I do not know when I shall next be able to write to you. Pray for me.

Yours in unfathomable revulsion,
Althea

HONEST JOHN FINDS A WAY

by Michael Dell

*Honest John Churchfield, the famed detective,
is on hand to solve the mysterious death
of Drysdale Tipton. Luckily for everyone present,
so is Constable Fairish. This Golden Age
delight is a marvelous turnaround.*

The men carrying the body stumbled on the stairs, and the late Drysdale Tipton thudding into the oak baluster drew the attention of everyone in the eerily silent sitting room. Everyone, that is, except the detective, Honest John Churchfield, who remained focused on the low neckline of Josephine DuMont's beaded evening dress. James DuMont, Josephine's brother, watched the men tighten their grips on the satin sheet encasing the deceased and then resumed his prodding of the fireplace's glowing embers. Constable Fairish scurried to assist the men in navigating the foyer and ushered them from the home, all under the watchful eye of Inspector Neville. The room remained hushed until the faint clopping of horse hooves and the moan of a distressed carriage wheel accompanied Fairish's return.

"He's on his way, sir."

Inspector Neville stood at the room's entrance like grim death itself. He held a small velvet bag in one sinewy hand and cast his cold gaze upon Churchfield. "Constable Fairish, I trust you will ensure that certain parties will finalize their statements tomorrow morning at Scotland Yard."

Churchfield sank deeper into his leather chair and draped his right leg over the armrest. "Certain parties will be sleeping."

"Ha ha, that's our Johnny," said Fairish, forcing an awkward laugh and stepping between the inspector and Churchfield. "Always the wise one, he is. But don't you worry, sir. I'll make sure he performs his duty."

"See that he does."

Neville glared once more at the detective before nodding a respectful farewell to the DuMonts and taking his leave. Fairish appeared not to risk another breath until the front door clicked shut. Then he removed his constable's helmet and wiped his sleeve across his forehead.

"Do you always have to be so bloody difficult?"

Churchfield yawned. "He loves it."

"He's going to take this out on me, you know," said Fairish. "He'll have me back patrolling Whitechapel. And I tell you, Church, that is no place for a delicate flower like myself. No place at all."

"Is the inspector always so grave?" asked Josephine.

"On a good day," said Fairish. "But Johnny here has a way of making him particularly sweet."

James placed the fireplace poker back in its stand. "The inspector should be grateful for Mr. Churchfield's help. Such dazzling detective work must be celebrated, not scorned. I daresay Sherlock Holmes himself would have struggled unraveling that mess."

"And so brave," said Josephine. "You should have seen him, Constable Fairish. The moment we heard the revolver, Mr. Churchfield ordered everyone to remain in the dining room, and then bolted up the stairs without any concern for his safety."

"It was nothing," said Churchfield, eyeing Josephine as if she were a chilled bottle of gin. "Any bloke with the courage of a lion and the strength of ten men would have done the same."

"So, so brave."

"And humble," said Fairish, his incredulous smirk tilting the ends of his waxed mustache.

"I'm not ashamed to admit I was terrified," said James. He lifted an intricately carved cigar box from the mantle. "And then when I finally did see . . . poor Tippy. Never thought he'd be the sort."

"You'd be surprised what people are capable of," said Churchfield.

James opened the box and presented Churchfield with a dozen crisp cigars. The musty tobacco smelled of old money and older resentment.

"No, thank you."

James pushed the box forward. "Go ahead. You've earned it."

Churchfield chose a cigar and slipped it into the interior breast pocket of his tweed coat. "Maybe later."

"Constable Fairish?" asked James.

"Don't mind if I do." Fairish selected a plump offering and dragged it beneath his nose, inhaling the wrapper's rich aroma. "You had no idea about this Tipton chap's dark past?"

James handed a silver cigar cutter to the constable. "He was always the kindest fellow back at school. To think, a jewel thief and murderer under our own roof."

"I'm just thankful Mr. Churchfield accepted our invitation to dinner," said Josephine. "I shudder to think what could have happened."

James struck a match and held it out for the constable.

Fairish slowly rotated the cigar while taking a few deep draws. "That Tipton fella must have been scared out of his mind when he realized he was sitting across the table from Honest John Churchfield."

"Why do they call you Honest John?" asked Josephine, twirling one of her golden curls.

Churchfield folded his hands on his lap. "Clean living."

"Don't let him fool you, miss," said Fairish. "Criminals call him Honest John because they always know what they're gonna get when they tangle with Johnny." Fairish pantomimed a flurry of punches. "He's crafty with his hands, he is."

"I can only imagine," said Josephine.

Churchfield gave her a sly wink.

"At least it didn't come to that," said James. He finished lighting his cigar and pulled the tip into a ripe cherry. "As gruesome as it was, at least Tippy surrendered to his guilty conscience before harming anyone else. But I still don't understand how you pieced things together, Mr. Churchfield. That room was a slaughterhouse." James turned to his sister, concerned. "Forgive me, Josephine. I don't mean to upset you."

"Please, James." She glanced at Churchfield. "I'm a grown woman."

"Don't I know it," said Churchfield under his breath.

"How's that?" asked James.

Churchfield cleared his throat. "I just mean I can understand how the scene upstairs could have confused anyone."

"It certainly didn't look like a suicide," said James. "And with all that ruckus we heard after the shot, I was afraid Tippy had encountered a burglar." He sat next to his sister on the wine-colored settee opposite Churchfield. "What was your first clue?"

Fairish stepped forward. "Excuse me, Mr. DuMont, but Johnny isn't much of a braggart. He's usually pretty shy about discussing his detective exploits. Isn't that right, Church?"

"Yes, well—"

"It's really just a simple matter of deductive reasoning. Once you know what to look for, the solution becomes obvious. But I have to give old sourpuss Neville credit. When Johnny first told him it was a suicide, Neville thought him daft. But Johnny insisted. The inspector wouldn't even listen to his explanation. The stubborn old goat had to figure it out on his own. Of course, he was just confirming what Johnny already knew." Fairish puffed his cigar. "Would hate to give away trade secrets, but would you mind if I explained to the DuMonts how you did it?"

Churchfield motioned him to take center stage. "By all means."

"Your evening began with an otherwise delightful dinner party," said Fairish. "However, unbeknownst to those in attendance, there was a killer in your midst. But one man sensed the truth. One man's keen eye and flawless instincts told him to be vigilant."

Churchfield shrugged. "I do what I can."

"When did you first suspect Tippy wasn't who he claimed?" asked James.

Fairish made a dramatic flourish with his cigar. "The first moment he saw him, that's when! There's no fooling Honest John. No, sir. Realizing that the famous Churchfield, the greatest detective in London if not the world, shared his dinner table and studied his every move and careless word thrust Tipton into panic. And as the dinner progressed, Tipton's fear consumed him. Each passing second brought him closer to the end, to being exposed for what he truly was. When would the great Churchfield leap across the table and deliver justice with a jaw-splintering blow from his legendary right hand? Would it be this second? Or the next? What about now?" Fairish took a healthy drag from his cigar and allowed the pendulum of the room's imposing grandfather clock to provide narration. "Finally, after a lifetime of nefarious behavior and crippling guilt, Tipton was unable to bear Churchfield's mental torture a moment longer and excused himself from the table."

Josephine leaned toward Churchfield and placed her hand modestly over her décolletage. "I had no idea you were doing all of that while we were chatting."

"That's the sign of true genius, miss," said Fairish. "The great detectives are always aware of their surroundings, and their minds are constantly spinning, working multiple strategies at once to ensnare the criminal. But note, Johnny didn't pursue his prey right away. No, he allowed Tipton to adjourn upstairs, knowing full well that the man had neared his breaking point. When the fateful shot sounded, Church knew the outcome. He knew what he'd find when he went up those stairs."

"Perhaps that's true, Constable," said James, "but when Mr. Churchfield did permit me to enter the room to see Tippy, it certainly didn't appear to be a suicide. The window had been smashed. The room ransacked. Blood covered the floor, streaked the walls. And poor Tippy was crumpled on the ground like a ragdoll with what appeared to be a burn across his forehead, a slashed throat, and no gun in sight."

"I'll admit," said Fairish, "if not for Johnny insisting it was a suicide, I would have assumed it was a burglary gone wrong or perhaps a military sniper tucked away in an abandoned house across the street. But this is where deductive reasoning wins the day. Present the most confounding scene and circumstances, and the skilled detective can discern the truth with little more than sound logic and workmanlike persistence. Churchfield's uncanny senses told him that the shot came from inside the house, so any foolishness about a sniper was quickly scuttled. That left two possibilities: a burglar or suicide. The shattering glass and sounds of struggle you heard following the shot would certainly indicate an intruder, but while everyone else at the party had paid little attention to Tipton's departure and merely went about their cheerful conversations, Churchfield had been marking time and analyzing the slightest sound for hints of danger. He could hear Tipton's footsteps as he entered his room. He heard the door shut. The several minutes that passed between Tipton entering his room and the revolver crack made it clear that he had not confronted an intruder."

"By Jove," said James. "You must have the ears of an elephant, Mr. Churchfield. Tippy's room was on the third floor. How you could hear his movements above the din of the party is truly remarkable."

Josephine blushed. "And here I thought I had your undivided attention throughout dinner."

"Don't be insulted, miss," said Fairish. "Churchfield's actions were in no way a critique of your lovely charms but merely a testament to his daunting acumen."

Churchfield hitched his thumb at the constable. "What he said."

"I recall seeing Tippy leave the table," said James. He crossed his legs and tapped his cigar into a standing, cast-iron ashtray that resembled a metallic tulip. "But the shot didn't come for a good fifteen or twenty minutes. What do you suppose he was doing all that time?"

"Confronting a life of sin," said Fairish. "Those final moments of moral anguish convinced him to heft the revolver and end his misery."

"But there was no weapon in the room," said James. "And how did he get the ghastly wound on his throat?"

Fairish took a deliberate puff of his cigar. "A loose shoelace."

James and Josephine exchanged confused glances.

"We don't follow," said James.

"While most ordinary detectives would have been distracted by the excessive blood and the missing gun," said Fairish, "Church remained focused on the task at hand and noticed Tipton's left shoelace was undone. Surprised Neville spotted it like he did. It's these seemingly minor details, often overlooked, that solve the most perplexing mysteries. Once he noticed the shoelace, Johnny's mind began exploring the possible significance, instantly calculating potential scenarios until the truth revealed itself."

Fairish shifted his cigar to his left hand and cocked his right to resemble a gun, its barrel pressed to his temple. "Whether due to a sudden fit of cowardice or a last-second change of heart, Tipton's hand wavered . . ." Fairish shook, as if with palsy. "And when he pulled the trigger, the bullet creased his forehead and buried itself in the south wall. The recoil from the shot, or perhaps his attempt to jerk his head away at the last second, caused Tipton to stumble backwards." Fairish demonstrated. "Still staggered from the shot, Tipton clumsily stepped on the errant shoelace, sending him twisting and tumbling into the window." Fairish reenacted the tragic misstep, falling forward and bracing himself on Josephine's side of the settee. He looked into the young woman's horrified eyes. "His weight, and perhaps the butt of the revolver, smashed the glass." Fairish snapped upright and clutched his throat. "And a deadly shard succeeded where the bullet failed."

Josephine let out a squeal and covered her face.

"In grabbing at his mortal wound," said Fairish, "Tipton dropped the gun outside, and it was later retrieved from the street below." Fairish staggered about the room. "Desperately clinging to the life he had been so intent to end only moments earlier, Tipton clawed at the walls, toppled a chair, yanked out a desk drawer, and snatched at the bedding, his death throes accounting for the commotion heard downstairs. Until finally," Fairish said, collapsing atop the oriental rug like a severed marionette, "he succumbed."

"Incredible," said James. He looked to Churchfield. "And you got all that from a shoelace?"

"Apparently."

"But that still doesn't explain the jewels," said Josephine.

"She's right," said James. "How did you know they existed, let alone where to find them, and the identity of the man he killed to steal them? Why, you even knew Tippy had stomped the man to death."

Fairish, still prone on the floor, blew cigar smoke into the air. "Even Inspector Neville couldn't figure out how Johnny knew about the jewels. You should have seen his face when Johnny pried up that floor tile and pulled out that little velvet bag. Neville demanded to know how he did it, and Johnny wouldn't budge. Didn't give him a crumb. Only said 'Think harder.' Steamed Neville but good."

"He could use a steaming," said Churchfield. "Might get out some of the wrinkles."

Fairish scrambled to his feet, careful not to drop cigar ash on the carpet. "C'mon, Church. Neville's not here. Just between us, how'd you know about the jewels?"

"Not sure I should get into it . . ."

Josephine inched forward on the settee and clasped her hands in prayer. "Oh, please, Mr. Churchfield. Do share."

Churchfield weighed her hopeful plea and the possible expressions of gratitude. "I suppose it could be our little secret."

Josephine applauded. "Yay!"

"It all started at dinner," said Churchfield, relaxing into the armchair's supple leather. "As the Constable said, I was on to Tiblin from the start."

"Tipton," said Fairish.

"Him, too. But if he were willing to take his own life rather than risk me catching him, he must have been carrying a heavy burden. So I started looking for any clues to his past."

"Did you start with the closet?" asked Fairish. "I bet you started with the closet. That's what I'd do." He looked to Josephine and gave his mustache a twist. "You know, miss, I'm a pretty fair detective in my own right."

"Yeah," said Churchfield, "he finds his way home to his wife almost every night. But I didn't have to start with the closet. When Tipton was flailing about the room, he spilled the desk drawer. Among the contents was a crumpled train ticket from Shrewsbury. That sparked a memory. A few weeks back, I recall reading a small item in the *Times* about a retired jeweler named Pike being strangled and stomped to death in Shrewsbury, and the murderer was still at large. Seemed a long shot, but it got me thinking. That's when I tried the closet."

"Told you," said Fairish, his chest swelling with pride.

"He had a modest wardrobe. Not the clothes of a refined gentleman. Common tweeds. Sack suit. They didn't seem consistent with the tailored shirt and jacket he had worn to dinner. The clothes he died in were of a much finer quality, and the lining of his jacket had a tag for Castell and Son, a swank shop in Oxford. The jacket's seams were tight. No wear on the cuffs or elbows. Seemed a recent purchase. Where would a fellow with modest means get the money for such an outfit? Made me think there might be something to the Shrewsbury idea."

"Fascinating," said James.

"He had three grips piled into the back of the closet," continued Churchfield. "One of them held a pair of work boots. Heavy. Utilitarian. Reinforced toes."

"The precise kind of boots one could use to stomp someone to death," said Fairish.

"And the right toe and heel showed evidence of a reddish brown tinge."

Josephine crinkled her nose in disgust. "How dreadful."

"The boots seemed to further confirm the Shrewsbury theory," said Churchfield. "And since he only had the one set of fancy duds, I reckoned he hadn't been able to cash in all the jewels just yet. In fact, that was probably his true motivation for visiting London, to move the jewels through illegal means."

"So much for his looking up old university chums," said James. "I was but a means to an end."

"If he still had the jewels in his possession," said Churchfield, "he'd have to keep them somewhere in the room so they would be close at hand. I checked his luggage and wardrobe with no luck, and the mattress also proved fruitless. But he needed to ensure no servants could accidentally find them. That's when I noticed the room's parquet flooring. Mr. DuMont, when you introduced me to Tipton, you said you were former classmates at Oxford."

"Class of '85," said James.

"And what would you say was the most memorable Boat Race of your tenure there?"

"Easily the '83 run. The boys rowed through a blinding snow storm to beat those Cambridge dogs by more than three lengths."

"That's what I thought," said Churchfield. "Eight and three makes eleven. So, starting in the lower left corner of the room, I counted off eleven tiles. And that eleventh tile just happened to be under the rear right leg of the desk. I pushed the desk aside and inspected the flooring. There were tiny nicks along the tile's edges, as if it had been chiseled loose. I found a letter opener among the spilled drawer's contents and went to work. The tile popped with ease, exposing a secret cubbyhole and the stolen jewels."

Josephine bounced with glee. "Bravo, Mr. Churchfield!"

"What did I tell you?" said Fairish. "Johnny's the best. I'd like to see that fool Holmes try and top that."

James stood and shook the seated Churchfield's hand. "That, my good man, is the finest detective work imaginable."

Churchfield got to his feet and smiled. "You may be right."

Josephine hurried to Churchfield's side and hooked her arm in his. "You're not going, are you? I would love to hear more about your adventures."

"Perhaps another time," said Churchfield. "It's been a long night and I wouldn't want to overstay my welcome."

"Nonsense," said James. "You will always be welcome. And the same goes for you, Constable Fairish. Two finer gentlemen I've never met."

"Thank you, Mr. DuMont," said Fairish. "Hopefully next time we'll meet under happier circumstances."

James took a long drag of his cigar. "I still can't get over that Tippy was a murderer, and that he shot himself in my very home." He hesitated a moment. "He could have at least had the decency to leave a note."

Josephine squeezed Churchfield's arm tighter. "But then we would have been denied witnessing Mr. Churchfield's brilliance." She stretched on her tiptoes and planted a kiss on the detective's cheek. "My hero."

"Thank you, Miss Dumont," said Churchfield. He stepped back and offered a slight bow. "I'll be sure and call again."

"Please do."

After bidding their hosts farewell, Churchfield and Fairish stepped outside into the warm July air. Fairish hesitated on the front stoop and blew a chain of smoke rings toward the starless sky.

"That Josephine's a stunner," said Fairish. "If I weren't a married man—"

"She still wouldn't give you the time of day."

"Wouldn't be interested in the time." Fairish swatted Churchfield on the back. "Really was some splendid detective work, boyo. Proud of you."

"Then it was all worthwhile."

"DuMont was onto something, though, about the note. Could have saved you a whole heap of grief."

"Got a light?"

"Gonna have that victory smoke, eh?" Fairish chomped on his cigar and rummaged through his trouser pockets. A quick strike of flint and a match burst to life.

Churchfield reached into his coat's interior breast pocket and pulled out what appeared to be a handwritten letter that was neatly folded into thirds.

The match's glow illuminated Fairish's confused expression.

Churchfield held the paper to the flame until it ignited, and then he turned it slowly against the night sky and watched it burn, the fire's orange ribbon devouring the missive in a steady march toward his hand.

Fairish shook out the match. "Uh, Church. . . ."

"Never you mind."

SPIRITED DEATH

by Carole Nelson Douglas

*Oscar Wilde enlists Irene Adler to investigate
a medium who may be bilking a bereaved mother.
Mrs. Wellford is devastated by the loss of
her daughter -- who took an unexpected trip down
steep stairs.*

Oscar Wilde called on us again, and I am quite sure no good will come of it this time either.

Actually, he is one of the few people to call upon the both of us, having taken a mad fancy to me, a simple, plain parson's daughter who should be beneath notice from a presumptive poet who wears yellow neckcloths and green carnation lapel blossoms.

I answered the knock, for Irene was at the piano practicing for a soiree where she would sing.

"Ah, Miss Huxleigh," he greeted me in the minuscule vestibule. "Janus, the god of gateways, could not have a fairer representative in modern times than you."

Before I could answer that I recognized only one God and Janus had been two-faced, hardly a compliment, the piano keys stilled.

"Who is it, Nell?" Irene swiveled on her piano stool to face our visitor. In those days, our shared "rooms" were one large chamber with a daybed, and a cozy curtained bay window sleeping nook for me.

"Irene," Oscar cried, "weaving her web of music." He brushed past me. He was not only tall, but somewhat wide. Hanks of brown hair to his shoulders, he reminded me of a St. Bernard dog, and, in truth, his puppyish enthusiasm did sometimes win me over. Slightly.

"I've brought you an admirer," Oscar told Irene. He was followed inside by a shorter young man of conventional dress and rather grim expression.

"Charles Wellford," Oscar said, nodding to his companion. "May I present Miss Irene Adler, the sublime American soprano, and her indispensible companion, Miss Penelope Huxleigh, who wields as staccato a type-writer keyboard as adeptly as Miss Adler does a vocal glissando."

"Charmed, ladies." Mr. Wellford gave brief bows to us both. I did give Mr. Wilde credit for not introducing me as a "type-writer girl," as my newborn profession called its practitioners.

"We are Bohemian here," Irene said with a smile. "May we offer you tea?"

That is all we could provide from our small hearth.

"You can offer us something far more valuable, dear Irene." Oscar settled on the maroon mohair upholstery like some exotic frog, his long legs akimbo. "Charles is facing a domestic quandary. I mentioned you undertook certain 'problems' as a side endeavor to your singing career. And that you were very clever about people and puzzles."

"Thank you, Oscar." Irene beamed upon his homely countenance. She had immediately seen, as had I, that Mr. Charles Wellford was a wealthy young man as evidenced by the impeccable cut of his Savile Row suit.

With Irene's erratic luck at obtaining paid singing performances and my wages as minuscule as our vestibule, a paid investigation would be welcome.

Irene mock-admonished Oscar. "You will flatter me into a very vain woman."

She regarded Charles with a serious face. "I act, at times, as a private enquiry agent, and have worked at the Pinkerton agency in America. What problem is your family facing?"

Charles's first words were hoarse. I immediately knew that grief had been a close, recent companion. "I must say, Miss Adler, you are already right. It is indeed a wrenching family matter. My sister died most suddenly, and my parents are at distressing odds. My mother has gone mad, it seems." He looked around. "I feel half-mad myself for revealing such personal matters to strangers."

"Then," Irene said with a warm smile, "we must cease to be strangers. I assure you, Mr. Wellford, that should you open the curtains in the whole of London, you would see scenes of multiple tragedies and comedies playing out."

He laughed with relief. "Yes, what is happening would be a comedy if it were not so tragic."

"What is the immediate issue?" Irene asked.

He thought for a moment. "The latest stage of my mother's madness. She is hosting séances, and these so-called 'mediums' descend on the household. My father and I refuse to take part. She insists my sister's ghost remains on the premises."

"How did your sister die?" Irene asked.

"A puzzling tragedy. Evelina was just twenty. She fell down the stairs."

"Dreadful," Irene agreed. "Had she been ill?"

"She had been altered in mood, as you noticed I have been. I don't know why."

"And you live where?" Irene asked.

"In Berkley Square," he answered.

Even a country mouse like myself knew that was one of the wealthiest addresses in London.

Irene frowned. "Most ... puzzling, as you say, Mr. Wellford. How long has Evelina been gone?"

He slapped his thighs in a gesture of frustration. "That's just it. It's been eighteen months. Mother should be six months out of mourning by now."

"We should meet your mother and father," Irene said.

"We?"

"Miss Huxleigh and myself. Could we sit in on the next séance?"

Charles eyed me doubtfully. I knew I looked a very modest mouse.

So I spoke up. "I'm not an ideal person to attend a séance. I don't believe in any ghosts except the Holy Spirit."

"A skeptic is just what we need," Irene said, settling the matter by rising from her seat. "Oscar, I think you must leave the matter to us, however amusing it would be for you to partake in a séance. Mr. Wellford, you must think of a pretense for us to be present."

"Perhaps Miss Huxleigh has suggested the very stratagem," Charles said.

"I have?"

"Someone doubtful of séances, who hopes to extract my mother from the chicanery. My father would welcome such an intervention."

"Excellent," Irene said, escorting our guests to the door. "Send a message two hours before the next séance."

"Irene," I said after the door closed, "you can't mean to subject us both to table knocking and spirits talking and all that mummery."

"Such extended grieving isn't natural, Nell, I'm sure you agree. And a bereaved mother should not be manipulated."

"No, but you are not an alienist."

"I *am* a performer familiar with stage machinery and trickery. I'm curious to see the medium who has snatched such a long engagement at the Wellford household. And what, besides a deceased daughter, haunts that family."

I couldn't help shivering at her sober tone.

"That's the spirit, Nell," Irene said with a wicked smile. "We must pretend to believe the impossible to have a chance at discovering the natural human passions that lie beneath the quest to revive a dead daughter."

***

By the time Charles's page boy brought a message around dinnertime two days later, Irene had created our names, roles, and costumes.

"Irene," I said, shocked when I first saw her persona. "That mauve changeable silk is divine on you, with the silver-gray gloves and bonnet, but those are the colors of half-mourning. You are mourning no one."

"Perhaps I am. Perhaps I'm mourning the dearth of acceptable roles for a singer of my darker soprano range."

"You simply know you look spectacular in those colors."

"Well, yes," she admitted. "Then again, if we are to judge a medium, should we not see how she would react to another possible client coming on the scene? Is she a money-hungry fraud, or a true sympathetic searcher for the dead?"

"And who am I to be?"

"Yourself. It is always best for one new to presenting a partially fictional personage to keep close to her real self."

"Oh, I see. So I am Miss Huxleigh, the type-writer girl?"

"No."

"What am I then?"

"My personal secretary. I am Mrs. Devorah North. I am writing my memoirs and must contact my dear lost husband, Norbert."

I sighed, relieved to be out of the spotlight and subject to exposure as a fraud. I could not but be sympathetic to Irene and these small operettas she devised at times. To be a sublime singer struggling for roles all too often assigned by who is sharing whose immoral bed must be heartbreaking.

So, despite my excessively moral upbringing, I found myself abetting her private enquiry agent opportunities with rather more zeal than I should have.

***

The house was as imposing as could be, with its ranks of marble steps and black front door, absent any mourning wreath.

The butler relieved us of our elbow-length capes and led us into a side parlor.

There awaited the family, Charles looking more worried than before. Mr. Hector Wellford was a tall, vigorous man. The brocaded vest that covered his barrel-chest sported a heavy gold chain and hidden pocket watch. Thick curly hair threaded with silver ran riot on his head and sideburns. I inhaled an invisible wall of cigar smoke.

Mrs. Annabel Wellford was a thin, nervous skeleton of a woman attired in ruched black silk from jawline to hemline, ruffled and rustling and aggressively clad in full-mourning black like some disconcerted crow. A pale woven bracelet of hair circled her bony wrist. Wearing the hair of lost loved ones as jewelry was a custom . . . long dead . . . dating to Queen Victoria's heyday.

Mrs. Wellford's hair was, in horrid contrast with all the black, an almost albino-blonde. All in all, she was a most outré figure one could ponder whether to pity or fear.

Young Charles introduced us according to our professed roles.

"Mrs. North lost her husband recently and heard of the medium we know, Madame Sophistron. She's asked to attend the séance, Mother."

"The more hands upon hands and mind upon mind of the believer, the better the séance," Mrs. Wellford said. "And your—"

"Secretary," Irene said swiftly. "She has recorded every secret, hopeful thought of mine for my memoirs, which I cannot, cannot, finish until I know if my beloved Norbert is in any way reachable beyond that heavy black curtain between us and our loved ones on the other side."

Mrs. Wellford's pale thin face produced an anemic flush. "'Heavy black curtain.' Is that not remarkable, Hector? That is just the background we have for our séances. We set them up each time, so there can be no hint of manipulation by the medium."

"Wonderful," Irene said.

Only I heard the skepticism. Going to such lengths to avoid charges of fraud advertised the possibilities of fraud.

"Tell me of your lost daughter," Irene urged.

"She was a bit fragile in health, but otherwise perfect. Beautiful, sweet, talented. An accomplished sketcher. Her father and I could not have been more proud of her, or of our son. I can't believe she's gone. She cannot be gone. Her eyesight was perfect. Falling down the stairs is impossible to accept. And *those* stairs. Why?"

"May I see the site?" Irene asked, adding dramatically, "My Norbert has been appearing to me at the top of a flight of stairs. I feel . . . I feel I have been sent here, for my sake and yours."

Hector snorted softly.

It is true that women have often been diagnosed as subject to an ailment called "brain fever" in a crisis.

It is also true that Annabel Wellford looked to be a victim of such a nervous condition.

"Please," Irene said, in a tone of Oliver Twist asking for "more" at the orphanage.

"Of course. Hector, take her there."

"My dear . . ."

"Now, Hector." Mrs. Wellford's voice grew shrill.

Her husband almost clicked his heels before escorting Irene out. I scurried after her to keep up with his loud, long strides.

"There," he said after we'd followed him up and down along circuitous hallways.

The stairs he had indicated were so narrow and winding that only a small woman's foot could fit on one at its widest point.

I looked at the lumpy plaster walls, and then at the slanted ceiling. These were the steps from the maids' quarters at the top of the house. What was their only daughter doing here?

Mr. Wellford caught hold of Irene's elbow. She swayed a bit at his grip.

"What is your game, madam? Are you a rival medium here to siphon off more of my wife's money?" He seemed to have forgotten me, as people often do, and I quite welcomed it. However, I had my boot-heel poised to stomp on the instep of his shoe should he move one bit more to threaten Irene.

"No," Irene said. "I am sincere. I loved my late husband and only seek a true medium. I would pay all I own for one brief glimpse of his face."

I sensed tense muscles relaxing. Not mine.

"You should leave this place, madam." He seemed strongly moved. "It is not where I wish to glimpse my dead daughter again."

His heavy steps echoed as he returned to the main house.

"Lydies?" a timid woman's voice asked.

Irene turned with a smile to the white-capped maid who stood blinking at us.

"Lydies like you shouldn't be in this part of the 'ouse.'"

"We were just learning where Miss Evelina fell."

"Awful, that was. Lovely lyedy, the miss. Had a bit of the chest congestion. Needed the doctor. Dr. Henson as was. Such a kind, concerned young gentleman. Not a *gentleman*, as such, of course. But a lovely man. Always tipped us, though he needn't."

She looked down the long, twisting stairway. "I've been up and down these old stairs all me life, as like. How should the miss have fallen? Wot should she be doin' 'ere? The stair only goes down to the kitchen, deep down and out the coal man's entrance."

"Thank you," Irene said, tipping her from the gray silk reticule around her wrist. "We'd be obliged if you'd lead us back to the main house."

* * *

And what a domestic flutter we found when we got there.

A woman had arrived, a tall grave figure attired in the daring new style of flowing Greek drapery rather than corset and bustle. She stood almost six feet tall, with a pile of white hair worn half up. Perhaps she did conjure spirits, for her skin was smooth and pink. The white hair had to have been a very premature occurrence, perhaps from seeing a ghost. She wore no hat or gloves, and seemed perfectly at home.

We were shown into the card room, a chamber only used for festivities. It had three identical round tables under three matching crystal chandeliers. The candles not only illuminated the room and tabletops, but trembled on the brink of dropping hot waxen tears onto the tables, perhaps in mourning for the daughter of the house, I thought fancifully. Sharing a room with an aspiring prima donna did manage to magnify my imagination.

Madame Sophistron stepped to the central chandelier, which ended in a glass globe as large as . . . well, as I am a Shropshire country girl born . . . as a small pumpkin turned Cinderella's coach.

With her long-fingered bare hands she reached up and cradled the sphere as a fortune teller would a crystal ball, her fingertips tracing the glittering central spear of crystal icicle that dripped from it.

"These candles," Madam Sophistron said, "when I dampen them, the spirits will flock to the dimmer light."

"Madame Sophistron." Mrs. Wellford nodded to the butler who quickly summoned a footman with a long silver candle-snuffer. "Another seeker after solace is here tonight, if that is all right."

Madame lofted her hooked Roman nose as her sharp blue eyes inspected me from bonnet to boot-toe.

Mrs. Wellford hastened to correct her. "Not Miss Huxleigh, Madame. She is our guest's er, maid."

From secretary to maid within twenty minutes! What a come-down.

Irene tilted her head, with its charming arrangement of curls and furbelowed bonnet. "I should be ever so grateful if I could stay. I've never attended a séance before, but I feel my late husband's spirit present like a chill haunting space ever out of my reach. I know he needs to convey something to me, poor man, taken young, so fast. Can you help me? I have sufficient pounds in my purse, I trust."

Well, even a top-speed type-writer girl at her machine could not record all the artful pauses and poses of Irene's impersonation of a widow, which ended with a pathetic clutch at an obviously richly laden reticule.

Madame nodded. "First, we must arrange our usual banquet table for the spirits who now dine on sorrow and sincerity."

The footman stepped to the wall and pulled the side cords loose. Heavy black velveteen folds fell together, like a closing theatrical curtain, over the bay window niche.

Madame pointed to the chair in front of her, and the footman drew it before the draperies.

"And the table," Madame said.

A brocade cloth held in place by a glass top swayed as the footman and butler bent to lift and move that, too, not easily, close to her chair. The empty side chairs stood abandoned as if waiting for invisible occupants. The footman swiftly moved another chair to seat me at Madame Sophistron's left. Mrs. Wellford moved to take the chair the butler placed opposite the medium, but Irene was suddenly there, clutching the arm in her gloved hand and sinking into it.

"Oh, just in time," she murmured. "I feel so faint."

Mrs. Wellford hesitated to relinquish her obviously usual seat opposite the medium. Yet her hostess instincts sent her bustling to take another seat at Madame's right.

The man of the house, who had stood with arms crossed in a wide stance in front of the cold fireplace during the furniture rearrangement, cast one last look of contempt on us and excused himself for the night. His son followed, obviously confused.

I tried to believe that grief made Hector Wellford so gruff, but even my tendency to think the best of people could not dismiss the impression that he despised our gathering and its purpose.

As the servants followed the men of the house out and the double doors closed behind them, a draft from the unlit fireplace *hushed* through the room. Madame remained standing in front of her chair, then leaned slightly forward to cup her long fingers around the magnificent hanging crystal globe at the bottom of the chandelier. As she caressed it above the gleaming spike of crystal finial, some clear liquid came dripping down the glass through her fingers like water from a melting icicle.

Drop by drop slowly splashed onto the center of the glass-topped table, making not a sound, and forming a pathetic little puddle. Between her fingers, on the central globe, a ruby light appeared. I squeezed my eyes shut for a moment, expecting the glass to cut her and her fingers to be soon shedding blood.

She pulled her hands away with an abrupt, grand gesture.

Her palms were dry. She slowly looked down at the water.

"No gloves, ladies. The spirits require direct contact. Please."

How unconventional to be hatted yet gloveless, but I followed Irene's lead and obeyed. With her bare hand, Irene touched a fingertip to the miraculously appeared water and then to her lips.

"Salty," she declared. "So the dead weep?" she asked Madame.

"Yours do for you. And Miss Huxleigh?"

"I am quite fine dry."

With a smile of smug serenity, Madame rose and lifted a wand—no, wait—the silver candle snuffer. Then she glided around us, still seated at the table, and snuffed each candle along the chandelier's gracefully curved arms, herself reflected as small as a fairy in the crystal globe.

The room dimmed to faint pools of light from the distant wall sconces. The now ghostly-appearing chandelier was reflected in the newly bottomless black glass surface of the tabletop.

Madame used the cap of the candle snuffer to stir the puddle of tears into a larger circle on which a man's face now faintly floated!

Even Irene couldn't stifle a gasp.

"Norbert," Irene marveled under her breath. "How is he here?"

"It is he?" Madame asked. "You are sure?"

"His brow, his dark eyes. Yes. He, indeed."

Mrs. Wellford leaned forward. "There is a face." She eyed Irene with something like envy. "I have not yet seen my Evelina." She swept a hand through the trembling image, then sucked at her fingers as at a burn. "Perhaps she is here, in these tears. Perhaps that is all she has to send me, my poor darling lost child."

We each held our breath. The woman's suffering was indeed teetering on madness.

Madame's deep voice called out, "Peace, Annabel. Our new participant has a certain magnetic attraction for the dead."

Wonderful insight, thought I. Irene had certainly proved adept at solving death by misadventure during our association.

"Annabel," Irene said, her bare hand over the other woman's trembling one. "We all weep for our dead, and they for us. But if we keep faith and heed Madame, we can find at least the peace that they may be gone, but what we feel for them will not leave the earth until we do."

Annabel. I could not think of her as Mrs. Wellford any longer, but as a mourning mother passing damp fingers over her tear-soaked face.

That and her hysterical sobs, tended by Madame Sophistron, ended the séance.

Irene leaned back in the family carriage's creaking leather seat. Charles had sent us home.

"All right, Nell. It is as I suspected, but I don't know *who* and *why* just yet."

"Are they not the two most important elements of the case?"

"As always, Nell, you bring me back to earth."

"Where I am most pleased to be. It's disturbing that the veil between life and death seems to be a rather wet and unseemly business."

"You, of course, realized that my dear departed husband's image was not he."

"Of course. You do not have a dear husband of any sort. But how was a face for this fictional person summoned? Are there lines of deceased spouses in the Afterworld waiting for someone to call them back?"

"The visage of the man who appeared had eyebrows and the requisite eyes to accompany them. A suggestion of the bridge of the nose. No specific hairline, no discernible moustache or sideburns or beard."

"I must say I think that a rather attractive condition."

"Ah, then you favor the clean-shaven visage shown by Mr. Sherlock Holmes when we have met him not in disguise."

"Certainly not!"

Irene bit back a grin. She always knew when she had won. And she liked to win.

"The medium assumes the loved one will fill in more specific features from memory," she said. "Nell, I am no stranger to séances. When I worked for the Pinkertons in America—"

"Oh, am I to hear of those most inappropriate days investigating mountebanks and criminals again? At least now more of your time is devoted to pursuing your art, rather than private enquiries."

"Yes, amongst charlatans. That's why I was most interested in Oscar's friend's situation. This could be quite serious, Nell. A matter of life and death." She frowned and finally pulled on her silver-gray leather gloves, as a woman should wear outdoors.

"You realize that the 'tears' readily dropping from the chandelier globe to the needle-sharp pinpoint tip of the spike below were squeezed from a twist of saltwater-soaked cheesecloth Madame palmed from her long sleeves?"

"Cheesecloth. You mean the flimsy white material used in the kitchen to leech water out of soft cheese?"

"So useful to the medium. Some are adept at consuming lengths and regurgitating them as the spirit stuff called ectoplasm."

"Irene! This is too much to imagine."

Irene laughed. "Don't imagine, but know that everything we saw tonight was manipulated by light, and the refractive power of glass, and an array of tools Madame Sophistron has up her tight-wristed, voluminous sleeves. I'm amazed we didn't have the table hopping and knocking tonight, but she needed to gauge how gullible we were."

"If a distraught Annabel wishes to throw money at a medium, what can anybody do? No wonder her husband is so angry. Aren't we tormenting that poor woman, rather than helping her?"

"*Hmm*. More than a medium's money-lust is at work here. I don't yet know who is prey and who predator. Luckily, Madame used my testimony of seeing my late husband as good reason to invite us back, as we have given her true target more hope."

"We all did see some man's visage floating on wet glass."

"A photograph she pressed onto the chandelier's crystal ball reflected on the glass tabletop. I intend to have something up my own sleeve for the next séance."

"What? "

"At the least, my small but wicked pistol."

I did not dare enquire further.

***

The cast and scene were much the same as the previous evening when we returned to the Wellford home with Charles. He'd brought the carriage and he fretted the entire journey.

"Mother and Father had a terrible row last night in the bedroom wing," he said. "I couldn't help but hear. I fear that last séance released evil spirits into the house."

Irene and I sat spellbound as his restless feet tapped the carriage floor. "I'd been away at school for years when Evelina had her accident. My father said she was no 'mother's little angel,' but a disobedient, ungrateful child, and that she fell running away to be with a penniless doctor, taking her fortune from her maiden aunt with her."

"My mother screamed, 'So you only married me for my fortune. May you rot in the Afterworld with all the devils that have ever died tormenting you.'"

Charles thrust his fingers into his hair. "I suspected none of this. This morning they acted as if nothing had happened. When I mentioned fetching you and Miss Huxleigh for the séance, neither had any objection. I must be crazy. Maybe it was a waking nightmare."

"There is a nightmare in your house and it isn't Evelina's ghost, poor girl," Irene said. "Charles, stay by your father's side tonight. I expect things will be the same as last night. And that expectation on all fronts will allow me to change everything."

And so it was the same, as if in a dream: the men of the family withdrawing, the servants performing the ritual re-arrangement of the table and the chairs, we four women left alone. Irene had tangled her reticule drawstrings and fussed to undo them while Annabel took her usual chair opposite the medium. When Irene sat down across from me, she remained distracted.

I felt nervous. Would she be able to reach her pistol quickly? I gazed surreptitiously in the crystal globe and saw our small distorted images.

Madame Sophistron shook out her fluid gray sleeves against the solid black of the draperies.

Annabel twitched in her chair and clutched a white linen handkerchief in her right hand.

The medium ritually walked around the table to snuff the candles, all of us holding still as she passed.

Then she stopped to caress the globe. This time I watched the miniature people moving in that fractured scene. I saw a white wing pass over and the saltwater tears dripped again from the crystal icicle onto the scrying pool on the black tabletop.

Out of the corner of my eye, pale disembodied hands floated like seagulls against the black curtain. The central pool was larger. A beautiful moon of a face floated there, framed by ripples of golden-white hair.

"Evelina!" Annabel leaped up to drink in the image of her daughter, her fanned fingers wet with the saltwater of false cheesecloth tears.

I felt the table tremble and the top tipping up on Madame's side. Evelina's face elongated and slid slowly off the lowering table edge where her mother stood.

"No!" Annabel screamed. The tabletop turned vertical and cracked as a clap echoed from above. Irene pounced on Annabel and dragged her away, down to the floor as pounding footsteps crossed the carpet.

A cry of "You stupid woman!" brought Hector Wellford from the image of a tiny man in a shattering globe into a giant directly under the crystal chandelier, which descended with an avalanche of tinkling glass.

***

When the servants heard Hector's screams and rushed in to light the other two chandeliers and right the table, they found the fallen chandelier's sharp crystal spike had impaled their master's hand and left it bleeding into the saltwater pool, now becoming scarlet. The great round globe above had shattered, embedding his face with glass shards.

Had Irene not intervened, the falling spike would have impaled the back of Annabel's neck.

A doctor, not Henson, was called, as well as the police by a dazed Charles.

Annabel sat sobbing in one of the chairs. She had given her white handkerchief to her son to tend his father, but it was of little use. Hector sat rocking, his hand wrapped in a towel.

We four women had nowhere to sit but in our separate séance chairs.

"When," Irene asked an even whiter-faced Madam Sophistron, "did you become this murderer's mistress?"

"Sometime during the months and months that Annabel wailed over their daughter," she admitted wearily. "He pushed Evelina, you say, so her inheritance remained in the family? I didn't know that. No one can prove I knew anything."

"Your using the photograph of Evelina during the séance proves you're complicit in the attempt to kill Mrs. Wellford," Irene said. "Mediums have many clever ways to mimic the dead. You used your so-called talents in an attempt to kill. You are as heartless and greedy for money as he."

Irene stood, sighed, and went to pat Annabel on the shoulder.

I realized Irene had always suspected the séance seating arrangements because mediums always choreograph their tricks.

"Irene," I said quietly as we left, "who did Hector call 'you stupid woman'?"

"I'm afraid that was me," she said with a smile. "I'd ruined his plans. He probably considers both his wife and his lover that way, too. Once he crossed the threshold and pushed his own daughter down the stairs to her death, he could no longer hide his contempt for every woman."

As I joined her in treading carefully to avoid getting glass in the soles of our shoes, I couldn't help thinking about the people who get glass in their hearts and souls.

And then that black front door in Berkley Square closed on us forever.

HOME FRONT HOMICIDE

by Liz Milliron

*In Buffalo during the Second World War, most of the
workers are women. Not every male supervisor treats
them respectfully. When one of these men is found dead,
there are too many suspects and motives to count.
Tough, smart Betty decides to investigate.*

People say war is hell. Most of the time, they're talking about the boys on the front—bullets, explosions, and mortar fire. They forget war is hell at home, too.

I strode down Mackinaw, the First Ward coming to life around me. Men headed off to Bethlehem Steel. Housewives swept their front steps. In the distance, I could see gulls drifting over Lake Erie. This October was mild for Buffalo. I should enjoy it while it lasted. Soon I'd be hoofing it through snow.

A voice behind me. "Betty, wait."

Puffing on my cigarette, I stopped and turned to face Dot Kilbride. We'd been best friends forever. She was gonna be maid of honor when Tom got back. "Keep up. We miss the bus at Main and we'll be walking to Wheatfield."

Dot gasped as she scurried up to me. "I'm trying, but you got longer legs." She was a good six inches shorter than me. A lock of red hair fell over her forehead.

I clamped my cigarette between my lips and pinned back the stray hair. "I told you to use a bandanna." Like me. I'd cut my brown curls short, but it wasn't enough when I was working.

Dot smoothed her shirt. "I couldn't get one. Pop don't like me taking this job as it is."

"Wait 'til he sees the first check. He'll like it plenty. Plus, you're helping the war effort."

"I guess."

"You are. With all the men off fighting who else will build the planes?" I patted her hair. "I'll get you one. C'mon. Won't be a great impression to be late your first day. Catch some sleep on the bus if you can. Got your quarter?"

Dot held up the coin.

"Good. Let's go."

On the bus, I closed my eyes. The rumbling made it hard to get real sleep. But I always tried.

Today, Dot's chatter made it impossible. "What do I do again?"

I could picture her chewing at her plump bottom lip, the one the boys liked to kiss. Dot was Irish working class, but if you put her in a bathing suit, she could have held her own against any Hollywood pinup girl. Not like me, all angles and bones. Only guy who'd ever been sweet on me was Tom. "Go to Mr. Lippincott. He's the supervisor. He'll give you an assignment. Work. Break for lunch. Work some more. Go home."

"Is that all?"

"That's all." I'd smoked my cigarette on the walk. With Dot's yapping, I might as well have lit up again. I shouldn't be annoyed. Poor girl was nervous. Her family needed the money, same as mine.

We arrived at Bell Airplane in plenty of time. Girls lined up at the clock, punching in. "Hey, Betty. Who's the new girl?" Fran Calloway asked.

I made the introductions. "What d'ya think Bell has for us today?"

"Same as yesterday." Fran punched her card. "S'long as they pay me, what do I care?"

I punched my card and showed Dot how to do hers. Then I showed her where to stow her lunch pail and led her to the floor. Girls milled around without direction.

"Where's Mr. Lippincott?" one of them asked.

"Beats me. Maybe he slept in. Wish I could," another said.

"Come on, we know what to do," I said and shooed them to their places. I wasn't senior by a long shot, but I didn't put up with nonsense when there was work to be done, so leadership often fell to me whether I liked it or not. Pulling Dot behind me, I said, "Until Mr. Lippincott shows up, work next to me and I'll show you the ropes."

The hubbub was cut by a horror-picture scream. I headed toward the noise. "What's the racket?"

One of the girls was sobbing, her friend patting her back. "We found Mr. Lippincott," she said, pointing.

My gaze followed her finger, landing on a pair of scuffed shoes and legs bent at an angle nature never intended. I recognized Ed Lippincott, body all twisted, blond hair matted by blood pooled around his head, dark eyes glassy and staring.

I whistled. And here I was worried about being late.

***

We stood around in the parking lot. The police had arrived and herded us outside, telling us not to go anywhere. A couple cops in uniform stood nearby.

I lit up and leaned against a wall. It was bad Mr. Lippincott was dead. But I was concerned about the wasted time. Was Bell going to pay me for standing in the sunshine, looking at the browning Wheatfield grass?

The rest of 'em gossiped. I didn't have time for that on a good day. I sure didn't now.

"What're we gonna do?" Dot asked. She sat on the ground, knees pulled up to her chest, arms clasped around them.

I blew out smoke and slid down the wall to sit beside her. "We wait. Hopefully whatever the police are doing won't take the whole shift. Then we go in and get back to work."

"You're so practical, Betty. Wish I was like you."

I looked sideways at her. Nobody ever wanted to be like me. I bumped her shoulder with mine. "Cheer up. Everything will be fine."

A shadow fell over us. Fran. Of all the people who could have wandered over. "You think so?"

"Yeah, I do. Bell still needs things built. And we're here to build 'em."

"Did you know about Mr. Lippincott?" Fran stood over us and crossed her arms across her ample chest. Busty, Mom would call her. So was Dot, but she was curvy all over. The only thing curvy about Fran was her chest.

Fran's attitude never sat well with me. Like manual work was beneath her. "About him being dead? Not until I saw him," I said.

"No, about . . . things," Fran said, lowering her voice and looking around.

For cripe's sake. This wasn't a spy flick. Nobody was listening. "No. I bet you do though. Spit it out or go away."

Fran huffed and tossed her head, hair carefully waved and pinned. "Mr. Lippincott was frisky with the girls."

"Not with me," I said.

Dot shrugged. She didn't have much to contribute, so she kept her trap shut.

"You've got a man." Fran looked at the tiny diamond on my left hand. "Although that didn't stop him with Caroline or Georgia. Maybe he hadn't gotten around to you yet. Or maybe . . ." A sly grin appeared on her face.

I blew out a cloud of smoke. Real slow.

"Maybe you don't have the right goods."

Dot stood, face red. "Betty's a great girl," she said. "How'd she get a fiancé if she weren't? You're jealous."

What a sweetheart. "Relax, Dot." I puffed my cigarette one last time, then flicked it away onto asphalt that no longer gleamed with the morning dew. I stood. "Let's get something straight." I resisted poking Fran in that busty front. "I don't know why, but Ed Lippincott never got *frisky* with me. Now unless you've got something useful to say, scram."

Fran glared at me. But she didn't say nothing else, just flounced back to a group of her friends. Smart girl.

***

We waited forever. Long enough that even the weak October sun got hot. The cops would escort a girl inside every few minutes. They didn't come out. Prob'ly gone to work. The rest huddled together, whispering.

I was on my third smoke when my least favorite person at Bell appeared in the yard. Frank Satterwaite. Balding and paunchy, with watery blue eyes and a belt fastened so tight his gut hung over it. Put the right uniform on him and he'd be a ringer for those comedic German sergeants in the pictures. "Okay, ladies. Break time is over," he said.

Break? Only he would think so.

"Can't. We're waiting to be interviewed," one of the girls said.

"They couldn't find anyone other than Frank Satterwaite?" asked Minnie Westerson, who'd wandered over.

"Is he bad?" asked Dot, chewing her bottom lip.

I jammed my hands in my pockets. "Mr. Satterwaite doesn't like women in factories."

He was close enough to hear me. He looked over, narrowing his eyes. "That's right, Miss Ahern." He smiled, his voice sugar-sweet. "If I had my way, you'd all be out on your pretty little backsides before the end of this shift. I won't go easy on you like Lippincott did. Maybe with him gone, I'll be able to convince the higher-ups they've made a terrible mistake and send you homemakers back to the kitchen where you belong." He stopped smiling, which actually made him look less evil. "Have you been interviewed yet?"

"No," I said.

"As soon as you're finished, back at it." He walked off while a cop came over to fetch Minnie.

Dot tilted her head. "Can he do that? Get us sent home?"

"I don't think so." I stared in the direction Mr. Satterwaite had taken. "Just keep your head down and steer clear of him."

"He that bad?"

"He was real mad when Bell promoted Mr. Lippincott over

him," I said. "And it's true he doesn't like women workers. He doesn't keep that a secret."

"Will Bell listen to him?" Dot worried her lip some more. "I need this job."

Tell me about it. Dad was laid up from an accident at Bethlehem. My older brother Sean was in the Pacific. Mom cleaned houses and my next-youngest brother delivered papers, but that wasn't enough to feed six mouths. "We'll be fine," I said with bravado I didn't feel. I patted Dot's shoulder. "The menfolk aren't here and Bell doesn't have a lot of options. Don't you worry."

Dot may not have believed me, but she stopped chewing that lip before it started to look like chopped meat.

A cop walked over. "Dorothy Kilbride?"

Dot squeaked.

"Come with me." The cop led her away.

I was the only girl left. I wanted another cigarette, but the cop reappeared only a couple of minutes later.

"Elizabeth Ahern?" he asked.

"Yeah, I got it. Follow you." I straightened my shirt and adjusted my bandanna. I wasn't going to be all sloppy when I saw this detective.

The cop led me into the cool interior of the plant and to one of the muckety-muck's offices. It was spare, but better furnished than my house, with a wood desk and a brass lamp that had a green-glass shade. We'd had a lamp like that. Pawned it. Gray metal cabinets sat against walls that loomed despite being painted stark white.

The detective seated behind the desk reminded me of Mr. Lippincott. But the detective's blond hair was darker. He wore a suit with a sharp white shirt and a deep red tie. The shoes under the desk were brown and shiny. He was writing when I entered. Nice pen. Something Dad would like, but would cost a month's salary.

I cleared my throat. "You wanted to see me?"

The detective's eyes were dark like Mr. Lippincott's, blue instead of brown. Mid-thirties, maybe older. He projected an air of calm confidence. "If you're Elizabeth Ahern."

"Betty."

"Sit. Thank you, Officer. You can go."

I dropped into the shiny wood chair in front of the desk as the cop left. The door clicked shut and my gut tightened. Why be nervous? I didn't do nothing. I'd done nothing all morning. That was the problem.

The detective continued to write, ignoring me once I'd sat down.

"You gonna ask me any questions? They aren't paying me to jaw, you know."

He finished writing, laid down his pen, and looked at me, chuckling. "Your friend said you were direct. Detective Sam MacKinnon."

A fellow Irishman. From the First Ward?

"Tell me about this morning."

I ran over the story, from the time I left home to when we found Mr. Lippincott.

"How was your relationship with Mr. Lippincott?"

"Okay. He was the boss."

"Was he a good boss? Kind? Demanding? Did he ever . . . approach you?"

I stiffened. "I'm engaged."

Detective MacKinnon held up his hands. "Of course. I'm not suggesting you would respond to those advances. Is your fiancé in Buffalo or overseas?"

"He was in Ireland, but he's on his way to North Africa." And Rommel and his tanks.

"Some men like to take advantage of situations like that." Detective MacKinnon laid his hands on the desk and studied me. His gaze was kind. "Did Mr. Lippincott?"

I relaxed a bit. "Not with me. I heard he was . . . forward with some of the others. This morning I heard that."

"What about Mr. Satterwaite? Do you know him?"

"Not really. I've never worked for him." I glanced back at the door. "Was Mr. Lippincott murdered? Your questions make it sound like he was."

"We don't know yet." The kind look disappeared.

"Do you . . ." I swallowed. "Do you think any of us are involved? Or Mr. Satterwaite?"

No answer.

"See, my brother, Sean, is overseas, so not much dough there. My family, I don't work—"

"I understand your situation, but I can't say." Detective MacKinnon's gaze turned stern. "I strongly encourage you not to try and find out."

What made him say that? "What am I gonna do?"

"You don't seem like the kind of person who waits well." He continued to study me like a gull sizing up scraps on the beach. "Anything else you care to tell me?"

I shook my head "Can I get to work?"

The detective waited a moment, then nodded. "If you remember anything, please tell Mr. Satterwaite. He'll know how to get in touch with me."

Talk to Mr. Satterwaite? On purpose? Not on your life. But I nodded politely, like Mom taught me. Then I left. I had a paycheck to earn.

***

The rest of the shift was filled by girls jabbering about Mr. Lippincott and wondering if Mr. Satterwaite could really get us thrown out of Bell. I stayed out of it, even skipping my afternoon break. Mr. Satterwaite prowled around, snapping at everyone except Fran. The one person he *should* have been coming down on like a load of airplane parts. She didn't do much all afternoon, just primped her hair and fussed with her lipstick. Maybe Fran was fooling around with Mr. Satterwaite.

No way.

I shook Dot awake when the bus reached our stop on Main and pulled her back to Mackinaw. Men from Bethlehem hustled past us, filling the air with the scent of grease and coke from the mill. "Get some sleep," I said. "Another early day tomorrow."

Someone had put the milk bottles out and the glass shone as the sun dipped over Lake Erie. The bustle of the street was cut off as I kicked the door shut. "I'm home."

Dad was in his armchair, snoozing. The youngest two were playing war on the floor with some tiny soldiers. "We're thumping the Nazis," Jimmy, the second youngest, said. "Wanna play?"

"Nah, I'm tired. Give Adolf a kick for me." I trudged to the kitchen, where Mom and Mary were making dinner. Meager as it was.

"What's it tonight?" I asked, ruffling Mary's hair and giving Mom a quick kiss.

"Beans, bread, butter, a little meat I picked up cheap at the Broadway Market," she said, stirring the pot. "How was your day?"

"Don't really know." I filled her in. "Everybody's nervous, 'course."

Mom's lips thinned. She didn't like my working at Bell, even if I did bring in good money. "P'raps it's for the best."

"The best?" I waved at dinner. "Only reason you can fill that pot is 'cause I work. Cleaning houses and delivering papers won't do it."

"Jimmy could pick up another route."

"When's he gonna do that?"

"He'd have to leave school. Do it in the mornings." Mom

stirred the contents of the pot, not looking at me.

"He's gonna finish school. Maybe go to college." Bright, thoughtful Jimmy was our future college boy.

Mom sniffed. "Your dad didn't go to college. Neither did Sean."

"I don't give a—"

"Elizabeth. Language." Mom rapped my knuckles with her wooden spoon, leaving a smear of gravy.

I balled my fists. "Jimmy is staying in school." I didn't bring up Sean. A fact prob'ly not lost on my mother, but she didn't say nothing.

"Dinner'll be ready soon. You should go change." She didn't like the smell of my work clothes. She didn't mind Dad coming home dirty from the mill, but I had to be clean.

I wiped my hand and stomped out of the kitchen, swallowing my words. I needed this job. We needed it. Until Sean came home. In my room I knelt and said a quick prayer. For Sean. For Tom. For me. 'Cause Mr. Satterwaite couldn't win. The best way I could see to keep my job was to show Bell I was too smart to lose. And the way to do that was to find out who killed Mr. Lippincott.

***

Dot didn't talk on the bus ride Tuesday morning. That was good, 'cause I needed to work on my plan. How did private dicks do it in the movies? First, they examined the scene. That shouldn't be hard. I'd be working there.

Except it was. Mr. Satterwaite resumed his stalking, like a tiger in a zoo. This tiger made comments under his breath, though. Comments about how it wouldn't be long until things were right at Bell. Until there were men at the factory.

I don't know where he planned to get 'em. These P39s weren't gonna build themselves.

I dawdled when it came time for lunch. Once I was alone, I looked where we'd found Mr. Lippincott. But the spot had been scrubbed clean. No blood, no weapons, no clues.

"What're you doing?" Mr. Satterwaite said, appearing from around the machine.

I jumped. "Just looking."

"At what?"

"Nothing."

Mr. Satterwaite jerked his head in the direction of the cafeteria. "Go. You're wasting your lunch hour and if you think I'm going to give you extra time, Miss Detective, think again. Yeah, I know what you're up to. You fancy yourself a sleuth. Well, you ain't, so get outta here."

I scrammed, plopping next to Dot where I unpacked my baloney sandwich as I mumbled to myself.

"Where've you been?" Dot asked. "What are you cussing about? Your mom would wash your mouth out with lye, she heard you talking like that."

That just made me swear more. 'Cause it was true.

At the table next to us, Fran was holding court. "Big changes coming. New management, new ideas. I might not be with you much longer."

No doubt she meant Mr. Satterwaite. But Fran was talking like she welcomed the change. Change that would mean putting us out on the curb. Where did she think she was going?

Then again, she was the only one Mr. Satterwaite hadn't yelled at today.

Could she be involved in Mr. Lippincott's death? Silly. Fran was short. Short as Dot and scrawnier than me. Her overpower Lippincott?

I mentioned my suspicions to the table and Sally Newcomb shook her head. "Bet she sees a position for herself in the front office. Thinks her uncle is going to take care of her."

"What uncle?" I asked. Fran had an uncle at Bell?

"Didn't you know?" Sally's eyes got wide. "Mr. Satterwaite is Fran's uncle."

***

Mr. Satterwaite was true to his word. I barely had time to finish my lunch. On the way back to the line, I passed Detective MacKinnon, who'd must've come back to ask more questions. "Detective, I need to talk to you."

"Certainly, Miss Ahern."

"In private."

He raised his eyebrows. "It's private here."

Most of the others had gone back to work. There was no one nearby and the noise made talking hard. I pushed him into the cafeteria anyway. "This is better."

"I thought you were engaged."

"I am. Get your mind back on track, mister. You're too old for me."

The corners of his mouth twitched. "What is it you'd like to say?"

"I've been thinking." I told him about Mr. Satterwaite's relationship to Fran, the way he'd been favoring her, and her predictions at lunch.

Detective MacKinnon chuckled. "You think we haven't found this out? You don't even know Lippincott was murdered."

"I checked where we found him. Nothing he could have bashed his head on, even in a fall. Someone hit him. I've been to the movies. Who had a motive? Mr. Satterwaite got passed over for promotion, d'you know that?"

"We do."

"Fran says Mr. Lippincott was coming on to some of the girls. If Mr. Lippincott insulted Fran, and her uncle got mad—plus he's sore he didn't get the promotion—"

"Stop right there." Detective MacKinnon didn't look amused any more. "Thank you very much for the information, although you haven't told us anything we didn't know. I suggest you get back to work and leave the murder solving to us. It isn't like what you see in the movies."

He nodded and walked off, leaving me fuming. He didn't think I could solve a murder, huh? Well, we'd see about that.

***

I cornered Dot near the assembly line. "I need you to do something for me."

"Anything."

"I need you to cause a distraction."

Her forehead puckered. "How?"

"I don't know. Use your imagination."

"Betty, you know I'd do anything for you." She glanced around and lowered her voice. "What're you gonna do?"

I didn't want to get Dot in trouble. "Just get me that distraction. Pronto."

Dot nodded, loyal to the core. Not five minutes later she yelped, clutching her hand in a very convincing act of being injured. Least I hoped it was an act.

The others gathered round Dot, but I snuck off to the shift supervisor's office. I left the door open just enough to let in light. Turning on the desk lamp would be a dead giveaway since the only people who should be in that office were supervisors. I conducted my search in the barely lit room.

It didn't take long. I had no clue what I was looking for. Something connecting Mr. Satterwaite to Fran or Mr. Lippincott. Or both. 'Course, that assumed Mr. Satterwaite was a sap and would hide something in the plant. If he was savvy enough to keep evidence at home, I was flat out of luck.

I didn't have a lot of time. The girls would notice Dot's injury was phony and I'd be missed in a New York second. Where would Mr. Satterwaite be likely to hide something? Fran's employee file? I tiptoed over to the cabinet and looked under "C" for Calloway. I found her file and flipped through the contents. Zilch.

I looked around the office. Where else? There was a safe, but other supervisors had to use that so any dirty secrets wouldn't stay hidden for long. I spotted a coat rack in the corner, no doubt shared. Next to it was a row of cubbies. Labels showed there was one for each supervisor.

I hustled over. My time was running out. There wasn't anything interesting in Mr. Satterwaite's cubby. Some gloves, lotion for his thinning hair, and a few snaps of a pudgy woman and some equally well-fed kids. The eating was good at the Satterwaite house.

Tick tock. I stared at Mr. Lippincott's cubby. The cops would have searched that. But after . . .

A few personal items. Hair tonic, cologne, a spare set of work gloves. Underneath it all, a folder.

Bingo.

The folder was unlabeled, but inside were notes. Mr. Satterwaite to Fran, Fran to her uncle. At first they were simple, a message that jobs were available. Fran complaining that she'd have to be a laborer, not work in an office. Her complaints continued, one a day. I could hear her tone, shrill as a Polish housewife arguing prices down at the Broadway Market.

Then the payoff. Mr. Satterwaite's reply, "Stop fussing. You'll get that office job."

I slipped the folder back into the cubby. That was it. Mr. Satterwaite had killed two birds with one stone. He'd gotten rid of his rival and taken care of his niece. He didn't care it would happen at the expense of the rest of us. He'd take over, get his way, and we'd be out on the bricks. But Fran'd be okay.

Sure would be nice if I could find the murder weapon. In the pictures, there was always a smoking gun, something pointing to the killer. But I didn't see nothing as I scanned the office. There weren't a lot of good hiding places anyway.

No matter. I had enough to corner Mr. Satterwaite. In a flash of inspiration, I scribbled my own note and stuffed it in his cubby. I'd meet him, force a confession and tie it up in a neat package to present to Detective MacKinnon. Who said I couldn't be a detective?

***

The whistle blew. End of the shift. Mr. Satterwaite shooed girls out the door while the new arrivals took their places.

Dot came up, carrying her lunch pail. "What're you doing? You don't want to miss the bus."

I shot a glance over my shoulder. Fran was messing with her hair. She didn't ride the bus back to Buffalo. But why wasn't she leaving? I had to get Mr. Satterwaite alone the way I planned. "I'll catch up." I turned back to Dot, who frowned. I waved her on. "Go on. I'm right behind you."

Dot walked away. I looked around. Fran was gone. So was Mr. Satterwaite.

Darn it. Where'd he go? My note had said to meet me. I'd seen him. Then poof! Gone.

I skulked in the shadow of an unused machine. Still no sign of Mr. Satterwaite. Time to come up with Plan B. Before I could do that, Fran strolled into view. "What're you doing here?" I asked.

"You said you wanted to meet me." She leaned, arms crossed. But not without first checking for stray grease.

"You? I wanted to meet Mr. Satterwaite. He—"

She laughed. "Lemme guess. You think he killed Mr. Lippincott. You thought you were gonna play hero, handing him over to the cops and saving the day."

Fran had read the note. The only reason she'd do that was…

"That's right, Miss Fancy Detective. Me." She looked like my neighbor's cat after he'd caught a particularly fat mouse.

"I don't understand. Why?"

"Because my uncle is stupid." Satisfaction was replaced with a scowl. "He was trying to get Mr. Lippincott fired with rumors he was *inappropriate* with us."

"That's why you were telling tales." Poor Mr. Lippincott. Murdered and his name smeared. "Office job that important to you? Money's better out here."

"But the office is cleaner. More chances to mingle with the men, maybe pick up a boyfriend. Or husband. One that isn't stranded in the African desert, stuck in a tin-can of a tank." She glanced at my ring.

I clenched my hand. "You decided to be more direct."

She straightened up. "I said I had information for Mr. Lippincott and arranged to meet him early. Then I bashed his head with a rock from the road and slipped out to join the rest of you. Easy as pie. Things were swell until my uncle showed me your note. He was too chicken to do what he had to."

"Which is?" But I knew.

"Get rid of you." Fran lunged at me.

She might have bested Mr. Lippincott with a rock and the element of surprise. But Fran was no street fighter. After about ten seconds, it was clear she didn't have brothers either. Brothers who taught you to fight dirty 'cause on the street that was the only way. Brothers like Sean.

She clawed at me, but I was able to trip her and tangle her in some chain. Then I delivered a light rabbit punch to her kidney as she struggled to her feet. I tripped her again as she lurched to her feet and shrieked.

"Police! Hands up!"

I'd moved in to deliver another sucker punch, but I stopped and looked up. Detective MacKinnon stood there, gun pointed my way, flanked by two uniformed cops. I backed up, hands palm out.

One of the cops hauled Fran to her feet. She was spitting like a wet cat. "I was gonna be in the office!"

"Get her outta here," Detective MacKinnon said to the cop. Then he turned to me. "I told you. Detective work isn't like it is in the pictures."

I straightened my bandanna. "I think it's pretty close. You arrived in the nick of time. She killed Mr. Lippincott. I found letters—"

"We know." He eyed me. "Should've known you couldn't stay away. Not a spirited Irish girl from the First Ward. You remind me of my sister."

"So you *are* a First Ward boy."

"Yeah, why?"

"I missed my bus. I need a ride home."

He grinned and holstered his gun. "After you."

I walked out into the yard, lit by the failing October sun. Then I opened the door of the sedan I assumed was Detective MacKinnon's car and got in. Maybe I should ditch Bell and become a private dick.

Nah.

THE UNSEEN OPPONENT
(from Judge Lu's Ming Dynasty Case Files)

by P. A. De Voe

*Wealthy Mr. Wang and his loved ones
(including his concubine) are celebrating his birthday
with a family kick ball-tournament. When death strikes,
they're lucky Judge Lu is there to get to the bottom of
the crime.*

It wasn't until later that Judge Lu realized he had witnessed a murder on the ball field. The game followed Mr. Wang's celebratory sixtieth birthday dinner. The wealthy patriarch of a notable merchant family in Lu's district favored the highly competitive game of kick-ball. Today the opposing teams were each led by one of Mr. Wang's two sons.

During the game's first half, Judge Lu had been captivated by Mr. Wang's concubine. Something Fu-hao, his younger brother and court secretary, hadn't failed to notice.

"She may be aggressive, but I'll bet Mr. Wang doesn't mind. I'd certainly be willing to bed her any day," Fu-hao said, grinning.

"Who?" Lu said, raising his eyebrows in response to his brother's comments and smirk.

Fu-hao bent closer to Lu's ear. "You don't have to pretend you can't see how striking she is. Any man would notice her."

"You're too much," Lu grumbled. "Always thinking about women."

"And you not enough. Life is more than work."

It wasn't that Lu hadn't noticed her. After all, how could he not? She was the only woman playing, aggressively attacking the ball, kicking it with a power he hadn't expected. While women had played the game for generations, since the beginning of the current Ming Dynasty, it had largely faded out as a woman's pastime. Scrutinizing the young woman more closely, he considered her attributes. She was athletic, and she didn't have the tiny lotus feet which were so prevalent among the Han women of her class. As an ethnic Mongolian, her feet remained unbound, thereby allowing her to participate in such games.

Nevertheless, Lu did think Mr. Wang's older son, Huai-liang, could have kept her from scoring points a couple of times. He shook his head. Did Huai-liang give way to her because she was a woman? He wasn't surprised that by the tea break the younger son's team was ahead.

During the time-out, Lu surveyed the guests. Except for the patriarch, he only knew his own brother and his coroner, a local healer. Lu's familiarity with Mr. Wang came through governmental meetings with city elders. He'd been invited for today's celebration, and had accepted because, as the district magistrate, such gatherings were a part of his social duties. Lu tugged impatiently at his long, dark, semi-formal robe. He admitted being more at ease working than socializing. Plus, he reflected, there was much to do back at the office and spending all day dining and watching a game meant a long night of work ahead.

Lu glanced at Fu-hao chatting amiably amongst a group of young men. His brother had natural social skills and moved easily among unlikely strangers.

"Are you enjoying the game?" the portly Mr. Wang asked.

"Your sons are excellent players."

"I've been fortunate," Mr. Wang said, rubbing a hand over his belly. "And my older son's boy looks like he will be a good player, too." The elder man nodded toward a youngster who was standing close to Huai-liang. Just then, one of the players tossed the ball, a red leather-encased animal bladder filled with air, toward the boy. He kicked it, keeping it in the air, never touching it with his hands or elbows.

"Indeed. You seem to have a family of team players," Lu said. "Even your concubine shows excellent skills."

Mr. Wang brightened. "When I took Xiao Tai-tai as mine, some said I was foolish. She's almost forty years younger. But why shouldn't I? Besides, she can run the household. My first wife is getting old and my younger son's mother, my second wife, died last year."

Soon the game resumed, with each side vying to breach the other team's line of defense by hitting the ball through a net placed in the middle of the field and to the other side.

As Qiu-lin, the younger son, surged toward the ball, feet flying, he fell. Mr. Wang's concubine seized the ball, kept it in the air and booted it through the net.

The audience cheered.

Lu leaned forward, his attention on Qiu-lin, who now lay sprawled out on the ground, vomiting and in convulsions. Lu jumped up and rushed onto the playing field, his coroner close behind.

By the time Lu reached the prostrate figure, he was still. His coroner and another older fellow came up behind and bent over the player.

"He's gone," the coroner said. The older man grimly nodded in agreement.

Lu knelt and touched the young man's hand, then his face. He was remarkably cold. Just moments ago he was full of vitality and dashing after the ball. Now his body had lost all its warmth, and a thick layer of vomit was smeared over his chin.

Mr. Wang and Huai-liang broke through the circle of people surrounding Qiu-lin's body. They had heard the coroner. At the sight of his son lying, unmoving, on the ground, Mr. Wang began to sway and leaned against his older son for support.

"Fu Zi poisoning," the coroner declared.

"No. That's not possible," the gaunt older man said. "I'm his doctor. He complained of suffering from yang depletion and wanted a tonic. I gave him the herb to restore his manliness. That's all. He's been under my care for several months. It couldn't be the medicine."

Eyes wide, Mr. Wang shook his head as if to push the words 'Fu Zi poisoning' away. Then, searching his dead son's face, his sobs overtook him and he collapsed, sliding to the ground. Huai-liang tried to lift him, but he resisted, remaining near the body. Finally, he raised his head and looked straight at his doctor. "I don't understand. What happened?"

The older brother again struggled to lift his father. "Father, come with me. Come." He looked at Lu, as if pleading for help.

Lu assisted in pulling the patriarch to his feet. "Go with your son. There's nothing you can do."

Devastation written on his face, Mr. Wang nodded and left the field, leaning heavily against his older son. They sat with his wife and grandson on the sidelines.

Lu ordered men to remove the body. He needed to examine it, for, as with any suspicious death, it was his responsibility as magistrate to personally determine if the cause of death was natural, accidental, or a homicide.

Lu glanced around for the family doctor and spotted him slinking away down the field. He promptly ordered a couple of men to stop the doctor and hold him for questioning.

At the table set up on the sidelines for keeping score, Lu grabbed a writing brush. Dabbing the brush into black ink, he quickly wrote a note to his court guards, telling them to come to the house and bring all of Fu-hao's court recording materials. It was imperative for the judge to have accurate notes of every stage of the proceedings. These notes would form the heart of his official report to his superiors.

***

Before questioning anyone, Lu examined the teapot and cup the deceased used during the break. He smelled the liquid left in the pot and, dipping his finger into it, tasted it. It was the same tea he'd been served. He was glad to see there were a few drops of liquid in the cup. He sniffed and discerned a distinctive acrid and slightly sweet aroma. He held the cup out to his coroner, who after checking it, nodded. "Fu Zi has been added to his tea."

"And it's not in the pot. So he's the only one to drink it," Lu said. "What do you know about Fu Zi?"

"It is an important medicine for people who are out of balance. Their system is too cold and they need more energy. And, of course, men often use it to increase their libido," the coroner said. "But an overdose means certain death. And, as we've seen, it's not pretty. Although death can be rather quick, the victim suffers dizziness and blurred vision, then severe pain along with vomiting and convulsions."

"He was murdered then?" Fu-hao asked, brush pausing in mid-air.

Lu shook his head. "We don't know yet. He could have taken too much by mistake. We'll know more after we question the key people involved." With that, he ordered his guard to bring in the family doctor.

"Why did you try to run away?" Lu demanded of the shaking elder.

"I didn't, Your Honor. I was merely, ah, merely going to offer my services to his mother, Madam Du."

"Then you were going in the wrong direction." Lu said coldly. "Tell me about your prescription."

"Mr. Wang's younger son has been married for a year and hasn't yet produced an heir. His wife is under the care of a woman specializing in such things. He came to me."

"And you prescribed Fu Zi," Lu said.

"It's often used for such purposes. I have many happy clients. I promise, Mr. Wang's son did not die because of my treatment." He clasped one hand over the other at chest level and bowed several times, begging, "You must believe me." He cast a glance around the room until he spotted the coroner. "Ask him, he knows."

"We saw him die," Lu thundered. "He was poisoned."

The old doctor seemed to shrink. "Yes," he said in a small voice. "It appears to be from too much Fu Zi, but I don't know how he could have taken so much. I warned him. I even had his mother keep the medicine in her care, so he wouldn't be tempted to take too much. Sometimes men do, impatient to boost their virility. But it's not hard to get it on the streets. Anyone could have put extra in his tea."

Lu let the family doctor stand off to the side, in case he was needed in further testimony.

Next he had Madam Du, Mr. Wang's wife, come before him.

Madam Du was the older son's mother and, as Mr. Wang's first wife, had always been responsible for running the household—even when his second wife was alive. And, while the younger son was by Mr. Wang's second wife, everyone expected Madam Du to share the role of mother to all her husband's children, however difficult such a feat may be.

The diminutive woman with steel gray hair stood ramrod erect in her black-on-black silk dress, only the white cross-over collar offering relief, her face a picture of concern and sorrow. She was impressive in spite of her age, or because of it, Lu thought.

"Madam Du, I'm sorry for your family's loss, but the court has to proceed as quickly as possible for the good of all, not the least your son."

She bowed in silence, indicating her understanding.

"Did you at any time go over to the players' tea table?"

"No, Your Honor. I remained with the women. The maids, under the direction of Mr. Wang's concubine, took care of the men's—" Her eyes flashed to the concubine standing on the side of the room next to Huai-liang. "—the players' needs," she amended. She had referred to her husband in the most formal manner, showing respect for him and the court.

"Did you know your son was taking medicine prescribed by the family doctor?"

"Yes."

"Did you know what it was and what it was for?"

"Yes. Mr. Wang's son wanted to increase his virility; he wanted an heir. He'd already been married a year and his wife wasn't yet pregnant. I told him it was her fault, but he insisted on increasing his yang energy."

"Where did you keep it?"

"In the storage area, where all the medicines are kept."

"Do you know if he took more than prescribed by the family doctor?"

"The doctor had his individual doses wrapped separately. I never gave him more than the proper amount at any one time."

"Who else had access to the medicine storage area?"

"Besides me, Mr. Wang's concubine. Just the two of us."

"Why did his concubine have such privileges? Isn't that unusual?"

"Perhaps, but I'm getting older, and I am gradually passing responsibilities to the younger generation." Madam Du kept her eyes downcast as she responded clearly and succinctly to each of his questions.

"Wouldn't your older son's wife normally take on such tasks?"

"Mr. Wang preferred his concubine be given that responsibility, not our son's wife."

Lu looked her over. There was nothing in her demeanor or voice indicating a fragile woman who needed to retire from the responsibilities—and power—of running the household.

"Did your son ask to increase his medicine recently? Perhaps to build his strength for today's ball game?"

She paused for a moment to consider the question before responding. "No, he didn't."

"And both you and the concubine have a key?"

She paused again. "No, I have the only key. Whenever someone needs medicine I give it to Mr. Wang's concubine. She retrieves whatever is requested."

"Did anyone require medicine recently?"

"Well, Xiao Tai-tai had a headache yesterday and wanted a dose. That's all. Except for Qiu-lin, of course."

Lu released her. Staring after her departing figure, he thought about her referring to the younger son as 'Mr. Wang's son,' but the older son as "our son."

Next he called in Mr. Wang's concubine. The tall, striking athlete moved with grace and feminine comportment as she approached him. Lu almost smiled. He wouldn't have guessed this was the same woman who so aggressively swept over the ball field.

"Xiao Tai-tai," he said, addressing her by the family's designation for her. "You were the one to oversee the tea and snacks given to the players at break. Did you personally give Qiu-lin his tea?"

In spite of herself, her shoulders slumped slightly. "Yes, Your Honor. I gave both of the teams' captains their tea. The maids served the others."

A movement to the side caused the judge to momentarily look up. He saw Huai-liang in mid-step, as if moving toward her.

The audience standing around the room, intently listening to the testimonies, gasped.

"But," she quickly asserted, "it was the same tea for both of them. I didn't—I wouldn't—alter it. Why would I? What would I have to gain? Perhaps if you look into the other team players' relationships and past, you might find a motive."

Lu was impressed by her self-control. The pluck and quick thinking she displayed earlier on the field was evident as she stood before him. She may be young, he mused, but already she possessed considerable poise. No wonder Mr. Wang was so taken with her. Still, the listeners in the room, all friends and family of the dead man, grumbled stridently. Judge Lu had no doubt they wanted this outsider and newest addition to the family to be the murderer. The alternative—as to who the murderer was—was too serious for them to contemplate.

The concubine also seemed to sense the hostility in the room.

"Master Wang won't be very happy if you blame the innocent," she said loudly.

Shocked at the inappropriate outburst, Lu was no longer impressed by her, but angry at her audacity. The room erupted in calls for her arrest.

"Anyone who speaks in the court without my permission will be removed and given a heavy fine," Lu bellowed. A hush instantly replaced the noise. He glared at the young woman and the crowd. He must maintain order as well as respect for the judicial process.

"And do you have anyone in mind?" Lu asked with an edge to his voice.

"You might ask the cripple, Kong," she said. "Ask what happened to his arm. He would have motive."

This accusation led to another outburst. Lu's rap on the table again brought quiet.

He glowered at the concubine. She remained defiant. Nevertheless, he ordered her to stand aside and called in Kong.

A man who had been on Qiu-lin's team stepped forward. Lu hadn't noticed it on the field—because the players couldn't touch the ball with their hands or arms and the long sleeves on his robe had hidden it—but now with the man standing before him, it was obvious his right arm ended at the elbow. "You heard Xiao Tai-tai's accusation. What do you have to say?"

A mixture of anxiety, fear, and anger crossed Kong's countenance. Finally, he said, "It was an accident. It happened a long time ago. Qiu-lin and I studied for our exams together. His father had gotten a large supply of fireworks to celebrate the New Year. Qiu-lin wanted to set them off. I didn't want to because they are so dangerous, but he talked his father into letting him do it. He could talk his father into anything. When I was holding one of the fireworks, he brought a light too close to it before I could move back. It tore my arm off." He shot a quick glance at the listeners. "It was fate."

"Did you learn how to use a writing brush with your left hand after that?" Lu asked.

"Yes, but not well. I admit that even today my handwriting looks childish."

Lu knew the significance of a good hand in writing when taking the all-important exams—the provincial and national exams that determined a man's success and place in life. "Did you go on to take the exams?" he asked quietly.

"I tried, but I failed several times at the provincial level."

A sigh of commiseration rose spontaneously from those in the room.

"How do you support your family today?"

Kong looked away. "I haven't married. Who wants a cripple for a son-in-law?" he asked bitterly.

Lu could feel the weight of Qiu-lin's thoughtless actions on the listeners in the room.

"But I didn't hurt him. We're like brothers. That accident, years ago, was my fate. Why would I wait until now to kill him?"

Lu asked a few more questions and then let him step to the side with the others.

Next he called Huai-liang, the older son, before him.

"Huai-liang, where were you during the tea break?"

"I was at the table with all the other players," he said.

"Did you notice anything unusual, anything that could help the court?"

"We were excited about the game. There was a lot of ribbing about which side was going to win and by how much. The usual."

"You brothers were always the captains on opposite teams?"

"Yes. We're competitive and play hard to win. Father likes a good game. He likes to see us pitted against each other. Let the best son and team win."

"Besides Xiao Tai-tai, did you see anyone else near your brother's teacup?"

He shot a quick glance at his father's concubine. Lu couldn't read the emotion on his face. "She filled his cup first, then mine. He drank his in one gulp. The maid Lily refilled it."

"Lily? Who does she normally attend?"

"Mother. She's a new maid with a tendency to get above herself. She has complete access to all of Mother's things."

"Everything?"

"Yes. From Mother's everyday items to her more protected things, like keys to various supply cupboards and rooms."

"You're sure?"

"Quite. Mother runs a tight household, but I've been in her

rooms when Lily appears to have too much freedom." Then, as if just thinking of it, he said, "She could easily have got hold of the keys to the medicine cabinet."

"Even so, what would be her motive?" Lu asked.

"Who knows? Maybe my brother asked her to get more Fu Zi for him. I know he desperately wanted to build up his energy, especially for our game today. He knew how much it meant to Father."

Lu excused Huai-liang and mulled over the testimonies he'd heard. Who was telling the truth and who was lying? He needed more information. He called in Mr. Wang, the patriarch.

"You are now sixty years old. At this stage in life, most men step down and enjoy the fruits of their labor. Were you planning on doing that?" Judge Lu asked.

Mr. Wang, who looked like he'd aged ten years in the last couple of hours, nodded. "I was going to divide my property between my sons, one-quarter each, and relax. Enter a new stage of life."

Lu stroked his chin. Such plans were typical. "And what about the other half of your property?"

Mr. Wang shrugged. "Of course, I need something to live on. My younger son would manage it for me until I died and then he would inherit my portion. Naturally, he would also continue to care for Madam Du and Xiao Tai-tai, should they survive me."

"Who else knew of your intentions?"

"My sons. And my wife. I told them last week. Such a plan is not unusual."

Yes, this was the normal course of events. As Mr. Wang told the court his plans, Lu watched the audience. He caught Huai-liang's momentary scowl and his eyes seeming to seek out Xiao Tai-tai. Was Huai-liang thinking of the expenses this new concubine added to his inheritance, or was there more?

Even with his younger brother dead, at hearing his father's words spoken in public, the idea of losing so much wealth seemed to have caused Huai-liang's visceral reaction. Lu considered the proposed uneven division of Mr. Wang's property: one-fourth to Huai-liang, his older, and three-fourths to Qiu-lin, his younger. Such a division could cause serious animosity between brothers.

What Lu hadn't expected was Mr. Wang's wife's reaction. A look of disgust, brief but definitely there, flashed across her face. As Lu watched her, he suspected she knew more than she'd told the court. He also began to suspect she was manipulating some of the scenes being played out before him. To get at the truth, he had to be careful in how he proceeded. Madam Du was both female and of the older generation, and the law severely limited how a judge could force information from her. While in the search for truth, the use of torture by the court was expected, mandated even, in many cases. When dealing with women, the disabled, and the elderly, however, such tools were sharply restricted or denied. Xiao Tai-tai was young, but as a female member of a distinguished family of his community, she also had to be treated with special care. Taking a chance, he decided to use guile.

He straightened up even more and called out, "Guards, I want you to arrest Xiao Tai-tai on the charge of murdering her master's son!"

Mr. Wang turned an ashen gray, eyes round as saucers. A satisfied smirk spread across Madam Du's lips. Stricken, Xiao Tai-tai turned toward Huai-liang. He returned a stunned look.

As the guard reached for the concubine, Huai-liang rushed between them. "No. Not her. She's innocent. I put the overdose into Qiu-lin's cup."

Now Madam Du swooned. Mr. Wang looked back and forth between his son and his concubine, totally confused. Pandemonium broke out among the listeners.

Judge Lu stared hard at the older son. "You killed your brother? Were others involved?"

"No. It was only me. Xiao Tai-tai is innocent. She didn't know anything."

"Why are you telling the court this now? Is it to save the life of this woman, your father's concubine?" He paused. "And your lover?"

Huai-liang hung his head. "Yes."

"Louder," Lu ordered.

"Yes. I admit we are lovers, but she had nothing to do with killing my brother."

At this, Mr. Wang staggered.

Madam Du seemed to spring to life. "No! No!" she cried. "I did it."

Lu flicked a hand at her, as if dismissing her. "You, madam, are his mother and simply want to save him, to protect him."

She drew herself up. Her tiny frame didn't hide her formidable character. "It was all me. My husband was going to give that gadfly Qiu-lin everything. He was no more than Mr. Wang's second wife's offspring. As the older and son of his first wife, Huai-liang should be his main heir. He worked hard all these years, yet all he and my grandchild were going to inherit was one-forth of the estate. It wasn't fair. I had to do something."

"And who would suspect the ever dutiful wife?" Lu asked,

watching her intently.

For a moment, only Fu-hao's brush rapidly sweeping across the paper could be heard.

"It was always about him. My husband never considered others in the family. What we did, how we worked, how we suffered. And then he brought in that concubine." She fairly spit out the last words. "That slip of a woman was to replace me and even deny Huai-liang's wife her place in running the household."

"And then finding out his decision on how to divide the inheritance was too much," Lu said.

"It was absurd. Something had to be done. All that was necessary was for me to put the overdose of Fu Zi into Qiu-lin's tea and have my maid serve it to him. No one knew anything."

"Then if anyone did suspect murder, you had set it up so that Xiao Tai-tai, who had access to the medicine room, would appear guilty."

"It was so simple," Mr. Wang's wife said.

Master Wang looked around the room, aghast. His younger son was dead, his wife of forty years had murdered him, and his concubine was having an affair with his own son. It was all he could do to remain standing before the judge and his community.

THE BLACK HAND

by Peter W. J. Hayes

*In a tale of multiple betrayals, tough guy Jake comes
back to Pittsburgh to discover the truth of his brother
David's death . . . and the murder of the woman they
both loved. But mobbed-up David was surrounded by
killers . . .*

The train ride from Minnesota started in sunshine that sparkled
across the January snow, hurting Jake's eyes, and ended in the
gathering black of Pittsburgh, the windows covered with grime and
streaked by a cold rain. It matched how he felt about returning. He
shifted his large frame in the second class seat and put aside the
Erie Daily Times someone had left in the compartment. During his
three years in Minnesota, the news hadn't really changed. It was
January 1928 and the Pittsburgh Police already had three unsolved
gang shootings. They blamed them on the Black Hand, but Jake
knew differently. The Black Hand didn't actually exist, but
Prohibition did, and the easy money from bootlegged liquor had
created a patchwork of neighborhood gangs, including the one run
by his brother, David. So the better questions, he thought, were
whether Stefan Monestaro still supplied the bootlegging barrels and
bottles out of his north side warehouse, if Joe Siragusa had finally
cornered the sugar and yeast business, and whether the Volpe
brothers still controlled Wilmerding.

And which one of them, if any, had ordered David's murder.

The train slowed. Through the back of his seat Jake felt the cars
nudge together at the couplings, and then, as the locomotive picked
up speed, the tug of them stretching apart. The rails ran alongside
the Ohio River in the final stretch to Pittsburgh. Just ahead, on the
far shore, recently poured slag glowed a fierce orange, lighting a
black river as flat and motionless as ice. Five days earlier someone
had fished his brother out of that same river near Brunot's Island,
the island where Meriwether Lewis had stayed on his first night
headed to the Louisiana territories. The Ojibwa he'd met in
Minnesota liked to say that in winter Lake Superior never gave up
her dead. Pittsburgh's rivers, he decided, were different.

They invited the living back for revenge.

From Penn Station he strode into the sulfurous coal smoke of Pittsburgh's mills and forges. He had never noticed the smell when he was growing up, but the years spent logging in Minnesota had cleaned it out of him. Now the stench settled in the back of his throat like a fishhook. He rolled his shoulders as he walked, glad to be moving again. New electric street lights guided him along Liberty Avenue eastward, the trolley and electric lines a crosshatch over his head. In Lawrenceville he turned left into a dirt alley, darkness enveloping him, the contours familiar to his feet. Fifty yards farther and the cold iron smell of the Allegheny River settled about him. He turned right and crossed a puddle-pitted backyard, guided by a candle lantern in a window.

The back door led into a cramped kitchen where his mother rose from a chair, her brown eyes haggard. He dropped his grip and folded his arms around her. She was tall and raw-boned, but felt smaller against him than he remembered.

"Thank you," she said softly, her face turned to his ear.

"Wouldn't have it any other way, Ma."

They separated and Jake turned to the man in the cassock and dog collar standing next to the kitchen table.

"Freddy."

"Father Crane," interrupted his mother, but Jake had already wrapped the man in his arms. They held one another for a moment, and when they separated, Freddy's cheeks were flushed.

Jake looked him up and down. "Still Freddy to me." He eyed the black leather gloves on Freddy's hands. "Jesus, Ma. You can't get a little heat in here? Freddy's freezing."

His mother tapped him on the arm. "Watch your language." A thin smile rose to her lips. "We had soup."

It was an old joke. Jake's mother brought Freddy home to live with them when he was seven, two years after his father died, and at the point when his mother was too drunk to care for him. All that first winter Freddy had complained about how cold he was, and even on the hottest summer days David would needle him about it, asking him if he needed them to light the stove.

Freddy found his voice. "I'm used to the clergy house now. Fireplaces in every room."

Jake grinned. "No wonder you fell for the church."

Freddy straightened. "It's a calling, Jake."

Jake held Freddy's blue eyes. He had seven inches of height on Freddy, and perhaps thirty pounds. A heavy silence that he wanted to avoid settled in the room.

"If you say so."

His mother touched his arm. "Father Crane has agreed to do the service."

Jake nodded. "Thanks, Freddy." He then added, "Father Crane."

"You're welcome, Jacob." Freddy's voice contained a new soothing tone Jake guessed he used on his parishioners.

"When is the funeral?"

"Day after tomorrow."

Jake turned to his mother. "I'm guessing the coppers still don't know what happened?"

Jake's mother shook her head, her eyes downcast.

Gently, Freddy said, "I'm sorry, but I should go." He hugged their mother and signaled Jake with his eyes.

"I'll walk you out," said Jake, and followed him into the alley. They stopped a couple of feet apart, the night so dark Jake couldn't see his eyes. When Freddy spoke the soothing tone was gone.

"Are you going to find who did this to David?"

"That's why I came. I want to get the guy."

"Nobody should be thrown off a bridge like that. Remember Connolley from when we boxed? He runs the precinct now."

"Figured I'd start with David's speakeasy."

"Which one?"

Jake settled on his heels. "He expanded?"

"Four speakeasies and two bawdy houses."

Jake collected his thoughts. "I didn't know."

"I was going to put it in the next letter."

Jake shrugged. "Did he take those speakeasies from anyone? Or the girls? Maybe that's it."

"I think he bought them square. He also bought Johnson's Diner last year. His boys use it for an office. They're there most mornings."

"Thanks." Jake fell silent, thinking about something else, and it was as if Freddy could hear his thoughts.

"I can tell you about Bridgid."

"Tell me," Jake said softly.

"I'm not going to ask what went on between you and David with her. But after you left, it was bad. Bridgid came to see me. She was desperate to find you."

Jake raised his face to the sky. Not a single star. He'd forgotten. Minnesota was a riot of stars, more than the trees in the never-ending pine forests. Pittsburgh's skies were as dense as its rivers. Freddy picked up the narrative again. "She'd guessed that I knew where you were, but I wouldn't tell her. And then she disappeared. Afterwards David showed up. He was sure she'd gone to find you.

It was bad."

"I'm sorry, Freddy. I didn't mean to put you in a tough spot."

"I was the one who said I'd write. Anyway, about a year went by and then Ma came to me. She took me to a house a few blocks from the church on Davison Street. The house that belonged to your aunt?"

"I remember. But she died years ago."

"OK, well, don't tell Ma I told you this, but she keeps the house for girls in trouble. Unmarried girls in the family way or ones beaten by their husbands. She takes them in. She asked me to pray with the girls, but you know Ma isn't religious. I think she really wanted the girls to get used to being around a man again. A lot of them have a hard time with that. Being a priest, I guess I'm not much of a threat."

Jake smiled at how well Freddy understood his mother's thinking. "How does she find these girls?"

"I think women tell her because she's a midwife. I hear about those things in confession but all I can do is pray."

"And Bridgid?"

"That's why she took me. Bridgid was there."

Jake's heart thumped harder. "David beat her?"

"I don't know. At first she wouldn't talk, just sat on her bed and stared out of the window. It was as if she'd lost something. She got better, but she was never the same."

"And then what?"

"She left. Ma tried to stop her, but it isn't a prison. She was a clerk at Kaufmann's department store. That's where David spotted her."

"And?"

"A couple of weeks later she was found dead in her boarding house. Beaten. Coppers never solved it."

Jake breathed out slowly. "How do you know David spotted her?"

"They had an argument in the store. Police questioned David, but he had an alibi."

"Which was?"

"His boys backed him up."

"Huh." Jake considered it, but he already knew the answer. "It wasn't David, he wasn't like that."

Freddy leaned in close, his eyes burning and angry. "Did he ever get mad when he didn't get his way? Tell me a time when he didn't."

Freddy was right. When one of David's rages descended, Jake either avoided him, or helped him do what he wanted, just to prevent trouble. He had gone along with him. He understood now that had been a mistake.

"Do you still fight?" Freddy stretched up toward him, his words sharper.

Jake shifted his weight. The fighting was something else he had gone along with. David had organized the fights for the swells who lived along Millionaire Row in Shadyside or drove in from Sewickley. Jake had won the first fifteen, all of them bare-knuckle, while Freddy, just out of seminary, held the bets. Then came the wiry, slack jawed man from Youngstown. In the two months Jake had spent recovering he'd thought a lot about why he'd lost. Overconfidence, certainly. But mostly it was distraction. David's new girlfriend, Bridgid, had come to the fight. She'd been there in the corner of his eye and he'd wanted to impress her.

"No more fighting," said Jake.

"You know, that last fight? That's when David made the money to buy the speakeasy."

Jake tried to blink away his confusion. "What?"

"I held the bets."

"He bet against me?"

Freddy's voice cracked. "He made me promise not to tell you."

***

That night Jake lay in his boyhood bed, David's empty one against the opposite wall. He wanted to remember David, but all that came to him was the memory of Bridgid and those few desperate nights when David was away. The feel of her body against his. The coursing guilt he'd felt afterward. At the time he had convinced himself that leaving for Minnesota was the right thing to do and that giving up Bridgid was honorable. Now he knew that decision was a mistake. In fact, his decision to leave was cowardice, just a way to avoid a confrontation.

And now Bridgid was dead.

He woke from a ragged sleep to find a note from his mother explaining she'd been called to a birth. He found Johnson's Diner later in the morning and spotted Louis, David's 300-pound partner, shoveling potatoes into his mouth at a table near the back. David's other partner, Doc, sat across from him. Jake started toward them but the man sitting at the next table rose, his eyes glittering, his right hand inside his brown suit coat. The diner fell silent. Jake stopped. Sensing the silence Louis looked up, still chewing on his potatoes. Jake nodded to him.

Louis dropped his fork, wiped his mouth with a napkin, and looked at the man with his hand inside his jacket.

"Geno," he called. "We're good. This is David's brother."

Geno didn't move, just blinked, then dropped his hand. Jake continued to the table as Louis rose and Doc slid a chair over with his foot so Jake could sit down.

"Jake," Louis said, and held out his hand. "I'm sorry about David. It's a mess."

"That's what I wanted to talk to you boys about."

Louis settled into his seat. From the corner of his eye Jake saw Geno collect a baseball bat from the wall and move to a stool about halfway down the counter. He reached over the counter and placed the bat out of sight. A waitress who Jake guessed was about 14 years old arrived and asked Jake if he wanted anything, carefully watching Geno the whole time. Jake smiled at her and shook his head.

"When's the funeral?" Louis' eyes searched Jake's face.

"Tomorrow. Allegheny Cemetery. Freddy's doing it."

"Father Crane." Doc smiled. "Who'd a thought it?"

"Yeah. But guys, tell me about it. What happened?"

Louis shrugged, picked up his fork and put it down again. "That's it. We don't know. Regular night, we close down the speaks. Doc goes to check on the girls. I went home, I thought David went home. Turned out he musta had plans to meet someone."

"He didn't ask you guys to go along?"

Doc shook his head. "Nah. Never said anything. You might want to ask Geno over there. David was his job."

Jake nodded toward Geno. "Yeah, explain that. I grew up with you guys, who the hell is he?"

Louis shook his large head. "You own a speak, you gotta gun up. Coupla guys took a run at the Polaks about a month ago. Siragusa is our boss. He brought Geno down from New York."

"He's itching for it," Jake said.

"What he's paid for." Louis stuffed another forkful of potatoes into his mouth.

Jake leaned in closer. "Someone take a run at you guys?"

Doc and Louis shook their heads. "Nah," said Louis.

"Then how come you need Geno?"

"In case some out of town guys hit us."

Jake nodded toward Geno. "But he's an out of town guy."

Louis and Doc glanced at one another.

"Jesus," said Doc. "Never thought of that."

"Christ." Louis put down his fork, his eyes wide.

Jake sat back, feeling sorry for them.

Louis leaned toward him. "Jake, you gonna stay around? You could take over for David. Everyone knows you from the fights.

They wouldn't mess with you. We wouldn't need Geno then."

Doc nodded. "Yeah, no one can complain about that, you being David's brother and all."

"I appreciate that." Jake glanced from one to the other. "I guess I like the air better in Minnesota."

Louis looked down and Doc grimaced. Neither seemed to know what to say next.

"C'mon guys, can't be that bad. You bought everything clean, right?"

Louis looked up, his voice almost pleading. "We did, but someone's gonna run us."

"Well, you got Geno."

Louis glanced in Geno's direction and Jake saw distrust in his eyes. Jake tapped his fingers on the table. "Hey, guys, what can you tell me about Bridgid?"

Louis sat back slowly and looked at the wall. Doc shifted in his seat.

"Guys?"

Louis turned his head back. "David was angry with you. You left and a month later Bridgid disappeared. He figured she went after you."

"You know that's not true, right?"

"How would I know?" Louis jammed a fat forefinger onto the tabletop. "All I know is that maybe a year and a half after she goes missing, David sees her at Kaufmann's. They fight, store dicks run him out. After that David was crap. Didn't come to work. Didn't do anything. Got so bad the bosses came around and told him to shape up. We got Geno a week later. Then Bridgid's dead. David sits around a coupla' weeks lookin' at the wall, then he comes around. But he's doing his job and he ain't, if you get my meaning. When I heard they found him in the river, I actually wondered if he dove in. But I guess he was beat up, so maybe not."

Louis fell silent. Jake shifted in his chair. "And you guys gave him an alibi for Bridgid?"

Louis tightened. "Yeah. Because David was eating with us when it happened."

Doc pushed his plate back. "It wasn't him, Jake. His hands were clean."

"What do you mean?"

"She was beat to death, right? But his hands were clean. No bruises or cuts. You remember what your hands were like after a fight? David had to feed you the first couple of days. His hands were clean."

"OK. I get that. I had to ask, guys, I'm sorry."

Louis shifted his belly against the table. "You think someone went after him because of Bridgid?"

Jake sat back. "I don't know."

Doc shook his head. "David had a temper, we all know that, but not like that. He never laid a finger on any of our girls."

"OK." Jake stood up, aware of Geno watching him. "See you guys tomorrow?"

They both nodded and Jake turned to leave. As he did Geno swiveled around on his stool and leaned back, his elbows on the counter and hands hanging limply beside his torso, a lazy smile on his lips. Jake nodded to him as he approached, then pivoted and rushed him, slamming his hands down on Geno's forearms, pinning him. Jake bent close to Geno's face.

"OK, asshole. You were supposed to keep my brother alive. So what the hell are you still doing here?"

Geno squirmed but Jake pushed down harder on his arms. The toothpick swirled between Geno's lips. "Screw you. He said he was going to bed. Went out after that."

"He didn't want you there?"

"Too damn stupid to know he did."

Jake searched his brown eyes. "Or maybe you did him."

"Somebody beat him. I'd a shot him."

"Yeah. You look like one of those guys who's scared to get close." Jake let go and stepped back. Geno's right hand darted under his coat and Jake launched an uppercut that landed with a flat smack under his jaw. Geno's head snapped back and his eyes turned the flat color of chocolate pudding. Jake watched him slide off the stool onto the floor. The toothpick, neatly bitten off, sat on his lower lip.

Jake shook out his hand and looked at Louis. Doc was twisted around, staring.

Jake called down to them, "Asshole can't take care of himself, no wonder he couldn't take care of David."

The young waitress grinned at him, her smile almost as broad as her face.

***

Jake flexed his hand as he walked to the police precinct, working out the stiffness. His memory of Connolley was of a tall, broad-faced Irishman at the Zivic brothers' gym, his feet too heavy and slow for success in the ring. At the precinct, the duty sergeant went in search of him, and ten minutes later motioned Jake through a side door.

Connolley was standing beside his desk, his blue uniform partially unbuttoned on one side. He was about thirty pounds heavier than Jake remembered, his face ruddy and hair already white. He held out his hand.

"Remember me?" asked Connolley. He gestured to a chair and perched himself on the corner of his desk next to a paint-chipped Underwood typewriter.

"The Zivic gym?"

Connolley smiled. "Yeah. We only sparred once. Jesus, you were fast. I never got the hang of moving my feet."

Jake nodded. "I remember. But you had me going for a while." Jake didn't remember, but the way Connolley's eyes lit up he knew he'd said the right thing.

"Hear you're in Minnesota now."

Jake nodded. "Yeah. Logging. I came in for the funeral. I was wondering if there was any news about David."

Connolley held up his palms. "We're working on it. Not a lot yet."

"Do you know which bridge he was thrown from?"

"Bridge? I don't know about that. Ain't clear how he got in the water."

"Maybe I heard wrong. Is anyone making a move on his speaks and bawdy houses?"

Connolley stiffened. "There's no bawdy houses or speaks in my precinct."

Jake stopped talking. He should have guessed. Of course Connolley was on David's payroll; it was the only way the speaks and bawdy houses could stay open. It meant Connolley wanted the case closed fast to keep his payments flowing. He spoke carefully. "I meant around Pittsburgh. Bloomfield, places like that."

Connolley scratched his chest, his face stone. "Nothing like that. Look, we're still figurin' out what happened, but I can give you this." From the desk he lifted a small cardboard box and held it out to him. "It's what we found on your brother. Keys, a pen knife, his wallet. Family should have them."

"Yeah." Jake took the box. "Thanks. One other question. Bridgid Devlin. I heard she was murdered a couple of months ago. I didn't hear about it until recently."

Connolley bobbed his head. "Not my precinct," he said finally. "What's your interest?"

Jake shrugged. "She and David were courting. I woulda visited her if she was still around."

Connolley straightened up slightly. "You know your brother was questioned about that?"

"Sure." As Jake answered he realized Connolley would have protected David from any investigation. He sat back. "I just figured you'd know the real story. Papers never get it right."

Connolley was silent for a couple of heartbeats and then leaned back. "Yeah, those newspaper shits always get it wrong. They said she was beaten to death. Uh-uh. Someone hit her with a club. Iron bar, bat, hard to say. Twice to the head. Clean and fast. But David had nothing to do with it."

Jake nodded, the box suddenly heavy in his hands. "Thanks. Yeah, the funeral is tomorrow at two. We need to get done before the shift whistles drown out the preacher."

Connolley stood up and extended his hand. "Yeah. There's that."

Jake stood and shook his hand. "There's that."

***

The next afternoon Freddy, Jake, and his mother stood at David's gravesite. Freddy's face was white against his black coat and boater hat. The sky was the color of pig iron. Louis and Doc joined them, then Connolley, and finally a black Cadillac V8 parked on the cemetery road and Joe Siragusa clambered out, his coat perfectly fitted. A bodyguard Jake's size followed him. Everyone waited as Siragusa walked over, skirting the grave plots.

Freddy took his time with the ceremony, his soothing voice mixing with the distant clanks and whistles that drifted up from the mills along the river valley. Jake tried to think about David but his mind drifted, reliving the conversations of the last two days, his mind realigning and reordering people's comments the same way he sorted and collected felled logs in the St. Croix river, grouping them for the downstream trip to the sawmills. As he did, something emerged, a truth logical and obscene. At first he fought it, but he couldn't take his eyes from the way Freddy struggled to turn the thin pages of his prayer book through his thick black gloves.

Finally, Freddy led them in the Lord's Prayer and closed the ceremony.

Joe Siragusa crossed to Jake's mother and said a few words, then took a narrow envelope from his jacket pocket and pressed it into her hands. He turned to Jake.

"You should come and see me."

"I'll be heading back to Minnesota soon."

"Think about it. You and I could do some good things." He turned and started toward his car, the bodyguard following. Jake hugged his mother and told her he would catch up. Finally, it was just him and Freddy at the foot of the grave, the others a small knot headed toward the cemetery's brick entrance arch. Casually, Jake reached out and took Freddy's right hand between his own hands.

He squeezed hard.

Freddy yelped and collapsed to one knee, his head down. Jake clamped Freddy's wrist in his right hand and yanked the glove off. Freddy's knuckles were bruised and red, the ring finger knuckle like a large split grape.

"You're the one," rasped Jake. "It had to be you. If you asked David to meet you, he'd go by himself. You he'd trust. And your right cross, you could take him. And you were the only one who knew he'd gone off a bridge." The shift-change whistles started, one after the other, wailing along the river valley.

Freddy choked out, "You don't understand. He killed Bridgid."

"He didn't kill Bridgid. But I got a good idea who did."

Freddy shuddered. "No! It was him!" He sucked air deep into his chest. Jake tightened his grip.

"Stand up," shouted Jake over the shift whistles.

Freddy staggered upright. "It was David!"

"David didn't beat women."

"She told me in confession."

"After I left, right? When she was at the house? You understand, dumbass? She made it up so you'd feel sorry for her. So you'd tell her where I was."

Freddy blinked hard and his pupils opened as if he were seeing something for the first time. "No," he gasped, but there was no argument in his voice.

"David didn't hit people, Freddy. He had me for that. Or Louis back before he got fat. Or that asshole Geno." The wind and shift whistles wailed in his ears. "So here it is. I can't give you to Connolley. He's on David's payroll and he'd just throw you in the river to keep everything quiet. Too easy. I want you thinking about this every day for the rest of your life. I want you praying for David every day. And Bridgid. And never get that hand fixed. I come back in a couple of years, I want to see that knuckle still broke. I want you to carry it. You're a mortal sinner, Freddy. Start making up for it."

Freddy sank to his knees, tears streaking his face. Jake dropped his wrist and reached back to hit him, but didn't have the energy. He was empty. He walked away and glanced back only once. Freddy was still on his knees, his hat on the grass, his face hidden behind his black gloved hands as he prayed.

***

At Penn Station Jake bought a ticket for the next day's 5:30 a.m. train. Then he searched David's speakeasies until he found Louis. Louis couldn't tell him what he needed to know fast enough. That night, over dinner, he said goodbye to his mother.

At 4:00 a.m. he rose, dressed, and pulled on an extra pair of pants. Walking briskly through the cold morning, grip in hand, he threaded his way to Johnson's Diner. From the box Connolley had given him, he removed a ring of keys and tried them in turn until the front door opened. Inside, he placed his grip near the door and waited until he could make out the looming darkness of the counter, then tiptoed behind it, passing the curtained entrance to the back of the diner. Geno's bat was exactly where he had left it. Jake hefted it, and in a single cutting motion knocked the cash register to the floor in a crash of wood and clattering coins. Swiftly, he crossed to the side of the curtained opening and pressed himself against the wall.

It took twenty seconds for Geno's hand to plunge between the curtains, pistol up. Geno followed, his eyes locked on the cash register. Jake brought the bat down on his wrist. Geno crashed to his knees, the gun skittering across the floor. He tried to rise but Jake swung the bat full arc onto the side of Geno's knee. He thudded to the floor with a keening wail. Jake recovered the pistol and squatted next to him.

"Geno," he said loudly enough to be heard above the man's sobs. "You listen now. It took me a while, but Louis explained it to me. I just didn't know how to listen. He said you showed up after David found Bridgid. Right when David was letting the business go to hell. Then a week later Bridgid is dead. I get it. Then Connolley told me that Bridgid wasn't beaten to death, someone used a bat. Like this one. And I know you aren't a guy who likes to get close. You're the kind who uses a weapon. And a bat is quieter than a gun, ain't it?"

He rose and kicked Geno in the side. "Convince me you didn't kill Bridgid, you asshole, and you got a chance. But I think Siragusa brought you in to kill Bridgid and get David back on track."

"Go to hell."

"That's not gonna get you out of this."

"It was business."

Jake looked away for a moment. A thick gray light glimmered over the roofs of the houses across of the street.

"No, you asshole. Bridgid was something between David and me. A family argument."

"Who gives a shit about your family? She was screwing up the business. You lose, asshole."

Jake stared at the man on the floor. "No, Geno. You do." He brought the bat down on the top of Geno's head and the crunch of bone vibrated up his arm. Geno went flat, his legs cycling. Jake brought the bat down one more time on his head and Geno was still. Jake checked that he was dead, then crossed to his grip. He stripped off his outer pair of pants and used them to wipe the blood and tissue from his shoes. He tossed the bat into the corner and dropped the pants in his grip. Let himself out and locked the door.

As he walked to the train he thought about Minnesota. The thousands of stars, the wind-whisper through the pines. A good place to sit and think. To get himself ready. They'd made so many mistakes. Freddy misunderstanding Bridgid's confession, him backing down when David was angry. How he fooled himself that running to Minnesota was the honorable thing to do. So no more mistakes, because getting Siragusa was going to be hard.

For Siragusa he would have to be perfect.

THE TRIAL OF MADAME PELLETIER

by Susanna Calkins

Maidservant Anna must testify in her employer's murder trial. Did Mme. Pelletier kill her husband? The evidence could argue either way. The answer is a chilling one in this tale set in 1840 in France.

April 1840
Tulle, Limousin, France

Anna Pequod stopped a few meters away from the entrance to the Tulle courthouse, closing her eyes to the madness that surrounded her and her parents.

Her father tugged her sleeve. "None of that, daughter."

Crowds milled about the judiciary grounds, many pleading with grim-faced guards to allow a few more curious onlookers inside the building. Everyone—from sewage workers to society women—wanted to witness the spectacle that would soon unfold inside the county's assize court.

"Trial of Madame Pelletier starts today!" the newsboys called. "Learn how the Lady Poisoner did her husband in!"

For weeks now, the scandalous poisoning of Monsieur Pelletier, Anna's former employer, had dominated *Le Figaro* and *La Presse,* relegating news of King Louis Phillippe I and his July Monarchy to the back pages. Even the recent assassination attempt on Queen Victoria in England could not compete with this juicy *cause célèbre.*

"Took Monsieur Pelletier two weeks to die!" the newsboys shouted gleefully.

Anna shivered. Her parents had served in M. Pelletier's household for over ten years, her father as his gardener and her mother as his cook and housekeeper. However, they'd only known Mme. Pelletier since last August, when their master had brought his new bride to Tulle, an unexpected act prompting a startling wagging of tongues.

"What kind of respectable woman is affianced through a marriage broker? Why was a match not made among her family's acquaintances?" Tulle's *le bon ton* had murmured behind their

fans as they strolled along the Rue de Corrèze. *"Perhaps she is ill-witted or lacking in the womanly graces."*

The shopkeepers' wives had been equally scathing, dissecting the newcomer while they waited for Mass to begin at Tulle's cathedral. *"Didn't even have a real wedding,"* they had sneered, having learned the couple were married by a judge rather than by a priest. *"Perhaps they* had *to get married."*

As for Anna's mother and the other servants of Tulle, an old city modernized by the lace industry, they were most disturbed by the bride's lack of adornment. *"Did you know that she had no lace or even a veil?"*

Mme. Pelletier's behavior after she arrived had only caused more gossip. Tearful and restless, the mistress had spent many hours walking alone on the grounds. She made no social calls and had refused all visitors throughout autumn. Most who met her pronounced her 'odd.'

However, everything had changed late last October when Mme. Pelletier's spirits seemed to lift. Unexpectedly she'd begun to cultivate her social equals, showing herself to be a lively and cultured woman. With that, her standing in the community improved greatly. Anna had been struck by her transformation, even more so when Mme. Pelletier had become almost gay in her husband's presence. *"Finally accepted her wifely duties,"* Anna's mother had whispered to her daughter, relieved that the family discord seemed to be dissipating. Of course, after M. Pelletier's death two months later at Christmas, the local gossips surmised that this change in spirits had marked the moment that Mme. Pelletier had begun to plot her husband's murder.

"She laughed, did you know, as he wretched his insides out," one matronly-looking woman muttered to another.

"Disgraceful," the other agreed. "It will be a short journey to hell for *that* one."

Anna's stomach lurched. Although Mme. Pelletier had been distant with her, she'd never been unkind.

Her father presented Judge Binet's summons to the guard, who looked it over with interest. Just then, there was a great commotion at the edge of the courtyard.

"Here she comes!" someone called, pointing to the eastern end of the wide-paved street.

"I see her carriage!" called another. The crowd began to jostle one another, everyone eager to catch a glimpse of Mme. Pelletier as she arrived.

"Wait here," the guard told them and pushed his way through the crowd down to the street.

From the steps, Anna watched as a hired carriage, pulled by two well-matched horses, drew up in front of the courthouse. The curtains had been pulled down over the windows, hiding the occupants within. The driver, smartly dressed in the carriage company's blue livery, hopped down in a practiced way and knocked on the carriage door.

An older gentleman, perhaps in his fifties, descended first. Anna recognized him. He was M. Le Bec, Mme. Pelletier's attorney. When he'd interviewed her at the Pelletier's home the week before, he'd been dressed as he was today, immaculate in a light gray morning suit, his cravat perfectly tied.

Extending his hand upwards, M. Le Bec helped a woman dressed in deep mourning step down from the carriage. Mme. Pelletier had a thick widow's veil covering her face and a small black handbag hanging from her wrist.

M. Le Bec and the driver flanked her while the assize guard swung his baton back and forth, clearing a path to the courthouse door. "Make way!" he called.

Around her the crowd hissed venomous words.

"Husband-killer!"

"Poisoner!"

"Murderess!"

Though the veil hid the woman's face from the crowd, Anna could tell from the way Mme. Pelletier shrank back against M. Le Bec that she was deeply frightened. He was supporting most of her weight as they moved into the old stone courthouse.

"May God have mercy on her soul!" Anna heard her mother whisper as Mme. Pelletier passed by. "Pray God forgive *us* for what we are about to do."

Her father grunted. "We are bid only to tell the truth. It is not our souls that will bear this wretched burden." But he allowed his wife and daughter to cling to him as they followed Mme. Pelletier into the courthouse.

Once inside, they were directed to a small chamber directly across from the courtroom where two other people were already seated. Anna recognized one of them as the local apothecary. She started to greet him but a heavy-set assize guard rapped his baton against the wall. "No talking," he said. "The trial is about to start."

Anna expected the courtroom doors to be shut, but they remained open, giving her clear access to the trial proceedings. The courthouse was quite warm; she could already see people fanning themselves with the trial pamphlets they had purchased outside the courthouse. At the bailiff's command, everyone rose when Judge Binet, wearing his heavy red judicial robes and great white wig, entered from a chamber to the right of the bench. Next, the jury filed in from a chamber to the left, seating themselves in long benches. Anna could see that her former mistress had removed her veil, perhaps at the order of the judge, and was now holding a small vial of smelling salts to her nose.

M. La Rousse, the prosecuting attorney, spoke first. "We have been convened to prosecute Mme. Violette Pelletier for the most heinous act of having willfully procured and administered poison with the express purpose of murdering her husband of just five months, Simon Pelletier."

The prosecutor then proceeded to speak at length, alluding to the evidence that he planned to lay before the judge and jury. Throughout his speech, the courtroom crowd murmured, exhaling when the more salacious details of the crime were touched upon.

When the prosecutor sat down, M. Le Bec rose and faced the jury. "I will tell you of a young noblewoman trying to make the best of an unexpected marriage. A woman whose undeserving husband racked up debt after debt without her knowledge, making many enemies in the process." M. Le Bec paused, allowing everyone to hear Mme. Pelletier's soft sobs. "A loving wife who tenderly nursed her husband until his untimely demise, becoming a widow before her time."

Anna could see many female spectators sniffling and wiping their eyes, while the men shifted their feet. The jurors, striving to look impassive, looked away from Mme. Pelletier.

"Very well," the judge said. "Let us hear from our first witness." He consulted a paper. To her surprise, Anna heard her own name being called. "Anna Lourdes Pequod, servant, Pelletier household, of Tulle."

The assize guard escorted her to the witness stand, where the bailiff stood with his Bible, waiting to swear her in.

Her heart pounding, Anna almost didn't want to touch the Bible. Her hands were so sweaty that she was sure she would leave a stain upon the ornately detailed leather cover. Nevertheless, she dutifully repeated the bailiff's statements. When the oath was completed, she climbed into the witness stand, her legs shaking.

The prosecutor smiled at her in a kindly way. "There's nothing to be afraid of, Mademoiselle Pequod. You are seventeen years old, is that correct?"

At her soft assent, he continued. "And you have been serving in the household of Monsieur Simon Pelletier for ten years?"

"Yes."

"Very good," he said. "Now I am going to ask you a few questions about your daily responsibilities—what you do for the

Pelletiers. Is that all right?"

"Yes," she replied. She noticed for the first time that a clerk was writing down their exchange, making her nervous again.

But the questions were not too hard. They were mostly about which rooms she cleaned, which ones she didn't. "So Madame Pelletier did not wish for you to clean the bedchamber she shared with her husband, is that correct?"

Anna glanced over at Mme. Pelletier who was still staring straight ahead. She did not even seem to be listening. "Yes, that is correct. I was to exchange her laundry and make the bed only in her presence."

"Do you know why?"

"No."

Anna bit her lip, remembering when Mme. Pelletier had first made the odd request. *This place is burdensome enough for three servants. I should not like to trouble you further.*

"...Is that correct, Mademoiselle Pequod?" The prosecutor's question cut into her reverie.

Anna flushed. She hadn't heard his next question. Perhaps sensing her distress, he smiled and repeated the question. "One of your duties was to purchase household goods from the market and other shops, is that correct?"

"Yes," she whispered.

"Did you purchase arsenic in October 1839 from Monsieur Schmidt, an apothecary located on *Rue du Canton*?"

"Yes, sir."

"For what purpose did you make that purchase?"

"I told Madame Pelletier I had seen rats in the pantry. The arsenic was for a rat-poison paste."

"Now think carefully. How much arsenic did you request?"

"I spoke to the apothecary and he made up a vial about this size." She held her fingers a few inches apart.

"Was this the vial?" M. La Rousse asked, holding up a small glass jar with a corked top, labeled *poison*.

"Yes."

"Please enter this into evidence." He handed the vial to the bailiff. "What did you do with the arsenic after you purchased it from the apothecary?"

Anna glanced at Mme. Pelletier. This time her former mistress was looking straight at her. She looked to have a slight smile on her face. Did she nod at Anna? Anna couldn't be sure.

"Mademoiselle Pequod? Please answer the question. What did you do with the arsenic after you received it from the apothecary?"

Anna gulped. "I gave it to Madame Pelletier. She wanted to

make the paste herself.'"

"Thank you," the prosecuting attorney said. .

M. Le Bec stood up. "Did you see the rat-poison paste after that?"

"Yes," Anna said. "We made sure it was everywhere we'd seen the rats."

The prosecuting attorney spoke again. "Now I'd like to ask you some questions about Monsieur Pelletier's illness that occurred during the Christmas period, which culminated in his death on January 8, 1840. When did you notice that your master first took sick?"

"He was ill when he returned from Paris on December twenty-seventh," Anna said. "I remember seeing him walk through the door. His face was green. Maman was worried we'd all get the Parisian sickness."

"You thought it was cholera?" The defense attorney interjected. "Is that what you mean?"

"Yes, sir. Ma mère thought so. But none of us took sick," Anna replied.

"Did Monsieur Pelletier think it was cholera too?" the prosecuting attorney asked.

"No," Anna admitted. She glanced at Mme. Pelletier, who had gone back to staring straight ahead. "The mistress had sent him a cake while he was in Paris. He told us he'd eaten a few slices but threw it away when he began getting sick. He thought maybe it had gone bad in transit."

"Your master attributed his illness to the cake your mistress—his wife—had sent him while he was in Paris. Is that correct?" the prosecutor asked.

"Yes, he told me that, sir," Anna recalled. "Said I needn't fear being near him."

The crowd murmured amongst themselves until the judge banged his gavel and called for order.

"Did Monsieur Pelletier's health improve?" the prosecuting attorney asked.

Anna considered. "At first he was able to eat. I remember he dined on goose and truffles."

"Goose and truffles? That is a surprising option for a man recovering from an illness, no?"

Before Anna could reply, the defense attorney interrupted. "Mademoiselle Pequod, as capable as she may be, is not a physician and cannot speak knowledgeably of medical treatments."

"Agreed," the judge replied. He waved his hand at the court reporter. "Strike the question from the record."

But goose and truffles had seemed an odd choice to Anna and her parents, too. Anna's mother had made a light broth that she thought might soothe the master's insides. *Goose and truffles,* her mother had tsk-tsked. *Whoever heard of such a thing?*

Anna frowned at the memory.

"What is it?" the prosecutor asked, evidently having caught her expression.

"It's true we were surprised by what Madame Pelletier chose to serve Monsieur Pelletier." Here, she saw her mistress raise an eyebrow, and she continued hastily. "Her devotion to her husband was touching."

Mme. Pelletier had hovered over her husband for hours, rarely leaving his side, even during the worst of his tribulations. Even when his relatives had come from Paris, she'd been the one to tend to his needs, feeding him, wiping his brow.

"Devotion and care were not enough, no?" the prosecutor prodded. "You sent for the doctor in early January?"

"Yes, my mother had me summon Dr. Bardot."

"Why? Was Monsieur Pelletier not improving?"

Anna sighed. She could not look at Mme. Pelletier. "Ma mère thought it best that the family physician attend to him."

"Why was that?" the prosecutor pressed. "Mademoiselle Pequod, what prompted your mother's belief that a doctor was now necessary?"

"I told her that I had seen Madame Pelletier sprinkle a white powder into my master's wine."

The crowd gasped, and again the judge pounded his gavel, calling for order.

"Did you ask Madame Pelletier what it was?"

"I did. She said it was gum arabic. To soothe his stomach."

The crowd murmured indignantly but settled down when the judge turned a baleful eye in their direction.

"Did it help him?"

Anna gulped again. "No," she whispered. "His legs began to cramp up terribly and he grew even more nauseous. Dr. Bardot prescribed eggnog."

Watching M. Pelletier flailing about in his tortured way had been excruciating. Over the next week he had succumbed to his malady, his body violently purging itself of the sickness within. He'd been such a large lumbering man in life, and in near-death he'd been a putrid hulking mass, alternately sobbing, praying, and groaning.

All the while, Mme. Pelletier had stayed by his side, holding his head while he sipped the eggnog in short labored bursts. Finally, they'd all heard the one last gurgle. Anna had kept her head buried in her hands and her parents had let her be.

"Thank you, Mademoiselle Pequod," M. La Rousse said, looking pleased.

Having completed her testimony, Anna squeezed onto a bench to view the rest of the trial. Her parents were called next—first her mother, then her father. They had little else to add except, to Anna's great embarrassment, her father was forced to explain how much in back wages the Pelletiers owed them. "His financial affairs were quite disastrous even before his marriage, it would seem," the defense attorney asserted to the jury.

Next, the judge called the apothecary to the stand. M. Schmidt confirmed that Anna had purchased the arsenic for rat-poison paste in October of 1839. He then added that Mme. Pelletier had sought to purchase more arsenic after Christmas. "She told me that Monsieur Pelletier had taken ill while in Paris and that the sound of scurrying rats was keeping him awake at night," the apothecary explained. "I was rather surprised to hear this, naturally, as the supply I'd provided in October should have been sufficient."

When the apothecary concluded his testimony, he slid in next to Anna on the bench at the back of the courthouse. She could see his hands were trembling as hers had been earlier.

After a short recess for a noon meal, the doctors were called in, beginning with Dr. Bardot.

"Dr. Bardot," the prosecuting attorney said, "tell us at what point you began to suspect something was amiss with your patient."

The physician nodded. "I had already heard about the cake, the goose, the truffles, and the gum arabic. I had also observed some white powder flakes near my patient's mouth. When I asked Madame Pelletier about it, she told me that she had added some orange-blossom sugar to sweeten his tea." Dr. Bardot paused. "As I could not yet rule out that my patient was suffering from a latent form of cholera, I then prescribed eggnog."

"And then?" M. La Rousse prompted. "Did the eggnog help him?"

Dr. Bardot shook his head. "No, it did not. As Monsieur Pelletier continued to decline, I called in Dr. Roque to consult on the case. When Monsieur Pelletier succumbed to his illness, Dr. Roque ordered an autopsy, as we were both suspicious of his death."

Shortly after, Judge Binet called Dr. Roque to the stand, who arrived directly to the point. "As soon as I laid eyes on Monsieur Pelletier, I had little doubt that he was in the final grips of arsenic poisoning. Upon his death, I called for an autopsy immediately, carrying out the analysis of the man's stomach contents myself."

"What did you discover?" the prosecutor asked.

"I found no poison in Monsieur Pelletier's stomach." Dr. Roque replied.

"Aha!" M. Le Bec exclaimed. "My client's husband may well have died of cholera then."

The spectators gasped and murmured among themselves.

The judge banged his gavel. "Order!" he called. "Order!"

"Not so," Dr. Roque replied to the defense attorney when the room had settled back down. "I then called for the Marsh test, which required the exhumation and study of the entire skeleton and remains." Now, the onlookers were sitting forward in their seats. "We took a carbonized mass consisting of the organs of the thorax and abdomen, the liver, part of the heart and the brain—which for brevity's sake, I shall refer to as the visceral mass—and boiled it with distilled matter."

"What did you discover, from this more thorough testing?" M. La Rousse asked.

"Arsenical crusts! M. Pelletier was most certainly poisoned, most likely over the course of several months. We checked the rat-poison paste, which was nearly devoid of arsenic. Yet, the box containing gum arabic contained traces of the poison."

"Murderess!" a spectator shouted, standing to her feet and pointing at Mme. Pelletier.

"Hang her!" called another, as Judge Binet banged his gavel again.

The apothecary glanced at Anna, a question on his face.

She shook her head. "I don't believe it," she whispered.

But M. Pelletier had been a brute of a man, a loud-mouthed lout. Anna remembered the bruises on her mistress's face and arms. The stiffness of her movements. The fear in her eyes. She knew why her mistress had not gone calling or sought out visitors in those first few months. She knew why poisoning might have seemed the only answer.

Watching her mistress now, she was dismayed to see the woman's eyes roll back in her head and her body slump over the table. "Madame Pelletier!" she shouted.

"Tend to your client," Judge Binet said sternly to M. Le Bec. "We will close the proceedings for the day."

***

The next day, Anna returned to the courthouse, unaccompanied by her parents. During the morning session, several members of M. Pelletier's family took the stand, testifying bitterly about how Mme. Pelletier had banished them from his bedchamber. "Why would she do that, if she had nothing to hide?" they accused.

Next, several of M. Pelletier's former business associates testified, their animosity towards the victim evident. "He made it clear that he would not be making good on his payments," one of them grumbled.

"Is that so?" M. Le Bec said, looking pointedly to the jury, who nodded in understanding.

When the local banker was called, he testified not only to M. Pelletier's dwindling funds, but also claimed that M. Pelletier had shown him several threatening letters he had received, to justify why he needed his line of credit extended.

"Threats were made against the victim's life?" M. Le Bec asked.

The banker nodded. "So he claimed."

Some other interesting things came to light as well. A clerk from the *Hôtel Meurice* in Paris, where M. Pelletier had stayed during Christmas, described the box that had contained the cake from Mme. Pelletier. "Most definitely, I remember noticing that someone had pried it open and re-nailed it rather shoddily." He looked disdainful. "It was held together with some twine."

"That someone had tampered with the cake box can most certainly be gleaned," M. Le Bec pointed out. "It stands to reason that someone might also have tampered with the cake."

Anna found herself nodding along with the spectators. Such a thing was certainly possible.

***

After lunch, Mme. Pelletier was finally called to the stand, a piteous creature in black.

M. La Rousse posed the first question. "Madame Pelletier, tell us. Was your marriage a happy one?"

The crowd sat up straight, straining to catch every word.

Mme. Pelletier's smile was tight. "I will admit that I was unhappy when Monsieur Pelletier and I first wed. My uncle had led me to believe that Simon was a friend of the family. It was only later that I discovered that my uncle had used the services of a marriage broker." Her voice wavered. "He had no personal knowledge of my husband's character when he agreed to the match."

The prosecutor waved a stack of letters in her general direction. "In fact, you wrote many letters to your uncle in which you pleaded with him to annul the marriage." M. La Rousse held up several sheets of paper. "Indeed, you sometimes wrote more than one a day, did you not?"

Always the feverish writing. The pleading in her eyes. 'Dearest Anna,' she would say. 'If you hurry, you can post this one as well. Perhaps they are not getting my letters.'

M. Le Bec stood up then. "I imagine you found your husband's manor to be very different from what you expected, is that so?"

"When I arrived, I discovered the 'manor' to be a shambles—a source of ridicule." Mme. Pelletier dabbed at her eyes, looking very much like a genteel lady. "Full of rats, it was! I have never seen such squalor!"

Perhaps noticing the scandalized faces of several jurors, the prosecutor switched tactics. "Why was your husband in Paris last Christmas, Madame?"

Mme. Pelletier sniffed. "He was attempting to negotiate some outstanding debts. He wasn't a very good businessman, I now understand."

M. La Rousse looked triumphant until the defense attorney interrupted. "For what purpose did your husband *tell* you that he was going to Paris?"

"He had promised me a special present. That is why I sent him the cake and a picture of myself, along with a letter, thanking him in advance for his kindness. You have *that* letter, too, I presume?" She asked, giving the prosecutor a hard look. "Has it been entered into evidence?"

The prosecutor frowned. "Yes, we have that letter in evidence." Again he switched tactics. "Why did you add gum arabic to your husband's food? There is no known medicinal value for doing so."

Mme. Pelletier shrugged. "My mother swore by it, as did many women in the community where I grew up. Ask anyone there. They will tell you that is so."

From the look on the prosecutor's face, it was evident he had done so and come up with nothing. Still he persisted with more questions. "How do you explain the traces of arsenic that the physicians discovered in that box of gum arabic?"

"I kept the box in an unlocked drawer by my husband's bedside," she replied. "There were many times I fell fast asleep, holding my husband's hand. Anyone could have added the arsenic had they so wished."

"Such as a servant?" M. Le Bec asked. "Perhaps one angry that your husband has not paid out wages in more than ten months?"

Anna felt her face flush. Out of the side of her eye she saw the apothecary glance at her.

"Perhaps," Mme. Pelletier answered. "But my husband had many enemies, as I've now learned. Given how long the Pequots have faithfully served my husband, I cannot imagine such disloyalty from *them*."

Seeing he wasn't getting anywhere, the prosecutor changed his line of questioning. "Can you explain, Madame Pelletier, why Dr. Roque discovered virtually no arsenic in the rat-poison paste we found all over the house?"

For the first time, something flickered in Mme. Pelletier's face. Guilt? Worry? Shame? "I may not have mixed it together very well," she replied finally. "Maybe I used too much flour and water and it grew diluted." She swayed a bit. "As I said before, I am unaccustomed to rats. It should not be surprising I did this incorrectly."

She swayed again, causing the crowd to exclaim.

"I beg you, Your Honor," her attorney implored the judge. "My client has answered all your questions to the best of her ability. Pray let her withdraw for a respite, lest we have two corpses to contend with, instead of one."

***

The trial continued over the next week. Throughout, Mme. Pelletier was interrogated by the prosecutor and the judge, submitting to their repeated browbeating, often answering the same questions several times. Though teary and wan, she did not waver in her testimony.

Finally, Judge Binet declared that he was satisfied that guilt or a presumption of innocence could be determined, and each lawyer issued a closing statement.

The jury returned to their chamber to deliberate. Anna, like most of the spectators, remained in her seat.

Within thirty minutes, the jury had arrived at their decision.

They could not prove that Mme. Pelletier had poisoned her husband.

Verdict: Not guilty.

***

An hour later, Anna sat alone on a low stone wall in the Pelletier garden. Her parents had been relieved when she'd told them the outcome of the trial. "Still, it's odd," her mother had said. Her father had just shrugged.

A crunch of sticks behind her caused her to turn around. It was Mme. Pelletier.

"You got me in a lot of trouble, Anna," her mistress murmured, sitting down beside her.

"You knew?" Anna replied. "How?"

"Those wretched rats. I could see the rat-poison paste wasn't working. That's why I asked the apothecary for more arsenic. Imagine my surprise when he told me you had just procured a whole vial the month before, not a half as you told me." Mme. Pelletier's voice hardened. "You started poisoning him then?"

Anna looked away. "It didn't make him very sick."

"You added the arsenic to the cake I made, too, didn't you?"

"It was easy enough to pry open the box and reseal it after. I thought that he'd die in Paris." Anna swallowed. "I hoped we'd never see him again."

"Did you want me to be blamed?" Mme. Pelletier asked, sounding more curious than indignant. "Did you hope that I would be imprisoned, even executed?"

"No! When I saw you sprinkle the gum arabic on his food, I thought maybe it was keeping the poison from working. I asked mother about its purpose." Anna sighed. "I didn't expect that she would summon the doctor."

Mme. Pelletier nodded. "I see."

"He was a monster!" Anna exclaimed. "I hated what he did to my parents—and to me." She rubbed the arm that he had broken when she was fifteen. She looked at Mme. Pelletier. "Why did you not tell on me?"

"As you say, he was a monster. I'd hardly turn on someone who had rid me of such a menace. Besides, I only had my suspicions. I could scarcely believe such a thing of you. Of your mother or father, perhaps."

Anna's heart lurched in her chest. "Will they be arrested?"

"Unlikely, given that your mother was the one who summoned the physicians. Besides, Momsieur La Rousse is convinced I am the murderess, so I don't think he'd prosecute anyone else for the crime." She put her lips close to Anna's ear. "Of course, he's not altogether wrong. I did add the rest of the arsenic to the gum arabic to finish what you had started." She laughed when Anna's mouth fell open. "Naturally, *I* cannot be tried again." She stood up. "I am leaving now, to take up residence in Paris. As you can imagine, I am quite in demand now."

"What will become of us?" Anna asked.

"I will sell the estate to pay off my husband's debts, including the back wages due your family, with a special bequest to *you.*" Leaning down, she kissed Anna's cheeks. "*Ma chérie,* this shall remain our secret. Let us hope our paths do not cross again."

Anna frowned. "Shall I make you a meal before your journey?"

Mme. Pelletier smiled slightly. "I think not, my dear. I think not."

HISTORICAL NOTE

The assize proceedings described in this short story were simplified for the sake of brevity and readability. In a French court of assizes, the President of the Court oversees the proceedings and is assisted by two *assesseurs*, or associate judges. In researching contemporary newspaper accounts and scholarly medical journals from the time period, which detailed similar criminal cases, I found that most only alluded to the President, referring to him commonly as the Judge, so I adhered to the same practice in this story.

S.C.

EATING CROW

by Carla Coupe

Emancipated Beryl Mayhew is incensed when her pet crow, Hermes, is accused of stealing a valuable necklace from the country house she is visiting. In defense of her pet, she must get to the bottom of the theft. Luckily, she can climb trees!

Dressed in their finest gowns, Beryl Mayhew and her Aunt Eleanora sat in the stylish barouche drawn by two grays as it made its stately way up the gravel drive toward Lytton House. The setting sun glinted off windows on the elegant Georgian façade, warming the pale Portland stone. A caw sounded in the distance. Beryl scanned the sky, smiling when she saw the black figure circling overhead. The barouche drew up to the front door, and they were handed out by the groom, then greeted by the butler and ushered inside.

After giving her shawl to the maid, Beryl smoothed her long gloves and smiled at the prospect of an evening of good company and fine food.

"Miss Beryl, Miss Mayhew!" Sir Denys Lytton crossed the receiving room, arms open in welcome. He was tall and lean, with a touch of gray at his temples, an expression of pleasure softening his austere features.

Aunt Eleanora took his hand. "Thank you for your kind invitation, Sir Denys, and for sending the carriage for us."

"Not at all," he said, leading them to the spacious drawing room. "And now I would like to introduce you to my niece and nephews, who are staying for the week."

Two men and a young woman turned from the garden window, and Beryl studied them as they drew closer. The men, James and Henry Alcott, smiled and bowed; they were smooth professional types, well dressed, with carefully tended mustaches and fair, Brilliantined hair. Their sister, Mrs. Caroline Devere, was in her early twenties, only a few years older than Beryl. Blond and delicate, she had the type of beauty Beryl admired, since it was the opposite of her own dark hair and sturdy form. Mrs. Devere wore the latest fashion from Paris as well as a sparkling emerald necklace. She clasped her hands tightly together and gave a frosty nod.

Her brothers' friendliness contrasted with her silent regard. Within a few minutes, Beryl was chatting freely with Henry, while James devoted himself to Aunt Eleanora. They continued their animated conversations as they went in to dinner. The party was small enough that the conversation remained general.

Henry turned to her. "Do you ride, Miss Beryl?"

At the mention of riding, Mrs. Devere looked up from her contemplation of the tableware.

"Yes, it's an enjoyable exercise." Beryl smiled and gave Sir Denys a sidelong glance.

Sir Denys laughed. "Oh, she does, but not sidesaddle, Henry."

"Not sidesaddle?" Mrs. Devere's frown deepened. "But what of your skirts?"

"I wear rationals when I ride."

"Turkish trousers?" Henry tilted his head. "I thought ladies only wore them for bicycling and athletics."

With a sniff, Mrs. Devere turned to Aunt Eleanora. "Miss Mayhew, what do you think of your niece's behavior?"

"I was the one who suggested that she adopt them," Aunt Eleanora said placidly. "If I still rode, I would wear rationals as well."

"Brava, Miss Mayhew." Sir Denys lifted his glass of wine. "Caroline is a devoted horsewoman," he continued, with a nod to his niece. "Perhaps you also should adopt rationals, my dear."

"Oh, Caro doesn't care about riding." James laughed as he speared a potato. "One does not wear rationals to wager on races at the Frying Pan."

Mrs. Devere raised an eyebrow. "At least I'm not at the gaming tables all evening, like some I could mention."

James opened his mouth, but Sir Denys turned to Henry and spoke quickly.

"Miss Beryl has a most interesting pet," he said. "It is named Hermes. Can you hazard a guess as to what creature it is from the name alone?"

"Hermes?" Henry set down his knife and fork and looked at his brother. "What were his symbols, James? You were always better at classics than I."

"Oh, dear." James thought for a moment. "A tortoise? A ram?"

"Not a snake!" said Henry.

Beryl chuckled. "No, definitely not a snake."

"A rooster?"

"Close!" cried Sir Denys.

"A chicken?" said Henry, grinning as he gestured at the roast chicken on his plate.

"A chicken? Oh dear, no," replied Beryl with another laugh. "Hermes is a crow."

"A crow? Truly?" Henry gazed at her, disbelieving.

Beryl nodded. "Truly."

"How does one acquire a crow as a pet?"

"He was just fledged when we met and he befriended me. Now he is independent, but still enjoys my company."

Sir Denys gave Beryl a fond look. "And two years ago he and Miss Beryl were instrumental in rescuing a young village woman who had been abducted."

"But now," said Beryl, after providing a brief explanation of the incident, "Hermes is being terribly naughty. He will come in an open window and abscond with anything of ours that is shiny— silver spoons, thimbles, sewing scissors, even a gold bracelet—and take them to his nest, so I have to traipse through the grove and retrieve them from his hiding place."

"Hermes is indeed a rogue!" said Sir Denys with a laugh. "Caroline, have a care of your emeralds, or you may find them snatched by a thieving crow."

Mrs. Devere gave Sir Denys a sour look, but when Beryl glanced at her a moment later, she was clutching her necklace, fingers wrapped protectively around the jewels.

***

The following evening, the sun disappeared behind the leafy canopy surrounding Ferndale, Aunt Eleanora's comfortable house. In the drawing room, Beryl laid aside her book at the sound of an approaching horse.

"Who could that be?" asked Aunt Eleanora, looking up from her own book.

Rising and glancing out the window, Beryl said, "It's Sir Denys. Whatever can he want?"

They did not have long to wait for an answer. A disheveled and red-faced Sir Denys hurried in on the heels of their maid.

"My apologies, ladies," he panted. "I am here on a rather delicate mission."

"Sit down and catch your breath," said Aunt Eleanora. "And then explain yourself."

After a restorative glass of brandy, he turned to Beryl.

"I hate to cast aspersions, but I suspect Hermes has graduated from petty larceny to major theft. This afternoon, Caroline left out her emerald necklace before bathing, and when she returned to her room, it was gone. She refuses to suspect any of the maids, and I cannot believe any of them are responsible."

"What of her brothers?" asked Beryl. "Were they in the house?"

Sir Denys shook his head. "Although James enjoys a flutter at the tables, he would never do such a thing. In any case, both James and Henry were out all afternoon, and had just returned when the loss was discovered."

Aunt Eleanora looked grave. "This is a heavy charge to lay upon Hermes."

"Especially without any evidence," said Beryl, not bothering to conceal her anger. "Where did she put the necklace? And was the window open?"

Sir Denys held up his hands, placating. "According to Caroline, and confirmed by her maid, she put it on her dressing table, which is next to the open window. It would have been a tempting prize."

"I don't believe it for a moment," said Beryl. "But there's a simple way to discover the truth. Will you come with me to the tree where Hermes keeps his treasures?"

She stalked from the room, Sir Denys trailing like a gosling behind its mother. As she walked across the lawn, her anger grew. How dare he accuse Hermes! Why, he only filched Beryl's and Aunt Eleanora's things. Besides, he would never take something as valuable as an emerald necklace . . . Would he? No, of course not.

They entered the grove at the edge of the lawn and made their way through the undergrowth to an old, gnarled yew tree. Perched on a nearby branch, a large crow regarded them with an inquisitive tilt of its head.

"Hello, Hermes," said Beryl. "We've just come for a quick visit."

With a croak, Hermes flew closer, his glittering black eyes fixed on them.

Sir Denys nodded approvingly at the yew. "Hermes has chosen his home well. Do you need assistance reaching his nest?"

Beryl snorted and ducked under a low branch. The yew was ancient, and at some point in its life had been struck by lightning. A portion of the trunk was cracked and falling away, devoid of branches, the bark blackened. Scrambling up, she reached a hollow filled with buttons, a dented fork, and a few pieces of broken glass . . . but no emeralds.

"There is no necklace here," she said, emerging empty-handed from the greenery. "Would you like to look yourself?"

Hermes cawed loudly as if in protest and left in a flurry of black feathers.

Sir Denys shook his head, his expression grave. "No, of course not. But you do understand why I had to ask."

Her ill-temper dissipated at his gentle tone.

"I do." She turned to retrace their path through the trees. "I suppose it's a police matter now."

"I would rather not involve the police just yet," he said. "All our servants have been with us for many years, and I would not like to repay their loyalty with unfounded accusations and mistrust."

"Constable Wright would not carry out an investigation with much tact or discretion," agreed Beryl, lifting a branch to allow Sir Denys to pass. "What will you do?"

They reached the lawn again, greeted by the sight of Hermes rooting in the grass. Sir Denys stopped and contemplated Beryl. "You have a sensible head on your shoulders and do not leap to conclusions. Would you be willing to look into the matter? I would ensure everyone knows you are acting on my behalf."

Beryl stared at him, overwhelmed by the responsibility and trust he placed in her. Could she do this? It was one thing to fight for her life when in danger, it was another to investigate a possible crime. She took a deep breath and released it slowly. "I can try, but I can't guarantee that I will discover the truth. Or if I do discover it, that you will like what I find."

"I accept both possibilities."

"And we may yet have to call in Constable Wright."

Sir Denys barked a laugh. "A dire possibility, but yes, I accept that as well."

Beryl straightened her shoulders and gave a sharp nod.

"Then expect me tomorrow after breakfast." She just hoped she would not disgrace herself or ruin an innocent life.

***

Sitting in the dog cart the next morning, Beryl flicked the reins over the back of Aerion. The pony trudged up the drive to Lytton House. Hermes had ridden part of the way, but obviously frustrated by the pony's slow pace, he eventually flew off and circled overhead while Beryl crept along, enviously eyeing the crow's freedom and speed.

After settling Aerion with a groom and a bag of oats, Beryl followed the butler to Sir Denys's study.

"Thank you again for agreeing to do this," he said. "I have spoken with the maids, and they will be excused from their work to speak with you at your convenience."

"And Mrs. Devere?"

Sir Denys sighed. "I have asked her to cooperate, but . . ."

Beryl bit back a rude reply. Without Mrs. Devere's cooperation, her investigation would indeed be hampered.

"Shall I begin with Mrs. Devere?" she said. "Perhaps the maids will fill in any information she . . . does not provide."

Sir Denys rang the bell and Beryl was escorted to Mrs. Devere's room. After a knock, she was bidden to enter.

The pleasant, sunny room boasted elegant furnishings and a large sitting area. A smiling Mrs. Devere tucked a sheaf of paper—could they be banknotes?—beneath her book and rose from her chair. "Miss Beryl, how lovely to meet you again." She extended her hand. "Please, do sit down."

Beryl stared. Was this friendly, warm woman the same one she had met two days ago? She did not at all resemble the frosty lady of their first dinner.

"I believe Uncle Denys has explained the situation to you." Mrs. Devere took a chair beside the cold fireplace. "About your Hermes making off with my emeralds."

Quashing the upsurge of anger, Beryl sat in the matching chair. "That's extremely unlikely. I searched his hiding place, and your necklace was not there."

"Ah, but he could have several caches, couldn't he?" Mrs. Devere pointed out. "No doubt he knew you would want to retrieve them, and secreted them in a place you haven't discovered."

"Perhaps." Beryl shrugged. "However, Sir Denys does not wish to call in the police, so he has asked me to look into the matter. I would be very interested in hearing the particulars."

Mrs. Devere rolled her eyes and sank back in the chair, looking for all the world like a sulky child. "Oh, very well. I laid out my emerald necklace on the dressing table over there. My maid discovered some of the stitching had come loose on my gown, so she took it off to repair. I went to bathe, and when I returned, the emeralds were gone. Claudette brought back my gown, and when I asked her about the necklace, she said she had been down in the servants' hall and had not returned in the meantime."

"Had anyone else entered your bedroom?"

"Not that I know of."

Beryl paused and studied Mrs. Devere. She was remarkably calm, indeed positively relaxed. "Why could it not have been taken by one of the maids, or another servant?"

Mrs. Devere waved her hand negligently. "Oh no! No, it could not be a servant. I refuse to countenance such a suggestion."

"I disagree. I find it a very compelling scenario," said Beryl. "A maid or valet overhears you discuss the emeralds with your maid, and when the room is vacated they enter and remove the jewels. We must at least search their rooms."

"Search their rooms?" Mrs. Devere rose and crossed to the

open window, where she stared out over the park. "Why, the idea is utterly ridiculous. Your crow took my jewels, hid them, and they cannot be found. The stones are insured, and the insurance company will reimburse us." She turned to Beryl with a dismissive shake of her head. "I have seen the harm caused by unmerited accusations, and I will not subject my servants to such."

Beryl stood. "And I must follow my investigation to its conclusion, wherever that may lead. Excuse me."

She made her way to the servants' hall, where Claudette and Betsy, the upstairs maid, joined Beryl at the long table. Claudette confirmed her mistress's account, and Betsy reported that she had only briefly been in James's and Henry's bedrooms.

"What of the valets?" asked Beryl. "Did you see anyone else during that time?"

According to both women, all three valets had been in the servants' hall during the time in question.

Betsy thought for a moment, frowning in concentration. "While I was in Mr. James's room, I looked out the window and saw Mrs. Devere's groom standing by the flower border at the front of the house. Well," she added primly, "grooms are supposed to stay near the stables and not wander the grounds. But when I went down to tell him, he was gone, and I didn't see him again that day. He certainly didn't turn up for his dinner."

Claudette shook her head. "It is impossible that he is involved! Ben is devoted to Mrs. Devere. He has worked for the family most of his life and would never think of stealing from her."

Beryl considered her words. That might be true under normal circumstances, but if he were in desperate need of money? Even the most loyal retainer could be tempted.

"I'd like to talk with Ben," she said, rising from the table and brushing off Claudette's offer to accompany her. "I'm familiar with the stables here, and would rather speak to Ben alone."

***

On her way to the stables, Beryl took a shortcut through the kitchen garden and was not surprised to see a familiar black figure land on a brick wall bordering the asparagus bed. Hermes greeted her with a harsh caw.

"Good morning to you, too. I suppose you haven't seen an emerald necklace about?" He regarded her inquisitively, but remained mute. "No, I didn't think you had." She sighed. "If you do find it, please inform me."

At that, he let out a croak and flew off.

She located Ben behind the stables, sitting on an overturned bucket and enjoying a quiet pipe. He stood and took off his cap as she approached, revealing grizzled hair and a weather-beaten face.

"Good morning." Beryl introduced herself, and he nodded.

"Yes, miss. Sir Denys, he tol' us'n you might ask us questions 'bout Mrs. Devere's necklace goin' missing." He offered her the bucket to sit on, and perched on an old packing crate.

Beryl settled on the bucket—it was even more uncomfortable than the local church pews—and studied him for a moment. Ben shifted under her regard.

"You were seen on the front lawn about the time Mrs. Devere's emeralds went missing. Why were you there?"

He rubbed the back of his neck and stared at the pipe in his hand. "'Twere a fine afternoon, and I had a fancy to see the house and gardens again. Mrs. Devere hasn't visited in donkey's years."

He obviously wasn't telling the truth. Beryl considered the matter for a moment. Perhaps making their conversation less of an interrogation would help win his cooperation, if not his trust.

"Please, go ahead and smoke your pipe," said Beryl.

"Gone out," he muttered. When he reached into his jacket pocket and pulled out a box of lucifers, a scrap of paper fluttered to the ground by Beryl's feet.

He bent and reached for it, but Beryl was faster.

"What's this?" She glanced at the paper. It displayed an address, written in an elegant, feminine hand: Austin's. Corner of Fore and Market Streets, Exeter.

She had heard of that name and address.

Could the answer be that simple? It would explain Mrs. Devere's changeable temperament, as well as Ben's actions.

She looked up at Ben. Color tinged his brown cheeks, and his lips were pinched together.

"Why did you visit this address?"

"It were a private errand for Mrs. Devere." His jaw set. "And that's all I'll say on the matter, miss. If you want to know more, you go to her."

"I believe I will." Standing, she dusted off her skirts and thanked him. It was time to reveal the truth, and she would begin with a small falsehood of her own.

***

Mrs. Devere was in the morning room, sitting at the escritoire beside the window. Although writing paper lay on the top and she held a pen, she was gazing out the open portal, her chin propped on her hand. She started and dropped her pen when Beryl entered. Ink spattered the paper.

"Oh! Well, I hope you are satisfied that the servants could not be involved."

Beryl crossed the room, her expression grave. "I believe the maids have nothing to do with the theft, but your groom is certainly guilty. I am going to inform Sir Denys, and he will have Constable Wright take him in charge."

"No!" Mrs. Devere's face paled, and she pressed a hand to her bosom. "You cannot!"

"He had a note with the name and address of a well-known pawn broker in Exeter. I'm certain if we question the owner, he will be able to identify Ben as the person who brought in the necklace." Turning and moving back toward the door, she said over her shoulder, "I wanted to tell you first, since you will need to hire a new groom."

"Wait!" Mrs. Devere leapt to her feet and dashed across the room, catching Beryl's arm. "Please, let me explain before you speak with my uncle."

Beryl allowed herself to be pulled to the settee. She sat silent and grave as Mrs. Devere paced from door to window and back again.

At last she stopped and faced Beryl, her hands clasped tightly before her.

"I love my husband, Miss Beryl. But he is exceedingly upright regarding morals, and can be . . . unforgiving to those who disappoint him. I have . . ." She stopped and bowed her head. "Many of my acquaintances run with a fast set, and I have allowed myself to act in ways contrary to what my husband believes."

"Such as wagering on horses at the track, and losing more money than you have available?" asked Beryl gently.

Mrs. Devere gasped. "How did you know?"

"Your brother James mentioned that you frequented the Frying Pan—isn't that the common name for the Alexandra Park track? Your demeanor changed once the jewels disappeared, as if a burden had been lifted from your shoulders. And there was the stack of banknotes I saw you tuck under a book when I entered your room this morning."

Mrs. Devere hesitated, then nodded, her shoulders bowing. "My losses grew to be greater than my allowance, and my creditors—one in particular, an odious man—threatened to approach my husband with evidence of my debts. My notes were due and I had no means to settle them, for I do not receive my allowance for another three weeks!"

"What about your brothers or uncle? Surely one of them would lend you the money."

She huffed a laugh. "My brothers already live up to their income, and do not have the money to spare. As for Uncle Denys, how could I admit such a failing to him? I tell you, I was at my wits end, and then you, Miss Beryl, provided a solution to my dilemma."

"Hermes," Beryl said dryly. "He supposedly steals your jewels so you can pawn them and use the money to pay your debts. But how will you redeem the emeralds once you receive your allowance?"

"I'm not certain," said Mrs. Devere with a sigh. "I could prolong my visit, or return home and send Ben with the money . . ." She gazed at Beryl. "What would you do?"

Beryl stifled her immediate response: avoid gambling in the first place. No, that was not helpful under the circumstances. "I would speak with your uncle, admit what you have done, and ask him to loan you the money to redeem your necklace."

"But that is impossible!" she said with a shake of her head. "Uncle Denys would tell my husband and never forgive me."

Beryl stood and walked over to her, taking her hand. "He will keep your secret and has already forgiven you."

Eyes wide, Mrs. Devere gasped. "What do you mean?"

"I informed Sir Denys of my suspicions before I came to see you. He is willing to loan you the money you need."

Mrs. Devere simply stared at Beryl, mouth agape.

Beryl gave her hand a squeeze. "He is waiting for us in his study."

* * *

The following afternoon, a breeze tossed leaves and branches in the grove, their shifting shade dappling Ferndale's lawn. Beryl's skirts flared and flapped as she paced on the terrace. Hermes flew down from the tallest oak in the grove, his feathers iridescent in the sunlight, and landed on the stone wall bordering the terrace.

Beryl stopped pacing. "I owe you an apology," she said.

Hermes croaked softly and hopped toward her.

"Yes, I know you understand, but it disturbs me to unjustly impugn your reputation. Although," she frowned, "I once found my good silver sewing scissors in your hiding place. I don't enjoy sewing, but that doesn't mean you may claim my scissors as your own."

With a flap of his wings, Hermes swooped to the lawn. There he prodded the grass with his beak, pulling a worm from the moist soil and eating it with relish.

Beryl nodded to herself as a carriage turned into the drive. Good. She wished to finish this.

A few minutes later, Mrs. Devere and Sir Denys stepped from the barouche.

Mrs. Devere smiled and offered her hand. Beryl shook it and turned to Sir Denys.

"Miss Beryl," said Sir Denys, glancing over at the crow. "And Hermes?"

"Yes. He is an inquisitive soul." Beryl gave Hermes a fond look. "And a hungry one."

"May I approach him?" asked Mrs. Devere. "I have a little present." She drew a buttonhook from her reticule, and held it up. Light glinted off the silvery surface.

"How thoughtful of you," said Beryl. "He will enjoy it. You can leave it on the wall."

Carefully placing the buttonhook on the stones, Mrs. Devere stepped back. Hermes, with a loud caw, flew to the wall and inspected the hook. He chuckled and picked it up in his beak, launching himself into the air, and disappearing into the grove.

Sir Denys offered Beryl his arm. "Shall we?"

"It would be my pleasure."

They quickly crossed the lawn and made their way through the grove to the yew tree.

"So this is the famous tree," said Mrs. Devere. "Hermes has a keen eye for good property."

For the second time that day, Beryl ducked beneath the low branch and once inside the leafy bower, climbed until she could see into the hollow. The buttonhook was already there. She reached inside and removed the emeralds she had placed there earlier, retracing her steps to stand before Mrs. Devere and Sir Denys.

"Your jewels, Mrs. Devere," she said, holding out the emerald necklace.

"Thank you, Miss Beryl." Mrs. Devere accepted the necklace with a twinkle in her eye. "How fortunate that you knew exactly where to find them."

"Indeed." Beryl laughed then, joined by Sir Denys and Mrs. Devere.

In the oak tree above them, Hermes cawed.

MR. NAKAMURA'S GARDEN

by Valerie O. Patterson

*This gem of a story is set in Hawaii just before the
Japanese bombing. One small boy is terrified of the
deep undercurrents in his household. His father is God,
his mother is helpless, and the servants are holding
their breath.*

December 6, 1941
Manoa Valley, Oahu

This is what the boy remembers.

The breeze through the palm trees sounds like his mother
walking in her taffeta party skirt. In the back yard, the gardener
picks up palm fronds that have fallen overnight.

They are seated on the *lanai*, his mother leaning over him, her
crisp shirt brushing his face. She holds his fingers just so and fits
the small rounded scissors into his hand. Then she places red and
green construction paper in front of him on the table. With pointed
pinking shears, she shows him how to cut even paper strips along
the lines she's drawn.

"And then what?" he asks, even though he knows. She has
promised him this time together, before the grown-ups' party.

"Then we'll glue the strips into rings and loop them together to
make a garland for the Christmas tree."

"*Mah-le Kah-kah-li—*" He stumbles over the words the cook
has been practicing with him.

"*Male Kalikimaka.*" His mother laughs. "That's right. Merry
Christmas." While he concentrates on cutting, his mother opens an
envelope stamped *airmail*. The cover of the greeting card inside is
Currier and Ives, a horse-drawn sleigh in a snowy woodland scene.
She props it up on the table between them.

The boy glances at it, imagining what snow must be like, so
white and cold. He stacks the red and green strips into separate
piles the way he does vegetables on his dinner plate.

From out front, the iceman rings the bell on his horse-drawn
wagon. "Fresh ice."

The boy almost abandons his project. He loves to pet the

iceman's horse, which wears rubber shoes and blinders. The boy calls them "eye patches."

"Keep cutting, I'll be right back," the boy's mother says. "We need extra ice for the party."

The boy keeps working. The swish of Mr. Nakamura raking gravel in the rock garden is rhythmic, steady. The boy likes the sound of Mr. Nakamura working, and the zebra doves cooing in the *ti* plants. When the sound of raking stops, the boy looks up at the gardener and waves. Mr. Nakamura bows before he begins raking again.

When his mother returns, the construction paper strips are ready.

"I'm going to show you how to make rings. We'll start with the first one." His mother brushes mucilage along one end of a red strip. Then she folds the paper over in a circle, and presses the two ends together. "You have to hold it a minute to make sure it sticks."

Voices come from the kitchen, the cook talking low, and then his father louder.

His mother's hand jerks to the right, and a streak of glue smears the table. Picking up a cloth, she scrubs at the glue spot before it dries and leaves a stain.

"Your father's home. Remember what I said? Speak up when he talks to you."

His mother always reminds him. He wants to tell her she doesn't need to remind him. He paints glue on the end of a green strip.

"Don't stick it together yet," she says. "See, now you have to loop the strip through the circle that was already made. If you don't, you can't link them."

The boy nods, and pushes the tip of his tongue against his teeth as he threads the green strip through the red circle. Then he pinches the ends together.

"Louise?"

"On the *lanai*, dear," his mother answers.

Footsteps clatter across the main floor. The boy knows his father doesn't take his shoes off at the door the way cook prefers. She's left to sigh and follow after him with a broom, as if she is sweeping away something more than just dirt.

"So here's where the party is," his father says. He stands in the doorway, dressed in his golfing pants and white shoes, swirling the ice in his drink.

The boy watches the amber liquid, the color of honey, swish inside the glass. Once when he was smaller, he tasted a drink of his father's. It burned his throat and made him cry, and he spit it out. His father made him scrub the spot on the floor until he'd rubbed the wax off. Now his father points toward the backyard, the *koi* pond. Toward the bent figure of Mr. Nakamura raking gravel in the rock garden.

"Why do we have a Jap gardener? How do you know he isn't a spy or a saboteur? I'm going to fire him. Hire a Filipino or Chinese instead. For cheaper, too. That's what they say at the club."

"Honey, shh," his mother says. "He can hear you."

"What do I care if he can hear?" His father sways and grabs the doorframe. "You know if anything happens, the Filipinos, they'll take care of things."

"What do you mean?"

"The paper says FDR's going to reject Japan's answer on China. Japan's amassed troops on the Thai border. War's coming to the Pacific."

His mother presses her hands on the edge of the table. "Mr. Nakamura is not a saboteur. His family's been in Hawaii for years. He's a gardener. This is Mr. Nakamura's garden."

His father slams his fist against the doorjamb. Drops of amber liquid splash against the floor, the table, and onto the strips of construction paper. The boy smoothes out the wet paper.

"Mr. Nakamura's garden. That's rich. It's ours. Paid for. Lock, stock, and barrel."

"The gardener conveyed." His mother's voice is light.

"Conveyed? He's hired help. Like most everyone else on this forsaken island, I tell you." His father stares into his drink. "Like I am," he adds in a low voice the boy barely hears. "And hired help can always be replaced."

The boy hunches his shoulders. He squeezes mucilage onto the paper, too hard. The paper tears. He edges the torn off piece toward the rest of the paper, trying to tack it back on. He holds it hard, forcing the lopsided strip into a circle.

The boy's mother nods to Charlie and gives him a small smile.

"You baby him," his father says. "Charlie has to start growing up."

"But we don't have to scare him," his mother says.

"You mean that *I* don't have to scare him." He reaches toward Charlie's arm.

Charlie flinches but he doesn't move away from this father.

His mother shakes her head.

"He needs to toughen up," his father says, dropping his hand without touching him. "War's coming. Everyone knows it. What's all this for anyway?"

Charlie sets aside the glue and paper. He holds one hand over the other one, in his lap, covering up the bruise on his wrist. His father's hands, ruddy from sunburn, pause near the table, as if they might pick up Charlie's work and inspect it. The faceted diamond in his father's college ring catches a bit of afternoon light and twinkles across the paper.

"Decorating, Charles. The Christmas tree, remember?" his mother says.

In the distance, Mr. Nakamura's rake swishes back and forth. The boy remembers that the patterns in the tiny gravel flow like water, and the three large stones are meant to be mountains or islands. Every few days the gardener rakes the gravel in different directions, and the boy can tell if the water is a river flowing to the sea, or a stormy ocean. One day Mr. Nakamura let him attempt a few strokes. It was harder than it looked. His pattern wobbled, as though tiny disturbances under the water disturbed the flow.

"The club party's tonight," his mother continues. "You wanted to host. A Christmas party needs decorations." His mother's voice is as smooth as water flowing over stones. It's the way she talks to him when he stumbles and skins his knee.

Charlie listens to his mother and to the garden sounds beyond. In the past, whenever Charlie entered the garden, Mr. Nakamura would bow to him, seeming to invite him into a magical kingdom. Mr. Nakamura bows to his mother and father, too, but it's as if his father never sees it.

Charlie hears his father now.

"This island only has enough rice for eight days," his father says. "You hear? Eight days. That's nothing. If the Japs surround us with subs, transports won't be able to get here when the war starts."

The boy's mother nods her head, and her fingers help him complete the last loop. Together they drape the still-damp garland onto the potted Cook pine tree.

***

Before the party, while his parents get ready, the boy wanders outside in his Sunday best. Mynah birds call in the distance. Mr. Nakamura is working out front, a last-minute survey to ensure the lawn is perfect before the party. In the back yard, the boy heads to the *koi* pond. Sometimes Mr. Nakamura lets him feed the fish. Kneeling by the pond, he opens his fist in the water. The *koi* know the shape of his hand, recognize his reflection on the surface of the water, too. They come to him as if he'd called them by name. The white, the red, the golden. They nudge his hand, the way the cat his mother once had did.

At the very back of the yard, before the greenery disappears into a steep lava wall, stands Mr. Nakamura's shed.

The boy peers inside. All the rakes and tools are upright in rows, all proper like soldiers marching in parade formation. A rolled-up *tatami* mat stands in the far corner. Two bowls, a basin of water, and folded clothes rest on a worktable.

"Charlie, come away now, people are starting to arrive." His mother has come from nowhere and rests her hand on his shoulder. "Remember, this is Mr. Nakamura's garden, and you mustn't disturb his things." The two walk hand-in-hand toward the house. Her skirt swishes.

"Your father talks about war. There's fear in the air, Charlie. I don't think it will come to anything, but some people don't like the Japanese. Even those Japanese who've lived in Hawaii for many years. That's why Mr. Nakamura stays here sometimes, in the shed."

Mr. Nakamura's folded clothes tug at the boy's memory. There was the time his mother packed her steamer trunk and a small suitcase for him, after his father had raged at them and driven off into the night, his car's headlights weaving madly along the Manoa Road. Before his father returned the next day, his mother had unpacked their things and put the empty suitcases back in the attic. Charlie's clothes were folded, back inside his chest of drawers.

"But, Charlie, it's a secret. Forget you saw Mr. Nakamura's things. It's like a dream. You know how dreams are. They feel real but they aren't."

Yes, he knows about dreams. At night sometimes he hears a shout from downstairs and then another, and glass breaking. Sometimes he hides under the bed until he falls asleep. But when he gets up in the morning, everything is quiet again. That's what dreams are like.

***

The boy stands near the door with his parents while the guests arrive. He says hello to each one of them.

"This is Bud Washington," his father says, a firm hand on the boy's shoulder, as if he might run away.

"Hello, Mr. Washington. My name is Charlie." The barrel-chested man pats him on the head and says he's a fine gentleman.

"A chip off the old block, Charles," Mr. Washington says, and everyone laughs. His father puts a drink in the man's hands.

As soon as introductions are over, his mother sends him into the kitchen to have his dinner with cook. And then he heads upstairs to bed.

Through the open window, white ginger sweetens the air. The

gibbous moon shines almost full, but not quite. His mother taught him all the moon's phases.

He crawls into bed. He imagines Mr. Nakamura asleep in the shed, close to the *koi* pond and rock garden. He imagines the smooth stones in the pond, the combed gravel, the zebra doves, and the hibiscus.

The later it gets, the louder the voices seeping up through the floor, until the party is as raucous as a flock of mynahs. Laughs puncture the air like machine gunfire.

The boy dreams. In his dream, the front door opens and closes, and the voices ebb and flow. Later he wakes, and he knows something woke him, but the house is quiet.

Outside, the wind stirs the balmy night. Palm fronds brush the sky.

Then he hears it, a shout downstairs. A curse. Murmuring. Glass breaking. All he hears is his father. But his mother must be there, too.

The boy crawls under the bed with his pillow. He waits for the sound of his father's footsteps on the stairs. He holds his breath. In a few minutes, though, the light coming from under the door goes out, and, somewhere, a door slams, and then another. The footsteps don't come. The moon reflects across the floorboards. Down the street, dogs bark.

***

In the morning, Charlie wakes under the bed to dove calls and wind rustling in the palm trees. Or, maybe it's his mother, still dressed in her taffeta party skirt as if she hadn't slept, hadn't been to bed at all.

Barefoot, he walks down the hallway. His parents' bedroom door is closed. Downstairs, martini and highball glasses are scattered across the sideboard and coffee table. Some still have liquid in them. He looks for broken glass but doesn't find any. The sharp scent of alcohol burns his nose.

In the kitchen, the cook runs water in the kitchen sink. The kitchen radio is turned on, the volume low. The church service broadcast starts with hymns.

The boy wanders through the hidden garden path that Mr. Nakamura showed him one day. It wends through the greenery, the vines, all the way to the back of the yard and the tool shed. There he touches the bamboo door, slightly ajar. It creaks open when he presses, and he steps inside.

There, the rakes rest askew, tumbled over like fallen soldiers. Empty clay pots lay scattered on the worktable. One has crashed to the floor, and a long crack cleaves it in half. The boy runs his finger along the crevice and gently rests the pot back on the worktable. Mr. Nakamura's clothes are piled in a heap like old rags, and the basin has tipped, leaving a puddle of water on the lava rock floor.

What does that mean?

Charlie stumbles out of the shed, suddenly unable to breathe.

Where is Mr. Nakamura? The boy runs toward the rock garden. Fear rises in him like the surf at Waikiki. His father said he was going to fire Mr. Nakamura. Did he? Just since yesterday? Did he send the gardener away? Who ransacked the shed?

The boy stops. Yesterday the Zen garden was a storm-tossed sea, with patterns of waves crashing onto the three rock islands, but the gravel was pristine. This morning, broken *ti* plants litter the path. Worse, footsteps cross the rock garden, zigzagging a trail from one side to the other, as if someone had wandered about lost. The boy has never seen footprints in the gravel before. Mr. Nakamura always walks backward, raking over his own steps with long, slow motions.

The track of footsteps ends at the edge of the garden. Two large stones—islands—lay untouched.

The footprints end at the edge of the rock garden, close to the *koi* pond.

There is the boy's father, lying forward over the edge of the *koi* pond as if he might be praying or feeding the fish. But he's unmoving. His head dips into the water, his lips open among the water lilies, as though he might be speaking to the fish in their own language. The golden and orange *koi* swim nearby, curious.

Charlie doesn't touch his father.

Don't touch me, boy. Don't make a sound. My head. . . . That's what he hears on mornings like this, when his mother hides in her room in the dark, shutters closed.

But this time his father doesn't speak at all.

The boy leans over the pond. A large stone sits at the bottom of the pool near his father's head. A jagged-edged stone.

He reaches for it.

Arms sweep him up. Mr. Nakamura's.

The boy will recall Mr. Nakamura cradling his face against his gaunt chest, shielding his eyes, and running toward the house.

Mr. Nakamura lowers him to his feet on the *lanai*. He bows over and over.

"Missus?" he asks.

The boy nods. He should wake his mother.

The cook comes to the door, wiping her hands on a linen cloth.

Mr. Nakamura points to the *koi* pond. He whispers something

Charlie can't hear. The woman's face droops, and her linen cloth flutters to the floor.

The boy picks up the linen. He loves the soft texture of it.

The cook motions for the boy. "You sit here," she says. "I get your mother."

The boy nods. He folds her linen cloth into smaller and smaller squares and presses it to his cheek. It feels like his mother's handkerchief, the one she gives him with an ice cube when a bruise aches, or when he's sick with fever. His body feels hot to his own touch, as if he's sick now.

Mr. Nakamura bows low and backs away. The boy watches him enter the shed and return to spread a tarp near the *koi* pond. Then he picks up the palm fronds that fell overnight and settles the third stone in the rock garden, where it begins to dry in the sun. He rakes the gravel, smoothing out the footprints.

Alone on the *lanai*, Charlie hears the radio, still on in the kitchen. It crackles, and an announcer breaks in on the sermon mid-sentence.

"We interrupt this program. Bombs are falling on Oahu. Eyewitness reports of an invading army on the north shore. Black smoke is rising over Hickam Air Force Base, near Pearl Harbor. Find your gas masks. All uniformed personnel report to duty."

The boy's mother dashes downstairs, still dressed in her taffeta party skirt, followed by the cook. She's changed blouses to one with a high neck and long sleeves. A hat perches on her head at an angle, hiding a bruise on her cheek in shadow. She might be dressed for church.

"Where is he? What's happened?" she asks.

"In the garden," the cook says.

The radio announcer repeats, "We interrupt this broadcast. Bombs have fallen over Oahu. We are at war in the Pacific."

The cook shies from the radio as if it is ready to detonate.

"War," his mother whispers. "Charlie, come here." She wraps her arms around him. "The world, Charlie. It's all a dream."

Whoosh.

A whistling sound arcs over the houses and pierces the trees. Doves scatter, their wings swishing. Then, *boom*.

Boom.

Charlie's mother jumps and hugs him closer.

Dogs bark from all the houses around them. Horns blow. In the distance, there's a siren.

Suddenly, the iceman's horse gallops past their house toward Manoa Falls, jerking the wagon behind him, the wheels rattling and creaking, and the iceman yelling "whoa, whoa."

After a moment, the sound of explosions fades.

"You better ring for the police," his mother says to the cook, who nods and scurries to the kitchen.

"Wait here, Charlie," his mother says, pushing her hat down on her head, and walking out.

Charlie nods, and he sits near the Christmas tree. He rearranges the paper garland he and his mother made, swirling it around the branches as high as he can reach. In the background, the radio announcer keeps a running commentary on the news. But Charlie focuses on the paper decoration, adjusting it just so.

When his mother returns, her face is white, even in the shade. She sinks into a chair on the *lanai*.

"Come here, Charlie," she says, and the boy sits in her lap and rests his head on her shoulder. Her skin smells of plumeria, of earth, of the ginger plants in Mr. Nakamura's garden. "There's been a terrible accident."

"Mr. Nakamura doesn't have to leave, does he?" Charlie asks. "Daddy said—"

"No, Charlie. Daddy didn't mean that."

When the policeman finally arrives, he's out of breath, as if he's run the whole way from the precinct.

"Charlie, go to your room. I'll come get you in a few minutes," his mother says, letting go of him and pressing her skirt flat with her hands. "I need to speak with the policeman."

"We have to hurry," the policeman says. His nametag reads *Hashiro*. "We have more to worry about than an accident. Your cook said it was an accident."

"Yes," his mother says. "Outside."

The boy stays inside his room. He stands away from the window, in the shadow so no one can see him if they look up at his window. So enemy pilots can't see him and drop a bomb on his house. But he can't help watching the policeman from his vantage point, the way he sometimes stood and watched Mr. Nakamura in the garden. The way he did so his father couldn't see him.

The policeman removes the tarp and walks around the boy's father. He circles the *koi* pond, as if seeing the body from all directions might tell him how his father fell. He speaks to Mr. Nakamura in the rock garden, but the policeman avoids stepping on the gravel path himself. Mr. Nakamura bows to the policeman, who also bows.

When the policeman finishes, he returns to the house.

"I'll write up the report. You better call Borthwick Mortuary. The funeral homes are all going to fill up, with all the casualties."

"Yes, we'll do that," his mother answers. She takes off her hat when the policeman leaves.

Charlie listens to her footsteps on the stairs, to the sound of her door closing.

Later, after the funeral home comes for the body and his mother is still in her room, Charlie returns to the garden. Everything is orderly. When he opens the door to the shed, all the rakes are present and accounted for as if someone had called roll. He touches each one in turn. The broken pot has been removed and the floor swept clean. Mr. Nakamura's clothes once again sit folded in their place.

Charlie visits the *koi* pond, too, and lets the fish nudge at his fingers while they swim lazily in circles. Around him the air is tinged with a hint of smoke and heavy with flowers.

***

The boy and his mother will stay in the Manoa house for months, unable to leave Hawaii because all civilian transport to California is cancelled for the foreseeable future. Mr. Nakamura will dig a victory garden plot for them in the front lawn. The coroner will rule his father's death an accident. Later still the army will issue a report attributing most of the bombs that hit civilian areas of Oahu to misfired U.S. shells, not Japanese bombers.

But, tonight, the boy and his mother stay in the house in darkness after the blackout is ordered. Civilians must stay off the streets. The *Honolulu Star Bulletin* prints its first extra edition, reporting early deaths at over four hundred.

> *The dead include a Portuguese girl, 10 years old, unidentified, puncture wound to the left temple…Migita Taro, 26, Schofield. Japanese girl, unidentified, age about 9, fur coat only identification. Mrs. White, 44 Dorsett Trace, puncture wound to the chest. Toshio Tokusaki, 5, Peleaula Lane….*

The army orders all moving picture theaters closed until further notice. All households must fill bathtubs and other receptacles with water in case of damage to the water works. No vessels may leave the harbor without special permission from the captain of the port.

The boy's mother reads an unsigned editorial:

> *"Governor Poindexter and the army and navy leaders have called upon the public to remain calm; for civilians who have no essential business on the streets to stay home; and for every man and woman to do their duty. Hawaii will do its part as a loyal American territory. In this crisis, every difference of race, creed, and*

color will be submerged in the one desire and determination to play the part that Americans always play in crisis."

The boy remembers the blackout that night. Not even candlelight could appear through the curtains. He crawled under the bed as soon as his mother left his room. The moon shone across the floor.

He dreams of the *koi* in the pond that he will get to feed in the morning. He dreams of holding the rake and smoothing the gravel path the way Mr. Nakamura taught him, all the lines even and unbroken. He will recall the peace of it.

This is what the boy remembers.

A BUTLER IS BORN

by Catriona McPherson

Early in his service career, Mr. Pallister must discover the truth about the death of a young (and dissolute) visitor to Thelpe Hall. He's up to the challenge . . . but is he going to be able to live with the consequences of his discovery?

Some men are born to lead. Some, so they tell us, are born to fish, travel, paint, or even dance. Such is the world's wide sweep. Mr. Pallister was born to buttle. The smooth running of a household swelled his heart, each rare stutter pained it, and the quick scurry of his staff to set matters right again soothed it, restoring as much order to his breast as to the great machine of which he was the chief engineer.

Despite this passion for rectitude, he was not a stodgy man or a stick-in-the-mud, although both slurs had come his way recently. His master, Mr. Gilver, carried on much as before—farming, with a little tractor in place of the plough; travelling to shooting parties, in his Daimler in place of the carriage; sitting in his library in the evenings, with voices quacking from the wireless in place of the former gentle sounds of logs in the grate and slumbering hounds on the hearthrug. But *Mrs.* Gilver, his master's wife (Mr. Pallister did not, even inside his own thoughts, call her his mistress), had abandoned the social round of her Victorian girlhood—letters, luncheons, and tennis—and had taken to detecting.

Mr. Pallister's face, after decades of stony reserve, betrayed him when first he heard the news. He flinched. "A detective?" he echoed with a shameful swoop in his voice, evidence that somewhere inside him there was, at least for that moment, an *emotion.* It had made the cook smile fondly when she thought he was not looking. He had never been smiled about fondly by a cook in his life. He cared little for it, now it had begun.

Besides, it was entirely unfair. What the other servants took to be disapproval was nothing of the kind. Rather, the thought of detectives, the notion of a crime to be solved, the very word "case" plunged Mr. Pallister back to that time, early in his career, from which he hoped to have turned his thoughts forever. He had not known then whether justice was served and he did not know now. All he knew was that his life was built upon the decision he made that night.

***

It was his first position. The year was 1886 and he was a junior footman at Thelpe Hall, still not quite decided between service and a job in his father's cousin's fish shop. The hours here were long and his calves sometimes ached from standing. But he wore a smart livery and it was a beautiful house. Fishmongers are on their feet all day, too, and they breathe very different air from that the young Mr. Pallister drank in as he walked up and down both sides of the dining table: hothouse flowers and beeswax polish and cherry logs burning.

This was to be a great dinner, the first really great dinner since he joined the staff, and he had caught some of the excitement beginning to simmer in the servants' hall. The only daughter of the house was newly betrothed to the eldest son of an earl, and the earl, countess, viscount, and another brother were arriving today to be shown the splendours of Thelpe, to be helped to the best of its cellar, and to gorge on the finest feast its kitchen had ever mustered.

Mr. Pallister, as the junior footman, was right at the end of the line when they all assembled on the gravel to welcome the visitors. But he still felt a leap of pride to be standing there with three other footmen, both the valets, and the butler, and eight maids in their black on the other side under the rapier gaze of the housekeeper, Mrs. Boyd.

The only sour note came from the look of the younger brother as he passed. He cast his eye over the eight maids in a way that made Mr. Pallister think of that fishmonger's shop again, of fresh goods laid on the slab and choosy customers making their selection. The earl and countess were ahead of their son and saw nothing, but the mistress of Thelpe shared a glance with her housekeeper and both their mouths pursed as though a string had drawn their lips tight shut.

The servants' hall was full of it when they gathered at the end of the day. It had quite taken over from the dinner, and even from the engagement, as the topic of the hour.

"Nasty," said the mistress's lady's maid, sitting over her stitching as she usually was. Her fingers flew and her silver thimble flashed. "I know his sort."

"Now, now, Belinda," said Mr. Cove, the butler. Belinda's needle glittered as her stitching grew faster yet. "The honourable gentleman is a favoured guest in our house and soon to be a connection of the family. Do not traduce his name or I shall be caused to—"

But he did not get to finish for at that moment the junior housemaid burst in. Her sleeves were rolled above her elbows and covered over with stout cuffs, and she was swathed in a twill apron.

"Lily?" said the housekeeper, with another of her sharp looks, this one delivered over the rim of her teacup.

"I went to see to his fire," Lily said. She had slammed shut the servants' hall door and was leaning against it.

"Whose fire?" asked Mr. Cove.

Belinda snorted.

"The brother," said Lily. "And he asked my name and I told him and he said lilies were his favourite flower and he came right up behind me and sniffed and told me I smelled sweeter than any lily he'd ever smelled before."

"Lily," said Mr. Cove, "if you would like to speak to Mrs. Boyd in private . . ."

Belinda delivered a snort so deep it made her cough afterwards. The butler glared but Mrs. Boyd was with her girls on this one.

"*Lily* has done no wrong, Mr. Cove," Mrs. Boyd said. "*Lily* has no need to be whispering in corners."

"Andrew," said Belinda, turning in her seat, "you'll go and light his fire in the morning, won't you?"

Mr. Pallister—"Andrew" as he was known back in those lowly days at the very start of his ascension—looked swiftly to Mr. Cove for permission.

Belinda opened her eyes wide. "Fine," she said. "Suit yourself." And she stuck her needle into the next stitch so wildly that her silver thimble was outwitted and her finger was pricked, which made her even crosser. "I'll ask somebody else who cares more about poor Lily than about keeping his own nose clean." She tutted as a spot of blood dropped onto the fine lawn of the mistress's nightgown, which she had been mending.

"Now, now," said the butler. "Of course, Andrew will light the morning fire. Quarter to five, mind. There's a day of grouse planned."

"Certainly, Mr. Cove," said Mr. Pallister, trying to sound dignified, though his cheeks—always ruddy—were now aflame. How dare she! Look at her sitting there, spitting on her finger and rubbing the spit on the blood spot. So uncouth, so un-dainty. She did it all the time, even took pride in it. Here she was regaling Lily, since the rest of them had heard it ten times before and were sick of listening.

"Moistening a blood spot right away with a wetted finger is better than all the soda and hot soaks in the world," she said, holding the nightgown out for inspection. "Look, it's quite gone."

Tchah! thought Mr. Pallister. If the mistress knew she had your spit on her nightie you'd get your jotters. But he said nothing and, to give Belinda her due, marveling at the vanished spot did take Lily's mind off her troubles.

"And don't tell him any more maids' names," Belinda said to Mr. Pallister.

"What do you take me for?" he demanded.

"I don't take you at all," said Belinda pertly. Then, snatching up the nightgown, she flounced off in such high dudgeon that she left behind not only her precious thimble, but even her sacred cloth shears—those perfectly ordinary scissors that the others touched only if they set their life's value at naught. Mrs. Boyd sighed and cleared the things off to the sideboard to let the kitchen maid give a last wipe over the table top before bedtime.

***

Mr. Pallister rose at four and by quarter to five was smoothly shaved and dressed in his livery with black cuffs over. He approached the door of the errant young gentleman and opened it softly. He was planning to behave with icy civility—not so much as smile, nothing so vulgar as a sneer—but he stopped short in the doorway and his mouth fell open.

The room was empty. The bed had been sat on—there was a dent halfway up one side—but had clearly not been slept in. Mr. Pallister stared. A pair of shoes lay on the rug under the creased dent in the bedclothes. The man had taken his boots off and then left to creep about the house in his stockinged soles.

Mr. Pallister thought swiftly. The only ladies in the house were the mistress, quite forty, and the girl to whom the man's brother was betrothed. He could not have fancied his chances with either of them. He must have gone after one of the maids. What on earth was to be done about it?

He had got as far as the landing when the question was taken out of his hands. Footsteps, fleet and light, were crossing the hall below. It did not sound like a man in socks but before Mr. Pallister looked over the banister he arranged his face into a look of haughty disdain.

It was Sarah, one of the housemaids, and she was racing upstairs, white-faced and trembling.

"Oh, Andrew!" she cried out in a kind of shrieking whisper

when she saw him. "I think he's dead!"

Mr. Pallister found himself at the first real crossroads of his young life. Should he, a lowly junior footman, obey the chain of command—in other words, wake the butler? Or should he, a red-blooded man in his own right after all, take charge and give aid to this damsel in distress?

"Where is he, Sarah?" he asked. Neither of them felt the need to specify the name of the unfortunate, possibly deceased, fellow.

"In the palm house," Sarah said. She was sobbing hard into her apron hem now, but Mr. Pallister was sure those were her words.

"The *palm* house?" he repeated, looking down to the double glass doors that led into it from the hall. The palm house was one of the glories of Thelpe, full not just of palms and ferns but of an abundance of exotic flowers, some of the blooms so large, bright, and pungent that Mr. Pallister always feared they must be vulgar, despite the mistress's fondness for them.

"He's lying on the floor just inside," said Sarah. "Oh, Andrew, I really do think he's gone and died there."

"Wait here," said Mr. Pallister and hurried downstairs.

The young man was indeed lying on the floor just inside the palm-house door, face down on the encaustic tiles at the bottom of the short flight of marble steps that led from one level to another (and still annoyed the master, who believed that if one paid an architect one should have things match up cleanly).

He was certainly unconscious. One arm was flung wide but one was tucked under his body in the most awkward fashion, so that he was quite humped up in the middle of his back. No one capable of movement would remain in such a position for a minute.

Mr. Pallister, with one finger, touched the out-flung hand. It was cold, wooden, and unfleshlike. He shrank away. Then, girding himself, he pushed back on one of the man's shoulders, just to see what might be causing that dreadful turtle-shell hunch, and caught sight of a gleam of copper inside a curled fist.

Gasping, Mr. Pallister stood up and backed off. The fellow had been carrying Belinda's cloth shears when he entered the palm house. He had stumbled on the unexpected flight of stairs and . . .

Mr. Pallister's thoughts flew round inside his head like moths in a bell jar. He should summon the master, the butler, the doctor. He should cover the man for decency's sake. At least, he should turn him over and close those dull, staring eyes. First things first though. This dreadful business was going to take a lot of dealing with over the course of the day.

Mr. Pallister made for the kitchen to start a kettle for tea.

At the kitchen door his feet stilled and his breath died.

Someone was in there, crouched at the range like a cloaked toad, stirring the fire.

"Wh-who is that?" he breathed.

The figure leapt up and clanged shut the firebox door.

"Oh! Andrew!" It was Hetty, one of the housemaids. "You startled me. What are you doing in *here*?"

"What are *you* doing?" asked Mr. Pallister. The girl was in her nightgown and a shawl.

"Just . . . burning rags," Hetty said, lifting her chin and looking him square in the eye.

"Burning rags?" he asked. "At five o'clock in the morning? What do you mean?"

Hetty's eyes were very small and round and dark and she regarded him without blinking.

"We always burn our rags early in the morning, if you must know," she said, an angry thrill in her voice. "When there's no menfolk about. I forgot you'd be up today."

"Oh!" said Mr. Pallister "Ah. Quite. Yes." He reeled away, his cheeks so far beyond red they were almost purple.

Sarah was still on the landing, still with her apron bunched in her hands, but her face was perhaps a little less stark.

"Is he really gone?" she asked.

"He fell and . . ." Mr. Pallister hesitated. *Hit his head* or even *broke his neck* were each preferable phrases to the horrid truth that ended with *on Belinda's cloth shears*. And it seemed so very unlikely. How had he got them from where they had lain on the servants' hall sideboard? And why had he taken them to the palm house anyway?

Mr. Pallister was seized with a sudden sick conviction that something quite different must have happened. Belinda must have come downstairs to fetch the precious object and perhaps she met him and they struggled and . . . Mr. Pallister turned smartly away from Sarah and, contravening every rule of the house, made a beeline for the women servants' staircase. He was rapping on Belinda's door not a minute later.

"Who is it?" she hissed in a low voice.

He opened the door, bold from relief, and strode in.

"I have some terrible news," he announced.

"Andrew!" she said. "What are you doing *here*?" She caught her lip. "You'll get flayed if they catch you. Get out of my bedroom."

"You're dressed and decent," said Mr. Pallister, which was half-true. She was dressed, but she was rather disheveled. Her hair was escaping its pins and her black dress was all over threads. She looked worn to a shred, too. "Your shears," he said. "Your blessed shears."

"What about them?" asked Belinda. "Did you mean to bring them up and forget? I left them downstairs last night. I'd leave my head behind if it wasn't screwed on."

"There's been a terrible accident," Mr. Pallister began. But even as he was wondering how to put it, the job of conveying the news was snatched away. Isabel, one of the tweenies, came rushing from the far-end stairs, sobbing as she ran.

"Oh! Oh! Belinda," she said. "You'll never guess! He's dead. He's dead."

"*Who's* dead?" Belinda asked. She looked more annoyed than alarmed.

"He went into the palm house to cut some flowers, the beast! He must have meant to take them when he went a-wooing. Oh! Lilies! He was cutting a bunch of *lilies* to try to turn the head of our poor little Lily herself when she went in to light his fire. Oh, the beast! The pig! And he went and tripped, carrying scissors, you see. And that was that."

"Ah," said Mr. Pallister. "That makes sense. I wondered what he was doing. That's very quick thinking, Isa."

One of the girls made a sound but for the life of him Mr Pallister could not have named it.

"Where *is* Lily?" he asked. "I took over *one* of her fires but she should have started the others by now. She's not in the kitchen."

"Dressing," said Belinda. The word came out like a bark. "Have *you* been in the kitchen?" she demanded.

Mr. Pallister stared at her, perplexed. She looked quite wild, her face shiny and her hair a scrambled nest. And those threads all over her dress.

"Have you been sewing, Belinda?" he asked. "Cutting cloth without your good shears? Did you search for them and wonder where they'd got to?"

"Sewing?" Belinda asked. "At five in the morning?" She curled her lip but before he could press his point further, the already ragged peace of the dawn was shattered completely. Someone was banging the dinner gong. The dead man was discovered.

***

Down in the servants' hall an hour later, Mr. Cove, the butler, and Mrs. Boyd, the housekeeper, held court. The entire staff was packed around the table and on it sat the three biggest brown teapots and a platter of toast made from two whole loaves. Some of the girls could only sip at very weak cupfuls as they fluttered their terrified thoughts into one another's ears. Poor little Lily could not manage even that, and just sat weeping. Most of the menfolk, made of coarser stuff, were slathering on marmalade and swiping extra sugar lumps while their bosses were distracted by the enormity of it all. The coarsest of them were trading bets about what the police sergeant would say and whether the wedding would go ahead after the mourning.

Mr. Pallister alone sat silent and puzzling. Why, he asked himself, would a gentleman visitor to the house come to the servants' hall to look for scissors? Didn't he have a pair of little clippers in his own dressing case? He glanced over at the sideboard where they had lain the night before. Was it his imagination or did it look different somehow? The shelves above, with their white cotton liners and their scalloped lacy edgings, bore the same willow-patterned plates as ever. And the deep shelf below held its burden of coppered kettles, too. He put his head on one side, the better to see what had changed, and a glint caught his eye. He bent over in his chair with his hands on his knees and peered closer. There under the deep bottom shelf, rolled right to the back until it stopped against the skirting, was Belinda's silver thimble. Mr. Pallister got to his feet and, stooping, stretched as far as he could to poke his finger into the thing and draw it out again. He breathed in from the effort of such an awkward pose and then coughed, such a very strong smell of bleach as there was. He straightened and coughed again.

The odour really was quite pronounced and the sideboard *did* look different. This little corner of the room had been scrubbed and scrubbed again. It was gleaming.

As he turned back towards the table where the menservants carried on scoffing and ragging, although—unless he was mistaken—the women had quieted down, his eye was caught for a second time. But it wasn't a glint this time. It was a spot. A murky brown spot on the snowy white cloth of one of the cotton shelf-liners. He bent closer and as he did so, a hand shot into view and grabbed the article, whipping it out from under the plates, rattling them against the rod that held them upright.

Belinda.

"It's got to be your own spit," she whispered. "The silly girl didn't listen."

"*Which* silly girl?" Mr. Pallister breathed. He swung round and raked a gaze up and down the table at all of the maids. Sarah, who had sounded so shocked when she broke the news; Hetty, who was certainly burning *something* in the range and picked the perfect way to stop him questioning her; Isabel, who had delivered the explanation so crisply but forgot to say the man's name. Lily, who sat there weeping; Rosie and Annie, such a sturdy pair, strong enough to drag a man from where he died to quite another part of the house and arrange him there. Or Belinda herself. Mr. Pallister reached out his hand and plucked from her dress one of the many threads, pale blue and frayed at the end, that clung to it.

Then suddenly a dozen chairs were scraping against the linoleum floor as the staff shot to its collective feet. The mistress had entered the room and stood, pale and regal, with one hand against the doorframe to support her.

"The police are satisfied that it was a terrible, terrible accident," she said. "As are both families. However, under the circumstances, the earl and countess and the viscount, too, will be leaving us this morning. I don't suppose they will return." She hesitated. "Yes," she said, "an accident. Such an unfortunate young man. They can tell, you see, that . . . the wound was caused from very close quarters. From *such* close quarters that it strains belief to imagine another person being able to inflict it. How could another person get so close to him, you see?"

There was a horrified silence in the servants' hall. How indeed?

"Yes," said the mistress again. "A most unfortunate young man in every way. Unlucky from the start. He was even left-handed, you know."

The silence deepened.

"But the police sergeant and both families are satisfied, as I say. If anyone else were involved in any way, that person would have been marked with blood. His clothes, from inflicting such a wound at such close quarters, would be quite grisl—" Her words died in her throat and her eyes flared. "Well, well," she said. "Carry on. What else can one do but carry on?"

Where had she been looking when her voice dried and failed, Mr. Pallister asked himself. He fixed his gaze where hers had been. Lily. Lily, who was still dressing at five when she should have been out and about at her chores. Lily, who was a silly girl and didn't listen. Lily, who unlike the others was looking so fresh and bright in her brand-new dress this morning, run up overnight by Belinda, even if the cutting out had gone badly without the special cloth shears.

What to do? Was this monstrous regiment of women above the law? Should the unfortunate young man evermore be laughed at for a foolish accidental death? Should a girl who struck out at an amorous pup with such deadly force walk free?

At that moment Mr. Pallister chose his path. He was not content to be merely a man, one of thousands. He meant to be a butler. He had a butler's heart, full of loyal discretion, and he had a butler's eye, too. Why even today, as a junior footman, he could tell that only one of the maids was turned out truly smartly. Lily was neat as a pin and the others, limp and crumpled, should smarten up to match her.

NIGHT AND FOG

by Marcia Talley

*Reporter Madison visits a survivor of the Liberation
of Paris, and hears a tale she hardly expected.
Margaret Price, awarded a medal by France, tells the
story of her friend Veronique, a spy during the German
occupation . . . a most dangerous game.*

Margaret Price could keep a secret, no doubt about that. When
Susan announced to the Methodist Women's Bible Study Group
that she was pregnant with twins, Meg was the only person in
town—other than Susan's husband and her gynecologist—who
wasn't surprised. Meg had known about the pregnancy for months,
ever since her friend's home pregnancy test had popped up
positive, but she had agreed to keep it secret in case the *in vitro* had
failed again. Joyfully, it hadn't.

I figure Meg would have taken her own amazing secret to the
grave, too, had an editor at the *Washington Gazette* not been
noshing on a chicken wrap at his desk while perusing a This Day in
History calendar.

"Madison!" he called out.

He meant me.

"Do you realize," Zack Bailey said when I appeared outside his
cubicle, a can of Diet Coke still sweating in my hand, "that August
twenty-fifth is the seventieth anniversary of the liberation of
Paris?"

I had been born during the post-Vietnam era, but thanks to an
AP European History course in high school, my background was
pretty solid. "When the Allies sent the Germans packing?"

"*Exactamente.*" He planted both feet on the floor, sat up
straight. "I'm thinking we need some sort of human interest story
for the Sunday edition. Liberation Day from the viewpoint of the
man on the street. Or woman," he added quickly. "Any ideas?"

My first thought was that ninety-nine percent of the Parisians
who had welcomed the Allies with cheers, flowers, and kisses on
that historic day were either long dead or confined to nursing
homes playing bingo for M&Ms. But the book in progress on my
bedside table was a Billy Boyle World War Two mystery, so after

a moment I said, "How 'bout the S.O.E.?"

"Es oh what?" History wasn't Zack's strong point.

"S.O.E.F. to be specific," I said. "Britain's Special Operations Executive. The F stands for France." I paused while he took that in. "They were spies."

Zack's left eyebrow quirked. He was a James Bond fan. I'd sparked his interest.

"They worked undercover during the occupation," I continued. "One out of five never made it home."

Zack tapped his nose and made a clicking noise with his tongue. In Zack-speak, that meant "Go for it, Madison."

I spent the rest of the day in my cubicle mining the internet. Then I made a few phone calls. By close of business, I'd tracked down the author of a recently published history of the S.O.E. to his flat in London. The following morning, in exchange for the promise of an Amazon link to his book in my article, he graciously agreed to share the names of his contacts. Which explains why two days later I was on American Eagle flight 3809 en route to Margaret Price's modest home near Scugog on the outskirts of Toronto.

Margaret—"please call me Meg"—had turned ninety-three on her last birthday but she didn't look a day over eighty. The former S.O.E. operative greeted me at the door wearing slim-cut blue jeans and a loose white t-shirt that said, "OOT & ABOOT." Neatly-pedicured toes, lacquered bold red to match her fingernails, peeked out from a pair of flat-heeled, open-toed sandals.

Between her front door and her living room, I learned that Meg was a widow and that until his death, she and her husband, a retired Canadian army colonel, had owned a Christmas tree farm.

We settled into matching chairs, upholstered in red damask, flanking a gas log fireplace. On the coffee table between us lay a staggering display of medals, ribbons, and assorted military insignia. "You asked to see these," she said as I leaned over the table for a closer look. "It's a little embarrassing, really."

Attached to a red ribbon, taking pride of place in a white silk-lined box labeled Toye, Kenning and Spencer Ltd, lay a gold cross engraved with *God and Empire*. "Wow," I said.

"That's an MBE," Meg explained, confirming my guess.

"I recognize this one," I said after a moment of awed silence. "May I?"

When she nodded, I picked up the Croix de Guerre, holding it carefully by the red and green-striped ribbon from which it hung. "The French don't give these out willy-nilly," I said. "You're a true heroine."

Her face flushed. "I'm not the heroine you're looking for," she whispered. "Veronique. She's the woman you should be talking to, not me." Meg pressed a hand to her chest, caught her breath. "Sadly, she passed away over ten years ago."

I laid the medal down, fingered an embroidered paratrooper patch. "I don't remember running across anyone named Veronique during my research," I said, glancing up.

She smiled. "You wouldn't."

"Can you tell me about her?"

Meg laced her fingers together and placed them in her lap. "Unlike most S.O.E. operatives who used aliases, Veronique Barbier was her real name," she began. "When the war broke out, Veronique was reading History at Somerville College in Oxford . . ."

I held up a hand, interrupting her story. "Do you mind if I take notes?" I was already pulling my notebook out of my bag.

"We trained together," Meg continued once I'd opened it to a fresh page and uncapped my pen. "First at Beaulieu down in Hampshire. As wireless operators." A corner of her mouth turned up wistfully at the memory. "My goodness, she was fast! Twenty-six words a minute. Most of us could manage only half that."

She placed her hands on her knees and leaned forward. "Speed was important, you see, or the Nazis would D.F. you."

"D.F.?"

Meg twirled a finger in the air. "Nazis crawled the streets in trucks with radio direction finders spinning around on top. The Germans could triangulate a radio signal in thirty minutes, so you had to get your messages out quickly."

"Did you work together, then?" I asked.

"Not really. Veronique made her way back to Paris via Spain. After I parachuted into the Mayenne in the spring of 1944 I didn't see her again until . . ." She paused. "Would you like some coffee?"

The cheddar cheese bagel I'd snagged at a Tim Horton's in Port Perry seemed like days in the past. I worried about the interruption—would Meg lose her train of thought?—but my empty stomach won out. "Yes, please."

Meg rose and motioned for me to follow her into the kitchen. Over the hiss and sputter of a Keurig coffee machine she told me, "Winston Churchill authorized the S.O.E. to set Europe ablaze, so there I was, running around the countryside pretending to be a simple French schoolgirl. Laughable when you think about it, really."

She handed me the mug. "Milk and sugar?"

When I nodded, she wagged a finger in my face. "*That* could get you killed, young lady."

"I beg your pardon?"

"Veronique liked her coffee white, too, but you not only had to *think* French, you had to *be* French, and the French drank their coffee black."

I took a sip of the dark, bitter brew and winced. Clearly, I'd have made a rotten spy.

Meg opened the nearby fridge, reached in, then handed me a container of half and half. "But we're not in hiding from the Nazis here, thank God." She pointed toward a sugar bowl on the counter. "Help yourself."

As I stirred a teaspoon of sugar into my cup, she added, "You had to totally immerse yourself in French life, Madison. We lost one agent when a German patrol caught him riding his bicycle on the wrong side of the road."

Maybe it was the jolt of caffeine, but something she had said earlier finally registered. "You said Veronique made her way *back* to Paris?"

Meg slotted another coffee pod into the brewer. "She did. Her mother had an apartment there. She was English, married to a French banker, but he died in 1939. Good thing, too. The sight of a swastika flying from the Arc de Triomphe would have killed him."

After her own cup of coffee had gurgled through the machine, Meg handed me a package of maple cream cookies and we returned to the living room.

"As I was saying earlier," Meg continued after we'd settled back into our chairs, "Veronique Barbier was much braver than I. While I was lodging with farmers, eating boiled rabbit and turnips, moving my wireless from barn to barn to avoid detection, she went undercover in Paris which was, quite literally, swarming with Nazis." She paused to nibble on a cookie. "Her mission got off to a rocky start."

"How so?" I asked.

"Veronique went to the address she'd been given, planning to meet her contact, code named Nicole, but minutes before she got there, the Germans raided. Her contact was arrested and the wireless seized.

"Veronique knew where Nicole had been taken, of course, almost everyone did. 84 Avenue Foch, the headquarters of the *Sicherheitsdienst,* the Nazi counter-intelligence service."

I scribbled and nodded, encouraging her to go on. I'd figure out how to spell *Sicherheitsdienst* later.

"They built cells on the fifth floor where prisoners were 'held for questioning.'" She drew quote marks in the air.

I winced. "I hate to imagine."

Something passed over Meg's face like a dark cloud, impossible to read. "Today, Veronique would have pulled out her cell phone and texted an S.O.S. back to headquarters, but in those days . . ." She let the thought die. "Figuring that her contact had been betrayed—she was right, as it turned out—she did the only thing she knew how to do. She went back to her mother's flat to lie low, waiting for London to miss Nicole's scheduled transmission.

"Have you ever been to Paris?" she asked suddenly.

"Never," I said, "but a gal can dream."

"Avenue Foch has a wide, park-like median," she explained, "so it was fairly easy for Veronique to keep an eye on the SS building from there. Sometimes she would walk her mother's dog, a little Bichon Frise named Mozart. Sometimes she'd simply sit on a park bench reading a novel, something uncontroversial, a Simenon mystery would be my guess. The Nazis shut down all the newspapers in 1940.

"It didn't take long for Veronique to observe that every day around mid-morning, German officers would begin to trickle out of the building. They liked to frequent *Le Poisson d'Or*, a cafe on Avenue Bugeaud near the Place du Marechal. So, Veronique started turning up at the cafe, too. Every day, regular as clockwork." Meg closed her eyes, as if the memory were a video spooling past inside. "She always wore a plain cotton dress, loosely belted. A short jacket, bought second-hand, a bit frayed at the cuffs. Smart, but well-worn shoes. Rayon hose, bagging slightly at the knees. Even the little red cloche she always wore soon became a familiar sight at *Le Poisson d'Or*, fading into the background like the waiters in their crisp, white jackets or the nouveau tulip wallpaper that decorated the vestibule."

Her eyes flew open. "Have a cookie, or don't you like them?"

I'd never had a maple leaf cream before, but I took one bite and rolled my eyes with pleasure.

Apparently satisfied that the cookie exceeded expectations, Meg continued her story. "Every day, out on the sidewalk if the weather was nice, she'd sit in a wicker chair at a little round table and order *une tasse d'espresso* and sip it slowly, making it last. Sometimes she'd bring little Mozart along, sometimes not. A book, perhaps. Her knitting, too. Always her knitting.

"They tested her, of course, the Nazis. '*Entschuldigen Sie bitte, haben Sie den zehn-Franc-Schein fallen lassen, der unter Ihrem Stuhl liegt?*'"

I paused in mid-scribble. "French major," I said. "Help me out here?"

Meg chuckled. "He was asking if she dropped a ten franc note under her chair. Veronique was fluent in German, of course, but she didn't move a muscle when she heard that. She simply sat, knitting calmly as if she hadn't heard the officer. Veronique was way too clever to fall for it, even though she was certain there must actually *be* a ten franc note under her chair. Eventually, the officer tapped her on the shoulder and called her attention to the money, speaking in fractured French." Meg sighed. "No reason for any of them to learn to speak the language. France was disappearing. All the street signs had been repainted. Buildings were being renamed. *Zentral Ersatzteillager. Wehrmachts-gottesdienst. Deutsches Rotes Kreuz.*" She sniffed, wrinkling her nose. "Certain books were banned, art was stolen, and as time went on, people began vanishing, too."

"*Nacht-und-Nebel,*" I said, recalling my research. "Night and fog. Hitler's top secret order."

"Yes. They were to be *vernebelt,*" she added. "Vanished. Transformed into mist. Nobody was ever to know what happened to them."

In spite of the warmth of the room, a chill ran along my spine.

"What was she knitting?" I asked in an attempt to lighten the mood.

Meg's eyebrows disappeared under her steel-gray bangs. "That's exactly what Major Kieffer asked her."

Kieffer. I searched my memory bank for the connection.

"Waffen SS Sturmbannführer Hans Josef Kieffer," Meg supplied, pronouncing each word with clear distaste, as if eager to get it off her tongue. "He was the senior officer in charge of the place."

I scribbled down the name so I could Google it later.

"Like so many things, wool was rationed. Sensing another trick question, Veronique explained that she'd unraveled a sweater that had once belonged to her father and was knitting a winter scarf. 'It's for my brother,' she told Major Kieffer. 'He's stationed in Berlin with the 33 Waffen Grenadiers.'"

Meg sniggered. "If Kieffer had decided to check, it wouldn't have been a lie. Not that Henri had wanted to go, you understand. Like so many French lads, her brother had been drafted by the Nazis and forced into service for the Reich."

"Did Henri survive the war?" I asked.

"Sadly, no. He died in the Soviet assault on Berlin." She sat quietly for a moment, then indicated the package of maple creams. "Have another cookie.

"After that, Kieffer left her in peace," Meg said, smiling with satisfaction as I reached into the bag. "Veronique was knitting from memory, you know. Printed patterns were not allowed."

"Why not?" I asked, munching greedily. Maple creams, as it turns out, are addictive.

"Messages could be concealed within the instructions," Meg explained. "Crossword puzzles were suspect, too. The clues might be used to pass intelligence to the enemy."

I felt the conversation drifting, so I said, "How long did it take for London to figure out that Nicole had been captured?"

"Ah, right. Well, there's the difficulty. On the second floor of Avenue Foch, the SS had set up a wireless room where operators sent bogus coded messages back to England. It took weeks before someone on our end realized that it wasn't Nicole's fist."

I thought I'd misheard. "Fist?"

"Sorry." She grinned at my confusion. "Every wireless operator has a distinct style of transmission. Maybe they use slightly longer dashes, or put shorter gaps between words. That's called their fist. Nicole had what's known as a good fist. Whoever was impersonating her was sloppy, harder to read. London should have twigged to it immediately, of course, especially when her messages didn't end with the prearranged code word that indicated everything was okay. But they were blooming idiots! What can I say?"

She pressed her hands together, fingertips touching as if in prayer. "Finally, after several weeks, London became suspicious and got word to me. They sent me to make contact with Veronique. Now that they knew Nicole must have been arrested, everyone was afraid that Veronique's cover might have been blown, especially if Nicole had broken under torture."

"And had she?" I asked.

Meg held up a hand, palm out. "I'm coming to that. Times were risky, Madison. There were Gestapo in plain clothes everywhere. Once I got into the city, I kept checking my reflection in the shop windows to make sure I wasn't being followed. And I didn't dare knock on the door of Veronique's apartment.

"One day, I followed her to *Le Poisson d'Or*. It was a mild, gloriously sunny day, the kind that Paris is famous for, so the café was busy. I waited for a table, keeping one eye on Veronique while chatting up a young couple and fussing over their baby who was napping in his pushchair. Eventually, Veronique noticed me and her face lit up. I'd taken a step in her direction when her eyes darted right, then left, then right again, warning me away. Hard to say exactly why, the place was so crowded. But I took the hint, stepped back and cooed over the baby some more. Eventually, two old codgers got up to leave, and I sat down at the table they'd vacated, ordered a beer and pretended to read the *Pariser Zeitung* one of them had left behind.

"When the waiter brought my beer, a dark, malty Doppelbock, I got distracted. Because of food shortages, we'd been starving in the country. I'd lost at least fifteen pounds." Again, she closed her eyes. "I can still taste that beer, Madison. Chocolaty, almost fruit-like." After a moment, her eyes flew open. "I practically inhaled it. Lord knows I needed the calories. Next thing I knew, Veronique was gone! Did she expect me to follow her? Honestly, I didn't know what to do. And then I saw that she'd left her knitting behind."

Meg paused, inhaled deeply.

I did, too. I was so engrossed by her story that I'd almost forgotten to breathe. "And you picked it up."

"That scarf made all the difference," she said after a moment. "Would you like to see it?"

"You still have it?" I asked, feeling stupid the minute the words left my mouth.

Without answering me directly, she pattered away, her sandals slapping the hardwood floor. When she returned a few minutes later, she carried a white Hudson's Bay department store box. After she removed the top, I could see it was lined with tissue paper.

"Do you knit?" she asked as she began peeling the tissue paper aside.

"Back in college, but I wasn't very good at it," I confessed. "I kept dropping stitches."

"So you know the basics."

I nodded. No matter how complicated the pattern, knitting involves only two simple stitches: knit and purl. Knits resemble tiny arrowheads while purls turn into bumps. The sweater I'd knitted for my father had been a disaster by any measure, but the crooked ribbing and the cabling that snaked erratically up the front had been a combination of just those two stitches, however amateurishly rendered.

Meg lifted the scarf out of its box. She held it in front of her chest and allowed it to unroll like a scroll, a scroll so long that one end puddled at her feet. "What do you see?" she asked.

Meg had mentioned Veronique couldn't use a pattern. Perhaps that explained the eccentric, almost schizophrenic design. "Looks like she took knitting lessons from me," I joked, stepping closer. I squinted, trying to sort the random knits and purls into some coherent pattern.

"Oh my gosh," I said after a moment, feeling like I'd stepped into a novel by John Le Carre. "It's a code!"

Meg beamed as if I were a prize student. If she hadn't been holding the scarf, she might have patted me on the head. "Every day as Veronique sat, she listened. She recorded—here— everything important the Nazis said." Meg ran her hand along the length of the scarf, caressing it. "It's in Morse code, as you guessed. Knit, purl, knit, purl—dash, dot, dash, dot. That's Morse code for N.N."

My heart flopped in my chest. "*Nacht und Nebel.*"

She nodded. "And here," she said, fingering a section of the scarf about halfway down. "Purl, knit; knit, purl; knit, knit, knit, purl. R-A-V and so on. Ravensbrück. Followed by a list of names."

She looked up, her eyes glistening with unshed tears. "As the Allies advanced, rather than release their captives, the Nazis pushed their prisoners deeper into Germany. Ravensbrück was one of the places they sent the women. Many of them died, some quite horribly.

"Veronique recorded troop movements, too, but . . ." She paused, began to refold the scarf, perhaps as a distraction while she regained her composure. "Other camps are listed here, as well: Dachau, Pforzheim, Natzweiler. Other names. If it hadn't been for Veronique, they might have vanished into mist, just as Hitler intended."

"And Nicole?" I asked.

Meg dredged up a smile from somewhere. "She survived. We didn't get to all of our people in time, of course. Of the thirty-nine women sent to France, twelve perished in the camps, but at least we *knew*. We could give their families closure."

Meg fixed me with tired, gray eyes. "I hate that word. Closure."

With some difficulty, I fought back tears.

Meg reached for the box.

I swallowed hard. "Before you put it away, do you mind if I take a photograph?"

"Not at all." Meg unfolded the scarf, draped it over both arms and turned her body sideways so the scarf's impressive length would fit in the frame.

"Ironic, really," she said as I fiddled with my iPhone and set up the shot. "Josef Kieffer was tried for his war crimes and condemned to death by a British military tribunal. They hanged him in 1947."

I snapped one photo, then another. "Why ironic?"

"When Veronique and I saw one another again, many months after the Armistice, she confessed that she'd often fanaticized about wrapping this scarf around Herr Kieffer's neck, and pulling it tight, then tighter . . ."

She began to giggle. "In the end, it was the information she encoded here that helped dispatch that monster to Valhalla," she said, once she'd reined herself in. "Veronique's scarf did him in. It hanged him good and proper!"

THE SEVEN

by Elaine Viets

*The members of this small women's club in 1950s
St. Louis do not discuss gardening or recipes.
Betty has agreed to follow the club rules, or suffer the
consequences. Her husband unwittingly makes this
easier . . .*

Betty checked herself once more in the bedroom mirror. Her short black hair was stylishly curled, and defiantly unwilted in the sweltering St. Louis heat. She thought her Besame Red lipstick was bold, but it went well with her pale skin. Betty's red-and-white polka dot dress was cinched with a wide, white patent leather belt that matched her white heels. It was June 1950, so it was safe to wear white shoes. Betty wouldn't dare wear white before Memorial Day. The starched, frilly apron over her full skirt was a sweet domestic touch.

Portrait of the Perfect Atomic Age Housewife, Betty thought. *Bill's always liked this outfit. I've made his favorite dinner tonight, too. That will put him in a good mood. This has to work. I don't want to kill him, but if Bill doesn't change his mind tonight, either he dies—or I do.*

She heard his Chevy pull into the driveway, and hurried to meet her man, heels clicking across the waxed kitchen linoleum. She greeted her husband of five years with a kiss and his favorite drink, a light scotch. With his chiseled chin and Princeton cut, Bill looked like the perfect young insurance executive. He also looked beat by the heat. He'd rolled up his white shirtsleeves and loosened his tie. His seersucker jacket hung over one arm, covering his monogrammed briefcase.

"Daddy's home," squealed four-year-old Pattie. She wrapped her short, plump arms around Bill's pants leg.

"Careful there, sweetie," Bill said, his voice sharp. "Don't spill Daddy's drink."

Pattie's lower lip trembled, but she knew better than to cry. Daddy didn't like crying children after a long day at the office. Betty fought to hide her panic. She couldn't have her plan unravel because of Pattie. Not tonight. It was Number Seven.

"Why don't you wash up, honey," Betty said. "Pattie and I will finish getting dinner ready."

"I can't wait to get out of this suit," Bill said. "It's ninety-two degrees."

While Bill changed in the bedroom, Betty turned up the kitchen window fan, and under the cover of its soothing whirr said, "You look so cute in your ruffled pink playsuit, darling. You know Daddy doesn't mean to snap at you. He's just tired."

Pattie nodded, her soft dark curls bobbing in the fan's breeze.

"Sit at the table," Betty said, helping her into her booster seat, "and I'll fix you your own cocktail."

Betty poured 7-Up over ice in a plastic glass, and added maraschino cherry juice and two fat cherries, then a candy-striped straw. "Cheers!"

Pattie managed a smile.

Betty prepared the summer salad: cool lime Jell-O with chopped celery and radishes on iceberg lettuce leaves, and poured tall glasses of iced tea for Bill and herself.

She heard the shower shut off. Time to take the casserole out of the warming oven. Perfect. It wasn't dried out at all. She heaped Bill's plate with tuna-noodle casserole topped with her secret ingredient for extra crunch—cornflakes—then dished out smaller portions for herself and Pattie.

Bill strolled into the kitchen, looking cool and refreshed in a short-sleeved plaid shirt and khakis. "Well, what have we here? Tuna-noodle casserole!" He smiled at Betty.

"It's not too hot for a casserole, is it?" she asked, her voice anxious. Everything depended on pleasing him tonight.

"Never! Nobody makes tuna and noodles like you do, sweetie. It's even better than my mother's."

Betty knew that. That's why she'd made it.

Number Seven was Bill's last chance. And hers. It was Wednesday. The Seven meeting was tomorrow night at seven. If she couldn't get him to say yes, then Friday it was curtains for one of them, and she sure wasn't going to be the one to get killed.

Betty was too tense to eat more than a few bites, but Bill didn't notice. She asked about his workday. "Miserable," he said. "The ceiling fans just moved the hot air around, and my desk fan was broken. By noon, I was sweating like a stevedore. The stupid secretary couldn't find my paperweight and the ceiling fan nearly blew my paperwork out the window. I had to use my coffee cup to keep it on the desk."

Betty made sympathetic noises while she cleared his plate, then served homemade brownies and vanilla ice cream. He wolfed down his dessert while she talked about her day. "I washed and ironed two loads of laundry in the basement, where it's reasonably cool. After lunch, I read Pattie a story at naptime. She's starting to read, Bill. Our Pattie is so smart." Pattie smiled at her mother.

"Too bad those brains are wasted on a girl," Bill said. Pattie stared at her dessert plate, her smile gone.

Betty wanted to say it was important for women to be smart, too, but she bit back her comment. She couldn't afford an argument. Not on Number Seven. "While Pattie napped, I waxed the kitchen floor," she said, "then . . ."

Bill wasn't interested, and Betty couldn't blame him. She knew her day was boring.

He interrupted her. "Another good dinner, sweetie. Your brownies are the best."

"Thank you, honey," Betty said, carrying his dessert plate to the sink.

"Can I have more brownies?" Pattie asked, her voice small and crushed down.

"*May* I have more brownies, *please?*" Betty corrected. "Yes, you may have one more. And you may watch television while I talk to Daddy."

She carried Pattie's brownie on a paper plate into the den and turned on the Philco. Once her little girl was settled, Betty took a deep breath, then rushed into the bedroom to fluff her hair and put on fresh lipstick. This was it. Number Seven had to work or she'd have to kill him. She had no choice.

She freshened Bill's tea. *Here goes*, she thought, and plunged ahead.

"Bill, dear, remember Mike Roberts? I worked at his law office before the war. He wants me to come back and be his executive secretary."

"What?" Bill set down his glass so hard tea slopped onto the tablecloth. "Betty, we've had this conversation before. Five times."

Six, Betty thought, but rushed on with her rehearsed reasons.

"Yes, I know, but he's offering more money—five cents an hour more. I want to go back to work." *Deep breaths*, she reminded herself. *Don't sound hysterical. Be reasonable.*

"With all the men out of work, Mike should be able to find a good executive secretary. I've told you before: no wife of mine is working."

Bill's face was bright red with fury, his thin lips were pulled into a snarl, and his voice was steadily rising. Betty reached over and turned up the window fan to the highest speed. Mrs. Raines next door was pretty deaf, but she couldn't risk the neighbors hearing them argue.

"What will people say?" Bill said. "They'll think I can't support you."

Betty twisted her starched apron under the table, so he couldn't see how nervous she was. *Don't offend him*, she thought. *Convince him.* "Bill, please. I'm trapped in this house all day. I need to get out. I need a job."

"You have a job!" he said. "Your job is taking care of my house, cooking and cleaning, darning my socks, ironing my shirts and rearing my daughter. That's your job—your only job. If you went to work who'd watch Pattie?"

"My mother," Betty said. Her heart was beating faster now. She had to make him understand. For her sake—and his. "Pattie goes to kiddie summer camp for a half-day now, and she'll start kindergarten in September. Mother said she'd enjoy watching her grandchild after school."

"And what about my dinner?" Bill said. It was a demand.

"You'll still have your dinner." She hated the way she had to wheedle and soothe him, as if he were a spoiled child. She no longer loved him, but she had to save him. "I'll get home an hour before you. Plenty of time to cook a nourishing meal. You love casseroles. I'll prepare them the night before and pop them in the oven. I'll make all your favorites: my green bean bake, Hawaiian ham casserole, chicken casserole…"

Bill cut her off. "And the housework?"

"I can do it in my spare time. On weekends." She was sounding desperate. He wasn't listening, and his stubbornness was going to kill him.

Bill talked to her as if she were a disobedient child. "Betty, I've given you everything a woman could want. You have a new brick home in Clayton, one of the best suburbs in St. Louis. You have a patio with sliding glass doors and huge walk-in closets to hold all the clothes I buy you. I gave you a new stove, a washing machine, a refrigerator, and you have the first television on the block. I put this food on the table. What more could you want?"

"I want to do something meaningful, Bill, like I did in the war. I was a third officer in the Women's Army Corps."

"And I was a second lieutenant. Now I'm a paper pusher at an insurance agency."

"You're not, Bill," she said. "You're a rising young executive."

"Who can provide for his family," Bill said. "You'll hurt my prospects if you get a job. Our daughter will grow up to be a juvenile delinquent. Motherhood is a woman's highest calling."

Betty chose her next words carefully. The wrong ones would

send one of them to their death. "I agree, Bill. I love being Pattie's mother, watching her discover the world. But a woman can have other callings besides motherhood. I was an officer just like you during the war. A third officer in the WACs was the same rank as a second lieutenant."

Bill's laugh was cruel. "You can't compare your war work with mine, Betty. I was part of the Normandy invasion. You were one of our *crack* troops."

Betty flinched at the insult. "Bill! Don't you dare use that vulgar term for a WAC. I took a job in the military to free up a man for the front."

"Where he could get killed! Everyone knows WACs were hookers in uniform, Victory Girls eager to give relief to the troops."

"You, of all people, know that's not true," Betty said. "I was a virgin on our wedding night."

"Of course you were, or I wouldn't have married you," he said. "The war's over. I've had to join the rat race. And I don't understand why any woman would want an office job when you could stay home in a nice house."

Please listen to me, she thought. *I don't want to kill you.* "Bill, every day I vacuum, dust, make the beds and mop the floors. I cook your meals. But it's the same thing over and over."

"That's life, Betty. You have plenty of diversions. How many clubs have you joined?"

"Three. The book club, the church's ladies' auxiliary, and the Seven."

"That should be enough," he said. "The Seven was hard to get into. It took you more than a year to become a full member."

"It's very exclusive, Bill. I was lucky to be accepted. I met Claire at the book club, and we went for coffee afterward."

That's where our friendship started, Betty thought. Claire has a sixth sense for finding women like me. Restless women who want more. Week after week, we drank coffee while she carefully sounded me out. What did I do during the war? Did I want to be a housewife? Was I happy in a new subdivision house with all the modern conveniences? Was it enough?

Little by little, I told Claire how I really felt. How I'd enjoyed my wartime freedom and missed it when it was taken away. Claire understood. She'd been there. She'd been a radio operator in the WACs, just like me. Only the brightest women were chosen for that job.

After fourteen months of coffee, Claire invited me to the first meeting of the Seven: seven smart, educated, accomplished women, all widows, except for Muriel, the newest member. I wanted to join this dazzling, sophisticated group.

"All the other Seven work, Bill," Betty said. "They have important jobs. Alice is an office manager. Louise is director of nursing at the hospital. Mitzi's an accountant. Ann is head of the notions department at Famous-Barr. Claire teaches deaf students. Edith is a college professor."

"At a girls' school," Bill said. She hated his sneer, as if teaching young women wasn't as important as teaching men. "Are these women putting this crazy idea about getting a job in your head?"

"No," Betty said. "This is my own idea. I only see them once a week on Thursday night."

"Maybe you should see them less," Bill said.

"You need them, too, Bill. They're very influential. Mitzi's husband, Tom, hired you."

"I liked Tom," Bill said. "He died too young. A heart attack at thirty-five. See, that's what I mean about the rat race."

"But your new supervisor, Bryson, likes you, too. Maybe more than Tom," Betty said. "You're on the fast track to promotion. Please, Bill, don't say no. Please let me go back to work."

"If you want something to do, give me a son."

"But we have Pattie." One child was more than enough. They'd agreed on that before they were married. When Bill started climbing the corporate ladder, he changed his mind. He wanted two children, a boy and a girl, like the other top executives. Betty's opinion no longer mattered.

"She's cute, but a man needs a son. Someone I can take to the ball game and play catch with in the yard."

"You can do those things with Pattie. She loves the Browns."

"I won't have a tomboy. She's going to be a girl, a real girl who plays with dolls. No more of those playsuits, Betty. My daughter should know that men wear the pants. America went off the rails during the war, but it's been over for five years."

He slapped five dollars on the table. "Here. Buy yourself something. Whatever you want. Don't ever say I don't give you enough money."

Betty didn't want money. She wanted a job with money she earned. Fear gripped her heart. She made one last effort to save her husband. "Bill, what if I put my salary in an account for Pattie, so she can go to college?"

"Girls don't need college. She's going to get married."

"All right then, I'll use the money for her wedding."

"No!" Bill pounded the table. "No! No! You are a mother and a housewife, Betty, and that's enough for any woman. This is my final word on the subject. Understand? MY FINAL WORD."

"As you wish," Betty said.

"I'm going to read my newspaper," he said.

Betty was relieved when he stomped out of the kitchen. As she washed the dishes, she told herself, *You tried. It's not your fault. If you don't kill him, you'll die. And then what will happen to your daughter? Bill won't send your smart little girl to college. She'll be trapped just like her mother.*

Betty's tears dripped into the dishpan as she scrubbed at the baked-on noodles in the casserole dish. She rinsed it clean, took out a fresh dishtowel, and began drying. Bill didn't like dishes in the drainer overnight.

When did my husband turn into a tyrant? she wondered. She'd thought he was her soul mate when she met him in 1944. Unlike many soldiers, he was respectful and a little shy. They'd talked about everything, especially the war, and he'd listened—really listened.

She knew then that Bill was the man for her. They were discharged about the same time, and he'd proposed. They were married in December 1945. Betty wore a wedding dress made of parachute silk and her mother's veil. She carried gardenias. And Bill had looked so handsome. She got pregnant on their honeymoon. She was delighted to be a mother. Bill seemed happy when Pattie was born, but as their little girl started growing, he often mentioned how he wanted a boy—as if Pattie was nothing.

That night, Betty waited until Bill was asleep before she climbed into bed. The heat gave her a good excuse to hug her side. Only one more night of sharing a bed with him.

Thursday flew by. Bill let her serve Swanson TV dinners to him and Pattie on the Seven meeting nights. Betty baked two pineapple upside-down cakes, one for dinner and another for the Seven meeting. She made sure Bill and Pattie were eating at their TV trays in front of the Philco. Pattie had been bathed and dressed in her pjs, so Bill could put her in bed. Betty thanked her husband for babysitting, then carried her cake to Claire's house, two blocks away, where the Seven would deliver the inevitable verdict.

Claire's ranch house was tastefully furnished. Five of the Seven were chatting on the matching Danish modern living room suite, nibbling Trix Mix and garlic olives. The dining room table held a buffet: pineapple fingers wrapped in bacon, deviled eggs, pinwheel sandwiches, and cream puffs filled with hot chicken salad, served in a silver chafing dish. She saw a rainbow pudding made with Del Monte fruit cocktail. Betty's cake and a bouquet of red garden roses were the centerpiece. They drank Lipton Tea planter's punch, made with tea and frozen lemonade. Betty was glad the Seven did not drink at meetings. They had to make sober decisions. Besides, if she came home with alcohol on her breath, Bill would never let her go to another meeting.

"Help yourselves to the buffet, ladies," Claire said. "Then we'll start the meeting."

Betty put a cream puff stuffed with chicken salad and a pineapple finger on her plate to be polite, but she wasn't hungry. She already knew the verdict. She also knew what would happen if she lost her nerve. No one understood how Muriel Johnson had fallen in front of the Clayton-Skinker bus. No one except the Seven. Muriel had lost her nerve to kill Roger at the last minute, and lost her life.

Louise had been with Muriel that fatal afternoon. They'd gone to lunch and then shopping. Louise told the police that Muriel had had a manhattan at lunch and was a little unsteady. She must have tripped running for the bus. Muriel's untimely death opened up a spot for Betty as one of the Seven, and now it was her turn to prove herself.

Claire took a club chair. Once the rest of the Seven were seated, Claire called the meeting to order.

"Today we begin with a celebration. Edith is engaged! She's marrying Dr. Jack Gatesworth, a professor of mathematics. They're moving to San Francisco, where they both have professorships at local colleges."

"Ooh," said the other women, gathering to admire Edith's engagement ring. Betty praised the sparkling square-cut diamond, but she was too nervous to join in the excited chatter.

"Edith will be a member of the Seven in San Francisco," Claire said. "We're a nationwide organization, Betty dear, but we keep a low profile."

"Publicity would be unladylike," giggled Mitzi.

"Thanks to you, I can marry my dream man," Edith said, blushing prettily.

"You've caught a good one," Mitzi said.

"There are lots of good men," Edith said. "We're not man haters. We give even the most difficult men seven chances to see reason before we declare them incorrigible."

And put them down like dogs, Betty thought. *Like I'm going to do.*

"I have a new recruit," Claire said. "We'll meet her at our next meeting when we'll have an opening. Or maybe two."

Everyone applauded, except Betty. She'd just received her

death threat.

Betty was trembling when Claire said, "Betty, let's hear your report."

She told them about last night. Everything. They gasped at Bill's insults about WACs and looked sad when Betty said her husband had reprimanded Pattie for hugging him and nearly spilling his drink.

"I'm so sorry that he makes your little girl feel unwanted," Mitzi said.

"Children are resilient," Edith said, with professorial authority. "And you'll do your best to give her confidence once this is over."

"Is that all?" Claire asked. "Ladies, shall we put this to a vote?"

The verdict was swift and unanimous. While Bill was pronounced "incorrigible, without hope of redemption," Betty folded her hands in her lap to keep them from shaking.

"Before we proceed, let me ask a few questions," Claire said. "You and Bill haven't had a fight recently?"

"No, I've been very careful. We had that disagreement last night, that's all."

"But nothing the neighbors could hear?" Claire asked.

"No. I was careful to turn up the window fan to the highest speed beforehand, and my neighbor on the kitchen window side, Mrs. Raines, is seventy and deaf."

"Good," Claire said. "And Bill's life insurance is paid up?"

"Oh, yes," Betty said. "We also have mortgage insurance, so if anything happens to him, I'll own the house free and clear. We made our wills when I was carrying Pattie. Our affairs are in order."

"Good," Claire said. "Now, for the details of your mission. It's my turn to help you." She handed Betty a Welch's jelly jar filled with about thirty shiny light brown beans with dark brown spots. They were about the size of pinto beans, and Betty thought they were pretty.

"These are castor beans," Claire said. "From the ornamental plants in my backyard."

"The tall ones that grow along the edge of your patio?" Edith asked. "I've always admired those plants with their big purplish, red-veined leaves."

"They're a super privacy barrier," Claire said. "I can't see the neighbors on the other side."

"Who would guess such a cute plant is poisonous?" Ann said. She wore a cool yellow sundress. Ann was the best dressed of the Seven, since she got her clothes at a discount at the department store.

"Castor beans are one of the deadliest poisons on earth," Claire said.

Betty looked alarmed. "But I give my little girl castor oil," she said.

"Every mother does," Claire said. "Castor oil is perfectly safe. I think the heat during the treatment destroys the poison. I do know that castor beans are poison if the outer shell is broken or chewed. It's the pulp that's fatal. Three beans are enough to kill a grown man, but you should use all of them, just to be safe."

"How do you know this?" Betty asked, forcing her voice not to tremble.

"My husband was a chemist," she said.

"Late husband, thanks to me," Mitzi said. She giggled again and sipped her punch. Mitzi came straight from the office and still wore her summer-weight beige business suit. Her untidy blond hair was frizzy.

Claire said, "You will serve your husband castor beans tomorrow night with his dinner. Will your mother watch Pattie?"

"Of course."

"Tell her you want a second honeymoon with Bill. Pattie shouldn't be around when the police are at your house or when he's in the hospital. That's too difficult for a child. When you go home tonight, tell Bill we talked you into having that son, and you want to have the whole weekend with him. He'll spend Friday at work in a good mood. That will give you the perfect alibi."

"Bill is too much of a gentleman to mention our private life," Betty said.

"Maybe," Claire said. "But his co-workers will notice he's happy and whistling in this dreadful heat. He may even drop a few hints. What's Bill's favorite appetizer?"

"Sour cream-and-chive dip with lots of garlic. Real garlic, not garlic powder. I chop my own."

"Perfect," Claire said. "Add extra garlic this time, and chop up the castor beans with the garlic. The garlic and chives should mask any unusual taste, if there is one. Give Bill a double scotch tomorrow night and have him eat as much dip as possible. Does Bill like steak?"

"What man doesn't?" Betty said.

"Then broil him a big juicy T-bone."

"But it's fifty-nine cents a pound," Betty said. "That will blow my household budget for the month."

"He gave you that five dollars," Claire said. "You can afford it."

"And he told you to buy something you wanted," Louise said. The other women laughed.

"Exactly," Claire said. "Serve him baked potatoes heaped with butter and sour cream. I gather he likes chives in his sour cream?"

"Loves it," Betty said. "And garlic, too."

"A double dose," Claire said. "The more the better."

"I can put garlic in his mashed potatoes, too," Betty said.

"You can, but don't bother putting castor beans in the mashed potatoes. The heat may make the poison ineffective. Don't forget to bake his favorite cake for dessert. Do you wear rubber gloves when you clean?" Claire glanced at Betty's smooth, white hands and perfect manicure. Betty nodded.

"Wear them when you peel and mash the beans. Throw out anything you use to prepare the castor beans. Break the bowl and toss it in the trash, along with the cutting board. Hide the rubber gloves, paring knife, the seed peelings, this jelly jar and anything else you use to chop and prepare the castor beans, until you can safely dispose of them."

"Where will I hide them if the police search the house?" Betty's voice was shaking.

Claire lowered her voice. "In a Kotex box. You keep one in the bathroom, right?"

"Yes, in the linen closet, behind the hamper. Bill doesn't even like to see the box. He says it's disgusting."

"Most men feel that way," Claire said. "Including the police. Put a few pads on top and they'll never check. After the funeral, when the fuss has died down, you can throw that box away. But not in your trash can."

Claire patted Betty's hand. "Don't worry, darling. No one will ever suspect you. And the symptoms of castor bean poisoning are similar to so many other things. Depending on how many beans he eats, the symptoms will show up in about three or four hours."

The other women toasted Betty with their punch.

As she left, Claire told her, "Remember, Betty. You owe this to your daughter. To all our daughters."

"And our sons," said Alice, who had a six-year-old boy. "We can't have them growing up to be men who don't respect women."

The Seven wished her luck, and Betty left.

***

She was surprised how well the plan worked. Bill was ecstatic that she wanted to be alone with him for the weekend. It was a muggy eighty-seven degrees when he went to work Friday morning, but he was whistling cheerfully. Pattie was excited to spend the whole weekend with Grandma. And Betty spent the day slaving in the hot kitchen, baking a sensational banana chocolate layer cake, and chopping heaps of garlic and all thirty castor beans.

By the time Bill came home, the kitchen was cleaned, the potatoes were baked and the steaks were ready for broiling. Betty wore her slinky black dress. The table was set with flowers and candles. She greeted Bill with a double scotch and a kiss, and tonight, Bill's kiss lingered. After he showered, she brought his favorite dip into the den and sat on his lap, feeding him chunks of rye bread dunked in the dip. He never noticed that she didn't eat any. An hour later, only a few spoonfuls remained. "Why don't you finish the dip, honey, and I'll put the steaks on?"

"Can't wait," he said. "I'm still hungry as a bear."

Bill looked a little shamefaced when she called him into dinner. "I'm glad you weren't watching me," he said. "I used the rest of the rye bread to mop up the last of that dip."

He ate every bite of his T-bone and heaped all the sour cream on his baked potato. "None for me, thanks," Betty said. "I'll never fit into this dress again if I eat sour cream."

Betty cut him a thick slice of cake. Bill watched TV patiently while she did the dishes. Betty washed the dip bowl, the sour cream bowl, and the cutting board separately after the other dishes, and stacked them on the counter. She'd throw them out later.

"Oh, Betty," Bill called from the den. "Are you ready yet?"

"Almost," Betty said. She blew out the candles and hurried to him. Bill led her into the bedroom and unzipped her dress with trembling fingers, then doubled over in pain.

"Honey, what's wrong?" she asked.

"Some kind of flu bug," he said, running for the bathroom.

***

Bill's flu worsened. He was sweating and running a temperature, mumbling things that didn't make sense. His heart was racing and his skin was waxy-gray. Betty called an ambulance and went with Bill to the hospital. While she waited through the long night, she called her mother, who promised to take care of Pattie.

When the doctor asked what Bill had eaten, she told them about her special meal. "The sour cream must have gone off in the heat," the doctor said.

Bill died Saturday afternoon. Food poisoning was the most likely cause. An exhausted Betty accompanied the kindly police detective back to her home. He took the empty sour cream container and denuded T-bones in the trash under the sink, along with the rest of the cake. Bill's neighbors and co-workers all said he had a perfect marriage. The tests found nothing wrong with the food. The doctors concluded Bill died of a mysterious virus.

Bill's wake and funeral overflowed with friends and co-workers. Every one of the Seven sent flowers to the funeral home or to the house. The most dramatic arrangement was from clever Claire. It included gladioli and the huge, starfish-shaped leaves of the castor bean plant. *We will never forget*, the card read.

Betty got the message. She would be the next one to set another woman free.

She waited for a week after the funeral before she called Mike Roberts and said she'd take the job.

"No, next week's not too soon to go back to work, Mr. Roberts," Betty said. "It will take my mind off Bill."

THE LADY'S MAID VANISHES

by Susan Daly

Lady Byng is about to return to England after her husband's duty in Canada is done, but when her maid Vaughan vanishes at a rustic retreat, she's determined to find out what happened to the young woman. A bear attack? A fall in the woods? Or something much more sinister?

I returned from a late luncheon at the Lady Evelyn Hotel to our rustic lodge to be greeted by two of my three staff members, looking none too happy. As Mr. McKuen and I stepped out of the motor car, I could see my companion, Miss Tempest, was actually wringing her hands. The always imperturbable Mr. Adrian Charles, my invaluable secretary-cum-aide-de-camp, was clearly on the verge of severe agitation.

"What is it, Mr. Charles?"

"We can't find Miss Vaughan, my lady."

"Can't find her?" I admit to being a trifle impatient, since I wanted to change into clothes more suitable for walking by the shore. "Has she been carried off by a bear? Gone fishing and fallen into the lake?"

Likely my maid had gone off into the woods to use the admittedly primitive facilities and was taking her time getting back.

I knew better than to despair immediately. In my recent career as the viceregal consort in Canada, I'd served my role without turning a hair at any number of challenges. Such as when the second course of a state dinner was declared unsafe for human consumption twenty minutes before the arrival of the American president. Or when faced with the news that the King's cousin, on a goodwill tour across Canada, had suffered a fatal heart attack in his bedroom at Rideau Hall. Not alone. Not with a woman.

So until I had definite cause to worry, I could cope with a missing maid.

"How long has she been gone?" Mr. McKuen asked.

"Two hours!" Miss Tempest wailed. Yes, wailed. Most unlike her.

Well, that put a different complexion on the matter.

"She went for a walk along the trail by the lake," Mr. Charles said. "It seemed safe enough."

"Mr. Thomson didn't go with her?" I asked.

Mr. Thomson was the excellent local guide hired to handle all the details of our Rocky Mountain adventure: equipment, provisions, canoes, fires, and cooking. Nature treks to beaver dams and waterfalls.

And to keep us safe in the woods.

"She didn't want him." Miss Tempest sounded hurt. "She didn't want any of us."

"She was adamant she could look after herself," Mr. Charles added. "Even Mr. Thomson didn't think she could get lost."

"Where's Thomson now?" Mr. McKuen asked. He'd arranged our stay at the lodge and hired the guide, so I could see how he might feel responsible.

Mr. Charles told us Mr. Thomson had gone out looking for her an hour ago, and hadn't yet returned.

I knew from experience how easy it was to get turned around in the woods, so I suggested we leave it in Mr. Thomson's hands for the moment.

But a few minutes later, Mr. Thomson was back. He didn't look happy.

"No sign of her, ma'am."

Mr. McKuen's look grew dark. He got back into his automobile. "Keep searching. I'm going for the police."

***

We weren't exactly isolated in the wilderness. The Lady Evelyn Hotel was one of the grand hotels built amidst the spectacular scenery of the Rockies. The two main railway companies, Canadian National and Canadian Pacific, had been outdoing each other since the 1880s, building competing hotels across Canada in stunning beauty spots. Now, in 1931, the Lady Evelyn was the jewel in the crown of its owners.

Marie Lake Lodge had been designed for guests who wanted to rough it without dealing with the rough. It was a twenty-minute drive from the hotel over a bumpy, winding road through the forest. The idea was to give an illusion of wilderness seclusion rather than the actuality.

Unfortunately, it was sufficiently remote that Vaughan had managed to thoroughly lose herself in the woods.

The capable Mr. McKuen was western hospitality manager for the railway. I'd met him a few times in our respective travels, since his position included arranging all VIP rail travel and accommodation in meticulous detail. As wife of the former

Governor General, the King's representative in Canada, I still qualify as a VVIP.

It had been at Mr. McKuen's invitation I'd enjoyed luncheon with his fiancée, Miss Agnes Lacey, and her father. Sir William Lacey was the managing director of the railway's entire hotel chain. Miss Lacey had summoned her fiancé to join us for dessert, and then to drive me back to the lodge. This turned out to be fortuitous, since he was now on hand to assist us.

***

I was resting in a canvas deck chair, dispirited and hoarse from having called Vaughan's name for an hour, when Mr. McKuen returned with Captain Northam of the RCMP and two constables. The constables were immediately dispatched to assist Mr. Thomson, who had organized the local guides into a wide-ranging search party.

I greeted Captain Northam and bade them sit, along with Mr. Charles and Miss Tempest.

"Captain Northam, thank you for coming so quickly. Although I hope your visit will prove unnecessary." It seemed curiously surreal, surrounded as we were by imposing mountains and lofty pines, yet the scenario was pure English country house mystery. (I am an aficionado of detective tales and whodunnits, though my husband Julian has never approved.)

"So do I, Your Excellency."

"Just 'Lady Byng' please, Captain." My days of being addressed in the viceregal style were past.

He nodded. "If you could start by telling me about your visit here? I understand you arrived only yesterday afternoon and came straight to Marie Lake Lodge?"

"Yes. I wanted a few days in the woods, hiking and canoeing and fishing. The sort of adventure frowned on when I held an official role." I explained that at the end of his five-year term as Governor General, Lord Byng had been posted to Hong Kong for six months. I'd taken the opportunity to enjoy one last trip across Canada before returning to our home in East Anglia.

"And Miss Vaughan? She was happy to join the expedition?"

"Poor Vaughan. I was surprised she seemed so keen to come with me, since she's a city girl at heart. I doubt she'd know a loon's cry from the call of a moose. But she's a game girl, Captain, and was eager to try it."

I added that she was a parlor maid who had stepped into the breach when Ellis, my personal maid, had suddenly taken ill just before our departure from Ottawa.

"And she's coping with these rustic conditions?"

"She seems to be. I wouldn't say we have all the comforts of home, but certainly all the comforts of camp."

In the early days of my marriage, I had often accompanied my husband, then a lieutenant-colonel, when his regiment was sent to South Africa and the Near East, so I was no stranger to field conditions. Compared with those long-ago nights spent among potentially hostile neighbors on the brink of war, staying in a well-catered lodge in one of the more civilized countries of the Empire was scarcely more adventurous than a stroll in a city park.

But not, perhaps, to Vaughan.

Captain Northam reviewed the afternoon's events with Mr. Charles, who repeated the details I'd heard earlier. Miss Tempest added, "And she was wearing those frivolous shoes!"

I hadn't realized that. "If you mean those flimsy pumps instead of the sturdy walking shoes I bought her, she may have turned an ankle."

Captain Northam shut his notebook. "I'll speak to Mr. Thomson when he returns."

Mr. Charles nodded. "He suggested we light a fire at the shore when it gets dark, so she might see it from some other part of the lake."

"Dark!" Miss Tempest looked appalled. "Oh dear. And her wearing just that light pink frock. Surely she'll be back before then."

I glanced at the western sky, where the sun had already dipped behind the glacier-capped peaks. It could get cold after sundown, even in late August.

"We can only hope," I said.

But all hopes were dashed an hour later when Mr. Thomson returned, his face carved in stone. They'd found Rose Vaughan's lifeless body in the lake, lying face down near the shore, about a mile from the lodge.

She must have fallen from the rocky ledge about ten yards above, striking her head on one of the boulders in the water below. And drowned.

***

Nothing would persuade Miss Tempest to spend another night at the lodge, and I admit I hadn't the heart for our continued wilderness experience, so we all decamped to the safety and luxury of the Lady Evelyn Hotel.

There would be an autopsy and an inquest as soon as the coroner and the pathologist arrived from Calgary, some hundred miles to the east. Mr. Charles sent a telegram back to Ottawa to advise my staff about what happened before they could read it in the papers.

He also wired my maid Ellis directly, saying that if she'd sufficiently recovered from her attack of flu, would she please pack her bag and catch the next train west. The rail journey across Canada from the nation's capital to the Rockies would take her three days.

***

The next afternoon, Miss Tempest and I sat at one end of the spacious hotel verandah, I ostensibly writing picture postcards to friends in Ottawa and relatives in England, while my companion flipped idly through an illustrated magazine. I compared the tinted view on the card with the reality laid out before me. The stunning panorama of Lady Evelyn Lake and the mountain peaks beyond were identical.

But I could take no joy in my surroundings or the comfort of the hotel, my heart and mind overwhelmed by Vaughan's tragic death. All I wanted was to cancel the rest of the trip and return to Ottawa. We'd have to take Vaughan's body back with us in a box in the baggage car.

Mr. McKuen would see to it all, of course, as soon as the Mounties released her to us.

I made another feeble attempt at writing, but what could I say? *Enjoying the trip. Magnificent views. Wish you were here.* Of course I didn't. I wished I were there.

"May I join you, Lady Byng?"

I looked up and nodded. Before Captain Northam sat down, I could see there was more bad news.

"We have the initial medical report," he said. "I'm afraid Miss Vaughan didn't simply fall and hit her head. The examining doctor found marks on both her wrists, recent marks, consistent with, well, some kind of restraint."

As Miss Tempest gasped, a series of horrors ran through my mind.

"Do you mean . . .? Was she bound?"

"It looks like someone grasped her wrists to overpower her before sending her over the edge of the rocks."

I was choking with anger, unable to speak. Poor, faithful Vaughan. She'd come out west as a favor to me, filled with a spirit of anticipation, as if embarking on a new adventure.

Some evil, vile person had put an end to her adventure. Her life.

"Captain Northam, I must ask . . ." I hesitated, hating the question. "Was Miss Vaughan . . . sexually violated?"

A whimper came from Miss Tempest's direction, but Captain Northam looked at me steadily.

"She was not, I'm relieved to say. Her clothing showed no disarray of that sort. There were only some tears where they caught on a branch. Although—" He cut himself off and I had the impression there was something he preferred to keep to himself. I didn't push him.

"Who could have done this?" My question sounded foolishly rhetorical, but I meant it literally. Was there someone in the vicinity capable of such a despicable crime?

Before I could reword it more diplomatically, Miss Tempest took up the idea.

"A passing tramp!" she cried. "A primitive backwoodsman. A Red Indian savage. These woods must be full of wild and disreputable men who would think nothing of attacking a defenseless woman."

I levelled a quelling look at her.

"I can assure you, Miss Tempest," the captain said in a dry but courteous tone, "we have all the passing tramps and wild backwoodsmen in this area under control. And as for Red Indian savages—" He paused.

"I think perhaps Miss Tempest is overly fond of American movies," I suggested, to relieve him of having to be polite. "But still, Captain, someone did this. What are your men doing?"

He told us a contingent of constables was searching the woods, looking for evidence of who else might have been there. He himself was poring over records looking for potential assailants in the area.

Well, it was a start.

***

That evening, Mr. McKuen invited me to join him and Miss Lacey for dinner in the dining room. His idea was to take my mind off the tragedy, but of course, we couldn't ignore it.

"You've heard what Captain Northam learned about Miss Vaughan's being attacked?" Agnes Lacey might look like a delicately nurtured girl, but she was quite human when it came to discussing morbid details. Her fiancé cast her a mildly reproving glance.

"Yes, I'm afraid so," I said. "It puts the matter in a seriously different light."

"And they have no idea who could have done it?"

Mr. McKuen patted his lips with his linen napkin. "Some transient ruffian—" He cut himself off, possibly realizing the effect this suggestion might have on his intended. "Long gone, of course. No doubt halfway to Moosejaw by now."

"Really, you sound like Miss Tempest," I said. "I have never believed in the theory of a passing tramp. They are often fingered as the convenient culprit in detective stories, but in the end it's always disproved."

"In fiction perhaps—"

Agnes cut him off, sounding equal parts aghast and thrilled. "Are you suggesting she was killed by someone she knew?"

"Well, she seemed adamant she wanted to take this walk alone. Rather unlike her. In fact, even coming out west on this trip was unlike her."

"But she didn't know anyone." Mr. McKuen looked displeased that I was encouraging Miss Lacey's blood lust. "And didn't you tell us yesterday that until just before you left Ottawa, it was your other maid who was to come with you?"

"Ellis." That had been bothering me a lot. "Yes. Vaughan should have been safely at home in Ottawa."

"You mean," Miss Lacey said, wide-eyed, "if Ellis had come as planned, she might have met with this fate?"

"No, of course not. For one thing—" But I didn't like to say it. Ellis, being a more practical girl, wouldn't have wandered off in the woods alone. Or if she had, she'd have kept an eye out for landmarks to guide her home again. But saying that, or even thinking it, implied Vaughan had somehow contributed to her own doom.

"Oh, and her shoes," Miss Lacey said. "Miss Tempest was telling me about the flimsy shoes Miss Vaughan was wearing."

"Agnes, my dear, I don't think gossip is quite—"

"Oh, Ian, don't be so prim. It's all anyone is talking about, all over the hotel." She went on, undeterred, "I understand they were thin-soled kid leather, rather attractive. Useless in the woods, but just the sort of shoes she might wear if she were going to meet someone."

"Yes, exactly." I also recalled she'd been wearing her favorite pink dress. "Between her apparent eagerness to come on the trip, and then to walk alone in the woods and dress up for it . . . Well, it all seems to come together, in a way."

Mr. McKuen cleared his throat slightly. "Ladies, it can't be good for you to dwell on these events. I understand, my lady, how this tragedy is affecting you, but I suggest you leave it in the hands of the police, and focus on continuing your journey."

"You may suggest it, but my heart isn't in it." I took a sip of my wine. "As soon as expedient, I and my entourage will be heading back to Ottawa."

"Good idea. I'll make the arrangements. What day would suit you?"

"Oh, not yet. I'm not leaving until Captain Northam has found out who did this terrible thing."

He opened his mouth to comment, but I went on, no longer able to hold back my anger, "When I think of that poor girl alone with her killer in the woods, horribly aware that no one could come to her aid. I just hope it was swift."

Miss Lacey nodded, her eyes filling with tears.

I found myself hoping equally that her killer would suffer long and miserably before he died at the end of the hangman's rope.

***

By the time Ellis arrived from Ottawa, the police still had nothing definitive. They'd found unmistakable signs of a struggle—crushed plants and broken stems and branches—near the top of the rocky outcrop, and even a scrap of the pink dress caught on a thorn.

But nothing to identify the man who'd attacked and killed Rose Vaughan. No other bits of fabric, nor those useful finds in detective stories, the monogrammed handkerchief or the unique cigarette end.

The moment Ellis arrived in my suite, looking more than a little travel weary, she dropped her bag and burst into tears.

"Oh, my lady! Poor Rose! I haven't stopped thinking about her the whole trip."

I made her sit down and phoned down for tea and a plate of sandwiches. I'm not wholly dependent on having a personal maid all the time, but this was the first time the tables had been turned. I put a comforting hand on her shoulder and when the food arrived, encouraged her to calm down and eat something.

Eventually Ellis did so. It turned out the foolish girl had purchased a coach ticket, not a berth, and had spent the last three nights trying to sleep sitting up through four provinces and three time zones.

My suite contained a small dressing room with a cot, suitable for a maid's room, and I packed her off for a bath and a nap.

***

After tea, I returned to my room to find Ellis on duty, examining my wardrobe for possible attention.

"You know, Ellis, I appreciate your coming so quickly, especially after that sudden bout of influenza. You're quite recovered, I hope?" I looked closely at her, concerned she might have made the trip before she should have, out of her sense of duty.

"Yes—" Ellis turned her attention to my travel suit.

"Are you still unwell?"

"Oh, no, my lady."

Such a vehement denial aroused my suspicions. But why sound evasive? She seemed well enough. In fact, she'd seemed perfectly well right up to the day before our departure. Some inkling nudged at me.

"Was it Rose's idea?"

She looked like she'd rather be back in Ottawa. "Oh, my lady, she made me promise never to tell! And now she's dead."

Fingers of fear and dismay crept into my brain. "Yes, now she's dead. And if there's anything you know that might help us catch her killer—?"

"Her killer!" Her face turned a startling shade of gray and she dropped into the nearest chair. "No one said . . ."

I now recalled Mr. Charles had sent his wire to Ottawa before we knew the extent of the tragedy. Ellis had already been on her way across country when he'd notified my staff of the new information.

Once again, I comforted my maid, who appeared wrapped in horror. Now the secret was coming out, a few words at a time.

"But she was so happy. This trip was perfect timing, she said . . . she was looking forward to seeing him again."

Oh my dear Lord. I forced myself to remain calm.

"Now then, Ellis, think carefully. Who was she meeting?"

"The man she'd been writing to. They were in love. They were going to get m-m-married." She burst into a fresh flood of tears.

"Listen, Ellis." I put on a stern tone. "You have to bear up and tell me straight if the police are to find out who did this terrible thing to Rose "

"The police?"

"Tell me, when and where did she meet this man?"

"She didn't say. I asked her, but . . ." Ellis bit her lip. "I got an idea he was, well, a travelling man. Perhaps a salesman, working mostly in the west."

"I see." But I didn't see enough. "And how long had she known him?"

"I think . . . since Christmas? That's when she started being really, well, excited. Giggling a lot. And then," Ellis paused, as though assembling her thoughts. "Around St. Valentine's Day, she became miserable. Terrible upset at times. Moody, you know?"

I nodded. "And by the time I started planning this trip out west, did things change?"

"Yes. When she heard about it, she asked if you'd need two maids. I said not likely, and then she asked if I'd be willing to let her go in my place. Well, it's not for me to decide, is it? And anyway, I really wanted to come. That's when she told me about this man she'd met, and how they were in love, and how they were separated by his job when he went out west, and how, if she could just get out here and see him again, then they could be married."

"She actually said that? Married?"

"Yes, my lady. She told me they were engaged, though . . . well, you know. Men will say anything to get what they want. Especially if they're leaving."

"Indeed they will." It sounded as though Vaughan had fallen for a man who'd had a passing fancy for her, talked of love and the future, and then had gone away. As men have always done. And always will do.

"The day before you left, I finally agreed to pretend to be sick. Because she'd told me she'd already written to him, telling him she was coming, and, well, especially since . . ."

Her hesitation reminded me of a similar pause I'd heard recently. Captain Northam, reporting the medical findings. Had the examining doctor told him Vaughan was not a virgin?

"Especially since you suspected Vaughan might have . . . given herself to him?"

Ellis hesitated, then nodded.

I didn't speak for a minute as I envisaged the whole picture, growing ever more furious with such men who play on a girl's innocence. Even if they don't then murder them.

"My lady. . . I know it was wrong of her, and it was wrong of me to deceive you. But I really, really hoped I could help Rose get what she wanted so badly."

"It's all right, Ellis. I'm not angry with you. Nor with Vaughan. You've been a good and faithful friend to her. I'm angry with the fiend who perpetrated this horrible plot."

I gave it some more thought, then said, "When she told him she was coming out west, he must have been shocked. I suppose he wrote that he would meet her here at Marie Lake. It would be a perfect chance to draw her away. 'Tell no one,' he probably said. A secret meeting in the woods, near the lake. They embrace, he grabs her—"

"Oh don't! I can't bear to think of it, my lady."

"Of course not, Ellis. That was thoughtless of me." I needed to turn her thoughts elsewhere. "There was no letter like that among her things." The police had looked. "Might she have destroyed it?"

Ellis shook her head. "No, she'd never. Although…if he wrote directions in the letter about where to meet, and made them complicated, then she'd have to bring it with her, wouldn't she? And then he'd take it from her."

"Excellent, Ellis! Well thought out."

She blushed at these words, then gasped. "Ian! That's what she called him. Just the once, that morning before she left for the train."

"Ian!"

"Oh my lady, how could anyone be so wicked, when she loved him and just wanted to be with him. Do you think he was already married?"

"Yes." My brain went into a vortex of shock. "Or engaged."

***

"Am I disturbing you?" I said to Mr. McKuen. I had tracked him down in his well-appointed office in the managerial wing.

"Lady Byng!" He stood up behind his massive oak desk. "No, of course not. Won't you be seated?"

"I prefer to stand, thank you." I stayed near the door, which was nearly shut to give the illusion of privacy. But not quite shut.

Protocol demanded he remain standing as well.

"I have a question. When did you meet Miss Vaughan?"

He gave an admirable impression of a man with no idea what I was getting at. "I never met her. I wasn't at the hotel to greet your party the day you arrived, remember?"

"Yes, even though that was part of your job, being in charge of all VIP guests. Convenient for you, of course, since she'd have seen you then."

He stared at me, still doing a good 'why are you saying these things?' act.

"You'd already met her, hadn't you? Just before Christmas, when Lord Byng and I were celebrating our final official occasion at Rideau Hall. You were travelling, representing the railway on a cross-country trip lasting several months. You stayed with us one night."

"I remember that occasion, certainly. You and your husband were most gracious hosts. But I was hardly in a position to have met your personal maid."

"Vaughan was my parlor maid. Quite a pretty girl. Noticeable. She was serving at table that night." Ellis, prompted by my questions, had gradually remembered more details about that evening.

I could see the hint of nervousness in his eyes, but he held his ground.

"Even if I'd noticed one of the servants, why would I remember her?"

"Why indeed? Even though you persuaded her to slip up to your room for a few hours. Why should you remember just another girl you'd seduced, however sweet and pretty she was?"

"My lady—"

"But she certainly remembered you. She wrote to you at the hotel after you'd disappeared from her life."

He stood straighter, now openly angry. And who could blame him?

"Lady Byng, you have no business making these absurd allegations."

"Oh goodness, how clichéd your words sound. Tell me, were you already engaged to Miss Lacey when you seduced my maid? Or was it only afterwards that you proposed to her, and then heard from Miss Vaughan, and realized she could do serious damage to your plan to marry the daughter of the managing director of the railway's hotel chain?"

"Are you seriously suggesting that I killed her?"

"You met Miss Vaughan in the woods near Marie Lake Lodge, exactly as arranged in the letter you'd sent her. After all, who else knew our travel itinerary in such detail?"

"Fanciful, my lady, but you no doubt remember that at the time you claim I was murdering your maid in the woods, I was, in fact, having lunch with you, Miss Lacey, and Sir William."

"Not quite. You joined us for dessert, and Miss Lacey asked you to drive me back to the lodge. Of course, it worked well for you, since it put you on the scene when Miss Vaughan was discovered missing, and you could run for the police."

He stood his ground. "Lady Byng, you may be one of the highest ranking women in Canada—"

"The highest ranking," I couldn't resist pointing out, "since Queen Mary is not here in the country and the new Governor General is a bachelor."

"—But I must ask you to leave my office. I will not listen to your scurrilous suggestions."

I raised a single eyebrow (one of my many accomplishments). "Did she tell you she was with child?"

"She wasn't!" he snapped.

A mistake. Until now he'd reacted exactly as an outraged innocent man would to my scurrilous suggestions.

"And why would you think that?" I asked.

He went deathly pale and couldn't find a response.

"Because you took precautions?" I continued. "You, a well-travelled man of the world, must know ways to avoid impregnating trusting young women. A French letter, perhaps? Or maybe you just don't want to believe that by killing that sweet girl who adored you, you also killed your own child?"

"She was not with child. She told me—"

He stopped and inhaled sharply, as though trying to pull those last words back into his treacherous mouth.

"You know, Mr. McKuen, you could have said that the examining doctor had not reported her pregnant."

In fact, she was not. Ellis had told me her friend was having her monthlies regularly. There had been that, at least, to be thankful for.

Mr. McKuen visibly recomposed himself, and turned a more natural shade of pink. "I am glad to hear it. That unfortunate girl, misguided as she was, suffered enough without the added stigma of—"

"Oh, give it up! You've already let slip too much."

"Since only you heard me, I will deny anything I may have said that led you to erroneously believe I knew Miss Vaughan."

"Oh, I wasn't the only one who heard you. Gentlemen?"

The door opened to reveal Captain Northam and Mr. Charles, who had taken in every word.

Mr. McKuen's demeanor collapsed. He dropped to his chair and groaned.

"Yes, Mr. McKuen, perhaps the ruse of hidden witnesses is a standard of detective stories. But then, I'm such a fan, despite Julian's disdain."

YOU ALWAYS HURT THE ONE YOU LOVE

by Shawn Reilly Simmons

This very short story packs a big, big punch. Two thugs transporting a man in their car trunk, taking him to his death, both give—and receive—big surprises.

"You have to learn to let things go."

Sanders shot an irritated glance at his bulky partner in the passenger seat, then pulled his eyes back to the road. The headlight beams poked weakly through the mist, reflecting silver particles in the air.

"You're too young to be wound as tight as you are. Keep it up you'll give yourself an ulcer." Johnson bit into his corned beef sandwich and orange sauce oozed through his fingers.

Sanders cut his eyes to the beefy hand. "Keep that mess off the leather or I'll shoot you where you sit."

Johnson snorted laughter, opening his mouth to reveal pink wads of partially chewed meat. "You wouldn't shoot me in here, your precious Roadmaster," Johnson said, taking another hearty bite. "Sometimes I think you like this car more than your girl."

"Leave Martha out of it." Sanders glared out the windshield, tapping the brakes as he came to the turnoff. He eased the shiny black Buick onto the sand-covered asphalt leading to the shore.

"How much farther is it?" Sanders asked, irritation clipping through his words.

Johnson motioned with his sandwich at the windshield. "Two miles to the water." A piece of sauce-covered lettuce fell onto his lap and he brushed it onto the floor mat.

"Hey!" Sanders shouted. He stomped on the brakes and the car lurched forward. Johnson slapped the dashboard heavily with his free hand before he was jerked back against the seat.

"Pick that up."

"What?" Johnson said, a warning edge coming into his voice.

"You know what. The piece of your disgusting sandwich that just landed on my floorboard. It's probably leaving a grease stain as we speak."

"Like I said, you need to relax, kid," Johnson said with a smile that didn't reach his eyes.

A rapid succession of loud bangs broke the tension.

"Dammit!" Sanders shouted. He threw the car into park and stalked to the trunk, lifting the lid and pointing his gun at the man's nose. "Kick the car again and see what happens."

The man's cheeks puffed around the necktie that gagged his mouth. His hands and feet were tied behind him with rope, and his gray hair was matted to his sweaty forehead.

Johnson lumbered over to the trunk from his side of the car. "Nice going, kid. Now he's seen your face."

"Like I care. He's a dead man anyway," Sanders said, staring at his captive's wing-tipped shoes. "Especially if he puts a dent in Betty."

The man grunted frantically from behind the necktie.

"Yeah, yeah, we know. We've got the wrong guy. It's all a big mistake, right?" Johnson taunted him.

The man nodded frantically as Sanders slammed the trunk lid down.

***

"What's the deal with this guy anyway?" Sanders asked as they bounced along the road a few minutes later. They would have reached the shore already except Sanders kept coming to nearly a complete stop whenever there was a rut in the pavement.

"What guy?" Johnson asked, picking his teeth with his thick fingernail.

"The guy in the trunk," Sanders said impatiently. "Obviously."

Johnson snorted another laugh and dug deeper into his gum, dislodging something and wiping it onto his tongue. "Got caught ripping off the casino. Boss wants us to teach him a lesson, get the money back. He works in the office, a little too free with his hands, if you know what I mean."

"I've never seen him before. What office?" Sanders asked.

"Out on the Island. Near where we grabbed him up."

Sanders nodded. "I've only been out there once before, making a delivery."

"You'll go out more soon. You're still green, kid. Once they get to know you, you'll get sent more places."

Sanders smiled and tapped the brakes.

"So how's Martha doing anyway?" Johnson asked. "Haven't seen her since that time we gave her a ride. You two are serous, huh?"

"Yep, so she says," Sanders said. "You checking up on me?"

"Nah. I see her downtown sometimes outside the insurance office where she works. Cute girl," Johnson said, shrugging.

"Martha's nice, and young enough to be your granddaughter, old man. She thinks I'm in insurance, too," Sanders said.

"Guess you are, in a way," Johnson said. "You make sure people pay up. Anyway, what's a nice-looking girl like that see in a stiff like you?"

"I guess you'd have to ask her," Sanders said, giving him a sly smile.

"Didn't stop you from slipping your number to the girl at the sandwich shop back there," Johnson said, giving Sanders a light punch on the upper arm.

Sanders brushed at the spot on his jacket with his hand. "So what? I'm not married. Anyway, sandwich girl is probably too far from the city to be worth it. Then again, not having my girls running into each other on the street is a bonus."

Johnson nodded. "True. This is it, pull up onto the dock."

"What is this place anyway?" Sanders asked, easing the car across the wooden planks.

"Again with the questions," Johnson said. "This is the spot we were told. The Boss said a hundred each to take care of this, so let's get on with it."

Sanders's jaw tightened as he pulled to a stop near the end of the dock. He switched off the ignition, then went around to the trunk, yanking the man to his feet by his collar. He shuffled him across the boards, Johnson thudding along behind them. Sanders forced the man to his knees when they reached the end of the dock, facing him away from the water.

Johnson sighed and pulled his gun from his shoulder holster, holding it lazily up, level with the man's head. Sanders pulled the necktie, damp from spit, from the man's mouth.

"Now he's quiet," Sanders said, shrugging. "First he wouldn't shut up and now look at him."

"That's how they always are. Start off begging and then dead quiet at the end," Johnson said. "Okay, guy, tell us where you hid the money."

"I swear, it wasn't me," the man stammered. His eyes flashed with fear, bouncing between their faces.

"The problem is, we don't believe you," Sanders said, raising his gun higher.

"Okay, okay," the man said, his voice breaking. "I'll pay it back. It wasn't that much . . . My mom, she needs an operation."

"Yeah, we all got a story. So where's the cash?" Sanders asked.

"At my apartment. I'll take you there," the man pleaded.

Johnson shook his head. "Too late for that, my friend. We'll find it without you."

"No, you won't! It's not in my apartment, it's in the building. You need me to show you where," he said, shifting his weight from knee to knee.

Johnson sighed with irritation. "What, it's in the laundry room? Your storage space, where?"

The man's face became still and he locked eyes with Sanders. "It's in Martha's room, in her underwear drawer."

Sanders squinted at him in the dark, searching his face. A gunshot cracked open the night and everything before him turned bright white, and then was gone.

Sanders's body toppled sideways, his calves catching on the edge of the dock as he fell into the water. Blood poured from the side of his head, turning the black water shiny for a moment before he began to sink.

Johnson lumbered over to the kneeling man, helped him to his feet, and sliced the rope from his wrists with his pocketknife. "You okay, Boss?"

The Boss rubbed the rope burns on his wrists and nodded. He walked to the edge of the dock and spit into the water where Sanders's body bobbed beneath the surface.

"Stupid kid. Bad luck to be the one to mess around on my daughter like that. Broke her heart, all those other girls."

Johnson nodded sympathetically and studied his shoes. "Kid didn't know who you were, and definitely didn't know Martha was connected to the family."

"Makes no difference to me," the Boss said, wiping his lips. "It's done. Let's get out of here."

Johnson got behind the wheel and the Boss slipped into the passenger seat.

"Nice car," the Boss said as they reversed back up the dock.

THE HAND OF AN ANGRY GOD

by K.B. Inglee

Faith Ivey must solve a locked-room mystery in the early days of Massachusetts. Everyone in the small settlement had reason to want Elder Hicks dead. But how was he killed, and by whose hand?

"Come at once, Mistress Ivey." Hosea Beeson pounded on her door. "Elder Hicks . . ."

The urgency in his voice drove Faith from her bed. She slipped her bare feet into her shoes, threw on her daytime clothes over her shift, and wrapped herself in her blue wool cloak. She wished her husband were here. He was due back from Boston later that day or early the next.

She went to open the door and found the latch bar was stuck in the keeper. With a flare of frustration, she gave a great tug on the string. Thomas would have to fix that when he returned. Before she closed the door behind her, she slipped the latch string through the small hole so that the door could be opened from the outside.

The wooden knob at the end of the latch string beat rhythmically against the door as she ran to catch up with Hosea. The partially risen sun had melted the snow on the rutted track that served as a road between the meeting house and the harbor. The rocks were wet and slippery with mud between, and the snow lay undisturbed on either side. Smoke rose from chimneys as hearth fires were raked into life. The households were beginning to stir.

Beneath Hosea's urgency Faith could sense a lingering sadness. His mother had died in a tragic accident barely a week earlier. Everyone in the settlement lived constantly on the margin between life and death. The hard work of daily existence left little time for grieving.

Elder Hicks had the grandest house in the village, two rooms and a buttery, and no one to share it with. The snow lay undisturbed around it except where Hosea had trod, first to the door and then to the tiny window beside it.

"Here, Mistress." Hosea pushed on the glass panes to show that the window was secured from the inside. "The door is barred as well, but you can see inside through the glass." A shaft of early morning sunshine left diamond patterns across the body of Elder Hicks as he lay sprawled, fully clothed and face down, on the floor. At the door she discovered that the latch string had been withdrawn, in effect, locking the door from the inside.

"Can you lift the latch with your knife?" Faith asked.

"No, Mistress. Remember, in the spring the Elder fitted an iron plate on the inside to cover the space between the door and the jamb? No one can open this door from the outside if the latch string is pulled in."

Faith ran her fingers over the freezing cold iron nail heads on the door, then over the leading in the window.

"Fetch your father while I try to find another way in."

Hosea turned and ran down the hill toward the blacksmith shop. His father had been teaching him the trade since he was old enough to lift a heavy hammer. While the young man's mind might not be sharp, his hands had learned the trade quickly. With a bit more experience he would be as fine a smith as his father.

Faith made her way around the house, leaving tracks in the pristine snow. The west-facing window was secured and she found no way in there, either. Her shoes were wet through and she wished she had tarried to put on her stockings.

No one in the village secured their dwelling so firmly for the night. Was Bradford Hicks afraid of something? Faith remembered the rage he had flown into accusing everyone of entering his house while he was away overnight. It was then that he had made the improvements to his lock system that now kept them from coming to his aid.

Faith returned to the front to find a host of villagers jostling each other to peer in through the windows.

"Is he dead?" asked Mother Vickery. "I would not be displeased," she muttered under her breath.

Bradford Hicks had always looked askance at Mother Vickery's use of herbs to heal and cure. She had spent time with the natives learning the uses of local plants. Everyone knew he thought her part witch and part Indian. He had not made life easy for her.

Faith realized that few of the people who were now gathered at the door would be upset by the loss of Elder Hicks.

Hosea had been berated time and again by the Elder for his inability to remember Bible passages for more than a few minutes. Elder Hicks had been trying to replace Hosea's father with a more docile blacksmith for some time. Only the fact that he was the best, yea, the only smith around, kept him at the forge.

Benjamin Kydd had been fined for missing a Sabbath service

when, in fact, his boat had been blown off course in a storm and he was far from the village on Sunday morning.

Goodwife Kydd had been found guilty of gossip.

Nicholas Corley had been publicly shamed the length of the street for firing his gun during a day of atonement. He had been trying to frighten wolves away from the carcass of a deer that was hanging from a tree just outside the stockade gates.

Faith herself had spent an afternoon in the stocks for uttering, in public, that which most took to be a prayer, but which Elder Hicks took to be an oath. Each time she thought of it she could feel the pain through her whole body as though it had just happened.

"There is no way in," Faith reported to them. "The windows are too small for any of us to fit through. The door is barred."

"Let us put Absalom Kydd down the chimney," said Smith Beeson, the only man in the village bedsides Thomas Ivey to stand up to the Elder.

The chimney was the biggest entry into the house after the door, and it would be easy to lower someone as small as the Kydd boy. He was instructed to come straight to the door and open it without touching anything else or stopping to see if the Elder were dead.

Once again Faith wished Thomas had returned. He carried authority in the village second only to that of Elder Hicks. He would know what to do and the people would listen to him. She was not sure she would be offered that courtesy in his absence.

Faith and Hosea, with the others pressed close behind them, watched as the boy came down onto the wide hearth. The fire had gone out long ago, but the ashes were scattered. Absalom walked directly to the door, leaving clumps of ash in his wake.

Once they had gained access, Mother Vickery knelt beside the Elder. She ran her hands over his face and neck, looked at Faith, and shook her head. Muttering to herself as she worked, she began an examination of his clothing. Faith saw that the man's limbs were not yet stiff as they would have been had he died before bed. So he had met his end sometime early this morning.

At Mother Vickery's request, Captain Richard Watkins, the peace keeper, turned the body so that the Elder's open eyes stared up at the rafters. There were no signs of violence on the body or in the room, no clothing askew, no chairs overturned.

"Seems to be a natural death," said Mother Vickery. "We need to prepare the body. Faith, stay and help. Everyone else out."

Faith heard a few rumblings about 'God's will' as Watkins herded the others out onto the street. Once the room was empty save the two of them, Mother Vickery asked Faith to bar the door.

Faith pushed the door shut and set the latch bar in place. It was like no other in the village. The workings were the same, but the bar was twice the width of that in the other homes. The latch string was a strong jute twine. The keeper that the bar fell into was deeper than the others. The iron plate fitted perfectly behind the bar and covered the opening to keep anyone from lifting the latch from the outside. The house was a fortress.

Without thinking, she lifted the latch string but did not feed it through the door. Something was beginning to bother her, but she was not sure what. It was clear enough that the Elder had risen early, dressed, and started to stir the fire back to life. He had then been struck down by some sudden affliction.

"The latch string is wet. No one but the Kydd boy touched it. Why would it be wet if it had not been outside the door during the snow?"

Mother Vickery glanced up, but went back to her work without comment.

"I sent the others away and asked you to stay because you are by far the most level-headed of them all, and your husband is now the highest authority in the village. I fear Elder Hicks has been murdered."

Faith took a sudden step back from the body. "What makes you think that?"

"When I went to turn him I felt a tear in his jerkin. When I pulled my hand away, there was blood on my fingertip. Let us look more closely."

There was indeed a hole in his clothing, too small to slip a finger through. When they removed the outer layers, they found a similar tear in his shirt and singlet. Beneath his garments they found a small hole in his side just under his ribs. It had seeped a few drops of blood onto his snow-white undergarments. Mother Vickery's touch had brought the blood to the surface of his clothing.

"He has been stabbed," said Faith. She was about to add that there would be ample suspects in the village, Mother and herself among them. She thought better of it and held her tongue.

Mother Vickery signaled for Faith to bring the knife from her kit on the table. Making a cut to enlarge the wound, she inserted two fingers and drew out a thin iron rod about six inches long. It was darkened from age and use, but the tip was bright, as though it had recently been sharpened.

"Looks like part of a ramrod that someone has taken a lot of trouble over. How many guns are there in the village?" asked Mother Vickery.

Faith thought for a minute. "Probably four muskets and two pistols. Both Thomas and Captain Watkins would know exactly."

Mother Vickery began to wash the body. It was some time before she said, "We must keep this between ourselves until your husband returns."

Faith agreed. "Yes, it would be important to have someone with authority here when it becomes common knowledge. Thomas will know what to do."

The two women prepared the body of Bradford Hicks for his grave.

The sun was high overhead before the women were startled by the sound of a tapping at the door. Faith rose from her work to peer out the window. She opened the door, and Thomas strode into the room. She secured the latch behind him.

He cast a quick glance and a half smile toward his wife. Village business came before happy reunions.

"I was met about half a mile from the village with word that the Wrath of God had taken the Elder. What did he die of, Mother Vickery? Can you tell?"

Faith handed him the weapon.

"Looks more like the wrath of a man. Could it have been an accident?" he asked.

Mother Vickery indicated the polished tip of the weapon. "It would appear that someone thrust it into him, then broke it off. The iron is old and in poor repair. It would be brittle and easy to break."

"Thomas, something has been bothering me. The house was secured from inside when we got here this morning. The windows were barred and the latch string was inside. We had to send Absalom Kydd down the chimney to let us in. How could someone have stabbed the Elder and gotten out? There was a dusting of snow with no tracks in it until I made them as I walked around the house."

"Could the snow have fallen after the murder?" he asked.

"No," Mother Vickery replied. "He had been dead only a short time when we found him. The body was still warm and the blood on the wound still wet. It was early and he was fully clothed, so he had made his morning toilet. Do you think he was expecting someone?"

Thomas considered the question for a moment, then said, "We will do nothing for the time being. For the moment let them think he died naturally."

"Will you look for the broken ramrod?" asked Faith.

"Not until we have thought about it some."

Faith felt a rush of joy at his inclusion of Mother Vickery and herself in the search for the truth.

**

The sun was halfway down the western sky. Faith had told Thomas of her part in the discovery of Elder Hicks three times. Each time he sat for a bit before asking her more questions. At last he seemed satisfied.

"We know the why of it," he said. "There is no man, yea, no single person who would not rejoice to see the man gone to his rewards, and happy to give credit to the Almighty. The questions remain: which one took action, and how was the deed accomplished?"

"Should we look at all the guns in the village?" she asked.

"Yes, I will put out the word that we are all to assemble in the meeting house at sunset and that each man is to bring his gun. It would be well if we could figure this out before we go. If we do not know how it was accomplished, at least the community should be told what actually happened to Hicks."

Thomas was the only person in the village who did not use an honorific before Hicks's family name. Most thought it was to show he was socially his equal, but Faith knew it was out of contempt for the man who ruled his people without compassion.

**

By the time of the meeting, most of the snow had melted, except in the deepest shadows. As they passed by the Hicks house, Faith saw the door had been pelted with snowballs, the remains of which showed as white circles that were slowly slipping down the wood toward the door step.

She stopped abruptly. "I think I know how it was done, Thomas. Now all we have to do is figure out who is guilty."

Faith explained her idea to him as they climbed the hill to the meeting house.

The hall, that once had held every member of the community easily, was now crowded almost to overflowing. Those who had come to the New World as children were now grown with children of their own and the prosperity of the community had attracted new residents.

Torches on the wall gave light but also heated the room so that it was uncomfortably warm. Damp wool clothing steamed and filled the air with the smell of unwashed bodies. The mood was glum. Once more there were murmurings that the Elder had not been cast down by the hand of man.

Thomas called the meeting to order and made a formal announcement of the death of the Elder, still unable to link the man's name and title in the same breath. "This morning, before sunrise, someone met with the Elder at his bidding. The Elder was fully clothed. The sun had barely risen before my wife was summoned to his house where his body was found on the floor. The house was secured as it might have been for the night. When the body was washed, it was found that he had been stabbed with this." Thomas drew out the piece of ramrod that had been imbedded in the body. There were gasps here and there. "I asked you to bring your weapons so we could find out which ramrod was used."

Faith watched the faces of each man as, one by one, they drew the rods from their guns. Not one seemed the least disturbed by the request. The fourth to comply was Benjamin Kydd. The rod he drew from his musket was missing its bottom third.

The look of astonishment on his face gave testament to his innocence. The tenor of the room was both relief that the gun had been identified and sympathy for the gun owner who had done away with the universally hated man.

Thomas reached out for the ramrod. A puzzled and somewhat frightened Kydd put it in his hand.

"It may have been Kydd's gun, but it was the hand of God that did the deed." The cry came from the middle of the group. Faith did not see who said it. She had heard similar statements several times, starting before they ever entered the house of the dead man.

Faith almost laughed out loud when she realized how ridiculous it was that she had been put in the stocks for saying "God, preserve us," when most of those in the room were accusing God of murder without a second thought.

"What did you do yesterday?" Thomas asked Kydd. "Did you take your musket out? Did anyone come to your house who might have taken it without your knowledge?"

"I spent the morning in the fields with Peirce clearing rocks. In the afternoon I went to the harbor to unload fish. I took the musket in the morning but not in the afternoon."

"Even if it was his weapon, how could he have done it?" asked Smith Beeson. "You yourself walked around the building looking for a way in."

"Yes, I did," said Faith. "There were no tracks in the snow but mine. But I think I know how it was done."

The room filled with the buzz of whispered comments. Thomas pounded his fist on the table in front of him to restore order. He glanced at Faith.

She continued the story. "You all know that Elder Hicks had modified his latch to keep everyone out of his house. As with all of our latches, the string needed to be outside the door in order to lift it or set it in the catch from the outside. But the string was inside when we arrived and found the body. It was wet, which might have been the case if it had been outside all night. Some of you mentioned the snow stopped around midnight. The death happened just before sunrise."

Mother Vickery rose and said, "It is well known that Elder Hicks was a suspicious man with great power but even he could not get up after being killed and draw in his latch string."

Faith agreed that it had not happened that way. She continued the story. "The snow had stopped but it was an inch or so thick when the murderer entered the house, let in by the Elder. The deed was done, and the killer slipped from the house, setting the bar in place in the usual manner."

Nicholas Corley spoke up. "But the latch could not be secured if the string were inside as we found it."

Faith went on with her explanation. "Before the murderer shut the door behind him, he formed a ball of snow around the string. The wad was sufficiently heavy to draw the sting inside. The snow had melted enough to drop off the string by the time we arrived to view the body. Any un-melted ice or wet spot on the floor was obscured by the feet of the people going in and out after we found the body."

During her explanation Thomas had been watching one particular face. When Faith was finished, Thomas pointed his finger at Smith Beeson. "I accuse you of the murder of Elder Bradford Hicks."

The expression on the smith's face changed from one of awe to one of fear and defiance. "I could not have done it. It was the hand of God. Everyone agrees."

It was clear that everyone did not agree.

Captain Watkins, the peace keeper, rose to stand beside the smith.

"How did you know it was him?" asked Kydd, clearly relived to have the burden of guilt removed.

Mother Vickery spoke. "In the afternoon when you were out in your boat, Smith Beeson brought your wife the fire shovel he had mended for her. He could have taken the ramrod at that time."

"He had the skill and tools to sharpen the point. It had to slip easily though clothing and flesh," Faith added. "He might also have weakened the rod so that it would break off easily."

Kydd's wife rose. "He came back very early this morning to see if the shovel met my standards. He could have slipped the ramrod back in place when my back was turned."

Smith Beeson shrugged but offered no defense. Captain

Watkins stood by his side, clearly reluctant to seize this man who was his friend.

At last the smith spoke. "The man killed my wife."

There were gasps from those around him.

The whole village knew that a week earlier, during a spate of icy weather, the Elder had sent Goodwife Beeson to the harbor to fetch a package that had arrived on a packet from Boston. She slipped on the icy gangplank and tumbled into the harbor, still clutching the new coat from Boston. She was dead before she could be pulled from the freezing water.

The village held no gaol. No one cared to bind Beeson in the stocks on such a cold winter night. Thomas posted a guard on the smith's house. In the morning he would be transported to a nearby village with a secure cell.

It snowed again in the night. Before morning the smith had slipped by his guards. At first light his body was found in the harbor where his wife had died.

As they carried the body to the meeting house to be prepared for burial, Faith could see in her mind's eye Elder Hicks and Smith Beeson facing the throne of the Almighty for judgement. Which, she wondered, would receive the harsher judgment?

THE COTTAGE

by Charles Todd

Who's rearranging Miss Barrington's furniture in between-the-wars Welsh Marches? Inspector Rutledge arrives in the tiny village, expecting to discover young Miss Barrington is a lunatic. But instead, the crime that's been committed is much more serious.

She stood in the doorway of her cottage, pointing. "Just look! Everything has been rearranged!"

Rutledge had come to this tiny village on the Welsh Marches because Miss Barrington was related to Viscount Barrington, and Chief Superintendent Bowles had heeded her request for Scotland Yard to look into the problem at her cottage.

"Batty, very likely," Bowles had said, handing Rutledge the file. "Lost her fiancé in the war, I've been told. Turned her mind. Do what you can to settle the matter. The local man is no doubt at his wits' end."

Miss Barrington appeared to be anything but batty when Rutledge met her at the village's only inn. She had been waiting in the entry, fending off the hovering owner, a man she called Waters. Scowling, he left, and Rutledge quietly introduced himself.

"Six months ago," she began straightaway as she folded her umbrella and led him to a quiet corner. It had been raining all morning, and the sky was black and thunderous again. "An elderly woman, Mrs. Grayling, died, and I bought her cottage, lock, stock, and teapot. I didn't want to bring anything from my parents' house, I just wanted to live quietly here and get used to the fact that Danny is dead. He died three days before the Armistice. Can you imagine? At home I've been surrounded by sympathy, and even the servants try to see to it that I'm kept too busy to mourn. Well, I need to mourn. At least for a while."

She was quite attractive, soft fair hair, dark blue eyes, and a pleasant smile. He could understand why her parents didn't want her to shut herself away and dwell on the past. On the other hand, he could also understand why she needed a little time.

"What went wrong?" Rutledge asked.

"I came down with my sister and her husband, then sent them

away as soon as I was settled in. It really is quite a lovely cottage, and the furnishings are very comfortable. I went to Gloucester one weekend to visit Daniel's sister, and when I came home, every change I'd made had been put back the way it was when I first crossed the threshold. And since then it has happened every time I leave."

"Did you speak to the local constable?"

"Constable Barnes? Yes, I did, and he treated me like a silly girl who couldn't remember how her own home looked. He even called me dearie!"

Rutledge fought down a grin. "Yes, well, London claims he grew up in Delwyn. He should know his patch better than anyone." He could see she was about to argue with him, and added quickly, "It can also mean that he's blind to what he doesn't want to see."

"Blind is a very good description."

"You've been away from the cottage for two days now?"

"Yes, I deliberately went off to visit my old nanny when I learned that the Yard was sending someone down. Now you can see for yourself what I go through on my return."

"I have no feeling for how the cottage looked before you set out," he reminded her.

"That's why I've made a map of each room and put down every piece of furniture, every lamp, every photograph, indeed, even the plants in the window and the dishes in the tall dresser." She reached into her coat pocket and took out several folded sheets of paper, passing them to him.

He was quite surprised to find that she was a very fine draftsman. The pen and ink sketches of each room were detailed and even colored in with pencil, so that the cottage was vividly portrayed on paper. He spent several minutes studying the drawings as she finished her tea, observing him over the rim of her teacup.

"Well done," he said, folding the pages and returning them to her. "I have a very good feeling for what to expect. Shall we drive to your cottage?"

There was a brief respite from the heavy rain as he helped her into the motorcar and asked for directions.

"Turn right just beyond the church. Bluebell Cottage is on your left."

It was easy to find, and he stopped before the gate. The front garden, flattened and dripping from the storm, was vivid with color. But Rutledge was more interested in the cottage's isolation, set off from its neighbors by a thick stand of trees.

"The garden is a legacy from the former owner. She was

obviously quite good with plants and won several prizes for her roses and her delphiniums. I have only to pull a weed here and there, and deadhead the blossoms, and it minds itself."

She opened the gate and they walked up the flagstone path. Miss Barrington took a deep breath, put her key in the lock, and then flung open the door. "Go on, see for yourself."

He stepped past her, regarded the entry with interest and then moved into the front room, her parlor.

It was quite a pretty room, with a colorful carpet on the floor, comfortable chairs arranged by the hearth, a window seat with embroidered cushions, and a small desk against an interior wall.

It was then that she followed him into the cottage and made her comment through a sweeping gesture with her hand.

Rutledge said, "You're right. Charming—but changed."

"Yes," she said. "And while I like it this way well enough, I enjoyed adding my own touches—moving that tea table nearer the chairs, putting the desk between the windows rather than against the far wall, and so on. That bookcase belongs against the wall, in fact, as you saw in my drawing. I liked the floral print above the bookcase with the rose vase beneath it. But the vase is now on the mantelpiece, and the floral print is over there."

"And this is true everywhere in the house?"

"See for yourself. I'll wait here."

He did, and found she was right. The changes were evident everywhere he looked. No harm done, nothing stolen or damaged, just a rearrangement that was unsettling. It meant, too, that someone had been inside, something a woman would find particularly disturbing. He came back to the parlor, took the chair opposite the one where she was sitting, and asked, "Who else has a key to this house?"

"As far as I know, no one. Why should they?"

"Not even an old servant of the previous owner's? Someone who remembers her mistress by trying to keep the house just the way she liked it?"

"I never thought of that."

"We'll call on the rector. He'll be able to tell us."

And Rutledge was right. The rector, Mr. Tomlinson, looked more like a rugby player than a man of God, broad-shouldered and tall, with unruly dark hair and a crooked nose.

He smiled when he saw Miss Barrington at his door, and said in a pleasant baritone, "At it again, are they?"

"Yes, and this time I have someone here to help me."

The two men shook hands and Rutledge said, after they'd been seated and refused the offer of tea, "Did the former owner of Miss

Barrington's cottage have anyone who cleaned or cooked for her?"

Tomlinson's eyebrows went up in surprise. "Yes, Gracie Barrow. She was pensioned off when Mrs. Grayling died. She lives with her brother on a small holding just outside the village. Surely you don't think—but of course you must, or you wouldn't have asked! Still, I can't see Gracie doing such a thing. She was quite happy to learn that the cottage had a new owner so quickly. Too small for a family, too dear for a single person." He smiled at Miss Barrington. "Because it was in good repair and had land around it, it was rather out of reach for most people."

"I wasn't told the price included a ghost!" Miss Barrington retorted.

"Then I think we must call on Gracie Barrow," Rutledge replied, rising.

Tomlinson reluctantly gave him directions to the farm. Halfway to the turning, another motorcar came down the same road and slowed, preparing to stop.

"It's Dr. Taylor. He's another one who believes I'm seeing things," Rutledge's companion said softly.

As the two vehicles met, Dr. Taylor leaned out his window. A gruff man with graying hair and an abrupt manner, he said to Miss Barrington, speaking across Rutledge, "You haven't found a buyer for the property! It would be a shame to lose you as a neighbor."

The inn's owner had been gossiping.

Before she could answer, Rutledge replied for her. "Dr. Taylor? Just the man I wished to see."

"I'm coming from a rather difficult confinement, but later today perhaps—"

"Actually, I can deal with the matter here and now. Before I decide to propose marriage to Miss Barrington, I should like to know if she is—well—not herself." He could feel Miss Barrington bristling beside him, and he put a friendly hand on hers. It was also a warning.

The doctor stared at Rutledge. "You do come to the point," he replied after a moment. "But to answer you, I've felt from the start that Miss Barrington was under great strain when she arrived in the village, and one of the manifestations of great strain is sleep-walking. It's my opinion that she rearranges the house in her sleep to prove to herself that she is not benefitting from another tragedy. Women take such guilt to heart, more so than men."

Rutledge knew something about guilt. And so did Hamish, in the back of his mind. "Then you feel she would make a good wife and mother?"

"Indeed. Most particularly if you chose another residence as your home and removed her from her present surroundings."

"And you can assure me that the former owner died of natural causes? That if we choose to live in the cottage, we will not be awakened in the night by a murderer looking for something he couldn't find in previous attempts?"

The doctor's face was a picture of shock. "Good God, how could you imagine such a thing? No, the previous owner was old and her heart simply stopped. Or she had a dizzy turn when she stood, and the heart stopped from the force of her fall. I don't remember the last murder we had here. Fifteen years ago? Twenty?"

"Thank you, Doctor. You've been very helpful," Rutledge said with a smile. He put in the clutch, moving on just as Taylor was about to ask another question.

When they were far enough away not to be overheard, Rutledge cast a quick glance at his passenger and saw that Miss Barrington was flushed and angry.

"No, listen. A doctor wouldn't discuss a patient with a stranger, or even someone interested in buying the cottage," he said. "But your fiancé asking about the stability of the woman he wishes to marry is another matter. I'm sorry if I upset you, but I needed to know what explanation he would offer for your circumstances."

She managed a smile. "I expect it was worth it to see the doctor's face when you asked if I were batty. But you could have warned me."

"There was no time. Still, it was interesting to see that he would be delighted for you to marry and leave the village for good. I daresay you've been a disturbing influence. I wonder why. Ah, I think that's the turning we're after."

A rutted lane lined with maples on either side led to a farmhouse that was so old it seemed to hunch on its foundations to keep from falling down. The sign in the yard read *Maple Farm— brown eggs, butter, apples in season, clotted cream.* The barn doors were open, and from the field beyond they could hear a male voice calling to his team.

Gracie Barrow answered their knock, her lined face lighting up as she recognized Miss Barrington, who once more introduced Rutledge as a friend.

"Do come in," she said. "I've fresh buttermilk, if you'd care for a glass, or there's lemonade as well."

"A glass of buttermilk would be welcome," Rutledge said affably, as they followed her through to the kitchen. "I'm from Scotland Yard. We've come about Bluebell Cottage. Someone has been moving the furniture about, changing pictures on the wall, and so on. Was it you?"

"Scotland Yard?" she asked. "You'll have some identification, will you not?"

He handed it to her and she scanned it carefully, squinting a little. Then she passed it back to him, nodding. "I've been hoping someone would come," she said. "I couldn't speak to Constable Barnes, could I? His sister is married to that man, Morton. The undertaker. And I don't trust him to cross the street in a straight line! If I said anything to Constable Barnes, Susan would hear of it soon enough, and what Susan hears, she tells her husband. And he's the one I'm afraid of!"

The last words caught Rutledge off guard. "Afraid of?

"Because he killed Elizabeth Grayling, that's why. Poor soul."

"Killed her?" Miss Barrington said quickly. "What do you mean?"

"Just that. It was said her heart gave out, but she had no trouble with her heart. Seventy-five and as fit as a fiddle. Well, look at that garden! She kept it herself, and she walked every day, looking for wildflowers to add to it."

"What did the doctor say?" Rutledge asked. "What did he put down as the cause of death?"

"Dr. Taylor said she had no history of heart disease, but that didn't mean her heart didn't simply stop. It happened sometimes, he said, and was a better way to go than most of the ailments of age. I was at the inquest. I heard him myself."

"Was he lying?" Rutledge asked.

"I dunno. I found her with her head against the edge of the bookcase, its corner as bloody as her hair. They claimed she'd fallen against it as she died. But I don't think that's what killed her. There's a bookend up the stairs on the table by the bed. It has a sharp edge too. I didn't find any blood on it, but it wasn't where it ought to be. Nor was the chair by the window. And haven't I dusted both every day for twenty years? I ask you. When I gave my evidence at the inquest, they said I'd been in a state of shock."

"According to the inquest report, which I read in London, nothing was taken from the cottage. What motive would this man Morton have for murder?"

"There was the prize she got for her winning rose at the fair in Hereford. Fifty pounds."

"That's rather a large sum for a prize," Rutledge commented.

"It was given in memory of the Lord Mayor's son, who died in the war. He was a breeder of roses. And I know for a fact she never spent the money. She valued it too much as a prize. But I don't know what she did with it."

"How many other people knew the money was in the cottage?"

"Lord love you, sir, most of the village, but they wouldn't touch it. Morton's the one needed it. He's mad for the horses, everyone knows that."

"Surely her solicitor looked for the prize and saw to it that her heirs received it."

"What heirs? Her daughter died of typhoid when she was a child, and her husband died of a cancer in 1910. He wasn't much of a farmer, but he worked hard."

"Then who benefited from the sale of the cottage?"

"I was never told," she answered. "I thought—well, the truth is, I never thought. It was the prize money crossed my mind. But now you ask, it's a good question. Some distant cousin?"

Curious, Miss Barrington asked, "Did you yourself look for the prize?"

Gracie Barrow flushed. "And what if I did? The solicitor, Mr. Gifford, told me there was no money to settle the bequest in her will. She left me fifty pounds. She said it was all she had to leave me."

"There should have been sufficient sums from the sale of the cottage," Rutledge reminded her. "Without touching the prize money."

"He killed her for both. He must've. Else, where is it?"

But Rutledge didn't think Morton had done. Fifty pounds was a great sum to Gracie Barrow, but not to a man who gambled. "Did she leave any bequests to charity? The church roof? Widows and orphans? The old age pensioners' fund?"

"Mrs. Grayling? Charity began at home with her."

"When you were looking for the prize money, did you decide to move the furnishings about? To cover up your search?"

"What if I did? That money is mine, and with all respect, Miss Barrington doesn't need it."

"Perhaps not. But you are in danger of being taken up for criminal trespass."

Startled, Gracie Barrow said, "Here, I wasn't stealing. That money is mine."

"But the cottage is not yours. If you search for it again, I shall take you into custody. Is that understood?"

***

As Rutledge and Miss Barrington drove back to Delwyn, she said, "You've solved my mystery very nicely. Thank you. But do you think Miss Barrow is right, that Mrs. Grayling was murdered for that fifty pounds?"

"Not for fifty pounds. But the question remains, why didn't

anyone insist that Gracie Barrow receive her bequest once the cottage was sold? If only to keep her quiet? Someone must have known she was behind your problems at the cottage. Why wasn't she killed to stop her from stirring up trouble?" He was silent for a time, then said pensively as they turned toward the High Street, "The solicitor, the doctor, the constable's brother-in-law. For all I know, the landlord of the inn. Why kill Mrs. Grayling, but draw the line at Gracie Barrow?"

"You're the man from Scotland Yard," she retorted. "It's why I sent for you. To find out such things."

"But why not give Gracie Barrow her pittance? Why deny her?"

It was an interesting question. Who had been so greedy?

In the hierarchy of a village, there was the squire, the doctor, the rector, and the solicitor. But he thought Delwyn was too small for a squire. What did the rest have in common?

For the first time since he'd arrived in the village, Hamish spoke from the deep recesses of his mind. "Ask yon rector."

"A good idea." But he had answered aloud. As Miss Barrington turned, brows raised, he quickly added, "Don't you think? To speak to the rector again?"

She smiled. "Yes, if you say so. But why?"

"We'll find out."

The rector was surprised to see them. He led them to the parlor and said, "Did you talk to Gracie Barrow?"

"Tell me a little about Mrs. Grayling." Rutledge said, taking the seat he was offered.

Tomlinson answered uneasily. "Elderly. Came regularly to services. I'm late to Delwyn, I only knew her the last eight years of her life."

"Where were you before you came to this church?"

"I—Gloucester. St. Stephen's."

The tiny church in Delwyn was a comedown from the prominent St. Stephen's. Had the handsome rector been disciplined by his bishop? Why? For stealing from the church? Hardly. For having an affair with one of his women parishioners? Very likely.

And that explained everything.

Rutledge asked bluntly, "Was Mrs. Grayling blackmailing you?"

Tomlinson's expression was all the proof Rutledge needed. But the rector made an effort to keep his voice steady as he said, "Good heavens, whatever gave you—don't be ridiculous! She was a good Christian woman."

Miss Barrington said almost at the same time, "The owner of

my cottage? You've taken leave of your senses, Inspector. Everyone, from the owner of the inn to the rector here, had only the nicest things to say about her."

"I'm not at all surprised. They wanted you to buy the cottage, and help them recoup their losses," Rutledge told her grimly. "Blackmail is the only thing that explains the murder, the doctor's verdict, the solicitor's greed, the constable's blindness, and the rector's complicity. The sale of the cottage repaid everyone except for Gracie Barrow, who only wanted her promised fifty pounds, and she saw through the charade. The question is, who actually killed Mrs. Grayling?"

The rector said quickly, "Here, I didn't have anything to do with murder!"

"Gracie believes it was Morton, the constable's brother-in-law," Miss Barrington said.

"No doubt they drew straws." Rutledge wouldn't have put it past the lot of them.

"No—I would never be a part of such a thing!"

"Who conducted the inquest?"

Tomlinson said, "Waters—the owner of the pub, since the solicitor handled Mrs. Grayling's affairs and Dr. Taylor performed the autopsy."

"There's your answer, then. If he was conducting the inquest, he wouldn't have to give evidence or lie under oath."

Miss Barrington said, "But you haven't even spoken to these other men!"

"Believe me, I shall."

"Why would Mrs. Grayling stoop to blackmail?" Tomlinson demanded in a last desperate attempt to stop Rutledge.

"Miss Barrington bought the cottage lock, stock, and teapot. I've seen it—quite a handsome property. Mrs. Grayling was a farmer's wife, her husband barely able to provide for her while he was alive, and surely he had little to leave her at his death. And yet a number of pieces of furniture are of excellent quality. Where did Mrs. Grayling find the money to buy those? Unless she had a steady source of income."

Tomlinson collapsed in his chair. "All right. I bought that desk and the bookcase for her. I gave her that painting of the seaside. I don't know what the others contributed."

"Were you repaid what you had spent to buy them?"

"God help me. Yes. I'm not rich, I depend on my living. And she was insatiable, I knew I couldn't satisfy her forever. But I swear I didn't know she'd been murdered! I believed the doctor when he swore she'd died of natural causes."

"How did she find out the secrets these men were hiding?" Miss Barrington argued.

"I expect Gracie helped there. She must know the other women in the village who did for their betters. A little gossip over a cup of tea? And Mrs. Grayling must have been quick to see when Gracie was bursting with a new secret." Rutledge turned to Tomlinson. "How did she learn of your indiscretions? I can't imagine you talking to a housekeeper."

"She kept asking me questions about St. Stephen's. I expect she wrote to someone in the Women's Institute in my last parish. There were several who would gladly tell her what was being whispered. I don't know how she discovered what the others had done, but the doctor swore she must have located his nurse in the first office he'd had in Hereford. Something to do with the wrong diagnosis, he said. He asked the postmistress, but she didn't remember Mrs. Grayling ever mailing a letter. All of us had secrets."

Rutledge had been listening with interest. Mrs. Grayling had played a dangerous game, and in the end she'd paid for it. But he didn't think she'd ever written to anyone. She'd lived in Delwyn all her life, and she knew a thing or two about her village. Gracie's gossip had just made her task simpler. Had she only needed to hint at knowledge, and let the guilty identify themselves? A word dropped here or there, a knowing smile, the quiet mention of needing a new bed or a new desk, admiring a painting or coveting a bookcase . . . had she lived a very comfortable life built on nothing more than understanding human nature?

He said to Miss Barrington, "Will you stay with the rector while I go and speak to the innkeeper, Waters? I shouldn't like to find he'd been warned. Or any of the others for that matter. And I rather think Waters could be the more dangerous of the conspirators."

She asked skeptically. "Do you think he'll confess to you?"

Rutledge smiled. "Two can play at Mrs. Grayling's game. Wait and see."

With that he was gone, leaving Tomlinson sitting there with his head in his hands.

When Rutledge walked into the inn, he saw Waters standing in the dining room, staring across the tables at him. The man turned and made his way to the kitchen without looking back.

Rutledge followed him into the kitchen and through a door that led into a storeroom where sacks of flour and sugar, tins of fruit and vegetables, jars of spices, large containers of lard, and boxes of tea jostled each other on shelves along the wall. There was a door at the other end that opened onto the kitchen garden. Rutledge swore when he glimpsed Waters disappearing around the corner of the inn.

He went after Waters, picking up his pace until he broke into a trot on the street.

Waters was just disappearing through a dark green door with a brass knocker in the shape of a pineapple, the symbol of hospitality. Rutledge crossed the street, dodged a woman pushing a pram, and went through the door after his quarry.

He realized he was in the office of the solicitor, Gifford. A clerk barred his way, but Rutledge had his identification in his hand.

"Step aside."

The clerk hesitated, then moved out of his way. Rutledge walked through the door to the private offices and down the passage. Voices came from one of the rooms, and he stepped inside without knocking.

Waters was standing by the window, Gifford behind his desk. A heavyset man with a receding hairline, he raised a hand as Rutledge faced them.

"Who are you?"

"Inspector Rutledge, Scotland Yard. I'm taking this man into custody for the murder of Mrs. Elizabeth Grayling."

Gifford turned to Waters. "Murder? Do you know anything about this? I don't understand."

Waters came away from the window. "Oh, no, don't pretend innocence. You are as deep in this as I am."

Gifford got to his feet. "I don't know what you're talking about. As your solicitor, I advise you to say no more."

The two men glared at each other.

"And what did the two of you contribute to the cottage? The new cooker in the kitchen? Perhaps the handsome bedstead upstairs? We'll find out, you needn't bother to deny it."

Despite his words, he was in a quandary. The doctor, the solicitor, the rector, the owner of the pub, the constable, the constable's brother-in-law. Was the local jail large enough to hold all of them?

Six cells, he discovered, when he had brought in the six of them, and locked them up until the Chief Constable could send someone to collect them.

Afterward, Miss Barrington invited him to tea, saying as she brought in the tray, "I must thank you for solving my problem. Although I shall have to strike six of my neighbors from my circle of friends. "

He laughed, accepting a teacup from her. The tall ormolu clock on the mantelpiece struck the hour, its flat note reminding him he must report to the Chief Constable.

"I'll sleep soundly now," she was saying.

"I'm surprised that the invasion of your peace hasn't set you against Delwyn altogether."

"No. I've found what I'm looking for in my cottage, and I was determined to get to the bottom of my trouble. Thank God the Yard agreed to help."

Finishing his tea, Rutledge rose to leave. As he said goodbye, Hamish was busy in the back of his mind, and he tried to ignore him. But it was nearly impossible.

She was just closing the door after him when he stopped her.

"Does that clock sound right to you?"

Surprised, she said, "The clock? I've been meaning to find a clockmaker. It needs a good cleaning."

"Let me have a look."

Miss Barrington smiled. "Does Scotland Yard have no end of skills?"

But he was already crossing to the hearth and lifting the clock from the mantelpiece.

Opening the back, he reached inside, and pulled out a packet. "This is what muffled your chimes. Have you never looked in here?"

"I've never needed to. One winds at the face."

Rutledge opened the packet and counted out five ten-pound notes.

Miss Barrington stared. "Gracie's fifty pounds!" she exclaimed. "Miss Grayling's prize money."

"I'm not sure Gracie deserves it—not if she was rearranging your furniture. But the will was specific, she was bequeathed this amount."

"I'll see that she gets it," Miss Barrington told him. "If only for helping us uncover and find six evil men. And to think I'd considered asking around for someone to clean for me. What if I'd taken on Gracie? Would the good citizens of Delwyn have decided to rid themselves of both of us? For fear the blackmail would begin again?"

Rutledge said reassuringly, "I doubt it. You're safe enough now."

But as he cranked the motorcar, he thought it very likely that she would have been the next victim. In his experience, the second murder was always easier.

THE MEASURED CHEST

by Mark Thielman

*In the early part of the nineteenth century, ship's
carpenter Marshall is asked to investigate a
disappearance. Of course the purser went over the side
– but was it an accident, or the act of a malignant
spirit?*

"Do you believe in the Devil?"

"Aye, Captain, I am a Christian man."

"What about other dark spirits? Do you put credence in them?"

My general nervousness at being summoned to the captain's
quarters was not quelled by his interrogation regarding the nature
of evil. I paused before answering, my eyes wandering about the
small room tucked in the stern below the quarterdeck. Though the
space was easily scanned, I could find no clues to assist me in
offering the correct answer.

"It is a direct question, Mr. Marshall."

I chose my words carefully, attempting to include just enough
vagueness that I might wiggle out of any theological fish trap the
captain had set. I settled my gaze on the center of the small desk
behind which he sat.

"Having seen the Southern Cross and the glory of the sunrise, it
is impossible for me to doubt the existence of God," I said, looking
for confirmation in the old man's face. He, however, remained
inscrutable. I continued, speaking slowly so that I might adjust
course if necessary. "I have seen enough cruelty in storm and battle
to believe that evil lurks among us. The good do not always
prosper and sinners are not always punished in this life in measure
to their transgressions. The iniquity of man, in my experience, far
exceeds God's storms in ruinous capacity."

I looked to his face in hopes of affirmation. He held me with an
appraising stare that seemed to bore directly through my sockets. I
withered under his scrutiny and raised my eyes to look just over the
top of his head and out the small stern windows of the *Fury*. As I
had been summoned before the aurora, I saw nothing but darkness.

"Do you consider yourself inordinately superstitious, Chippy?"

The use of the nickname surprised me, as if we were two mates discussing the nature of things over a pot rather than the ship's carpenter having an audience before the captain of a sloop of war. I looked again into his face and found his eyes, still intense, but perhaps a bit less hard.

"I do not wish to set sail on a Friday, nor do I allow myself to whistle while aboard ship. I like the sign of the red sky at night," I said. "I do not know that I put great stock that consequences will befall me should circumstance cause me to violate one of these superstitions, but I see no profit in the risk, and only downside."

"That is a reasoned, well-measured response, Chippy."

"Thank you, Captain," I said.

He held up his hand, cutting off any further comment.

"Our purser has disappeared, Chippy," Captain Gregory said.

"Disappeared, sir? But we're at sea."

The captain ignored my statement of the obvious. "He is no longer aboard this ship. I have had the vessel discretely searched. Some members of the crew may soon suspect that he has been collected by a phantasm. What do you say to that, Mr. Marshall?"

"Sea spirits may claim prizes, as do we all," I said. "It is possible, although—"

The captain again interrupted my sentence. "Exactly why I wanted you for this task, Mr. Marshall. You will not rule it out although you are not automatically predisposed to believing in sea spirits. I find it more likely that our purser befell some accident and went overboard or . . ."

"Or what, sir?"

"Or was murdered. We make port in two days' time. If he was murdered, the guilty soul will likely jump ship when we reach Charleston. I want your report before then. You are temporarily relieved of your other duties except sounding the well. That is all." He turned his head back toward the paperwork across his desk.

"Begging the captain's pardon?"

"What is it, Chippy?"

"I am a carpenter, sir. How might I make such a determination?"

The captain fixed me again with his look. "I have seen your work, Chippy. You display imagination. Your craftsmanship is meticulous. You are intelligent, particularly for one born to your station. As a warrant officer, you sit between the ranks. You berth and move among the men. The officers know to rely upon you. You are the best man for this responsibility."

"Aye, sir."

"And you are the only carpenter I have ever caught reading a book."

"My father taught me sums and a bit of reading. He believed it was every man's duty to read his Bible," I said by way of explanation.

"I'm also told that you have a London-born cousin who is a Bow Street Runner."

"'Tis true, Captain," I said. "But my loyalty . . . "

The captain raised a hand and cut me off midsentence.

"I, myself, have English relatives, Chippy. I do not doubt your loyalty in this 1812 war. I only mean that this sort of inquiry is in your blood."

My cousin, indeed, served under Fielding, the renowned London magistrate. I, a second son of a Connecticut farmer, spent my early years on Father's farm learning to craft with tools. I lived an ocean away from Bow Street, but, looking at the captain's face, I could see that even in private, he would brook no argument.

"Aye, sir."

"Two days, Chippy," the captain repeated.

"Aye, sir. Two days."

This time I stood my place before his cramped desk.

"Is there something else?" he asked, a hint of irritation in his voice.

"I should like to examine his berth," I said. "And speak with the officers regarding the purser. But . . . "

"Continue," he said in the voice of command.

"Well, I anticipate reluctance on the part of the officers to submit to an interrogation by someone not of rank, sir." I said. "It would be unnatural."

The captain glowered at me. "Forthrightness is a characteristic of an officer. That will be all."

"Yes, sir."

I saluted and spun on my heel, making move to leave.

"Mr. Marshall."

I turned back around, completing the circle.

"Yes, Captain."

"If you encounter difficulties with the officers, please inform me."

"Aye, sir."

"Lieutenant Robinson," the captain called.

A young blond officer appeared in the doorway.

"Assist Mr. Marshall with whatever he requires," the captain said as he handed him a brass key. "You are relieved of watch responsibilities until this task is complete. Dismissed."

I saluted and, this time, made it out the door cut into the bulkhead.

"How am I to help, Chippy?" Lieutenant Robinson asked, his look grim.

I wondered to myself if I heard condescension in his tone.

Before I could decide, my thoughts were interrupted by seven bells. Middle watch would be ending soon. It was, however, still too dark to look about the deck for clues to spiritual activity.

"Let us go to the purser's stores," I said.

Robinson led me onto the quarterdeck and down the ladder. Although he had only recently been assigned to the *Fury*, I watched him walk confidently along the main deck, even in the dark. He prowled it like the ship's cat. After cruising upon her for two years, I knew every strake and stanchion aboard the ship . Yet, I doubted I could move about her any more assuredly than Lieutenant Robinson did.

Using Captain Gregory's key, he unlocked the door to the store. From here, the purser stocked his slopchest with goods, then sold them to sailors below the mainmast. I entered and Robinson followed. Finding the lantern, I raised the light. Turning, I saw the lieutenant eyeing me.

"For what do we seek?" Lieutenant Robinson asked. He began to move around the small room, looking at the stores. I stayed him with my hand.

"I wanted a private place to speak with you," I said. "Do you know of my assignment?"

"Captain wants to know what happened to the purser," he answered. "You're to tell him."

"How well did you know the purser?" I asked.

"As well as any, I guess." As he spoke, his fists clenched and his arms pulled in tighter to his body. As a commissioned officer, his discomfort at being questioned by a warrant was etched on his posture.

"How did you find him?"

"A copper-bottomed fellow," he answered, "a worthy servant of the service."

I doubted that he could see my look of disdain in the dim light of the single tallow lantern.

"Then you did not know the man very well," I said.

"I beg your pardon?"

"He sold second-rate goods at first-rate prices because men at sea have no choice. He was duplicitous to the crew and truckling to the officers. Jones would, in my opinion, have stolen from his own mother were he birthed of woman. My question, Lieutenant Robinson, is does your opinion of purser comport with or differ from my own?"

"You sound as if you should be investigating yourself, Chippy," he said.

"During the pendency of our inquiry, Lieutenant, I think it best we avoid nicknames. Please call me Mr. Marshall."

Although the light remained dim, I could see his arms pull in tighter and the muscles at the back of his jaw quiver.

"What was your opinion of the purser?" I asked again.

The lieutenant took a long moment before answering. "Mr. Marshall," he nearly spat, "you've got grit, I'll give you that." He sighed. "I have heard of some games he played with the account books, receipts, and certificates."

"When did you last see Purser Jones?"

"Early last evening, prior to dinner."

"And did it appear to you that he had been drinking?"

"I saw no indication of it," he said, frowning.

"If you had, it would not be commonplace for you to admit so to the carpenter." When Robinson did not answer, I continued, "To disparage the character of a deceased officer is contrary to the comradery of command. Yet, it is essential for me to determine matters such as this if I am to give the captain a reliable answer. If we need to include the captain in our conversation, you need only tell me."

Tight-jawed, he thought hard before answering. Then, as I had all but decided we were headed back to the captain's quarters, he nodded.

"The logic is sound, Chippy . . . Mr. Marshall. Though I had the late dogwatch and honestly did not see the man during the evening meal."

"Then I must find another."

"Mr. Marshall," the lieutenant began, speaking slowly. "If I might make a suggestion."

I nodded.

"As you have sensed, we officers are unused to speaking candidly to men such as yourself. I apologize for my earlier reluctance but we can both foresee that this will be a continuing problem. You do not wish to bluster with the threat of the captain at every interview. Someone, likely, will call your bluff and that will be awkward for all concerned. If you have tasks that you wish to accomplish in connection with this inquiry, then may I request that I be allowed to question the officers privately? I shall report back to you directly whether Purser Jones was in his cups last night."

My mind turned over the lieutenant's suggestion. His reasoning was sound and the separation of tasks would improve our speed.

"And I apologize as well for my heavy-handedness," I said. "Such an inquiry as we are about is new to me. I am more comfortable with a piece of wood. Your suggestion is much appreciated."

The lieutenant smiled for the first time since receiving the assignment. "Then I shall be off."

"Let us endeavor to meet back here at four bells, morning watch," I said.

"Aye, Mr. Marshall." The lieutenant made a point of emphasizing the word 'mister,' but this time I heard no anger in the tone.

Making peace with the lieutenant proved necessary. I needed the time from first light to four bells to examine the ship. The first duty of the day for those sailors not on watch would be to swab the *Fury* with holystones, to clean the deck of oozed pitch and tar. My search must precede their swabbing. I felt certain that a coarse rubbing with the sandstones followed by a flushing with seawater would remove whatever it was I hoped to find. As such, I did not have time to engage in half-hearted answers and threats with the commissioned officers.

Though I did not know what I was searching for, I felt confident that the living *Fury* would reveal her secrets to me. We had a relationship similar to that between a sailor and the surgeon. This ship-rigged sloop and I had served together for two years. Although I could leave after each cruise, I elected to stay, loyal to ship and captain. As often as I had bandaged her, I assured myself that her living essence would speak to me without reticence.

The *Fury* was a sloop of war. Most sloops of the fleet carried only a single deck. Unique to the *Fury*, an aft quarterdeck allowed the officers to observe the crews' actions on the main deck. As a warrant officer, I was entitled to venture there, though I rarely had occasion to go. This, however, was where I began my search.

I walked slowly around the quarterdeck looking for anything out of the ordinary. The helmsman, stationed at the wheel, watched me but soon lost interest and turned his attention back to the horizon. The carnation dawn brought enough light for me to examine the planks. I carried the lantern we had obtained in the purser's store should I need additional illumination.

Finding nothing noteworthy, I stood at the break of the quarterdeck and looked out over the ship. A breeze, which the log book would record as light, blew across me as I considered my course. I could, for a better bird's-eye view, go aloft the main mast. Walking the deck would take longer but provide me a more detailed view. Deciding, I descended the ladder and moved toward the bowsprit.

I walked deliberately, working my way up the port side. I kept a hand on the bulwark, took a step and paused to survey the oak on which I lived. Feeling the familiar wood beneath my hand, my mind drifted back across my service with her. I remembered the battles, not in the details of the engagements, but rather in the necessary repairs.

Athwart the mainmast, the *Fury* snapped me from my reverie and beckoned me to examine the deck. Holding the lantern close, I saw a circular drop of dried blood on the bulwark. Not unusual on a ship of war, but it prodded me to search the area more closely. Immediately behind me, I found another, also round, and then another behind it. The drops formed a faint trail that I had passed by completely.

Cursing my inattention and retracing my steps, I found another drop, this one disturbed as if swiped at. Someone had made a crude attempt to wipe this one or had inadvertently dragged something through it. The trail led me back to a location just below the quarterdeck in the shadow of the mizzenmast. I held my lantern aloft and examined the bulkhead of the quarterdeck.

Faintly, I saw wisps of blood like the high thin clouds on a clear day. Gathering a line, I sectioned off the area from the corner of the quarterdeck and lashed it to the bulwark. Marking off the area for future study, I continued my survey of the deck.

Because the captain had praised my thoroughness, I felt compelled to complete the examination. The review, however, was perfunctory. I knew in my heart I had located the area that concerned me. Still, I proceeded up the port side to the bow and then back down the starboard. The additional search, not surprisingly, yielded nothing except the curious looks of seamen beginning to turn to topside. As I passed, I heard the low rumble of speculation. Word was beginning to spread about the purser's mysterious disappearance.

I needed to find Lieutenant Robinson. Looking in the cockpit where the junior officers berthed, I saw him centered amid a company of two midshipmen and an ensign, engaged in earnest conversation. One of the midshipmen noticed me as I approached and signaled to the others. Silence fell over the group immediately.

"Mr. Marshall," the lieutenant said, "it is not yet four bells."

"I realize that I am early, Lieutenant. At your convenience, might I request assistance?"

He and I both knew it was a summons. We also knew that this inquiry would end in a day and we would return to our roles in the hierarchy of the navy. It served neither of us to flaunt my temporary status before the lower ranks of commissioned officers. I, therefore, snapped off a salute, turned on my heel, and made my way back to the deck, confident that Robinson would join me directly.

When he arrived. I pointed out the area that I had marked off with the roband and requested that he dispatch a sentry to secure the area. I did not want this portion of the deck scrubbed until we were finished. Although questions registered on his face, Robinson nodded. He located the captain of the marines and spoke to him. A guard took up his position. The task complete, Robinson returned to where I stood.

"I have spoken with three of the messmates who dined with Jones last night," Robinson said. "No one believed him to be in his cups. They commented that he seemed quite cheerful, sharing a bit of monkey blood with them from his stores, something he typically reserves for the higher-ranking officers. The ensign said Jones spoke rather brazenly of the money he expected to pocket when he left the service. It's unlikely that he fell overboard in some drunken stupor. Perhaps he tripped while dancing his own private jig."

"More likely thrown," I said and led him closer to the roped-off area. I pointed to the line of blood drops leading up the wall, then directed his attention to the diversity of the drops' shapes.

Lieutenant Robinson inspected the blood with the nonchalance of a veteran officer who had seen combat. The significance of the drop forms, however, appeared lost upon him.

"Walk with me. You have seen a great amount of shed blood, I don't doubt." I said. "The exigencies of massed battle, however, leave little time for contemplation. Carpentry is a more solitary activity. Alas, with edged tools the occasional bloody injury is a part of the process."

He nodded in agreement. It is the rare man at sea who has not known a four-fingered Chippy.

"A curious mind, a bit of blood, and some quiet allows one to notice the elegance of a pattern," I said. When we arrived at the taffrail I excused myself. I returned shortly with my tools: a plank, a pot of red paint, and a hammer.

I laid the plank flat atop the deck, dipped the tip of the hammer into the pot, and watched the drips of paint fall, the small stains on the wood near perfect circles. Taking up a rag, I wiped the hammer clean and then dragged the head through one of the drops, streaking it and watching it thin as it pulled.

Turning to the lieutenant, I spoke. "Do you see how fallen liquid creates the circular drops? I can assure you that it is the same with blood."

Lieutenant Robinson nodded. "And if something is dragged through the drop, the tails . . ."

"The thinning tails give an indication of the course of travel," I said, completing his thought.

"Like the wake of our sloop."

"From which direction was the wind last night, sir?"

"South southeast."

"Making the area where I found the drops the lee side," I said. As I spoke I carried the plank to the lee side of the quarterdeck and leaned it against the bulwark. "You might stand to the side, sir."

Robinson moved over a step, clearly torn between adhering to my admonition and curious as what might occur next.

I dipped the hammer back into the pot, then swung it violently, staining the board with long thin streaks, less resembling drops than a school of tiny red pilchards. I set down the hammer and turned toward Robinson.

"If you've ever hit your off-hand whilst swinging a sharp tool, you'll have seen these marks."

"That is, if you're not too preoccupied with shouting and oaths," he said.

I agreed.

"So what have you surmised?" he asked.

"Purser Jones was murdered," I said resolutely. "Clubbed down with a belaying pin or some such in the darkness created by the shadows of the quarterdeck and the mizzenmast. 'Twas on the lee side last night, and any sound would be carried to the open sea. The killer dragged him to the bulwark, Jones dripping blood as they went. He was then discarded over the side."

"And who committed this deed?" Robinson asked.

The question had already been turning in my head. "Assuming one man . . . strong enough to drag the bulk of Jones . . . he is likely to have served larboard watch."

Robinson looked at me skeptically.

"Those serving port-side watch would have had greater opportunity to notice the dark corner in which the attack occurred."

He nodded in agreement.

"We should examine the account book. Debt can be a powerful motive," I said.

Robinson paused. "Justice, perhaps."

"What?" I asked.

"A peculiar justice if Jones were to be thrown overboard in the shadow of the mainmast, given to the sea within steps of where he cheated the men from his purser's chest."

Whether the action be just was a question for a stiller time. I needed to see the account book.

We made our way back to the purser's stores. Robinson again produced the key and allowed us inside, leaving the door open for the additional light. There was no point in secrecy now, news of the disappearance had spread from foretop to bilge.

The account book was not among the ship's supplies, so we turned our attention to Jones' chest and dunning. Lifting the chest's lid, I found the record secured to the underside. Together we leaned over the columns and studied them, doing our best to make sense of the entries. The sums my father had taught me were not fully up to the challenge of the accounts. Robinson seemed to move through it with more facility. I looked at him nearly as much as the ledger, his lips silently calculating the figures. When he finished, he pushed back from the book.

"These accounts seem in order," he said. "Purser Jones makes a profit on his sales, that is indisputable, but the amount does not seem unduly excessive."

I turned and looked down at the sea chest. I could feel Robinson's steely gaze on my back. I had accused the purser of cheating the men and gotten Robinson to disparage a fellow officer. The records now shamed us both.

"Let me put the book back," I said. Closing the cover, I returned it to its resting place beneath the lid.

As I made move to replace the lid on the chest, however, I felt an irregularity. Although I could not readily identify it, my hands, which had held so much wood, detected an imbalance in the proportion. I brought the lid near the lantern and studied it more closely. Soon I discovered a false bottom. Inside lay a second book.

Robinson and I traded looks as we opened up the ledger. This time, I stepped back and allowed him full access to the account tables.

"You'd think he was selling suits and not sailcloth breeches and spotted handkerchiefs," he muttered as his finger traced down the page.

Another time I heard the phrase 'for candles' uttered like an oath.

He raised his head and looked at me. "I should hide this book, too, were I he."

We made a list of the debtors and crossed from the list those we did not believe were strong enough or had stood larboard watch.

I pointed out three ordinary seamen from the list who had recently purchased new breeches. I proposed that a premeditated killer would surely have realized that an attack might leave revealing blood on his own clothing.

"Shall we interrogate these three now?" he asked.

"If we are correct," I said, "the killer thought through his plan. It seems unlikely that confronting him would elicit an acknowledgement."

"Then whatever shall we do?" he asked.

I closed the book and thought through our predicament. I tried to concentrate, but again found my mind drifting. Sailors gathered around the roped-off area where the sentry stood. As I watched, they acted out the preservation rituals of superstitious men, attempting to appease the boggart. I could see now why the captain needed an inquiry before fears of ghostly kidnappings seized control of the crew. I watched a sailor having a pig tattooed on his arm as a talisman of good luck. I suddenly found myself remembering an old farmer's story.

"I have an idea," I said, "but we will need the captain."

***

The captain increased the work around the ship as we made ready for port. Make-work though it may have been, the tasks kept the men's attention focused on their duties and less on spirits haunting the ship. When we were in sight of Charleston, he allowed Lieutenant Robinson and me to be rowed into port ahead of the ship in order to make the necessary arrangements. Upon our afternoon return, he ordered the bosun's mate to pipe "all hands." The men gathered expectantly below the quarterdeck.

"Men," he began. God, himself, likely sounded no more authoritative. "On this voyage, we have suffered the grievous loss of Purser Jones."

Here, I could see in the flat expressions of a few of the men that the loss was not necessarily deemed grievous.

"The inquiry into his death is continuing. No man will be released to port until it is complete."

A low murmur moved through the assembly.

The captain paused for a moment before continuing. "Seamen Gilley, Francis, and Tuck, come forward." He instructed the bosun's mate to dismiss the remainder of the crew.

The three seaman, accompanied by musket-ready marines fore and aft, were escorted to the gunroom where officers took meals. All three wide-eyed sailors stood on one side of the officers' dining table. The captain sat opposite them, and Robinson and I took flanking seats at both ends of the table. Accustomed to the tight confines of their quarters, the seamen looked to be alone in a palatial hall of justice, the dark and gloom of the windowless, below-deck space matching their moods.

"One of you murdered Purser Jones," the captain said. "Was it you, Seaman Gilley?"

"No, sir. I swear it," the man answered, voice shaking.

The other two proclaimed innocence as well.

"I expected as much," the captain said solemnly. "Prior to committing to the service, Mr. Marshall was a Connecticut farmer. From his agricultural studies, he knows that donkeys are well recognized for their ability to detect falsehood." The captain paused and allowed the statement to settle before continuing in his stentorian voice. "I, too, have found donkeys to be effective truth engines. Lieutenant Robinson has, therefore, arranged for a jack to be brought quayside. Each of you shall seize his tail and swear to your role in this matter. The donkey will bray upon hearing the lie. Marines, take these men."

The sentries marched the men back to the rowboat. The captain, Lieutenant Robinson, and I joined them, and we were rowed to shore.

***

As darkness settled upon the quay, we led the three seamen to a small tent we had erected. The tent flap was pulled back and a chaplain emerged from the darkness of the interior. The three men stood hunched, shaking in the line, their pigtails rocking like clock pendulums.

"Has the donkey been blessed?" the captain asked.

"As God's agent," the chaplain confirmed.

"Gilley, the donkey inside is now an instrument of truth, of God, and of the naval service. You are instructed to enter the tent. Take the tail within your hand, proclaim in a clear voice whether you committed this crime, and then pull the donkey's tail. Do you understand your orders?"

"Aye, Captain," the seaman answered in a quaking voice.

"Proceed."

The man disappeared as if into Hell. A marine closed the flap. Silence shrouded the field.

A faint mumbling came through the canvas.

"Louder!" the captain ordered.

"I swear I did nothing," came Gilley's trembled testimony.

Suddenly, the tent flap flew back and Gilley stood there with a broad smile across his face.

"The ass didn't say nothin," he cried out in relief.

The marine marched him back to the line and picked Seaman Francis. He, too, entered the tent on shaking knees but emerged triumphant. The donkey remained quiet during Tuck's visit as well.

All three men stood in line, posture more erect now than when they had marched tent-side. Infectious smiles moved back and forth among them.

"Marines," the captain said, "take Seaman Francis into custody."

"Captain," he cried, "the donkey never brayed!"

"Look at your hands, Francis," the captain said solemnly. "We smeared the donkey's tail with soot. You are the only man standing with clean hands. You were afraid to touch his tail."

The eyes of all three men looked down, first at their own hands and then at Francis' palms.

Suddenly Francis pawed at his lanyard and retrieved the rigging knife that hung from his neck. He wagged the blade as he backed away from the rest of us.

The forward marine shouldered and fired his musket.

As the shore authorities carried the body away, Lieutenant Robinson came to where I stood.

"Next time, we must remember to disarm the accused men, Mr. Marshall."

"Lieutenant Robinson, you may call me Chippy."

HE DONE HER WRONG

by Kathryn O'Sullivan

*Mae West's sister has been arrested, and the diamonds
she was wearing are missing. The sister's arrest is not
too surprising, but the missing diamonds were Mae's,
and she's determined to discover the thief . . . with
George Raft's help.*

"Is that a pistol in your pocket or are you just happy to see me?" I
gave Captain Sweeney of the Los Angeles police department the
onceover.

The captain blushed and his fellas snickered.

Jim Timony, my manager and lawyer, cleared his throat. "Miss
West is here to sign the papers. If we could get on with it."

"Aw, what's the rush?" asked Sweeney. "It's not every day we
get a movie star at the station."

You may be wondering what Hollywood's biggest box office
star was doing at the police station on a Saturday night. Believe
me, it was the last place I wanted to be. You see, that evening
Paramount was throwing me a little soiree on account of the
success of my pictures, *She Done Him Wrong* and *I'm No Angel*.
The year 1933 was giving me a lot to celebrate and I was in the
mood for a party. But when my spiritual advisor read me my
horoscope, well, plans changed.

Reverend Edmund Schilling tells my fortune and, on occasion,
holds séances at my apartment. As the cosmos would have it,
Saturday wasn't going to be lucky for me. When I heard Edmund
say the words 'grave danger,' the party was out and I was in.
Needless to say, I was disappointed. It was a big night. I had picked
out a new sequined number and it was a real flash. But the reverend
hasn't been wrong so far, so I stayed in and told my sister, Bev, she
could go in my place since her horoscope was fine.

When I say I 'stayed in,' I don't mean knitting. I was
entertaining a gentleman in my boudoir and the only thing on was
the record player. Then the cops called. Seems Bev was in a
speakeasy instead of at the party with the swells, and I had a pretty
good idea why. Bev has a soft spot for tough men and sweet liquor.

The men I understand, but the liquor—I don't touch the stuff. Don't get me wrong. I'm no angel. I had my share of run-ins with the cops back in New York. Even went to jail for my play, *Sex*. What a stir that caused with the bluenoses. But I know how to wiggle out of a tight spot. Bev's a pretty thing, but she doesn't have my assets.

I called Jim and gave him the lowdown. I asked him to go ahead, find out the particulars, and see if he could get Bev out. When he didn't have any luck, it became clear the situation needed a woman's touch.

I added an extra wiggle when I sashayed into the station. A pug-faced cop sat slumped over the paper at the front desk. When he saw me, he straightened up. Several fellas eyeballed me from a doorway. Nothing I like better than a room full of strong men. Then the captain made his entrance and, as you already know, I admired his pistol.

"So you're the boss," I said to Sweeney. I ran my fingers over his badge and purred. "Fascinating."

Sweeney's cheeks reddened. "We've read good things about you in the papers, Miss West," he said.

"Good, you say? Hmm, I better talk to them. They'll ruin my reputation."

I flashed him a smile. The fellas and Sweeney had a good laugh.

I crossed the room to the pug and leaned against the counter. "So what's this about you fellas arresting my sister?"

The pug got fidgety. "I wouldn't do that," he said. "It was the captain's idea."

I raised a brow at Sweeney. "Is that so?"

"Now don't be sore, Miss West. We didn't know she was your sister when we raided Flynn's. She kept mumbling about some fella stealing her jewels."

"Someone stole my diamonds?"

I had loaned those jewels to Bev on account I thought she was attending a party with the high hats. The jewel set was a real pretty platinum and diamond necklace and bracelet from Paris. Cost me ten grand. That Bev went to a speakeasy was bad; that she lost my diamonds, worse.

"Where is she?" I asked.

The men looked at one another uncomfortable-like and scrammed.

"Right this way," said Sweeney.

The captain ushered Jim and me to the holding cell, then beat a hasty retreat.

Bev caught my eye and hung her head. Her hair and dress were a mess and she stank of booze.

"So you went to a speak and lost my jewels," I said.

"The party was a drag—everyone saying 'Where's Mae?' and 'We thought Miss West was coming.'"

"So it's my fault, is it?"

Bev sniffled.

"Come on, Mae. Don't be so hard on the kid," Jim said.

Like most men, Jim was a sucker for a lady's tears.

"Alright, no waterworks. You'll ruin your paint." I handed Bev a handkerchief. "So what gave you the fool idea to go to a joint like Flynn's?"

"You're not the only one with admirers."

"I got nothing against you having fellas, Bev. It's the kind of fellas you've been seeing that worries me."

"And what kind is that?"

"The kind that get you arrested and my diamonds stolen," I said, trying not to lose my patience.

"That's all you care about. Your precious rocks." She folded her arms and sat down hard on the bench.

I put a hand on my hip. "That's a lousy thing to say." I was good to Bev and she knew it.

Bev wilted like a week-old rose. She had been seeing a lot of men since Sergei divorced her and, in the process, attracting trouble. Me, I never trouble trouble until trouble troubles me. And Bev being in such a state and losing my diamonds troubled me a great deal. Like most dames, Bev was known to do foolish things for a man. I didn't like to think ill of my sister, but I had to consider she might have done something she regretted. I joined her on the bench.

"Okay, honey," I said and brushed a blonde lock from her forehead. "So you blew the party and went to Flynn's."

For the next twenty minutes Bev went on about a fella named Ivan she met at the party. Said he was a real gentleman, got her glass after glass of champagne—the skunk. Bev told Ivan she wanted to dance. Next thing she knew, she was at Flynn's having a swell time—until the joint was raided and my diamonds were pinched. I found it hard to believe she didn't feel the bum lifting my jewels, but that's what she told Jim and me. Then Ivan split and she was in the paddy wagon.

I stole a look at Jim as she finished. Bev seemed dopey. Made me wonder if she'd been slipped a mickey. She broke down sobbing. I signed the release papers and Jim took her home. Then I called George and asked him to meet me at Flynn's. I wanted to find Ivan. Nobody does that to my sister, steals my jewels, and gets away with it.

George Raft and me grew up in New York. Back then, he was part of Owney 'The Killer' Madden's mob and got into his share of fights—most of which I hear he started. Funny how he went out West and made good in pictures playing gangsters. People speculate he's a real-life criminal, maybe on account of his dark features, the scar on his neck from a broad attacking him with a hat pin, and his temper. Him being friends with Lucky Luciano and Mickey Cohen didn't help. But with me, George was on the level. He did me a square and gave me my first part in pictures. *Night After Night* it was called. I played Maudie Triplett. So I called George because he has two things going for him: he's my pal and he can handle himself in a brawl.

I had my chauffeur pull across the street from Flynn's until George got there. The establishment wasn't much to look at. A sign reading Flynn's Grocery hung over a dark wood door. Funny door for a grocery. Two mugs approached the joint and knocked. The door opened and they disappeared inside. I sank back in my seat. I didn't like the looks of those guys. I studied the stones on my fingers. Reverend Schilling had warned me about going out tonight. Maybe coming here wasn't such a good idea.

Headlights approached. George hopped from a Chrysler and signaled the driver to pull into the alley. He spotted me and strolled over.

"Hiya, Mae," he said. "Sorry to keep you."

"Oh, that's okay, Georgie. It gave me time to think."

I touched the side of my chin. He opened the door.

"Don't worry, Mae. I won't let anything happen to that face."

"You better not. It's my fortune."

He closed the door and extended an arm to escort me. "How's Bev?"

"She'll be fine once she sobers up."

He shook his head. "That stuff is poison."

George hates liquor. One of the things I like about him. That, and his good heart. His love of the horses? Well, that I'm not so crazy about. George knocked on the door—once, then three quick times, then once more. The door opened a crack.

"How ya' doing, Charlie?" George said.

"Hey, Georgie," a burly man said and then saw me. "Say, if it ain't Mae West."

Charlie admired me a moment. I didn't mind.

"You gonna let us in?" George asked.

"Sorry. Come in, Miss West."

Charlie was big with strong arms. I resisted squeezing his muscles as I entered. I was here to find the skunk who deserted Bev and took my things.

We followed Charlie past the butcher case. "Didn't expect you back so soon after the raid," he said.

"Didn't expect to be back," George said.

I stole a sideways glance at George. He hadn't mentioned being at Flynn's during the raid when I talked to him on the telephone. George had a habit of taking things that didn't belong to him, especially in speaks like Flynn's.

"Here we are."

Charlie pulled back a curtain in the storage room, revealing a dumbwaiter big enough for two.

"You expect me to get in there?" I asked.

"Unless you prefer the tunnel we use to bring in the hooch."

I took George's hand and squeezed into the lift.

"Nice to meet you, Miss West."

Charlie yanked the rope pulley. The elevator jerked. We went down and Charlie vanished like in one of them vaudeville disappearing acts. There was a dim light in the ceiling. So this was the kind of joint Bev was frequenting. It was a wonder she still had her stockings. Maybe I should have been keeping a better eye on her.

Jazz and laughter echoed up the shaft. Seems the raid hadn't closed the place for long. The cops must have taken a bribe. Smoke wafted into the elevator. I pulled my collar over my face. I hate cigars. Never could understand why Father smoked them. The music got louder. It had a nice sound. George wrapped an arm around my waist.

"Something on your mind?" I said.

"You know what."

"I don't do encores, you rascal," I said and gently pulled away.

George smiled. He has a nice smile. Too bad you don't see it in his pictures. I guess the studio doesn't think audiences will buy him as a gangster if he shows his pearly whites. The elevator shook.

"Looks like we're here," George said and pulled back a curtain.

The room was all dark mahogany wood and warm lights from Tiffany lampshades. Everywhere, Johns and Janes. The band played in a corner.

"Hey, look who it is," someone said.

I shook hands and signed autographs as we made our way to a table. One fella had me sign his shirt. He'd have a time explaining that to his missus. I locked eyes with a debonair fella watching from across the room. He tipped his hat. I gave him the onceover.

Hmm. Not bad.

"Alright, alright, let's give Miss West some air," George said.

The crowd dispersed. George showed me to a table along the wall and signaled a waiter to wipe off my chair.

"Why didn't you tell me you were here tonight?" I asked when George was seated.

"You act like I pulled a fast one. I figured it would be better to talk in person. You asked me here, remember?"

He had me there. "I appreciate it, George, really I do. I guess this thing with Bev has me more upset than I realized. She knows better than to go to a honky-tonk with a strange man. Something worse than losing my diamonds could have happened. Why would she do such a thing?"

"Don't worry. I was keeping an eye on things. It's just hard on the kid, being the sister of Mae West."

"Try being the sister of Beverly West," I said, my dander up.

"Yeah, but you pulled Paramount outta bankruptcy. I mean look at you. The hair, the hips, the—"

"Are you helping me or cataloging my assets?"

George laughed. "You have a lot to catalog."

"Hey, no cracks now."

George waved over a man in a nice suit. I figured he was the manager on account of how he watched the room.

"To what do we owe the honor of your presence, Miss West?" he asked.

"I understand my sister, Beverly, was here tonight."

"Blonde like Mae. Wearing a lot of sparklers," George said.

"Ah, yes," the manager said. "She was here with a Russian gentleman. I think he said his name was Ivan, or maybe Igor. His accent was hard to understand. You remember, Georgie. You said he looked familiar."

"Yeah," George said and then snapped his fingers. "I know where I seen him."

"Where?" I said, anxious to know the identity of the Russian thief.

"At the studio. He wants to be an actor."

I raised a brow. "Does he know we do talkies now?"

"Well, waddya know," the manager said. "There he is."

The manager pointed to the debonair fella with the hat. So, that's Ivan. George sprang from his chair, charged through the crowd, grabbed Ivan by the collar, and cocked a fist.

"Where's the jewels?" George said.

"You gotta stop him," I said to the manager. I wanted George to help, but not that much.

The manager pulled George back but not before George had roughed the Russian up a bit. I actually felt sorry for the fella. I crossed the room. Ivan stumbled to his feet. Despite being knocked about, the man bowed when I reached him. I had to hand it to him. He knew how to play a part.

"So you think it's alright to slip my sister a mickey?"

Ivan looked confused.

"Don't act like you don't know what Miss West is talking about," George said. "Did you put something in the lady's drink?"

"No," he said. "I have no mickey."

The guy's accent was thick as molasses. Too bad. With a face like that, he could have been big.

"Then what about my diamonds?" I said. "The ones you stole from Bev."

"I have no mickey and no diamonds."

"I'll beat the truth outta you," George said.

Ivan shrunk against the wall.

"Easy," I said and patted George's chest to calm him. Ivan wasn't any good to me unconscious. "What did you want with my sister then?"

"I thought she could introduce me to the enchanting Mae West."

So that was his angle. He was using Bev to get to me. "Why'd you want to meet me?"

Ivan looked at his feet. Peculiar fella. That's not where men usually look when they meet me.

"Answer the lady," George said.

"It was my hope you could put me in picture. Like you did Mr. Grant," Ivan said.

So he wanted me to pluck him off the lot like I did Cary. That gave me an idea. "I'm having a little get-together tomorrow night. Why don't you come?"

"You give me screen test?" Ivan asked.

Just like that, the mug forgot all about Bev and the trouble he was in.

"Yeah," I said. "A screen test."

"Have you lost your mind?" George said.

"Will Mr. Grant be there?" Ivan asked.

"Sure," I said, ignoring George poking me in the side. "I'm at the Ravenswood on North Rossmore, near Paramount. Tell the doorman and he'll ring you up."

"Thank you, Miss West," Ivan said and kissed my hand.

"Don't thank me yet," I said. "Now scram before I change my mind."

Ivan beat it. George stared at me in disbelief.

"Don't worry, Georgie," I said. "I got it all figured out."

I hadn't been fixing to have a party, but after my visit to Flynn's I had a plan about how to trap the Russian and get my jewels back. I'd invite Reverend Schilling and have him read Ivan's future. Schilling is also psychic and could tell me if Ivan was lying.

I told George to meet me at my apartment the next night and leave the fisticuffs at home. Then I had Jim invite Bev, Sweeney, and Cary. I needed Bev there to see what a rat her beau was and to find out if she had a hand in my diamonds going missing. Sweeney was there to arrest the hoodlum. As for Cary, well, I couldn't have Ivan knowing what I was up to, so I invited him. Plus, Cary would be nice to look at.

I was finishing getting dressed for the evening when there was a knock on my bedroom door. Jim peeked in.

"Everyone's here," he said.

"Help me with this zipper, would ya'?"

Jim closed the door, came over and pulled up the zipper on the back of my dress.

"How do I look?"

Jim stared at me in the vanity mirror. "Lovely."

"Lovely enough to catch a thief?"

"You caught me," he said and touched my shoulders.

"Now don't start with that. I need you focused." Jim and me had had a thing once, but that was ancient history, at least for me.

Thunder rumbled. Even Mother Nature was mad about my diamonds.

I took Jim's arm and strolled into the living room. Ivan talked to Cary by the piano, Bev sulked on the chaise, George paced by the door, Sweeney admired the view out my window, and Edmund—that is Reverend Schilling—set up his table. I had told Edmund to dress the part, but I didn't expect the lavender ascot, headdress, and sequin jacket.

"Good evening," I said.

"Is it?" Bev snapped.

Ivan had thrown Bev over for Cary and she was none too happy about it.

"I see you've met Ivan," I said to Cary.

Cary gave me one of his amused looks. "You're up to something."

"Hmm, you outta know," I said.

How I liked that guy. Maybe I'd put him in a third picture.

"I'm ready for screen test," Ivan said.

"No need to rush," I said and sat at a round table in the middle of the room. "Reverend Schilling's gonna tell our fortunes."

Edmund made sure everyone sat in a particular spot. George sat next to me, Bev next to him, then Edmund, Ivan and the captain. Cary said he didn't believe in fortunes so he'd watch from the wings. I didn't suspect him so that was fine. Jim stood guard at the door in case the Russian made a run for it.

"Looks like we're all here," I said to Edmund.

Edmund arranged crystals, Tarot cards, and incense on the table. "Who would like to go first?" he asked.

Bev stole a look at Ivan who squirmed in his chair. George tensed. I put my hand on his leg. I didn't need him blowing things. The captain wiped sweat from his lip. Odd because my apartment was cool. Maybe it was his uniform. I would have told him to wear something regular but he was here to make an arrest.

"Ivan wants to be in pictures like you, Cary," I said, breaking the silence.

"So I understand," Cary said.

"He's handsome enough, don't you think, Bev?" I asked.

Ivan puffed like a peacock.

Bev scowled. She was thinking I had designs on her beau, but it was her I was testing. If she was sweet on the fella, she'd cover for him. But if Ivan threw her over for me and a chance at being in a picture, Bev might not be so loyal.

"Maybe you could tell Ivan about his future in the movies," I said to Edmund.

"Yes," Ivan said with enthusiasm.

Edmund closed his eyes.

"What do you see?" Ivan asked.

"I see a man. You two are struggling."

Ivan shot George a worried look.

"And Miss West is there," Edmund said.

Bev glared at me. "Ivan's with you, is he?" she said as if she had caught me cheating with her man behind her back. "You just couldn't leave him alone. Had to take him for yourself." Bev rose and flung herself on the chaise.

"Continue," I said. I didn't want Bev's fella, but I didn't want her knowing that. Not yet. "Where is Ivan during this struggle?" I asked.

"A very beautiful place with soft lights and satin."

Ivan looked less worried.

"Sounds like this apartment," Sweeney said.

"Yes," Edmund said.

"Why am I fighting in Miss West's apartment? I come for

screen test."

"I'll give you a screen test," George said under his breath.

I shot George a look. Thunder rumbled.

"Perhaps you're rehearsing a scene," Edmund said.

"With Mr. Raft?" I asked.

Edmund's brows furrowed. "No." He suddenly opened his eyes, pulled a handkerchief from his jacket, and dabbed his forehead.

"What did you see?" I asked. "Something about my diamonds?"

"Again, the diamonds," Ivan said. "Beverly, tell Miss West I am innocent."

"Why? So you can be with her in her pictures?" Bev said through tears. Poor kid. She was really sweet on the Russian.

Ivan rose. So did George. The Russian crossed to Bev and sat next to her.

"I am not ashamed of wanting to be in pictures," Ivan said. "Please, tell your sister I do not have her jewelry. I am gentleman."

I had seen that look in a lot of fellas' eyes. It was clear as crystal Ivan had taken a shine to Bev. I stole a look at Edmund, my human lie detector, to be certain I was right. There he was dabbing his forehead again. What did he have to be nervous about? And then it hit me. Him warning me not to go to the party and knowing Bev would. Why that double-crossing rat.

"Tell me, Reverend," I said, rising. "When you told me not to go out last night because it was bad luck, it wasn't because you read it in my stars, was it?"

Thunder rumbled. Edmund backed away from the table.

"You wanted Bev to go out instead of me. You knew I'd lend her my jewels, figured she'd be an easy mark. Isn't that right?"

Edmund looked at the captain.

"What are you looking at him for?" I said.

"Why don't you ask him?" Edmund asked.

"Are you saying Sweeney had something to do with it?" I asked.

Sweeney wiped his brow. "You're all screwy," he said.

"Of all the low . . ." George said and reached for Sweeney.

I stepped between the captain and George. "You made me a promise," I said. I didn't want George messing up my beautiful apartment. "So that's why you're all wet," I said to Sweeney. "You planned the raid to cover lifting my jewels and now you're found out."

"That's not true, Miss West," said Sweeney. "Schilling set it up with one of my guys, but I didn't know about the scheme until just before I came here. I have men searching my fella's place for your diamonds right now."

"Why didn't you tell me, you big mug?"

"I suspected an inside job. I didn't know it was Schilling until now. Besides," he said and rubbed his neck, "it's not every day I get invited to a Hollywood party."

"What a load of bull," George said. "Why the LA coppers are as crooked as a dog's hind leg."

George had a point. But even if the captain had a hand in the heist, it would be tough proving it. I strolled to Sweeney with my hand on my hip and stared him straight in the eyes. "Are you on the level?"

"I may not be Einstein but I'm not dumb enough to pinch the sister of Mae West. We have enough bad publicity."

One thing I knew was how to read men. "I believe you," I said and patted his chest. "As for you," I said turning to Edmund. "Shame on you for using my belief in the spiritual against me. Upsetting my sister. Making her land in stir. Haven't I shown you respect? Paid you fair? Well? Haven't I?"

"Yes," Edmund said.

"So why'd you do it?"

"He owes Jack Tarantelli dough," George said.

"How do you know that?" Edmund was stunned. I was, too.

"Jackie's my bookie," George said.

"This is a misunderstanding, Miss West," Edmund said. "I'm innocent."

"Tell it to Sweeney," I said and signaled the captain.

Then the rat pulled a gun on me. Before George or Sweeney could grab the pistol, Ivan crossed the room faster than the lightning outside my window and tackled Edmund. The men wrestled, arms and legs flying, until George and Jim grabbed them and Sweeney took the gun. It was a miracle nothing got broken.

"Well done," Cary said and shook the Russian's hand.

Jim and Sweeney lifted Edmund to his feet.

"Say," George said to Ivan. "Jackie's looking for a guy to settle accounts for—"

"No, you don't, George Raft," Bev said, pulling Ivan away and hugging him tightly.

The doorbell rang. "I'll get it," I said and opened the door.

Two cops dragged the pug in. He looked like he had been gone over pretty good. So the pug was really a weasel.

"Are these your rocks, Miss West?" a cop asked and handed me a sack.

I pulled out a necklace and bracelet. "These are them."

Sweeney put the cuffs on Edmund and left with his men and the pug.

The next day LAPD took credit for the arrest. They left out details about Edmund being my advisor and them having a crooked cop. It's the one time I was happy not to have publicity. Why, if word got out I solved the case, people would think I was a regular Bulldog Drummond. I can see the shingle now: MAE WEST. MOVIE STAR. PRIVATE EYE. COME UP AND SEE ME. Say. That's not bad. Not bad at all.

THE CORPSE CANDLE

by Martin Edwards

Lowborn, beautiful Rhiannon marries Prince Brochwel
after he spies her in a crowd, but this fairytale
beginning may not have a happy ending. In a story with
many twists and turns, the end will make you gasp.

A few hours ago, I feared I would die before the night was out.
Now all is quiet. We are alone with each other, and safe. I shall
dare to tell you the story of the murders, but after tonight, you will
never hear me speak of them again.

At least Father's passing was natural. I had cared for him, as
well as for my brother Owain, since we lost our mother when I was
eleven years old. The farm was set in a scrap of pasture amidst the
moorland, under the forbidding shadow of Foel Eryr. It took the
efforts of all three of us to scratch a living and keep body and soul
together. I am sure Father realised that his time was short, for he
was frequently unwell and often spoke of how we would cope after
his passing. While Owain was to take charge of the farm, I should
keep house. I suspect that my brother found the prospect as
unappealing as I did. Owain had a sweetheart in Morfil, and
Kenedlon was a fiery woman who would have no wish to share her
home with a spinster sister-in-law. For my part, I had no wish to
spend the rest of my life as an unpaid drudge for a married couple.

Our life was not unrelieved gloom. The harshness of our
existence was softened by those evenings when my father would
call Owain and me together in front of the fire and recount stories
that the two of us always found thrilling. Tales of the Otherworld,
of mermaids and giants, of the little fair people and the Sunken
Lands. The legends unlocked my imagination, and from an early
age I repeated the stories to myself in bed, dreaming of a life
overflowing with miracles and untold riches.

One chilly night at the end of May, I had a taste of freedom
when Owain took me to the market at St David's. I was to be his
excuse, so that he could conduct an illicit tryst with Kenedlon. I
readily agreed, since the trip gave me the opportunity, however
briefly, to spread my own wings. The visit to St David's made me
all the more determined to break away from the lower slopes of the

Preseli Hills. The chance came all too soon. One night, Father started with a hoarse, racking cough. Within hours, the first man I ever loved was dead.

***

"Rhiannon," my brother said in a low voice after the funeral. "Did you see the Corpse Candle?"

I stared at him. "What are you talking about?"

"I saw it, Sister," he whispered. "Just as Father described it. You remember, surely? The sign that St David prayed for, so that people should be able to prepare themselves for a death?"

"I know the story, of course," I said reluctantly. The only way to cope with our father's death, I had decided, was not to dwell upon it, but rather to think about anything other than the old man with the tender smile, and here was my brother, reminding me of our nights spent listening to him. "The Corpse Candle is seen passing along the route of a funeral, or hovering near the spot where someone is to die. But . . . "

"On the evening Father took ill, I saw from outside a light in the room next to the kitchen. Yet when I entered the house, I found no light," Owain said.

"Your mind was playing tricks," I said. "It was only a story, like that of the Water Horse of St Bride's Bay or the Mermaid at Aberbach."

He shook his head. "That room where I saw the light, it is the same room where we laid Father to rest, when he was coughing so terribly and could not manage to reach his bed."

"What's this?" a high-pitched voice demanded. "Owain, shame on you! You are terrifying the poor girl!"

We had been joined by Kenedlon. She linked arms with Owain and I saw a possessive gleam in her hazel eyes. I felt a sudden rush of sympathy for my brother. He was no match for her and I was reaffirmed in my determination to carve out a new life.

"The legend came true," he said mulishly.

Kenedlon simply laughed and led her trophy away to be admired by her proud and stupid parents.

I did not waste time. My father had a cousin, Rhodri, who lived a little way outside Pembroke and I persuaded him to offer me lodging at his farm in return for keeping his house. One day, when Rhodri was out in the fields, I walked into the centre of the town to watch a procession of soldiers heading towards the castle.

That was the first time I saw Brochwel. It would have been impossible to miss him. He led the procession, a tall and fearsomely dressed man, with long flowing hair and a beard, resembling one of the giants my father had loved to describe. This was a man capable of the tremendous feats of strength recounted in legend, of tearing up trees or hurling the great stone from the summit of Freni Fawr to Llanfyrnach far below.

I made no effort to conceal my admiration or my sense of awe. Our eyes met and his gaze lingered upon me. I felt the heat of his stare, imagined him picturing what lay beneath my simple dress. My whole body tingled. It was as if at last I had cause to believe that dreams could indeed come true.

He gave me a quick nod before marching on. I turned to a wizened old woman standing beside me in the crowd.

"Who was that?" I asked innocently.

She treated me to a gap-toothed grin. "Do you not know, my dear?"

"Would I need to ask the question if I did?"

"That is Brochwel."

My mouth fell open. "But . . . "

Her laugh reminded me of the cackling witches my father used to describe. "Yes, my dear, I saw the way he looked at you. He is a man, after all. More than that, he is a prince of Dyfed."

"He is very handsome," I said.

"Well, he is a fine figure of a man," the old woman chuckled. "And you know, he is not spoken for. His wife died last year and he has yet to return to the altar. His mistresses are two-a-penny, my dear, and you are so lovely. Now you've caught his eye, I bet he'll not spare them a second glance."

I had no reason to doubt her honesty. She had, as she said, seen how he looked at me. With, I told myself—although still hardly daring to credit it—love in his eyes.

As I drifted away from the crowd, a young man approached me.

"Excuse me, but I am Pryderi, cousin and aide to Brochwel of Dyfed. The prince asked me to enquire your name."

"And why does he trouble to put the question?" I asked boldly.

"He says you will learn the answer tonight, in the castle hall."

"I will?"

"Assuredly. A feast is being held to celebrate my cousin's triumph in battle against the brigands from the north."

"What if I am unable to attend?"

"An invitation from a prince is not to be spurned."

"Very well, I accept his invitation."

He allowed himself a smile. "Thank you. And your name?"

"It is Rhiannon," I said. To myself, I said: Rhiannon and Brochwel. Trying out the names together. The coupling had a certain charm.

***

Brochwel was waiting for me at the castle gate that evening. As I approached, Pryderi, who was standing at the prince's side, gave me a quick wave of greeting then slipped away, leaving the two of us alone.

"Rhiannon," Brochwel said simply. I liked his voice. It was deep and strong.

I bowed. "My lord."

"You will sit by my side at the feast."

"I am honoured," I said quietly. "But there are many other women, far worthier than—"

"You are the one whose company I seek."

"I do not understand, my lord. You do not even know me."

"I have seen you," he said, "and that is enough. You were watching the procession."

At close quarters I was struck by the sheer size and physical power of the man. He was no longer young, but he was taller and broader than anyone I had ever known. Yet I was aware of an uncertainty inside the vast frame, a hidden weakness that few would even guess at.

"Celebrating your triumph," I said.

He laughed, a sound like a thunderclap. "You think me immodest?"

"Not at all, my lord. You have vanquished your enemies, your people are devoted to you. You have earned your garlands."

"So you think I have everything, do you, Rhiannon?"

I looked into his eyes. "Surely, my lord."

"I'm afraid I do not," he said.

"Well," I rejoined, my gaze unwavering, "I am sure at least that you can have everything you want."

"Everything?" he asked.

This was my moment. I smiled and said, "Everything."

***

The betrothal of Brochwel, prince of Dyfed, to an unknown young woman from a remote farming community was announced the day after the feast. I had not left Brochwel's side since he beckoned me to join him at the castle gate. In a few short hours, we had become as one. My lover was captivated by me. He told me so, time and again but even if his tongue had been cut out, I could have read the devotion in his eyes. I felt intoxicated. For so long I had dreamed of a better life, and now it was coming true.

Yet soon clouds emerged on the horizon. I suspected that not everyone was pleased by my arrival in the castle. In particular, I worried how Gowein, Brochwel's devoted mother, would regard me. Thus I took special pains to establish friendly relations with her. I told her the story of my own mother's death and of how since childhood I had missed the wise counsel of an older woman. When I said I prayed that she might supply the lack, she nodded gravely.

"You will be wife to my first born," she said. "I wish the two of you a long, happy, and fruitful life together."

Something in my expression must have given me away, for she clutched my hand and said earnestly, "Fruitful, yes. Brochwel must have told you of our family's great sadness when both his children died in infancy."

I nodded. Disease had carried off first the little boy and then his sister. Brochwel's wife had striven in vain to give him an heir before dying in childbirth. The tragedy of her passing had deterred him from seeking a hasty remarriage, but he was keenly aware of the need to continue the line. I did not doubt his love for me, but I realised also that he saw in me a young, healthy woman, the ideal mother for a successor to his throne. I had no objection to that. I had always wanted to have children of my own, children of a man who adored me, children to whom I would recount legends in front of the fire, as Father had done to entertain Owain and me.

I cleared my throat. "Gowein, there is something I wish to raise with you."

She gripped my hand. "What is it, my dear?"

"It is about Elfin."

Yes, Elfin, brother to Brochwel.

Her face darkened. "What about Elfin?"

"I do not believe . . . " My voice faltered. "I am sorry, Gowein. It is nothing. Please forget that I mentioned his name."

She squeezed my hand more tightly. "Tell me, please."

Her voice was clear and firm. Although she was no longer a young woman, she was accustomed to obedience and I dared not refuse to speak.

"I fear . . . I believe that he dislikes me."

"What makes you think that?" she demanded.

"Oh, I do not know. Perhaps I am imagining it. I am sure I have done nothing to cause him offence."

"One need not provoke Elfin to earn his enmity," Gowein said softly.

I was shocked by her words. She was his mother, after all. "Forgive me," I said hurriedly. "It is just a fancy I have. He has not said anything unkind to me. At least, nothing deliberately unkind."

"Even though . . . " As Gowein began to speak, the door of the chamber swung open and a handsome dark-haired man appeared. He bore a resemblance to Brochwel in the shape of his cheeks and jaw, but the likeness was superficial. Where Brochwel was strong and commanding, this fellow was slender and almost womanish in the way he slipped into the room.

"I am sorry, Mother, if I am interrupting."

"Elfin," Gowein said dryly. "We were just talking about you."

"Oh, really?" He shot a glance in my direction. "Rhiannon, my dear. I shall soon have to learn to call you Sister, won't I? Were you confessing to second thoughts? Perhaps you aren't quite sure that you chose the right brother?"

I curled my lip. In a short time, I had gained a confidence undreamed of during those long years spent toiling at the foot of the Preseli Hills.

"I promise you, Elfin, I have made no mistake."

"Sure?" he prodded, a smirk upon his lips.

"Elfin!" his mother snapped. "It will be the worse for you if Brochwel gets to hear that you have tormented Rhiannon."

"I would sooner die than harm Rhiannon," he said, affecting a noble pose.

"Elfin! You have said enough."

"I only came to express my congratulations," he said, pretending innocence. "I have come from Brochwel's chamber. He tells me that the wedding is to take place on the last Saturday of this month. I tell you frankly, Rhiannon, my brother is besotted with you. It is as if you are a witch who has woven a spell upon him."

"I am no witch," I said, returning his gaze. "I merely wish to make my husband happy."

He gave me a frankly lascivious glance and said, "I am sure you will do just that."

He turned and, at the door, paused. To his mother he said, "Brochwel's tastes have always been simple to the point of crudity, have they not?"

When he was gone, I started to cry. Gowein came up to me and put an arm around my shoulder.

"Hush," she said. "You must take no notice of him. He was always a difficult boy. Where Brochwel was forthright and uncomplicated, Elfin always loved to plot and make mischief. Perhaps it is my fault. He was born when I thought I was past childbearing years. Brochwel was twenty and already hardened by battle. Perhaps that is why I spoiled Elfin. Besides, he has always possessed a certain charm."

"I'm afraid it has escaped me," I said, drying my tears.

"You must understand," Gowein said, "Elfin is jealous of his brother. He is intelligent and to him it seems unfair that he has no power. What he fails to realise is that he is no warrior, whereas

Brochwel is fearless. Elfin does not lack vanity, either. He is a well-favoured man. But a pretty young thing like you was bound to choose a strong man ahead of a weaker one."

I shivered. "He frightens me."

"There is no need." A note of decision entered Gowein's voice. I guessed that she had made up her mind about something. "I shall speak to Brochwel this very evening. He will despatch Elfin on business to Ireland where he can do no harm."

Although at first Brochwel was reluctant to send his brother across the sea, eventually he assented. I spoke to him that night about the matter and mentioned my dislike of Elfin.

"Ah, he is not as bad as you suggest," Brochwel said.

"I believe he is much worse."

Brochwel laughed. He was in high good humour and proved it by pushing his hand beneath my dress. I shrieked and tried in vain to dance out of his reach. Within a few moments, my apprehensions were forgotten.

Elfin did not return to Dyfed in time to attend the wedding. I was not sorry. I wanted nothing to distract me on that special day. Owain and Kenedlon did make the journey and it struck me as a delicious irony that after my long years of innocence, I had married before even they had taken their vows.

And what a marriage I had made! My husband looked every inch the prince he was. He towered over me, except when the two of us were alone and I could make him do my bidding, have him kneel and plead for my good word.

***

The showers of spring gave way to the burning sun of summer, the hottest I could recall. Shortly after our wedding, I discovered that I was with child. Gowein, as a woman would, guessed the truth, but before I was ready to give the news to my husband, I lost the baby. My indisposition caused me to be confined to a room of my own on the ground floor of the castle, but Brochwel and his mother were equally solicitous. One morning he admitted to me that Gowein had told him what had happened.

"You will have another baby," he announced.

I smiled. "As it happens, I felt better on waking than I have done since . . . since it happened."

"You are ready to return to the marriage bed?"

He was breathing heavily. I knew how impatient my husband was for an heir. The long years of battle had taken their toll. He had resolved to live each day as if it were his last.

"Tonight," I said, nodding.

He beamed and his happiness was so infectious that I smiled as

I said, "I have missed you, Brochwel."

"At last we can be man and wife again," he said eagerly, enfolding me in his bear-like embrace.

"You have been so patient . . . "

"It has not been easy."

"Then perhaps you deserve a reward."

He smiled at me, wondering what I had in mind. When I told him, he let out an exuberant shout of delight.

***

I had promised to give my husband his prize at a place which held special memories for us. On the afternoon following the feast, he had taken me to the coast and we had made love on the shore of a lonely cove. I took him back there and we walked hand in hand along the beach, teasing each other about names we might give to our child. It would, of course, be a boy.

Brochwel pulled me down onto the sand and started to undress, but I jumped up again and skipped out of reach. When he lumbered after me, I raised a hand and told him to shut his eyes and count to one hundred.

"What do you have in mind?" He was sweating in the heat. I could smell his excitement.

"Trust me."

He closed his eyes as instructed and I ran off, laughing as I scrambled up the steep slopes of the cliff. I could hear him counting, slowly, carefully.

"Seventeen, eighteen, nineteen . . . "

The way up the cliff was narrow and difficult. I suppose it was dangerous, but that did not concern me. Owain had nicknamed me The Sheep because of my surefooted climbing skills. This was no more of a challenge than the Freni Fawr at the eastern end of the Preseli mountains.

"Sixty-nine, seventy, seventy-one . . . "

Panting, I pulled myself up onto the summit. Once I was on firm ground, I began to tear off my clothes with reckless abandon. Brochwel's voice was distant now, drifting up in the light summer breeze.

"Ninety-two, ninety-three, ninety-four . . . "

Naked, I peered down to sea level and my husband. The drop was almost sheer.

"Come to claim your reward!" I cried as he reached one hundred.

He opened his eyes and looked up at me. I smiled and waved. With a cry of pleasure, he began to clamber up the cliff. Not for one moment did I doubt that he would reach the peak. Although heavily built, he, too, was accustomed to rough terrain. I heard him panting as he climbed towards me. I moved back from the precipice and lay down on the parched grass, waiting for Brochwel to claim me.

We made love with a passion I had never known before and when we were done, I demanded more. He gave a roar of ecstasy and complied, but just as he entered me again, he let out a different kind of cry, a cry of pain and dismay.

"What is it?" I gasped.

Suddenly he pitched over and collapsed onto his side, clutching his heart.

"Brochwel?" I cried. "Brochwel?"

***

A week after the funeral, I was sitting alone in my chamber, as had become my custom since Brochwel's death. Elfin had returned to the castle as soon as he heard the news and taken charge. He was now the prince of Dyfed and I no more than a weeping widow. Small wonder that I stayed in my room, staring out of the little window at the moon which shone above the sleeping town, trying to conjure a picture in my mind of what the future might hold.

Gowein had told Elfin to show me kindness. He had assented readily enough; he could afford to be generous. I saw little of him, as he took pains to respect my mourning, but in his mother's presence he told me that I was welcome to treat the castle as my home. He said he was determined that he and I should become the best of friends.

Gowein was affected even more than I was by the death of her son. If Brochwel's heart had burst, hers had surely broken. I tried once or twice to engage her in conversation, but she did no more than indulge in a few banal pleasantries before saying that her head ached and that she needed rest.

Suddenly I heard a dreadful scream. My imagination playing tricks? Surely there could be no other explanation. I pulled my wrap around me and opened the door. I expected darkness, but instead I saw the faint flicker of a candle, hovering above the passageway. Chilled to the bone, I stopped in my tracks. In the dead of night, I could not help remembering my father's stories and his tale of the Corpse Candle.

How absurd. Even as I waited, the flame disappeared. I must have dreamed it, as well as the scream. I took a step forward, then paused again. I could hear footsteps coming in my direction. Holding my breath, I saw another flame lighting up the gloom, moving closer to me.

"Who is it?" I called out.

"It is me, Gowein."

My mother-in-law sounded strangely agitated. I waited as she approached.

"What are you doing abroad at this hour?" I asked.

Her face appeared, illumined by the flame. "Did you hear the scream?"

"I wondered if I had been having a nightmare."

"You did not dream that terrible noise," she said, reaching out and taking my hand.

"Gowein," I stammered. "I do not understand. What is happening?"

"You are afraid?"

"Yes."

"Afraid . . . of Elfin?"

"Of Elfin?" I repeated stupidly. "What do you mean?"

"I have always been afraid of Elfin," she said. "Ever since he was a small boy, tearing the wings off flies."

"Since his return he has been good to me," I said.

"Oh yes, now that he has what he always wanted." She gave a bitter laugh and led me into my room. "Come. I shall tell you about Elfin."

We sat down side by side on the edge of my rumpled bed. "Gowein," I said gently, for I had begun to suspect that the loss of her elder son had pushed her into madness. "You are talking in riddles. What is this about Elfin?"

"He was jealous of Brochwel," she said. "Even as a child, he envied his brother. I saw it, but I was too weak. There was an incident with an axe, passed off as horseplay, but Brochwel came within inches of losing his head."

"You cannot be saying that Elfin wanted Brochwel dead? I do not believe it!"

"It is true," Gowein insisted. "Later, while Brochwel travelled far and wide, Elfin retreated within himself. He was such a good-looking boy that I was ready to forgive and forget. Forgive his wickedness, forget the harm that he wanted to do to his brother. Stupid of me."

"Elfin is not violent!" I cried. "He is bookish, not in the least a warrior."

"Nonetheless, I hold him responsible for Brochwel's death."

"What are you talking about?" I cried, genuinely alarmed. "That was a tragic accident."

"I think not," Gowein said. "I believe my son was murdered, as truly as if Elfin plunged a dagger into his heart."

"This is madness!" I sobbed. "You do not know what you are saying."

She gazed into my eyes. "I know precisely what I am saying, Rhiannon. As you do."

"You accuse me?" I gasped.

"Something puzzled me," Gowein said in a faraway voice. "I believed that you and Elfin had plotted to kill Brochwel, but I did not understand how the conspiracy could have originated. Stray words from my late sister's boy, Pryderi, confirmed my suspicions of Elfin. I asked Pryderi to undertake some investigative work on my behalf, and he reported back this evening. I gather that you visited St David's at the same time as Elfin was there. That was where you met. I suppose the pair of you fell in love. At all events, you hatched your plot. You would travel to Pembroke with a view to seducing Brochwel and becoming his bride."

"Absurd!"

"No false modesty, Rhiannon, please. For such a beauty, it was not a difficult task. The first part of your plan accomplished, you had a further goal. Elfin confided in you that Brochwel's heart was frail, a secret known only to the three of us. Elfin wanted you to contrive the circumstances where his brother's heart would be strained to its bursting point. Then you could safely leave nature to take its course." She paused. "As it did when you lost Brochwel's child. Or are my darker suspicions founded in truth? Did you give nature a helping hand so that you would not give birth to a baby sired by a husband for whom you cared nothing?"

"This is intolerable!"

"I agree," Gowein said. "Alas, it is also true."

"You believe I betrayed my husband and contrived to ensure his death? You dare to suggest that I destroyed my own unborn child out of sheer malice?"

"Acts of such wickedness," she said evenly, "cannot go unpunished."

"I suppose," I murmured, "you claim that we wanted Elfin to be sent far away so that no one could hint that he played a part in Brochwel's death?"

"You acted so prettily," Gowein said. "I genuinely believed that you disliked Elfin. Instead, you lusted after him."

"I came to realise," I said slowly, "that much of what you said about him was true."

"You were his pawn," she said, not troubling to hide her scorn.

"He is your own flesh and blood—and yet you hate him."

"Even a mother cannot remain blind forever." Gowein said, shrugging. "But he will do no more harm."

"What do you mean?"

For an answer, she reached inside her gown and pulled out a knife. Touching the blade, I felt a warm stickiness upon it.

"I have killed my own son," she said in a hollow voice.

"And now you intend to kill me." I gave a bitter laugh. "I should have realised when I saw the Corpse Candle."

There was a look of sorrow in her eyes. "There is nothing else I can do. Brochwel must be avenged."

She lifted the knife, but I was younger and faster and more desperate. I seized her wrist and forced it downwards. I heard a bone snap and then the blade plunged into her breast. She cried out and fell backwards. I forced the knife home and within a moment I was standing over her body. Yes, the Corpse Candle had presaged another death. But not mine.

I heard footsteps in the darkness.

"They are all gone!" I cried. "Brochwel, Elfin, Gowein."

And Pryderi, my handsome Pryderi, came running down the corridor and into my arms.

***

Nine months have passed since then, my little one. Pryderi, the same Pryderi with whom I fell in love when he gave me Brochwel's message, is Prince of Dyfed and I am his proud consort. Tonight our union has been given a special blessing. I have presented him with a son and heir.

Your birth was slow and agonising, my sweet. There was a time when I believed that neither of us would survive. But now you are here in my arms, a small warm bundle of humanity. I have a child of my own, a child to love and cherish, a child to whom I shall tell stories of wizards and saints and fearsome beasts. Yet I shall make no further mention of the Corpse Candle. There will be no more deaths in this household. For you and I shall live happily ever after.

DEATH ON THE DUELING GROUNDS

by Verena Rose

*In 1859 Washington, freedman Noah Hackett calls
Constable Wallace to the site of a gruesome death. But
the dead man is a slave catcher, so many people had
good reason to wish him dead. Wallace is obliged to
discover the killer . . . but he doesn't have to like it.*

Washington City – 1859

Someone was beating on the door. Hezekiah "Zeke" Wallace had
only just fallen asleep after a long day on duty. As a constable, he
was responsible for patrolling a large section of the city and his last
shift had been a long one. He got up, stepped groggily over the cat
lying in the middle of the rug, and headed downstairs.

"Who is it?" he asked through the closed door.

"It's me, Noah, sir," came a muted reply. "Master Horace sent
me to fetch you right away."

Zeke opened the door. "Noah, what is so urgent that Horace
would send you here at night after curfew? It isn't safe for you to
be out after dark. Come inside and tell me what's happened."

"He knows, Mr. Zeke, but he couldn't leave to come get you
hisself. I said I'd come because I can get around the city without
being seen. There's been a murder at the old Bladensburg Dueling
Grounds. A man riding home was taking a shortcut through the
grounds and came across a body. He wouldn't have seen it except
his horse stumbled and almost threw him. Seeing as Master Horace
is the city coroner, the man went to him for help."

Zeke headed back to his bedroom to get dressed where he
discovered Lizzy, the family's ginger-furred cat, sleeping
comfortably on his pillow. Sighing he mumbled, "At least
someone's sleeping tonight." While his wife and children were
away visiting family in Baltimore, Lizzy was his only company. He
couldn't begrudge her a warm spot on the bed.

Zeke's late night visitor was Noah Hackett, a mulatto man of
25 years, born a slave to the Kingsley family on the White Oak
Plantation on Maryland's Eastern Shore. He'd been gifted to

Horace Kingsley at age thirteen. When Horace turned twenty, he left home to study medicine at the College of Philadelphia, bringing Noah along. In Philadelphia, the two became acquainted with members of the abolitionist movement. When Horace finished school, he told his family it wasn't right for one man to own another, and that he was leaving the plantation and accepting the position of coroner for Washington City. His father, outraged by his son's blasphemy, ordered him to leave and bade him never return.

Returning to the front hall, Zeke grabbed his coat and hat. "Come on, Noah. We'll go by the city stable and get a wagon, then head to the Dueling Grounds. I'm sure Horace doesn't want to wait all night for us."

"Yes, Master Horace will be pleased. With a wagon we can take the body directly to his surgery," said Noah. Zeke nodded his agreement and led the way to the stable.

***

About an hour later, Zeke and Noah arrived at the Dueling Grounds. Thankfully, Horace Kingsley had brought a lantern, and the murder site was visible even in the pitch black darkness of the moonless night. Even before they could get out of the wagon, Gulliver, Horace's Irish Wolfhound, was there to greet them.

"So, Horace, why did you have Noah rouse me from my warm bed? Couldn't this have waited 'til daylight?"

"No, Zeke, it couldn't. It would be unthinkable to leave a dead man lying out here all night. Besides, with Jelena and the children away, what else do you have to do? Not to put too fine a point on it, I am the coroner for both city and county, and I have the power to call out a constable to assist me."

"No need to get riled," said Zeke. "I'm cranky because of the hour, is all. Now, before the night is completely spent, where's the body?"

With Gulliver running ahead, the two men walked onto one of the most notorious dueling grounds in the nation. Lying on his stomach in a pool of blood was a large, roughly clothed man. "Have you made any examination yet, Horace?" asked Zeke.

"I've only taken a preliminary look. I wanted you here before I moved the body and besides, I need Noah to make notes to include in my official report. The victim appears to be a man in his middle years, tall of stature with a muscular build. I believe his death resulted from the obvious gunshot to the back. I've made no other determinations as yet."

Zeke looked down at the body and, in addition to Horace's observations, noted that the man was wearing well-worn homespun trousers, a jacket, and a pair of sturdy boots. Lifting the edge of the jacket he discovered a holster and pistol as well as a pair of shackles attached to his belt.

Zeke motioned to Noah. "Would you help me turn him over? I want to have a look at him."

The two men bent to the task, and when they revealed his face, Noah gasped.

Zeke turned to the young man. "What ails you, son?"

"I know this man, Mr. Zeke. He's a slave catcher named Jedidiah Trask. Most folks here abouts call him 'Die' Trask 'cause once he catches you, you think you're going to die before you make it back to your master."

Horace got closer, with Gulliver right behind, and knelt down to have a better look. "Noah, I need you to write down everything I tell you. Zeke, please hold the lantern directly over the body. Now then, the date is November 5, 1859. It is 1:30 in the morning and we are on the field known as the Bladensburg Dueling Grounds. We are examining the body of an adult male identified by my assistant as Jedidiah Trask. He is approximately 40 years of age, about six feet tall, and his physique is robust and muscular. He has reddish brown hair and a full bushy beard of the same color, lightly streaked with gray. The victim sustained a fatal shot that entered his back and exited to the left of the center of his chest. Noah, did you get all that?"

"Yes, Master Horace, I got it all down," said Noah proudly.

"Noah, how many times do I have to tell you not to call me master?" asked Horace, shaking his head with exasperation. "It's been three years since I freed you and gave you your papers. That gives you the right to go anywhere you choose. I was very pleased when you decided to become my assistant, but call me Horace or Mr. Horace, not master."

After a short silence, Zeke said, "It's going to be daylight shortly. Let's get the body loaded into the wagon and to the surgery. I'd like to keep this as quiet as possible for the time being."

***

In less than an hour the trio of men and one Irish Wolfhound arrived at the Washington Infirmary. Although it wasn't yet daybreak, they had managed to navigate the streets of Washington City without drawing any undue attention. Jumping down from the wagon, Zeke said, "Horace, go on ahead and open the door for us. Noah and I will carry the body to your examining room."

"Come on, Gully, let's get inside and light the lantern." Horace, Gulliver padding at his side, led them down a dim hallway and through a glass plated door marked CORONER, where he pointed to a long wooden table. "Put him down there and remove the tarp and bindings."

Once he finished helping Noah with the body, Zeke said, "I best be getting over to headquarters. I need to let the captain know about this as soon as possible. Given the fact that more and more slaves are making a run for the North, and there are many abolitionist sympathizers here in the city, this murder is going to cause a stir. I just heard of an arrest made over in New Windsor. A Dr. Boyd who lives here in the city was assisting two local runaway slaves by hiding them in a produce wagon and attempting to take them across the Mason-Dixon Line."

"You can be sure slavery is going to be a very important issue in the coming months. The abolitionists are growing stronger and are gaining a voice in politics. I don't see it ending peaceably," said Horace.

Zeke headed toward the door, then turned and said, "How long before you can give your final report?"

"You should have it by noon today. Come by then and I'll tell you my findings and treat you to a meal. I'm sure you haven't been eating properly with the family away," Horace said with a quick smile.

Zeke left and drove over to the city stable to return the horse and wagon. Then he walked several blocks to the station house to report to his captain. It was full daylight and Washington City was a beehive of activity.

After meeting with his captain, Zeke walked the streets and checked likely places, asking about Jedidiah Trask with little success. At about 11:30 he started the long walk back over to the infirmary, looking forward to a hot meal. He arrived just as Noah was leaving with Gulliver in tow.

"He's waiting for you, Mr. Zeke," said Noah. "I'm taking Gully back to the house, and I'll return later to walk Mr. Horace home."

Zeke gave Gulliver a scratch behind the ears. "You be careful out there. We don't want a slave catcher mistaking you for a runaway. You've got your papers on you, I trust."

"Yes, sir, I do, and I've got good protection with Gully. He wouldn't let any harm come to me or Mr. Horace."

Nodding farewell to Noah, Zeke entered the building and upon reaching Horace's door, knocked lightly.

"Come in," came the response. Looking up Horace said, "You're right on time. I've just finished cleaning up, and Noah completed the report. You just missed him and Gully."

"As it happens, I ran into Noah and that dog of yours as I was coming in. Noah said he'd be back to walk you home later. Does he always do that?" asked Zeke.

"When I'm here alone at the end of the day, he always comes back to accompany me through the city. He worries that someone may try to rob me. Noah thinks he's indebted to me for freeing him and is constantly doing things to prove how grateful he is. It is I who am grateful to him. He could have gone North and been out of this hotbed of pro and anti-slavery dissent," said Horace with concern and worry on his face.

"It's good you look out for each other," Zeke said.

Horace remained silent, but some of the concern left his expression.

"Okay you promised me a meal, and I'm mighty hungry. Where should we go?"

"I suggest the Ebbitt House. They serve a very respectable midday meal, and as we walk there I can give you my report," Horace said, putting on his coat and hat.

"Only if your report isn't going to ruin my appetite. I didn't take time for breakfast this morning, so I'm looking forward to enjoying this meal. If you're in no rush, I can wait for the report until after we've eaten."

Chuckling, Horace patted his friend on the back. "I'm in no rush. Thankfully there are no new bodies waiting for examination. And while I haven't anything too unsettling to report, I'll gladly wait to discuss my findings until after we've dined."

***

After a filling meal of roasted chicken, potatoes, chow-chow relish, and a delicious slice of apple pie, the two men settled back to enjoy a shot of single malt and a cup of coffee. By one o'clock, most of the other patrons had left, so the men were not concerned about their discussion being overheard.

"Alright, Horace, what can you tell me about your examination of Jedidiah Trask?"

"First of all, this is not the first time Mr. Trask has been shot."

"What?"

"His body shows scars from previous gunshot wounds as well as knifings. It's not too surprising, considering his line of work. As we observed at the Dueling Grounds, the gunshot to the back, which passed through his heart, was the cause of death. While it's looked upon as a cowardly act to shoot a man in the back, whoever shot him wasn't taking any chances. Jedidiah Trask had a well-deserved reputation for violence and those who confronted him lived or died regretting it."

"I assume the list of people wanting him dead is a long one," said Zeke, shaking his head as he realized he had his work cut out for him.

"Indeed, but I might be able to give you a place to start. When we searched his clothing, we found warrants for two runaway slaves and some notes Trask had made. The warrants were for a man and a woman who had been living with their owners here in Washington City. His notes indicate that their owners had allowed them to marry and that the slaves have family living in Foggy Bottom."

Zeke looked at his friend with appreciation. "You've learned more from the dead man than I did questioning his living associates this morning. You didn't happen to bring the warrants and notes with you, did you?"

"I thought you might ask for them," said Horace, reaching into his coat to pull out the packet of documents. Handing the papers over, he asked, "How are you planning to proceed with your inquiry? I'm sure you intend to go to Foggy Bottom, and if I might, I'd like to suggest that you take Noah with you. He knows his way around and has relatives there. The people in Foggy Bottom can be leery of strangers, especially a white constable."

Nodding in agreement, Zeke asked, "Will he be available to go with me tomorrow morning? I'd like to get there as soon as possible in case the runaways are hiding in the area. Not that I'm interested in capturing them, but they are possible suspects in the murder. Also, would you be willing to accompany me to question the people who hired Trask?"

"Of course I'll go with you. Would tomorrow after you and Noah return from Foggy Bottom be agreeable? You can stop by for Noah in the morning. I have a couple of horses the two of you can use. It's much too long a trip on foot."

Standing up to leave, Zeke shook hands with Horace. "Okay then, I'll meet Noah at your surgery at 8:00 tomorrow. Thank you again for the meal and, of course, the information. I'm sure you've saved me a lot of time."

***

Early the next morning, Zeke stopped by the police station to update his captain.

Arriving at Horace's surgery a few minutes before 8:00, Zeke found two saddled horses outside the infirmary entrance, Noah mounted on one and holding the reins of the other. "Good morning, Noah. It looks as though you're ready for a ride to Foggy Bottom."

"Yes, Mr. Zeke, I am. Do you know who we're looking for?"

"Two runaways. A black man of about 36 years named John Lee and a mulatto woman about 25 years named Lydia Taylor.

They have different owners but were allowed to marry. I gather from the slave catcher's notes the woman is pregnant. That may be why they ran, trying to give their child a life of freedom."

Noah furrowed his brow in thought. "As I recall, there are some Lees and Taylors in Foggy Bottom. When we get there, let me do most of the talking. They'll respond better to my questions."

"Lead on, Noah, lead on."

It only took a short while for the two riders to make their way to the Foggy Bottom section of the city, an area populated by both white and colored laborers who worked in the breweries and warehouses. After a few false leads, they finally found relatives of both John Lee and Lydia Taylor. No one admitted to knowing their whereabouts, but Noah was able to confirm that the couple were no longer in the city and hadn't been for over a week, long before Jedidiah Trask was murdered.

Noah came back from speaking to an elderly colored woman and told Zeke, "That lady is an aunt of mine. She says we should be looking for friends of Dr. Boyd."

"I've heard that name before. I believe he's the man arrested over in New Windsor who was caught attempting to transport two slaves out of the South. I just thought of something, Noah. We need to get back so I can ask Horace a question."

***

Back at the infirmary, Zeke and Noah found Horace in the midst of an autopsy. He held up his hand and said, "Zeke, I'm almost finished here if you want to wait for me."

"Yes, I will. I have a very important question to ask. I'm surprised I didn't think of it sooner. I'll be in your office."

A few minutes later, Horace joined him. "What's your question?"

"When Noah came to get me the other night, he told me that you were called to the Dueling Grounds by a man who found the body. Do you know who it was?"

"His name is Paddy Moran. He works for a Dr. Boyd who lives here in the city."

"What do you know about Moran or Dr. Boyd?" asked Zeke.

"Nothing."

"Where was Moran when Noah and I arrived at the Dueling Grounds?"

"He rode back out to the Grounds with me to show me where the body was and then said he needed to get home. I knew you'd be there soon, so I didn't see any reason to detain him further." Horace was starting to get a worried look.

"Did you see another horse? I should think there must have

been one. How else would Jedidiah Trask get out there?"

"No, I didn't notice a horse but then again it was pitch dark. My lantern didn't illuminate much of the grounds except around the body. What are you getting at, Zeke?"

"Dr. Boyd was arrested a few days ago over in Carroll County trying to smuggle two Washington City slaves to freedom. It concerns me that the man who found the body works for him. Maybe Trask had something to do with Boyd getting caught and Paddy Moran decided to exact revenge."

Horace sat for a while studying his friend and pondering the information he'd just heard. Then he said, "That sounds a very likely solution. What do you propose we do next? With Dr. Boyd in jail, Moran has probably left the area, in fact, he's sure to be over the Mason-Dixon line by now."

"I'm sure you have the right of it, Horace. But I think, if you loan me a horse again, I'll go over to New Windsor and speak with Dr. Boyd. He may know where to find Moran. If not I still can report to the captain that I followed all leads."

***

Zeke wasn't a skilled horseman, but Horace's hack was gentle and easy going. When he arrived in New Windsor, he entered the jail, showed his badge to the sheriff, and asked if he could speak with Dr. Boyd. The sheriff agreed and shortly afterwards, the doctor was seated in front of the sheriff's desk.

"Dr. Boyd, this is Constable Wallace from Washington City. He has some questions for you," said the sheriff.

"Dr. Boyd, I'm investigating the murder of a man named Jedidiah Trask. He's a known slave catcher and was found murdered out on the Bladensburg Dueling Grounds. The person who found him is an employee of yours by the name of Paddy Moran. I've been checking around, and Mr. Moran has disappeared. Sir, do you know his whereabouts?"

"No, Constable, I do not. The last time I saw Paddy was the morning of the day I was arrested. He was supposed to act as a diversion for me that night. Unfortunately, Paddy sometimes drinks too much and loses track of time, so he didn't meet me at the appointed place. I tried making the run without his assistance, but as you can see, I got caught. I can tell you this, though, Jedidiah Trask was part of the group who apprehended me. He had warrants for the two slaves I was trying to get to freedom."

"Do you think your man Moran would be capable of killing someone?" asked Zeke.

The doctor studied Zeke for a long moment, then said, "I can't answer you with absolute certainty. But I can say that Paddy feels very strongly about the abolitionist movement and that men like Jedidiah Trask are a blight on humanity."

Zeke got up and thanked the doctor. Turning to the sheriff, he said, "Thank you for your help. Any time you need anything in the city, let me know."

***

Zeke managed to get back to Horace's office before he left for the day. Zeke stopped only long enough to let Noah know he was back with the horse. Then he left to go check in with his captain. He believed he had a solution if not a resolution in the case of the murder of Jedidiah Trask.

The station house was quiet this time of day. The captain was still at work in his office, and looked up when he heard Zeke's footsteps. He put down his pen and said, "Well, Wallace, what have you got to report?"

"After a good bit of work, including a trip to Foggy Bottom and another over to New Windsor, I'm pretty sure I know who killed Jedidiah Trask."

"Excellent! Do you have the man in custody?"

"No, Captain, I do not, and I'm not likely to make an arrest anytime soon. It seems that several days ago, Jedidiah Trask was involved in the apprehension of a man by the name of Dr. William Boyd who was attempting to transport two runaway slaves to freedom. Boyd employed a man named Paddy Moran to assist him in this enterprise. However, Mr. Moran missed the rendezvous and Boyd was arrested. I believe that in retaliation for his boss's arrest, Moran lured Trask out to the Dueling Grounds and murdered him."

"Have you tried to find this Moran?" asked the captain.

"I have, Captain, and he hasn't been back to his lodgings or been seen around in several days. Dr. Boyd believes, and I agree, that Moran has most likely headed North. He's a staunch abolitionist and will have no trouble finding people to hide him."

"So it appears you still have an open case. Until you have conclusive proof that Moran is the murderer, I will not consider this matter at an end. Keep at it, but do not neglect your other cases, " said the captain dismissively.

"Yes, of course, Captain.," said Zeke as he turned to leave. Deciding there was nothing more he could accomplish that day, Zeke headed home, hoping to find his family returned from their trip.

***

"Is that you, Hezekiah Wallace?" came the call from the kitchen.

"It is, Jelena. I'm so glad you've finally come home. I've missed you and the children and I can't wait for a good meal again."

"I knew you wouldn't eat properly while I was away so I've been busy preparing some of your favorites for tonight's supper."

Taking his wife by the hand, Zeke looked into her eyes and said, "I have missed you, my dear."

***

Later that evening Zeke was comfortably settled in bed, dozing after a lovely reunion with his family and a delicious home-cooked meal. Suddenly, there came a loud knock at the door. He awoke with a start and looked over at his wife, who was still asleep with Lizzy curled up on her pillow. He quietly got out of bed and left the room to see who was at the door.

"Who's there?" he asked as quietly as he could.

"Western Union, sir. I have a telegram for you."

Opening the door, Zeke saw a young man covered in road dust holding the reins of his horse. He handed Zeke an envelope and turned to leave. Zeke closed the door and moved to the kitchen to light a lamp so he could read the telegram. Opening the envelope he read:

Constable Wallace STOP
Trask deserved to die STOP
I am out of reach STOP
Take care, and beware the storm STOP
PM

THE BARTER

by Su Kopil

*Child of the Depression Dani-Lou has to grow up fast
and she has to be tough. Young Dani-Lou and the older
Ruby hatch a plot to send Ruby on her way to
Hollywood. When a murder interrupts their plans,
Dani-Lou must find out who's responsible.*

Ruby stares at me hard from behind the mercantile counter. My daddy always said the trick to being a good pincher was to hide behind the obvious. Buy a pound of coffee, pinch a pack of ten-centers—nothing too big or too expensive. It's the ordinary, everyday stuff that goes unnoticed.

Mr. Nash, Ruby's father, is smoking one of his Turkish cigarettes out on the front stoop with Sheriff Gunther, leaving Ruby in charge of the store. I grin at her. It takes her a minute, but she grins back before disappearing to help a customer.

Pulling pennies from my pocket, I start to counting when someone bumps me. The coins clatter to the floor and the bell over the screen door jingles.

"You keep those gypsies off my property, Sheriff." Mr. Nash steps inside, the sheriff behind him.

"They's just looking for work same as everyone, Jack."

"Damn Depression's going to ruin us all." Mr. Nash's gaze goes directly to Ruby, who's back behind the counter.

Me, I'm on my knees after the pennies. I don't waste time looking for who hit me. I gather nine of the coins—all but the one rolling across the planks right beside Sheriff Gunther's boot.

He bends to retrieve it, and holds it out to me. "Need to keep a tighter hold on your money these days, Dani-Lou."

"Yes, sir." I take the coin. Feel it move among the others in my cupped hand.

"How's your mama getting on?" he asks.

"She's doing." I remember her telling us kids how she and Sheriff Gunther dated back in high school. "Why, he could have been your daddy," she used to say. That's before our real daddy took to hitting Mama. Back before the whole town heard he'd up and left us. Back before the crazy turned Mama into a stranger.

"Good to hear it." I can tell from his practiced smile he doesn't believe me. "She's a fine woman, your mama. You know, you take after her, same blonde hair and dimples."

Tucking my hair behind my ears, I figure he's just being polite. Mama's a looker, while boys look right past me.

"What's that sticking out of your overalls, Dani-Lou?" Mr. Nash eyes me like a piece of gristle he means to toss to the dogs.

I feel around to the gap on my left side where the PayDay candy bar I swiped mere seconds ago is protruding. The tips of my ears burn like they done since I was a kid whenever I got caught doing wrong.

"You plan on buying that?" Mr. Nash's arms are crossed. Ruby's staring, same as the dribble of customers hanging around gossiping. I can practically hear Widow Wren's drool hit the floor. At least it got her to quit griping about that old Tin Lizzie of hers.

I straighten—push my shoulders back like my daddy done whenever a bug crawled up his ass. "Course, I'm buying. I only stuck it there so I had two hands free to catch my money when it fell. I was near knocked off my feet in your store, Mr. Nash." I stretch my neck and look around the shop. That's the other thing I learned about pinching—sometimes you had to distract people like a magician does, so you don't see the card he stuck up his sleeve.

With one sweep, Mr. Nash's steely gaze takes in the perimeters of his store. Ruby herds Mrs. Wren and her companion around a bolt of blue satin she says she's making into a dress. A few old timers start their pool game up again in the back corner. There's a boy, about my age, seventeen, using the wall phone, receiver pressed to his ear, his back to us.

Mine and Mr. Nash's eyes meet and I know he doesn't believe me. So I rub my elbow, wince a little, and say, "I'd like to pay now. Mama and the kids are expecting me. Today's Henry's birthday. He'll be ten." I prattle on. "The candy's a present from Em and me." I place the candy bar on the counter and set five pennies in a straight line next to it. I was supposed to buy a quart of milk to go with the birthday cake Em made. That would have to wait now. I slip the rest of the coins in my pocket and find something else—a slip of paper. I pull it out and read, '*I know what you did.*'

"Here, are you going to take your candy or not?" Mr. Nash is frowning again.

Ruby is standing next to him now, looking at me funny. I stuff the note back into my pocket, grab the candy and run, the screen door slamming like a gunshot behind me.

***

It's not until later that night after eating the lopsided birthday cake and reminding Mama for the tenth time that Henry is her son and, no, she can't eat his candy, that I recognize the handwriting on the threatening note. The words are loose, sloping to the right like the letters are sliding down a hill. Sure as I'm sitting on the old porch swing listening to the katydids, I know it to be Ruby's writing. I ball the paper in my palm. What I can't figure out is why.

***

Ruby and me been friendly enough since the time I stopped her from drowning herself the day her mama run off. We'd gossip at the store, say hey at church. Two weeks ago, after rumors spread about Daddy taking off, Ruby showed up with a bottle of Old Crow she'd pinched from her father's stash. She said since I was there for her the day her Mama run off, she reckoned she'd do the same for me. Then we giggled because sharing a bottle of spirits ain't exactly like saving someone from killing themselves. And my daddy being gone wasn't exactly like her mama running off with another man.

But I guess it was close enough because our gloomy silence turned into a whole lot of sharing. The more whiskey we drank the more wild our talk until Ruby blurted out that she was going to New York City—leaving this dinky town and her suffocating father to be an actress.

"You can't tell anyone, Dani-Lou. No one." We were sitting together on a thick limb of an old oak tree in the farthest corner of my backyard. The branch hung so low our feet touched the ground.

"Who am I gonna tell?" I asked.

She turned to me, grabbed my shoulders. "You got to cross your heart and swear it."

I might have shrugged. Ruby had a way with the dramatics.

She shook me a little. "Swear it."

Her insistence and the spirits running through my blood fired me up. I was going to tell her to leave off, but then I looked in her eyes, and saw fear—real fear, which sobered me up some. I crossed my heart and said, "I swear it, Ruby. I won't tell nobody."

She leaned in and kissed me then—full on the mouth. Her lips were soft and warm with the sour taste of mash. "I come by your house some nights. Watch you through the windows," she said. "Is that weird?"

I didn't know what to say to that, but she expected something. "No." I couldn't look her in the eyes when I said it.

"Yeah, it is."

I did look at her then and we burst into giggles.

***

There's a crash from somewhere inside the house. I push off the porch swing and shove the crumpled paper back into my pocket. The night's turned dark. An owl hoots somewhere close by. I scan the shadows and wonder if Ruby's out there, but all I see are the winks of fireflies.

***

Next morning, Mama's in a bad way. Em wants to stay home from school, but I send her off with Henry. There's no money to pay for a doctor, besides I know what ails Mama and it's nothing a doctor can fix. Two days go by before Mama's well enough to stay alone with Em. I need to find Ruby.

When I get to the mercantile, she's sweeping the steps. Business is slow. The New Deal has yet to touch our little corner of North Carolina. A stone toss to the right sits the gypsies' bright red covered wagon. It's been parked there since their horse died a week ago. A woman in a blue dress with a matching scarf wrapped around her head is cooking under the shade of a tree, while an olive-skinned man sits and whittles, his gaze straying often to the front of the mercantile.

The shop's screen door squeals. Out steps Avery Lynch, his blond hair pale against his sun-scorched skin. He's a farmer's son. He steps right up to Ruby and tickles the back of her neck. She turns and swats him with the broom. He laughs and moves even closer.

"Howdy there, Ruby." I lengthen my strides. Nod to Avery. "I come to tell you about that new Jean Harlow film."

Avery is none too pleased to see me, nor I him. I caught him cornering Em once in the back of the schoolyard. Em's the one that's been cursed with mama's good looks.

"Since when you got money for the movies?" he asks.

"I don't think I was sharing my financials with you, Avery."

"Way I hear it the women in your family aren't big on sharing anything. That's why your daddy run off."

Ruby raises her broom. "You done your business here. Now git."

"Not yet, I ain't." Avery hops down the steps. "But I aim to come back, Ruby, and finish it. See if I don't."

I wait for Avery to become a blur in the distance, then I grab Ruby's arm. She drops the broom and I pull her off the steps and around the side of the store. "We need to talk. Why are you threatening me?"

"Threatening?" She shoves her hands onto her hips and scowls. Next thing I know she's doubled-over in hysterics, gasping for breath. "You should've seen your face, Dani-Lou, when you read that note."

"I don't understand you." I start to walk away.

Ruby catches my arm and yanks me around, tears glisten in the corners of her eyes from laughing so hard.

"Why would you do such a fool thing?" I ask.

"Don't be mad. This town's so boring. I got to do something for fun. Besides—" Her fingers slide down my arm and find my hand. "I need your help."

I try to ignore the pressure of her hand in mine. "What for?"

She lets go to dig into her pocket and pulls out a bus ticket. "I've got my ticket to New York, but I need a lift to Rock Springs."

"That's an hour away," I say. "Shouldn't you ask someone with a car, like Avery?"

Her face turns red. She shoves the ticket back into her pocket. "Avery's a crumb. You're the only one I can trust. We'll barter. You get me to the bus, I'll keep your secret."

I want to tell her that's more akin to blackmail than bartering. And that she's got her own secret that needs keeping. Instead, I say, "What makes you think I got a secret?"

"Might be I seen some things I shouldn't have while I was watching your house them nights." She picks at her fingernails, not looking at me.

"What things?" The day's heating up and I'm starting to feel sticky.

"Maybe your daddy never did leave Pine Mountain. Maybe he's still here." She lifts her head, her blue eyes gone almost gray.

I feel a slick of sweat shrivel under my shirt. Maybe Ruby's talking out of her ass, maybe she's not. Suddenly I'm glad she's going so far away.

"Ruby!" Mr. Nash's roar sounds like a lion I once heard at a traveling circus.

Ruby clutches my hands, her grip strong. "We got a deal?"

I'm not sure why I agree or how I'll get her to Rock Springs, but I nod.

"Friday before the sun comes up. I'll meet you at the crossroads." She plants a kiss on my cheek and strolls back to the shop, with the gypsy man watching, like she hasn't a care in the world. But she's not fooling me. That girl's strung as tight as a fiddle.

***

Dinner is a bowl of watery chicken soup, easy on the chicken, heavy on the parsley. The garden Em and me planted produced one good tomato before shriveling up to nothing, leaving us with a patch of wild herbs.

Mama and Henry are glued to the radio, listening to the Lone Ranger while Em reads in a corner. I sneak onto the front porch to think. I have less than forty-eight hours to figure out how to get Ruby to Rock Springs. But the question that won't leave my head is why is Ruby so fired up to escape Pine Mountain?

The screen door slams and Mama is there, her hair uncombed, her dress spotted with food stains. She sits next to me on the porch swing and I can feel her thin bones trembling. The full moon is playing with the shadows and the birds are singing their last goodnights.

"What is it, Mama?"

She leans back, closes her eyes. I think maybe she's fallen asleep until she whispers into the night, "He's dead."

My eyes scan the shadows. The birds stop singing.

"Daddy's dead," she says.

I stiffen. "Mama—"

"He's dead on the mountain. Won't be coming home no more."

And then I realize she's talking about her father who died in a mine explosion when she was a girl.

"We're going to get a puppy soon." Her eyes are bright as the stars in the dark.

I pat her thin arm, glad she can still pull happy memories from the jumble in her head.

She stands, and then leans down to kiss my forehead. "Goodnight, Dani-Lou."

My breath hitches at the sound of my name on her lips. She's half in the house before I'm able to reply. "Goodnight, Mama."

***

The plan comes to me in the night, triggered by Widow Wren's rants about her husband's old Tin Lizzie. "The fool thing run itself into the ground and him into the grave," she's always saying to anyone who'll listen.

Ruby might not know the first thing about bartering, but my daddy was an expert. Once he bartered a one-eyed rooster for a whole gaggle of egg-laying hens. Course, he lost the lot in a card game the next day, but that's hardly the point.

The point being, bartering is second cousin to pinching. I have faith my knack for one will carry over to the other. Of course, it wouldn't be a plan without a hitch. And that hitch is Avery Lynch.

I know nothing about automobiles except what Daddy taught me. Keep your right hand on the throttle, the left on the wheel. Brake a mile ahead of where you want to stop. I think he was mostly kidding about that last bit, but maybe not.

Besides Sheriff Gunther, and I aren't about to ask him, Avery is the only other person in my acquaintance who tinkers with cars. He's was just coming in from the fields, mopping his sweaty brow with a stained rag when I arrive at his parents' farm.

"I see Ruby sent her dog after me," he says.

"I ain't nobody's bitch, Avery. Would serve you to remember that."

"Men order. Women serve. Say what you come for, Dani-Lou, or beat it."

"I'm here to barter."

"Barter what?" He shoves the dirty blue rag into his back pocket. "You got nothing I want."

"I got a car that needs fixing. You fix it, twenty-four hours later, it's yours."

"You're as crazy as your Ma." He pulls half a ten-center from his pocket, strikes a match, and lights it.

I ignore the dig. "We got a deal?"

He blows a neat smoke ring into the air. "Why twenty-four hours?"

"None of your business. Fix the car, next day it's yours. No questions."

He drops the cigarette and grinds it into the dirt with the toe of his boot and holds out a beefy hand. We shake. "You wrong me. I'll be after you," he says.

* * *

I'd rather talk to a hundred Averys then face the Widow Wren with her snooping questions. She invites me into her kitchen, sets down a pitcher of iced tea, showing off how the cubes pop out of her new ice tray, and settles in for what I'm sure she hopes is a good long gossip.

"Yes, Henry is growing like a weed. Em is such a big help. Mama is doing better. No, I don't think she's up for visitors just yet. Yes, it's a shame Mama didn't marry Sheriff Gunther. Everyone thought they would. No, I don't know where my daddy took off to nor how he got there. He sold the car before he left."

"Speaking of cars . . . " I dutifully take a sip of the cold tea. "I heard you want to get rid of that old Tin Lizzie in your yard."

"That was Wilbur's Model-T. I warned him not to buy it, but he had to have it. Wouldn't listen to a word I said, but that was Wilbur."

"Bit of an eyesore," I say, "your garden being so beautiful and all."

"Right shamed I am to have it sitting out there this past year. Ann Peedle even suggested we hold bridge club elsewhere. Can you imagine? After ten years of hosting it here. I remember when your mama used to come. She made the best jam cake. I do surely wish I had that recipe. Would never give it up, though. Family secret, she'd say." Widow Wren removes her glasses and wipes the lenses with the end of her apron. "I tell you, Dani-Lou, I don't know what to do. Even the scrap metal man said it's too big for him to cart away."

I lay my hand over hers, the way I seen Mama do hundreds of times when consoling a friend. "Might be that I can help."

***

Ruby leaves tomorrow and I'm worried the Model-T won't be ready. It didn't help the gypsy man showed up at our house this morning trying to sell us chickens. I didn't ask how he came by them. Em was with me and I didn't like the way he kept looking at her, same way I seen him watching Ruby. I told him, "No, thank you" and shut the door. I warned Em not to answer if he showed back up while I was gone.

I'm halfway to Widow Wren's when Sheriff Gunther pulls up on the road. "Dani-Lou." He touches his cap. "You seen Avery Lynch today?"

"No, sir," I says. "What's he done?"

He doesn't answer, just says, "If you see him tell him to steer clear of the mercantile for a few days."

"I will, Sheriff."

"Can I give you a lift?"

I shake my head no and he rolls off in a cloud of dust.

***

Avery's under the hood of the Model-T, just where he's supposed to be, when I walk up to Widow Wren's place. "Sheriff's looking for you," I say. "Says to stay away from the store for a few days. You ain't been bothering Ruby again, have you?"

Avery straightens and slams the hood. He's got grease on his forehead and a wrench sticking out of his back pocket. "As I recall, I already got me a mama. You ready to start this clunker? Stand back."

I frown but do as he says as he starts cranking the engine. He adjusts the choke and the engine sputters. The back end smokes, but the engine holds.

"You did it." We grin at each other, a momentary truce.

Widow Wren comes out of the house, clapping her hands together. "Dear boy," she's saying over and over. "Dear boy."

I pull a folded sheet of paper from my pocket and hand it to her. "Mama says she was pleased you were thinking of her and would like you to have her jam cake recipe."

Widow Wren's eyes light up. She takes the recipe and scurries back to her nest. I figure Mama wouldn't be too mad if she knew, seeing as I might have left off an ingredient or two.

Avery looks pleased with himself and I'm feeling pleased, too. I want to go tell Ruby but figure it's wiser to stay away from the store for a while. Besides, we have an hour ride in the morning in which to say our goodbyes.

Avery drives himself home with me watching from the passenger seat. He's reluctant to turn the car over to me. Finally, he gets out. "Twenty-four hours," he says. "Then the car is mine."

"That's right," I say.

"I don't see why I just don't take it now. What can you need it for? You probably can't even drive it."

"Never you mind. I can drive it good enough. That's all you need to know." He steps back watching as the car jerks forward and nearly stalls. The engine sputters. A cloud of smoke rises, then engulfs the car. But I work the pedals and keep it going. By the time I get home, I'm feeling comfortable enough that I'm starting to believe we'll actually make it to Rock Springs.

Henry, Em, and Mama tumble out of the house when I pull up. Jumping and exclaiming and laughing. We get a blanket for Mama, and all squeeze into the car. I take them for a bumpy ride in the mountain air.

***

Next morning, I'm at the crossroads listening to the whippoorwills call to each other. They've been at it for at least an hour. The shadows beneath the trees are starting to lighten but still no sign of Ruby. Did she get cold feet? Did her daddy lock her in her room? I haven't seen her for two days so anything might have happened.

The mornings are starting to cool, giving me a shiver I can't shake. Plus I need to pee. I don't think I'll make it back to the house given how bumpy the ride is. No one's come by all morning so I walk into the woods far enough not to be seen by the road and trip over a log. Only it's not a log. I scuttle backwards through the pine needles trying not to scream or gag.

Ruby's staring at me from the ground, her face as blue and shiny as the material twisted around her neck. I force myself to crawl closer to see if she's still breathing. Her body is still. So very still. I see the bus ticket that must have fallen out of her pocket half buried in pine needles. Next to it is a half-smoked Murad.

This time I can't hold it in and I stumble away to get sick. I raise my head and wipe my face with the back of my hand. A branch snaps and I freeze. But only long enough to get my bearings, then I'm off. I forget about the car and run—cutting through the woods, a shortcut that takes me right to the back of the gypsy camp. The woman, wearing the same blue dress as the other day, stares at me, only this time her blue scarf is missing and something clicks in my head.

Past her I spot the sheriff's car parked in front of the mercantile. The sheriff's standing next to it with a red-faced Avery. Above them, looming on the stoop, stands Mr. Nash, his arms crossed.

Somehow Avery spots me and points. I look at the gypsy woman. She's shaking her head ever so slightly. I take a breath, push back my shoulders and make that long journey to the sheriff's car.

"She can tell you, Sheriff," Avery shouts, pointing at me. "She dropped me off at my house yesterday after I fixed Widow Wren's old Model-T."

"That right, Dani-Lou?" the sheriff asks.

I keep the car between me and them. "Yes, sir," I say.

"They's accusing me of robbing the store when I wasn't anywhere near it. Maybe it's those gypsies you should be talking too." Avery is pacing up a head full of steam while his hands twist and pull at a dirty blue rag.

I glance at the gypsy camp and see the olive-skinned man has joined the woman. They watch from a distance.

"Now just calm down, son," the sheriff is saying. "What are you doing out so early this morning. Shouldn't you be working your daddy's farm?"

"He's after my Ruby, that's what he's doing," Mr. Nash says. "Money from my register wasn't enough. First my wife runs off, now this one—this one plans to run off with my daughter."

No words, only spit flies from Avery's mouth.

"I found a bus ticket to New York." Mr. Nash stabs the air with his finger. "That's where he planned on taking her."

"That's a lie," Avery finally spits out.

"Where is Ruby?" the sheriff asks. "She can settle this for us here and now."

"That's why I called you, Sheriff. She's gone." Mr. Nash hangs his head. "Bed ain't been slept in."

"What about her dress?" I ask. "The one she was making? Is it gone, too? Or only part of it. 'Cause I don't think she ever did finish it, did she?"

I've got the sheriff's full attention now. "What are you talking about, Dani-Lou?"

"Ruby's dead, Sheriff. She's in the woods by the crossroads. We were supposed to meet this morning. I was going to drive her to Rock Springs. When she didn't show, I wandered a bit and there she was. Lying there by herself—strangled with a piece of blue satin. Killed," I say, "by her own daddy."

"That girl's crazy," shouts Mr. Nash. "As crazy as her mother."

The sheriff's face hardens.

"The girl does not lie."

I jump at the accented voice coming from behind me. It's the olive-skinned man. The woman, her head now wrapped in the blue scarf, stands just behind him.

"I saw the shop owner go into the woods after the girl. He returned alone. My wife, she says I should check, see if the girl is all right. I tell her we should stay out of it but—"

"He did it," Mr. Nash screams. "That gypsy killed my daughter."

"And how would he get a piece of the dress she was making?" The sheriff shifts so that the bulk of him is now blocking the bottom of the steps.

"He stole it. I told you there was a break-in yesterday."

"I also found a cigarette by her body. At first I thought it was Avery's." I nod in his direction but go on before he can blow his top. "But he only smokes ten-centers and he always crushes them with his foot. This one was half smoked, just lying there. A Murad."

"I don't know anyone else who smokes Turkish cigarettes in these here parts, do you, Jack?" Sheriff Gunther's got his foot on the bottom step.

Apparently Ruby wasn't the only one with a flair for the dramatics. With all pretenses gone, Mr. Nash seems to shrivel before us. "I owned that girl. She had no right to leave me like her mother did. I warned her. I begged—" His voice breaks and he turns to flee inside the store but the sheriff is quicker, taking the steps two at a time, with Avery right behind.

***

Later that night, Mama and me are rocking on the old porch swing. I don't know if she knows what's happened or not, or if she understands. But there's a pause in the winding down of the night chatter when she turns to me and says, "Sometimes people love too hard, Dani-Lou, like your daddy." Then she starts humming softly under her breath—an old nursery rhyme she sung to us when we were babies.

Em calls from inside and Mama leaves me alone on the porch. I stare out into the night and think of a girl with big dreams. When the last bird warbles, I say, "Goodnight, Ruby." I wait a beat, and then ever so softly whisper, "Goodnight, Daddy."

MISTRESS THREADNEEDLE'S QUEST

by Kathy Lynn Emerson

*In the London of 1562, Dowsabella Threadneedle
wonders how her neighbor, Edward Sturgeon, came to
be struck by lightning. Mistress Threadneedle visits the
bereaved widow, and in the course of helping her with
a household task, draws some unusual conclusions.*

London, 1562

On the day of Edward Sturgeon's funeral, I stood in my garden, staring at an upper window in his tall, narrow house. It had been a fine, large casement, made up of dozens of small, expensive triangles of colored glass held together by H-shaped lead rods. Now blackened wood and missing panes told a terrible story. I was at the same time fascinated and horrified. I could not look away.

Sturgeon had been standing just inside that window when he'd been struck by lightning. His death was quick, but it must have been excruciatingly painful. The stable boy who bore witness to his passing said Sturgeon looked as if he was wrapped in exploding fireworks. By the time the flames were extinguished, it was too late to save him.

You may well ask how such a thing could happen. Some said it was an act of God. Others called it a portent of disaster—a strange, unnatural death. I believe I am the only one in all of England to suspect that Edward Sturgeon was most foully murdered.

I am Mistress Dowsabella Threadneedle, childless relict of a prosperous mercer. I married beneath me, having been born the daughter of a knight. In my widowhood, I live in considerable comfort in a house in Catte Street in the parish of St. Lawrence Jewry. Most of my neighbors are well-to-do merchants of one sort or another. Edward Sturgeon was the richest of them all, not only a goldsmith, but a moneylender, too.

Even as I ruminated upon the strange manner of his death, the Goldsmiths of London were bearing his body in solemn procession from their guildhall to the churchyard. From where I stood, I could hear the wailing of professional mourners and imagined them in their new black gowns, tearing at their hair and weeping.

Inside the Sturgeon house, the new-made widow grieved in seclusion with her kinswomen and closest female friends. The spouse of the deceased never attends the funeral. I have no idea why this is the custom, but it was the same for me two years ago when my beloved Richard was taken from me.

Although I knew I would be welcome to mourn with Mary Sturgeon, I did not go to her. When we'd first met, she'd made it all too plain that she would value my acquaintance not because of any pleasant characteristics I might possess, but solely because my gentle birth made me desirable to know. I am related by blood to certain persons who have influence at the royal court. My husband benefitted from those connections, which brought additional custom to his mercery, but I am not inclined to ask my cousins to do similar favors for anyone else.

Instead of entering the Sturgeon house, I returned to my own. I would bide my time before confronting Mistress Sturgeon. I had much to ponder before I took action.

Why, you must be asking, did I imagine that a crime had been committed? No one has the power to call down lightning from the sky, let alone direct it at a specific target. Even the most powerful necromancer would be hard put to accomplish such a feat.

To explain, I must first tell you that my husband indulged me to a degree most people would find peculiar. Having been taught the skill at an early age, I had already developed a passion for reading by the time we wed. Knowing this, he made it his habit to gift me with books instead of jewelry. Thus have I acquired all manner of reading material, but in particular I am partial to the tales of brave knights, impossible quests, and strange happenings. As a widow with control over my late husband's entire fortune, I continue to purchase such stories. Anyone who hopes to persuade me to speak on his behalf to one of my kinsmen at court, or keep me sweet for any other reason, is encouraged to find an appropriate token in one of the booksellers' stalls in Paul's Churchyard. So it was that, about a year before Edward Sturgeon's strange death, I acquired a slim volume entitled *The Sorcerer Knight*.

This is the story of an arrogant knight's attempts to turn base metal into gold, raise the spirits of the dead, and find lost treasure. All these things defy both the law of man and the law of God, and when the knight seeks to call down the power of a storm by holding a sword over his head, he suffers divine retribution. He is struck by a bolt of lightning and dies.

I know for a certainty that Edward Sturgeon was familiar with the story. He was the one who presented me with the book.

The more I thought about the knight's tale and compared it to what happened to Master Sturgeon, the more convinced I became that the circumstances of Sturgeon's death were suspicious. If for no other reason than to ease my conscience, I felt compelled to investigate.

***

A week after the funeral, I paused once again in the garden. I studied the scorched and boarded-over casement for a long time before passing through the narrow alley between the houses. Like a proper visitor, I went to the door of the house that now belonged to the widow and was admitted by one of her maidservants.

Mary Sturgeon herself received me in an upper room at the front of the house. The faint smell of smoke still lingered in the air but we both ignored it.

"How kind of you to call." She seemed surprised by my visit.

"I have brought a gift to cheer you in this sad time," I said, presenting her with a small packet.

Her forced smile turned genuine as she opened it and found a sampling of the best my late husband's mercery had to offer—assorted ribbons and tassels and a decorative border for the front of a French hood. The latter was made of the finest black silk and garnished with jet beads.

"You are most generous, Mistress Threadneedle."

"It was the least I could do, Mistress Sturgeon, Even the deepest mourning allows for a few adornments." I glanced at the sewing abandoned beside my hostess's chair. She had been attaching a length of black cord to a black sleeve. "Shall I work on its mate?" I offered, catching sight of more of the same cord wound into a ball and tucked into a corner of her sewing basket.

I reached for it, but she stayed my hand, delving into the basket herself and producing a smaller segment of the cord, together with a needle and a short length of black thread. She was still rummaging after I had seated myself and taken up the materials she'd provided.

"What do you lack?"

She gave a nervous laugh. "I am unable to locate any pins. I have been more distraught of late than I realized. I forgot that I needed to buy more."

It was a trifling matter, but odd all the same. Pins, whether small fine ones or long dress pins, are customarily purchased a thousand at a time.

Together with Mary and her two maidservants, I sat and stitched. I offered news of the royal court, where there had been a recent outbreak of smallpox. A goodly number of highborn ladies in the service of Queen Elizabeth had been afflicted and those who survived were likely to be scarred for life.

Mary Sturgeon had little to offer in return, save that the butcher's wife had been delivered of twin sons. "They say twins are unlucky, but surely it is better to have two at a time than be barren." She sounded wistful and then, too late, remembered that I was also childless.

I let her comment pass unanswered, for to tell you true, I look upon my barren state as a blessing. Too many women, burdened with fatherless chicks, are pressured into remarrying and once again become little more than a husband's chattel. Now that it had been forced upon me, I prized my independence. I especially liked being answerable to no one but myself when it came to how I spent my money and managed my property.

After a little silence, I began, by a circuitous route, to approach the subject that had brought me to Mistress Sturgeon's door. "Will you need to replace your roof? I have heard that when the steeple of St. Paul's was struck by lightning last year, molten lead poured down onto the street below."

"There was no lead in my roof to melt. The tiles are scored but intact."

"I did not realize anyone had climbed up to inspect them," I said. "You must not think I spend all my time spying on my neighbors, but a ladder that tall would be most conspicuous."

"There is a trap door in the garret that gives access to the roof," she said. "It is not difficult to open and go through. Thus I have seen for myself that the roof does not need repairs. Only the window must be replaced."

I executed a few more careful stitches before I spoke again. "Did your husband stand at that window every time there was a storm?"

"Oh, yes—the more fool he!" Color rose in Mary's cheeks as she spat out heated words. "He said thunderstorms made him feel alive. He *lived* to watch lightning flash across the night sky. He had no one but himself to blame that such an ungodly habit killed him!"

Her anger at her late husband struck me as natural. He had been both careless and arrogant. "Sensible people are afraid of thunder and lightning, as well they should be."

Some believe thunderstorms are sent by the devil. Others see them as an expression of God's displeasure. Either way, almost everyone agrees that it is best to stay indoors with the shutters closed during violent storms.

"Edward thought himself sensible," she said. "He laughed at the superstitious things people do to repel lightning."

I nodded. Everyone knew such remedies. "I cannot see that

planting houseleeks on the roof or draping mistletoe over doors and windows offers much protection."

"And most foolish of all, or so Edward always said, is the belief that ringing church bells during a thunderstorm will drive away the devil. What more likely place, he used to say, than a church with a tall steeple to be struck by lightning? And what more dangerous occupation than bell ringer? It was his frequent observation that lightning seeks out the highest point in the landscape."

"I suppose that is why he thought himself safe. Your house is no taller than any of those surrounding it."

"He tempted fate. Worse, he mocked God." Mary Sturgeon's fingers flew faster and faster as her voice rose. Her two maidservants shrank away from her. "He paid the price for thinking too well of himself."

Sturgeon had been accustomed to having his own way. That was true enough. He'd trampled anyone who stood in his path. By one means or another, even threats of violence, he'd forced choices upon lesser men, and upon some women, too.

I reached for the sewing basket to retrieve more thread. My nose wrinkled as I caught a whiff of singed fabric. It was not coming from the room at the back of the house, the one where Edward Sturgeon had died. Instead, it seemed to emanate from within the basket.

Frowning, I bent closer. Surely the widow would not have kept any of the clothing her husband had been wearing when he died.

"What is it you need?" The sharpness in her voice made me jerk upright.

"Thread," I said.

She provided me with more and we all resumed stitching.

It was soon after that exchange that the glazier arrived.

When Mistress Sturgeon left the chamber to supervise his work in the other room, I seized the opportunity to examine the sewing basket. The smell was as strong as I remembered and led me straight to the roll of silk cord. I plucked it out to study more closely.

The outside was undamaged, but when I unrolled the cord, I at once found evidence of scorching. I might have attributed Mary Sturgeon's frugal reuse of expensive decoration to her upbringing—her father had been naught but a yeoman farmer and it was said that, because of her beauty, Sturgeon married her without a dowry—had I not noticed a second oddity. A great number of pinholes showed in the fabric. The pattern they made suggested that someone had inserted dozens of pins, overlapping, all along its length.

Pondering this curious discovery, I returned the cord to the sewing basket. I looked up in time to catch the maids exchanging a look. For once, I was glad of my superior birth. I had no power to enforce my will, but I could speak with convincing authority.

"You will say nothing to your mistress of anything you see me do this day," I said. "Do you understand?"

Identical nods answered me, although one maid was short and stout and the other tall and thin.

"Do you know what happened to the pins?" I felt certain they had seen the same thing I had.

The tall girl shook her had so vigorously that she nearly lost her cap. The other young woman worried her lower lip and tried to avoid meeting my eyes.

I waited, my hands busy with the sewing but my full attention on the maids. After a lengthy silence, my patience was rewarded. The one who had been gnawing on her lip spoke in a whisper.

"Threw them down the privy, she did."

"Why?" Pins might be a paltry expense to someone of Edward Sturgeon's wealth, but a frugal housewife would not carelessly discard so many of them, especially one who knew what it was to scrimp and save in order to afford the cheapest sort.

"All blackened and bent, they were." The expression of distaste on the maid's plump face convinced me that she'd had a good look at them.

"How did they get that way?" I asked.

Neither maidservant dared offer an opinion.

I felt certain that the pins were somehow connected to Sturgeon's death, but how had they been used? I pictured in my mind the illustration that accompanied *The Sorcerer's Tale*—the knight with his sword held high. Swords are made of metal, and so are pins, but how could pins draw down lightning from the sky?

I glanced toward the door through which Mary had disappeared. I had no business following her, but if I wished to examine the window before it was repaired, I had to at once. I set aside my sewing and stood. If all else failed, I could use that sad old excuse of needing to use the privy. The Sturgeons, having money enough to afford such a luxury, had a small chamber for that purpose right in the house. It could not be reached by passing through the room where Edward Sturgeon had died, but that was a minor concern. I could always claim, with some truth, that I had not visited Sturgeon's house often enough to be sure of the way.

The glazier, closely supervised by the widow, was busy measuring when I entered. Neither noticed me at first, giving me the opportunity to study the casement from the inside. It was easy to picture Sturgeon there in the opening. He'd been accustomed to standing in the center, hands braced on either side of him. Braced, I realized with a jolt, on the lead bars that framed each section of the window.

If it was not just the height of a steeple, but the lead roof and the bells within that attracted lightning to churches, then surely it was not a good idea to touch metal of any kind during a thunderstorm. Even so, this house was nowhere near as tall as a church tower. I was still missing a piece of the puzzle.

I learned no more that day, and although I had the most dire suspicions about what had happened to Edward Sturgeon, I still did not understand the mechanics of it.

That night I read the story of *The Sorcerer Knight* again.

The next day, I accosted the thin maidservant as she crossed Sturgeon's garden on an errand for her mistress.

"What else did your mistress throw away after your master died?" I asked her.

She cast a guilty look toward the house. "It means naught," she whined.

"Let me judge that." I resisted the urge to seize and shake her.

"Rope. A length of thin, fine rope."

"Was it blackened, too?"

She nodded, but before I could ask anything more, she fled.

***

That evening, I invited Mistress Sturgeon to sup with me. Afterward, I sent the servants away and fixed her with a steady gaze.

"At some time when you felt certain you would not be seen," I said, "mayhap in the dead of night, you climbed through the trapdoor to the roof and tied your husband's sword to the chimney. Then you attached a length of silk cord, bristling with pins, to the sword, let the other end down beside the window, and fastened it to the lead frame."

She had to swallow hard before she could speak. "What madness is this?"

"Not madness. Murder. And your victim was the one who devised the means of it. You took note of his observations about lightning and put them to good use."

"No one will believe a word of this." Her bravado was touching, if ill-founded.

"Perhaps not, but I might convince the church courts to charge you with sorcery."

"You can prove nothing!" She sprang to her feet. "And in my turn, I will accuse you of foul slander."

I rose, too, blocking her way to the door. "Just tell me why. Why did you want him dead?"

She started to laugh. "How can you ask? He was a cruel man who stopped at nothing to get his own way. He cheated his customers, lent money at a usurer's rates, and mistreated women."

I sighed. "Yes, he did."

"He deserved killing, and it must have been God's will that he die." She was frantic now, determined to convince me of the rightness of her actions. "How else could a sword and a few pins smite him? It was as you said. I listened to his speculations about storms and swords and steeples and tall trees and I devised a plan. When I heard distant thunder that afternoon, I was ready. All I had to do was attach the lower end of the cord to the window. He came into the room just as I finished and flung wide the casement. In the next moment, God struck him down."

Emotions flickered, one after another, across her pale face. Remorse was not one of them, nor was sorrow.

"I never thought it would work," she whispered, more to herself than to me. "I expected he would beat me when he discovered that his sword was missing."

I led her to a padded bench and tugged on her arm until she sat beside me. After a moment, I said, "You are fortunate the house did not catch fire."

"That was God's will, too."

Her voice was stronger and more confident again. Well, why not? She had the right of it. I could prove nothing. She had removed most of the evidence. The rest was now firmly affixed to the sleeves of her mourning gown.

"You have nothing to fear from me," I told her. "I have no intention of going to the justices to accuse you, or to the church courts, either. What would it avail me? No one would believe such a fanciful tale."

"You have powerful friends." She regarded me with wary eyes. "You could cause me a good deal of trouble. Why are you willing to forget what you know?"

"Because your husband deserved to die. He preyed on the weaknesses of women left alone in the world. Once one yielded her virtue to him, he expected her to yield in all things."

She heard the bitterness in my voice and knew my truth, just as I knew hers. At first, Edward Sturgeon had offered sympathy and kindness . . . and a book about a sorcerer knight. But in the end he had been greedy and demanding, angling to take control of my fortune as well as my body.

Had his wife not killed him first, I'd have had to murder him myself.

A ONE-PIPE PROBLEM

by John Gretory Betancourt

WWII veteran Joe Geller is working at building his plumbing business, so he's glad to work on the clogged drain of a Russian countess's bathtub. What he finds in it is a very unpleasant surprise.

Brooklyn
April 24, 1946

Late in the afternoon, a familiar-looking blue Packard Twelve sedan cruised slowly down the street. Boys playing stickball moved to let it pass. I'd seen the Packard a dozen times over the last few months, so I didn't give it a second thought. Its owner visited Madame Anastasia, our neighborhood crackpot spiritualist, on a regular basis.

As the Packard pulled even with my truck, I grabbed a rag and wiped grease from my hands. I'd spent the last half hour replacing spark plugs and tuning the engine till it gave a strong, throaty growl. Best you could expect from a fifteen-year-old Ford.

To my surprise, the Packard's driver stopped and rolled down his window. Mid twenties, dirty blond hair peeking out under his gray chauffer's cap, piercing blue eyes. Good looking in a James Stewart sort of way.

"Mr. Geller?" he asked.

"That's what is says on my truck." I grinned and jerked my thumb toward the side panel, which proclaimed—optimistically— GELLER & SON, PLUMBERS. My boy was not quite a year old and hardly ready for a partnership, but I liked the name. "What can I do you for?"

"I'm looking for Madame Anastasia. I can't seem to find the address. Do you know where . . . ?"

I pointed. "End of the block. The house is the one with the yellow pansies in the flowerbox. She has a sign in the window." I'd read it often enough—Madame Anastasia, Palmist.

"Thanks."

He drove half a block and double-parked. I watched, still cleaning my hands on the rag, as he leaped out and opened the rear door. Behind me, the boys returned to their stickball game, shouting something about Ed Head and the no-hitter he'd pitched for the Brooklyn Dodgers the day before. Someday my own boy would be doing that. I couldn't wait to take him to his first Dodgers game.

A woman dressed all in black emerged from the car. She spoke to the chauffeur, he nodded, and she went up the steps. Madame Anastasia's front door opened. In she went.

After the door closed, the chauffeur backed the Packard into the only empty space on the block, directly in front of my truck. He killed the engine and got out. His left knee was stiff; he had a slight limp.

"See action in the war?" I asked, folding my truck's hood closed with a heavy clang.

He nodded. "I was in the 7th Armored. Didn't make it to the end, though—I got shot up pretty good on D-Day. How about you?"

"The 81st Infantry." I'd spent my time slogging through mud in the South Pacific.

He pulled a pack of Fatimas from his shirt pocket. "Smoke?"

"Thanks." I pulled one from the pack. "Name's Joe. Joe Geller."

"Randall Carter. Randy to my friends."

We both lit up and puffed for a few minutes. He kept glancing toward Madame Anastasia's house.

I gave him one of my business cards. "If you ever need a plumber, give me a call. I do good work, and I'm reasonable on the prices." You never knew where your next job would come from. And with all the competition from newly-released G.I.s, I certainly needed it.

"Sure." He stuck it in his breast pocket.

"New chauffeur?" I guessed.

He nodded. "This is my first day driving for the countess. She doesn't pay attention to addresses. Couldn't tell Queens from Brooklyn."

That explained why he'd had to stop and ask for directions.

I said, "Countess?"

He closed his eyes. "Contesa Maria Habsburg Gruber von Osterling. Yeah, I think that's all of it."

"Sounds German."

"Russian. Second cousin to the last czar, according to her cook. She's a queer old bird. Kept escaping by the skin of her teeth—apparently she got out of St. Petersburg minutes ahead of the Bolshies, then out of Paris as Nazi tanks rolled down the Champs-

Élysées. Kept her cash and her family jewels both times, too."

I whistled. "Lucky."

"Yeah." He glanced up the block. "So what's the deal with this Madame Anastasia? You've never met her?"

"No. Never goes out. Never talks to anyone in the neighborhood. I hear she's some sort of spook chaser. Holds séances, talks to the dead, reads the future in tea leaves. All a bunch of hooey, if you ask me. Lots of women visit her trying to get in touch with dead husbands, or dead mothers or fathers. There oughta be a law against it."

He shook his head. Then Madame Anastasia's front door opened, and out came the countess. She couldn't have been inside more than five minutes. Shortest séance on record?

"Catch you later, Joe!" Randy threw his cigarette into the gutter and scrambled into the Packard. Gunning the motor, he raced to pick up his employer.

***

The next morning, the phone in our hallway rang at 8:30 sharp. Madge, my wife, took the call like a professional switchboard operator: "Geller Plumbing, how may I assist you?" She waited a heartbeat, then motioned me in from the kitchen.

"It's a Mr. Randall Carter, sir," she said, grinning.

I grinned back, passed over the baby who wasn't screaming for once, and picked up the receiver.

"Nice to hear from you, Randy!" I said.

"Glad I caught you," he said. "I thought I might throw some business your way. The countess has a clogged drain, and I haven't been able to fix it. Think you can take a look?"

"Sure. Let me check my schedule." Mentally, I ran down my list of appointments. One job the next afternoon, and that was it for the week. "It looks like I have some free time this morning. What's the address?"

He gave it to me, and I jotted it down: a brownstone in the East 50s, Manhattan.

***

Traffic over the Brooklyn Bridge wasn't bad, and I reached the countess's four-story brownstone a short time later. It was in a ritzy area. The houses all had intricate stained glass panels over doors and windows. Men in suits and ties headed for the subway.

I cruised around the block, found parking, and lugged my toolbox over to the countess's address. I rang the bell at the basement door, and a few moments later, a stern-faced maid in a black-and-white uniform opened up. She gave me the fish-eye, but when I introduced myself as the plumber, she nodded.

"Come in," she said, her voice heavy with a Russian accent. "It is this way." It came out, Eet ees zis vay.

She led me up a wide marble staircase. We passed oil paintings of sour-faced old men in 19th-century military uniforms, reached the second-floor hallway, and turned left into the countess's bedroom. Plush oriental rugs covered the floor, and a huge bed covered in white satin sat against the far wall. There were two dressing tables with round mirrors and two walk-in closets with open doors. It looked like the countess owned a lot of clothes.

The maid steered me to the countess's private bathroom, then left to go back downstairs. The bathroom floor was a mosaic of tiny pink tiles, and had a pink pedestal sink, a white porcelain toilet with an overhead tank and dangling flush chain, and an ancient bathtub with huge clawed feet. The white enamel had chipped in several placed along the tub's rim.

Randy, still in his chauffeur's uniform but with the jacket off and the shirt-sleeves rolled up, was having a go at the drain with a hand plunger. He set the plunger aside when he saw me.

"Thanks for the call, Randy," I said. "Let me see what I can do."

I set my toolbox down and peeked into the tub. Six inches of dirty brown water swirled slowly to a stop at the bottom.

Randy mopped his forehead with a hand towel. "Thanks for coming so fast, Joe. The drain is really jammed up."

"It's these old houses . . . The pipes aren't big enough. I get calls like this all the time. I'll have it open in a minute."

I rolled up my right sleeve, reached into the water, and felt around for the drain. At least the stopper had been removed. You'd think anyone with a clogged drain would check first for a stopper, but I'd found them wedged in place more than once over the years.

When I stuck my index finger down the hole, I felt no resistance. Probably a hair clog at the elbow joint.

Flipping back the toolbox lid with my left hand, I pulled out a coil of rough, triple-braided wire. The "drain buster," as I called it, had a hand crank at one end and a spray of iron bristles at the other. I'd built the gizmo myself from spare parts. It didn't look like much, but it usually did the trick.

I guided the bristle-end into the drain, stood up, and started cranking. The corkscrew action forced the bristles and wire down the pipe, and sure enough, after the first foot had played out, I saw a sudden rush of air bubbles. I'd reached the clog.

Giving a few more turns for good measure, I pulled the wire out. It came free with a gurgling pop, then a miniature whirlpool formed and dirty water began to empty.

As the last half inch flowed away, I reached down to clean the drain-buster . . . and froze. I'd expected a knot of soap-scum covered hair, and sure enough, a rat's nest of human hair was stuck to the bristles. But among the long, black hairs were shorter gray ones attached to what looked like a couple of half-inch chunks of very white, very human scalp. And—was that a broken tooth? I swallowed hard. I'd seen enough bits and pieces of dead bodies during the war to recognize stray bits of human anatomy.

I took the towel Randy had used and worked the clump free. Slowly I turned it over. It was definitely a tooth, complete with a gold filling. And those gray hairs went into the scalp . . . and they were so short, they could only have come from a man's head. The scalp part looked relatively fresh. No older than a day or two.

"Geez!" Randy said with a gulp, looking over my shoulder. "Is that . . . ?"

"Yes," I said. I straightened. "Is there anyone with hair like this in the house?" And is he missing a tooth?

"I—I don't think so. I'm the only guy here. All the countess's other servants are women."

"Is there a count?"

He shook his head. "Widowed. Years ago in Paris, I think."

A floorboard creaked behind us. I folded the towel over the tooth and hair, then glanced over my shoulder.

Countess von Osterling stood in the doorway. She wore black again, but with an old-fashioned white lace collar. She regarded us both with a cool, detached gaze, like a scientist examining insects through a magnifying glass.

I stood up. "Ma'am," I said.

"The job, is it finished?" She had the same accent as her maid, only not quite as heavy.

"Yes, ma'am," I said. "Just cleaning up."

"Leave your bill with Randall. He will see you out."

"Yes, ma'am."

She gave a short nod, turned, and continued down the hall. I heard slow, heavy steps on the staircase.

I don't know why, but I had been holding my breath. I let it out and looked at Randy.

"She gives me the creeps," I said softly.

"The old chauffeur!" he whispered. "The cook said he retired and went to Florida. He'd been with the countess since St. Petersburg."

"Do you know his name?"

"Fyodor . . . Klonski? Something like that. He left a few papers in my room."

I glanced at the towel again. If he's been with her since the days of the czar, Klonski would have been older . . . like the owner of the chunk of gray hair from the drain. But how could Klonski have lost a piece of his scalp in here? If he'd been hurt or killed he'd be in the hospital or the morgue, not Florida. A chill went through me. I placed the handtowel and its grisly contents inside my toolbox and shut the lid.

"Hey—why are you keeping that?" Randy said. "Shouldn't you flush it or something?"

"Think about it. How could part of a scalp and a tooth get lodged in this particular drain?"

"Maybe . . ." He bit his lip and looked away.

I said, "Maybe he was murdered. Maybe someone washed up in here. Or cleaned the murder weapon in the bathtub."

"That's crazy!"

"Is it?"

"The countess is an old lady. She doesn't go around murdering people. There has to be another explanation."

"If so, I want to know what it is."

"If we go to the cops, she'll fire me. I need this job, Joe. This is the best job I ever had."

I sighed, looked away. Still, I couldn't very well go to the cops and say, "I found some skin and hair in a drain, can you question everyone in the house?" They'd laugh me out of the police station.

"Okay. We won't do anything rash."

Randy gave a sigh of relief.

"But if it was a murder, she'd have to dispose of the body. Right?"

"I suppose so."

"Does she drive?" I asked.

"No."

"Then she would have to stash it in the house somewhere."

He nodded. "Maybe . . . the basement?"

"Makes sense. If we find a grave, we call the police."

"And if there's nothing, we forget about it."

"Agreed."

We shook on it.

***

Randy and I went to the basement to "check the pipes," which generated no suspicion from the maid who'd let me into the house, nor with the kitchen staff. We trooped down rickety wooden steps and found ourselves in a dim, dusty packrat's hoard. Evidently the basement had been used for storing everything unwanted or unneeded for generations. I had never seen such a jumble of broken furniture, old dishes, steamer trunks, and miscellany in all my life. A junk dealer would have had a field day.

Randy found an old hurricane lamp with some kerosene in the base and lit it, then we prowled through the dusty debris looking for evidence of murder. No bodies. No blood. Nothing. Even the pipes looked sound.

I was about to give up when, at the foot of the stairs, sitting atop an old desk, I spotted a shiny metal kitchen hammer, the kind my wife uses to tenderize meat. I waved Randy over and pointed to it.

"So what?" he said, frowning. "There are tools all over the place. I don't see any blood."

"Look at it," I said. "Then look at everything else on the desk."

He stared. Then he paled when he, too, realized a thick layer of dust coated everything except the hammer. It was spotlessly clean, as though recently scrubbed.

"But there's no body," he said. "Doesn't that count for something?"

"That has to be the murder weapon," I said, raising the lamp and turning it slowly, taking in the room. "Is there anything else down here that isn't covered in dust? And why wouldn't it be in the kitchen?"

He bit his lip, shrugged.

After that, we looked through the basement again, trying to hurry. Finally, as we were about to give up, I lowered the hurricane lamp and peered under the desk. I hadn't paid much attention to the boxes beneath it, since they weren't big enough to conceal a body, but this time one caught my eye. It was an old tin breadbox, and like the hammer, it had no dust on it.

I picked it up and set it on the desk. It was a lot heavier than it should have been.

I passed the lamp to Randy, then pulled open the little door. Inside sat a black leather notebook. I pulled it out, flipped it open, and found tables of numbers and plenty of writing in what looked like the Russian alphabet. I couldn't make sense of anything.

"What the Hell is that?" Randy whispered.

"I don't know. Maybe a codebook?"

"That's nuts! Why would the countess need a codebook? I bet it's a diary, or a log of household expenses."

"Well . . . maybe. But why hide it down here?"

He had no answer.

I put everything back in place, closed the little door, and stowed the breadbox under the desk where I'd found it.

"Are you doing anything tonight?" I asked Randy.

"If the countess doesn't need me to drive her anywhere, I get off at six."

"Come out and see me. And wear your civvies. I . . . I think we need to talk to Madame Anastasia."

"About the countess? Do you want to get me fired?"

"Would you rather go to the police? We can bring them the scalp, the tooth, and the codebook."

He shut up. But I could tell he wasn't happy.

"We'll be discreet," I promised.

"This was the best job I ever had," he muttered.

***

Randy showed up in front of my house at 6:40, dressed in a plain brown suit, an ugly brown necktie, and a brown fedora with a little white feather in the band. I was tinkering with my Ford's engine between sips of beer while the neighborhood boys played kick the can. Madge was inside with our son cooking dinner. Spaghetti, from the smell.

I'd already stopped by Madame Anastasia's place and made an appointment for us to see her. I'd told her a friend wanted to contact his dead uncle. Of course, she ate it up.

"Want a beer?" I asked.

"Maybe later." He looked like his dog just died.

"I know you don't want to see her," I said, "but if there's something fishy going on, we have a duty to find out. And if there isn't, well, the countess never needs to know."

In silence, he pulled out a pack of Fatimas and offered me one. I took it. We both lit up and watched the kids, who were now arguing about whether the Detroit Tigers or the Boston Red Sox had better pitchers. It almost came to a fist fight, but someone changed the subject to the Yankees. Everyone hated the Yankees.

I glanced at my watch. Almost 7:00. I stubbed out my cigarette, and Randy did the same—the smoke seemed to have steadied his nerves. Then I closed the hood of my truck, finished my beer, and wiped my hands clean. I put the rag and the empty beer can in the cab.

A six-inch piece of copper pipe sat on the passenger seat, left over from a small job I'd done for one of the neighbors that afternoon. I grabbed it and stuck it in my pocket. I didn't have my service rifle anymore, but I didn't want to go in defenseless. Semper Fi.

"Let's go," he said. "I want to get it over with."

"Remember, spring the old chauffeur's name on her. Try to catch her off guard."

"I know. I got it."

We might have been on a death march, from his expression. But he matched me step for step, and in a minute we were in front of Madame Anastasia's house. I climbed the steps and rang the bell.

A second later, the door swung open, and Madame Anastasia stood there: a heavyset woman in her late 50s, with dark hair, dark eyes, and yellow-toothed smile. She was dressed like the gypsy in *The Wolf Man*.

"Please, come in," she said, bowing slightly and stepping back. She had an accent similar to the countess's.

I followed her into a darkened front hall. On the left, a staircase led to the second floor. On the right was a closed door to what I imagined would be the parlor. Dark red drapes covered all the walls, and three red candles burned on a table at the far side of the room. A sickly sweet smell I couldn't identify hung in the air—herbs or incense of some kind, no doubt.

"This is the friend I told you about," I said, taking off my cap. "Randall Carter."

"Pleased to meet you, ma'am," Randy said. He took off his fedora, too.

"Young seeker of wisdom," she said. She smiled up at his face and patted his arm. "It is two dollars for the first reading."

"Two dollars!" Randy looked ready to throw up. And I didn't think he was acting.

"Here." I pulled out my wallet and gave Madame Anastasia a pair of bills before Randy could object.

"This way, young sir," she said, taking his arm and drawing him toward the door. It swung open at her touch, revealing a room lit by half a dozen candles. A small table with two chairs sat in the middle. She steered him to one of the chairs while motioning me to a bench beside the door. Apparently I would be permitted to stay and observe.

I sat heavily. The pipe in my pocket thumped against the wooden seat, then dug painfully into my leg. Shifting to one side, I pulled it out.

"You are grieving," she said to Randy. "I feel your pain."

"Yes," Randy said. "I—"

She raised one finger to silence him. "First," she said, settling herself across from him, "you must tell me the name of this dear departed relative."

"Fyodor," he said. "Fyodor Klonski."

She tensed. "What was that name?"

"Uncle Fyodor. Fyodor Klonski."

She shifted, and from my position, I saw her hand dart under the table. A finger stabbed upward—pushing a button? Over our heads, footsteps thumped on the second floor. A distant door slammed.

I leaped to my feet. "What did you do?" I pointed at her with the pipe. "I saw your hand—you did something under the table!"

She leaned back and folded her arms. "Who sent you? How do you know my Fyodor's name? What is this game?"

Randy said, "We think Fyodor Klonski's dead. The countess—"

A heavy tread sounded in the hallway. The door burst open, and a bald-headed man rushed in. I saw a pistol in his hand. Without thinking, I swung at it with my pipe.

Bone crunched, and he dropped the pistol, howling in pain. The gun hit the floor and discharged.

Baldy tried to turn, but I kicked his feet out from under him. Randy tackled him a second later, then sat on his back and pinned his arms behind him.

Madame Anastasia went for the pistol, but I leaped forward and scooped it up first. A German Mauser. I cocked the trigger and backed into the doorway.

"Let him up, Randy," I said, aiming for Baldy's chest.

Randy rose a little unsteadily and staggered to my side.

"Up against the wall," I said to Baldy. "Mach schnell!" It wasn't Russian, but it was as close as I could come.

He obeyed—sullenly, it seemed to me. Randy sagged against the wall, then slid to a seated position on the floor.

"What's wrong?" I asked.

"I—I think he winged me." His left hand glistened in the candlelight, dark and slick with blood. Adrenaline must have been keeping him going.

Madame Anastasia stared at us. "My Fyodor—why do you think he is dead?" she demanded. "Tell me!"

"I'm a plumber," I told her. "I went to the countess's house to clear a drain, and I found bits of gray hair and scalp, plus a tooth with a gold filling, caught in the drain. He was the only man in the house. Suddenly the countess is telling people he retired and went to Florida. You do the math."

She bit her lip, looked away. Tears trickled down her cheeks.

"You have a phone?" I asked her. I hadn't seen one on the way in.

She didn't answer. She probably did, but I didn't have time to search for it.

"You up for guarding them?" I asked Randy.

"Yeah. Give me that pistol."

I passed him the Mauser. He held the grip in his right hand, bracing the barrel on his knee. It pointed unwaveringly at Baldy.

"Can you hold on for a few minutes?" I asked. "There's a police station a block away."

"Go!" he said through gritted teeth. His eyes were bright in the flickering glow of the candles. "Just make it fast!"

I ran.

***

They called us heroes and patriots in the newspapers. We got our pictures in the *Brooklyn Eagle*, the *New York World-Telegram*, *The New York Times*, and a dozen other papers. Most of them ran banner headlines like "Local Boys Smash Spy Ring" or "Brooklyn Boys Nab Ruskie Spies." Never mind that Randy lived in Manhattan.

It seems Madame Anastasia had been pumping her clients for American secrets . . . not just A-Bomb stuff, but anything of interest to the Commies. And she turned over everything she learned to the countess, whose history—from escaping the Bolsheviks to fleeing Nazi occupation in Paris—had been invented wholesale for public consumption.

This time the countess didn't escape by the skin of her teeth. The Feds nabbed her in her brownstone, and they found the codebook exactly where Randy and I had left it. None of the spies were talking, but the Feds put together a pretty good case. They figured the countess and Baldy murdered the chauffeur in the bathroom. Apparently Klonski and Madame Anastasia fell in love and planned to quit the spy game. Of course, the countess couldn't let that happen. She lured Klonski to her bathroom on some pretext, then a quick blow with the meat hammer finished him off.

No one ever found the body. I figure Baldy must have taken the car and buried Klonski on Long Island, or maybe over in New Jersey.

***

Randy lost a lot of blood, but never was in any real danger. By the time he got out of the hospital, he had a dozen job offers waiting. He ended up driving for one of the Rockefellers.

And as for me . . . well, Geller & Son uses a real appointment book now. The Rockefellers have a lot of houses in Manhattan. Between Randy's referrals and the write-ups I got as a local hero, I have all the business I can handle.

THE KILLING GAME

by Victoria Thompson

*In 1917, grifter Elizabeth (in tandem with her mentor
The Old Man) is setting up a con called* The Killing
Game. *But nothing in their scheme turns out like they
expect.*

July 1917

"Don't you think you waited a little too long to take me on my very
first picnic?" Elizabeth asked the Old Man.

He shifted slightly, making himself more comfortable on the
richly upholstered seat of their hired motorcar. "It's the Fourth of
July, Lizzie. Everybody goes on a picnic on the Fourth of July."

"Not everybody." Especially not them, not ever. "And don't
pretend we're going all the way out to Long Island just so you can
take me on a picnic."

The Old Man smiled the smile that had bamboozled thousands
of gullible chumps. "Lizzie doesn't trust me, Max."

Their driver grinned at her over his shoulder. "Smart girl."

"Just tell me what the game is and what part I'm playing."

The Old Man sighed with so much long suffering that Lizzie
could almost believe he was aggrieved by her mistrust. Almost.
"I'm going to meet a Mr. Vandermere. He owns a lot of land on
Long Island, and I want to buy a place where I can train my
racehorses."

This was surprising, since the Old Man didn't own any
racehorses. But he did earn his very nice living by telling lies, so
Elizabeth was only a little surprised.

"And you want me to charm Mr. Vandermere?"

"No, his son. The son keeps a close eye on him, I'm told. I
want to invite the father to the racetrack so he can get interested in
my racehorses, but of course I don't want the son to know about
it." Ah, he was going to play the Killing Game, where the mark
thinks he'll make a killing on a fixed horserace. The horse farm
story was nothing but a fairy tale to get the Old Man on friendly
terms with his mark.

"So I'm just a distraction."

"Oh, Lizzie, you are so much more than that. But in this case, yes, you are a distraction. You'll play my daughter."

"That should be easy enough."

Max gave a snort of laughter.

The Old Man pretended not to notice.

The entire population of Long Grove was apparently attending the Fourth of July community picnic. They'd missed the parade that morning, thank heaven, but they'd arrived well in time for the pig roast and the foot races, and the pie eating contest and many other activities that Lizzie found more than a little amusing. They made no effort to find Mr. Vandermere, of course. That would have been foolish.

Instead, they wandered around and made small talk with the locals. As strangers, they were naturally objects of curiosity. Elizabeth's white summer frock was the height of fashion, and the Old Man's linen suit was a tailor's masterpiece. But their red Cadillac Town Car and uniformed driver attracted the most attention of all. The Old Man had hired the biggest, fanciest vehicle to be found in New York City, and he'd asked for Max to drive it. He'd used Max before and knew he was reliable.

Several young ladies immediately found Max in his uniform fascinating, and Lizzie had to admit he did look attractive. She just hoped he didn't get them run out of town by some irate father protecting his daughter's virtue.

At some point in the middle of the afternoon, the mayor got up on a makeshift stage in the middle of the town's park, made a short speech, and introduced some dignitaries. Mr. Vandermere was one of them. After what Lizzie considered way too much bluster about very little of importance, the mayor called Mr. Vandermere to the podium where he announced that some of the young men of the town would be passing baskets through the crowd so people could donate to support the local orphanage.

The Old Man had attracted his own group of followers through the course of the day, although his were middle-aged men in bespoke suits wearing diamond stick pins in their four-in-hand ties. They'd recognized him as one of their own, a successful businessman who might be interested in investing in their flea-bitten little town. Fat chance of that, but the Old Man did give this impression, with his handsome face, his expertly trimmed silver hair, and his fine clothes. His charming conversation and his lovely daughter didn't hurt, either.

As the young men passed the baskets, all of these businessmen pulled out their wallets and made a show of donating a fiver or a ten-spot. When the basket reached the Old Man, however, he casually dropped in twenty-five dollars. The boy holding the basket gasped.

"That's mighty generous of you, Mr. Miles," one of his new friends, a man named Snyder, marveled. "You aren't even from around here."

"Oh, the children need it more than I do," the Old Man said. "What's next on the schedule? We don't want to miss anything, do we, Lizzie?"

Several of his companions insisted on buying them some ice cream, and by the time they'd enjoyed their treat, Mr. Vandermere had made his appearance. He was a scrawny fellow with a shock of fading red hair who put her in mind of a banty rooster. He introduced himself as the president of the orphanage's board of directors and thanked the Old Man profusely for his contribution.

The Old Man waved him off, as if it were nothing. "I'm happy to help."

"May I ask what brings you to our town today? I know we have a first-class celebration here, but surely you could have found a bigger one in the city."

"As a matter of fact, I decided this would be a good opportunity to look around the area and get a feel for the people here. You see, I'm hoping to buy some land where I can set up a farm to raise and train my racehorses."

"What a lucky meeting," Vandermere said. "I happen to own some property that would be perfect for a horse farm."

The two men had just begun to discuss this interesting coincidence when a younger man hurried over. "Father, I thought I'd lost you."

He had his father's red hair but not his physique. He was a little on the pudgy side, and the July heat had turned his face an unbecoming shade of red beneath a generous sprinkling of freckles. He glared at the Old Man suspiciously.

Mr. Vandermere introduced his son, Joseph, so the Old Man turned to her. "And may I present my daughter, Elizabeth."

She gave the younger Vandermere her hand and her own version of the smile that had bamboozled many chumps. Not thousands yet, but she was still young. She mentally added one more to the tally when young Vandermere forgot to release her hand.

"Maybe you could escort Elizabeth over to watch the three-legged race, Joe," the Old Man said. "That would give me a chance to find a shady spot to sit down for a few minutes."

"I'd be happy to, Mr. Miles," Joe said, and he did.

Elizabeth managed to keep him enthralled and away from his

father for the better part of two hours, and by the time they found the two men again, Mr. Vandermere had agreed to be the Old Man's guest for a day at the racetrack where he could see some of his horses perform. Vandermere had also asked the Old Man not to say a word about it to his son.

Having accomplished what they'd set out to do, they took their leave and found Max entertaining a rather disheveled young lady in the back seat of the motorcar. She hurried off, giggling and blushing, while Max stared appreciatively after her, absently rearranging his uniform.

"I'm so glad you were able to amuse yourself while we were gone," the Old Man said.

Max grinned. "So am I."

"Until your wife finds out," Elizabeth added.

Max's grin turned sheepish. "If that ever happens, I'll be dead."

***

Two weeks later, Elizabeth was eating a late breakfast when somebody started pounding on the front door of the ramshackle house where she lived in Greenwich Village. Since her housemates were both already gone for the day, she had to answer it herself.

She sighed when she peeked out the window and saw Jake on the porch. She'd first met him when she was thirteen. Her mother had just died, and the Old Man had taken her to live with Jake and his mother, an arrangement that pleased no one. She and Jake had spent every minute since competing for the Old Man's attention.

She didn't even have a chance to ask him what he thought he was doing, pounding on the door like that, before he blurted, "The Old Man's been arrested."

It didn't happen often. The wily old devil was usually too clever to even let a mark know he'd been fleeced. But if it did happen, Jake had no reason to be upset. "You know what to do. Call his attorney and bail him out and—"

"You don't understand. He's been arrested for murder!"

"Murder? That's impossible. Who is he supposed to have killed?"

"That driver, Max."

***

By the time they arrived at the attorney's office, Elizabeth had almost recovered from her shock. When he wasn't drinking, Oscar Pendleton was an excellent attorney, and he never drank before five o'clock, thank heaven.

"I've spoken to the district attorney's office, and I think I can get him bailed out, but it looks very bad for him," Pendleton said.

"What on earth makes them think the Old Man killed Max?" Elizabeth asked.

"Two witnesses identified him."

"Witnesses? You mean somebody actually saw him do it?" Jake nearly shouted.

"No, nothing like that. This is what happened. It seems a well-dressed man went to the Plaza Hotel and asked the switchboard operator where he could hire a motorcar. He particularly wanted a red Cadillac Town Car. The operator suggested Dandy Dan's Garage, so he telephoned them and requested the vehicle, and he asked for Max by name to be his driver."

"That doesn't sound right," Elizabeth said. "The Old Man wouldn't need to ask a switchboard operator where to hire a motorcar."

"Of course not," Pendleton said. "So this fellow—he gave his name as Smith, of course—had them bring the motor to the hotel, and the doorman remembers helping him into it when it got there. Seems like the fellow didn't tip him as much as he'd expected."

"Which proves it wasn't the Old Man," Jake said. At least Jake was right about that.

"Anyway, the next morning they find the motor on the side of the road out on Long Island. Max is in the driver's seat, shot dead."

"Which also proves the Old Man didn't do it," Jake repeated. "He never carries a gun."

"We know that, but who else does?" Elizabeth asked. "Where on Long Island did they find him?"

"Near some little town called Long Grove."

Just as Elizabeth had feared. "I still don't understand why they think it was the Old Man who shot Max."

"That's where the witnesses come into it. Nobody had any idea who this Smith was, of course, but when they questioned Dandy Dan, he remembered the Old Man had hired the same motorcar to take him to Long Island and had asked for Max in particular, just like he always does. The cops took the Old Man's picture to the hotel and both the switchboard operator and the doorman identified him as the man who had hired the motor."

"But the Old Man would've just gone to Dandy Dan if he wanted to hire a motor," Elizabeth reminded him. "And Max is Dan's son-in-law, so he knows why the Old Man always asks for him."

"That's what I told them," Pendleton said. "But the district attorney thinks the Old Man was planning to kill Max all along, and he did it that way so Dan wouldn't know he was the one who hired the motor."

Jake swore and Elizabeth sighed in exasperation.

"What does the Old Man say?" Elizabeth asked.

"That he didn't do it, of course."

"Then all they have is these two witnesses," Elizabeth said. "We need to discredit them first and then figure out who really killed Max. That's the only way we can be sure the cops will leave the Old Man alone."

"How can we do that?" Jake asked.

Elizabeth smiled. "Well, first we bail him out."

***

"Are you sure this is going to work?" the Old Man asked as he and Elizabeth strolled over to the switchboard operator at the Plaza Hotel. He wasn't exactly nervous—she'd never really seen him nervous—but he did seem a trifle less confident than usual.

"Of course it is. Unless you really did kill Max."

He didn't even bother to reply.

As they reached the desk, he put a protective hand on Elizabeth's back and she affected a distressed expression.

"Excuse me, miss," he said to the operator. "This young lady needs to make an urgent telephone call. Can you help her?"

"Of course," the operator said. She was a middle-aged lady who apparently took great pride in her appearance, probably to ensure that she kept her job in the fancy hotel. "Just give me the number."

Elizabeth did and they waited while the operator made the connection and gave Elizabeth the telephone. She began a long conversation with an imaginary person about her missing, imaginary brother who was supposed to have met her at the hotel hours ago but never showed up. Meanwhile, the Old Man turned his attention to the operator.

"This must be an interesting job," he said, giving her his famous smile. "I'll bet you hear all sorts of things."

"You wouldn't believe it if I told you," she replied. "But of course, I can't say a word."

"I know he said he'd meet me today," Elizabeth said into the dead telephone. Jake had already hung up. "Do you suppose he's been in an accident?"

The Old Man and the operator ignored her. "I don't suppose you ever see anything really criminal here, though, not with the class of people who stay at the Plaza," he said.

"Oh, we do, but it's all very discreet," the operator assured him. "The house detective makes sure the police don't get involved."

"But didn't I read something in the newspaper this morning? Did somebody get murdered here?"

"Oh dear, no, not at the hotel. But the police were here the other day, questioning me."

"You? Whatever for?"

"But where could he be?" Elizabeth lamented into the telephone. "Can't you do something?"

The operator leaned closer so they wouldn't be overheard. "A gentleman came in a few days ago and asked me to help him hire a motorcar and driver."

"That doesn't sound like a police matter to me."

"Not normally, no, but the driver ended up murdered."

"Really? And they think this fellow who hired the motor did it?"

"Yes, and they asked me to identify him."

"You mean they brought him here in person?"

"Oh, no, they showed me a photograph. Just between us, it was a terrible photograph, but they told me he was the man who had hired the motorcar, so I said I recognized him."

Elizabeth wanted to slap the woman, but she turned her fury on the imaginary person on the other end of the telephone line. "If that's all you have to say then I suppose I'll have to find him myself." She argued a bit more while the Old Man continued to chat with the operator, finding out where she was from and how she'd become an operator.

As planned, Oscar Pendleton came strolling up. "Excuse me, I hate to interrupt old friends, but could you help me?"

"Oh, we aren't old friends," the operator said with a laugh.

"You're not? I could have sworn you were, the way you were chatting."

"Not at all," the operator said. "In fact, I've never seen this gentleman before in my life."

"Are you sure?" the Old Man asked with a teasing grin.

She grinned back. "Absolutely."

"Well, I wouldn't mind seeing you again," the Old Man said.

The operator seemed surprised, but very pleased. "I'm here every day."

Elizabeth let her argument trail off and ended her call, hanging up with an angry sigh.

"Is everything all right, miss?" the Old Man asked.

"I have no idea, but I need to go home immediately. Thank you so much for your help, sir, and you, too, miss," she added to the operator.

"No trouble at all," the Old Man said. "Let me escort you outside to get a cab." He gave the operator a wink and then walked away with Elizabeth.

"I told you it would work," she said when they were nearly to the door.

He just sighed.

Outside, the doorman greeted them and cheerfully tried to hail a cab for them, but none were immediately available. While they waited, the Old Man turned to the doorman and asked how he was doing on this fine summer's day. After a few minutes of conversation, the doorman mentioned, with some subtle prodding, having been questioned by the police about a murder. When he had finished telling the tale, Pendleton came out and did his little part of the drama again. When the doorman insisted he'd never seen the Old Man before in his life, Pendleton joined his client and Elizabeth in the cab, and they went straight to the district attorney's office.

***

"The district attorney was pretty annoyed with the cops who did the investigation," Pendleton explained to Elizabeth, Jake, and the Old Man when the four of them met up in his office that evening. "He sent us back to the Plaza with the lead detective to verify our story and the operator and the doorman both admitted that Mr. Miles wasn't the man who hired the motor from Dandy Dan's."

"I have to admit, I didn't think your plan would work, Lizzie," Jake said, annoying her as he loved to do.

"And you were wrong once again, Jake," she replied sweetly. "We're not done yet, though. The coppers will be really mad that we made them look like fools."

"But they are fools," Jake said.

"They're also coppers," Elizabeth said. "That means they can harass the Old Man so much he won't be able to work. And sooner or later they'll find something to charge him with that will stick."

The Old Man nodded grimly. "Lizzie is right. We've got to make it up to them by handing them the real killer."

"Do you know who the real killer is?" Elizabeth asked.

"Not exactly, but I have a suspicion."

"Does it have something to do with the game you're playing with Vandermere?"

"Not directly, but . . . do you remember that girl we saw with Max at the picnic?"

"What picnic?" Jake asked, jealous as always. "Don't tell me he took you on a picnic."

Lizzie just smiled.

"I needed her to deal with the mark's son," the Old Man said patiently.

"I could've done that," Jake said.

The Old Man gave him a pitying look and turned back to Elizabeth. "I made two trips out to Long Island afterward to look at the land he wanted to sell me. Max took me both times, and both times Vandermere insisted on driving me to his property himself. So I left Max and the motorcar in Long Grove for most of the day."

"And you think he was seeing this girl while you were off with Vandermere?" Elizabeth asked.

"He was doing something that made him very happy to wait for me, and very anxious to return."

Knowing Max, that meant a girl. "When did you plan to go back?"

"In a few days. I found some property I like, and I need to bring my architect to look at it. I was going to spend the night at Vandermere's house and get a telegram the next morning about the fixed horserace."

Yes, the Killing Game. Elizabeth turned to Jake and looked him up and down. "Nobody will believe Jake is an architect."

Jake started to protest, but the Old Man cut him off. "No, they won't. Handsome Willy is my architect. Jake will be my driver since Max is . . . unavailable."

"And I need to go along, too," Elizabeth said.

"Why? You don't need a twist for the Killing Game," Jake said.

Elizabeth gave him a glare that told him just how she felt about being called a twist. "No, but you'll need somebody to deal with the girl."

"What girl?"

"Max's girl."

***

They decided Mr. Vandermere didn't need to know Elizabeth had accompanied the Old Man and his architect, so Jake dropped the Old Man and Handsome Willy off at the bank where Vandermere was president. Then he drove Elizabeth to the park where Max had found a shady spot to park the red Cadillac Town Car they'd hired again today, and they waited.

"What makes you think this will work?" Jake grumbled after he'd cut off the engine.

"Nothing, but it stands to reason that if Max was meeting a girl when he came here, the sight of this motor parked in the usual place will bring her out."

"But wouldn't he have sent her some kind of message to let her know he was coming?"

"Maybe, but how would he contact her without her parents

finding out? I'm guessing she checks the park every day to see if the motorcar is here."

Jake muttered something she didn't want to hear, slumped down into his seat, and pulled his chauffeur's hat over his eyes. Elizabeth pulled a deck of cards from her purse and practiced dealing. Not that the Old Man would ever permit her to use her skills by actually gambling, but who knew when being able to deal from the bottom of the deck and palm the winning card would come in handy?

By the end of an hour, she was hot and cranky and more than ready to find a café where they could enjoy some lunch. Before she could suggest it to Jake, however, a shadow passed her window and a girl's voice said, "Max?"

Jake jolted awake, knocking his hat off his face. The girl jumped back a step and cried out in surprise.

"You're not Max," she said accusingly.

"Uh, no, I'm not."

"Where is he?"

"He's . . .uh . . . Lizzie?" the coward called, as she'd known he would.

Elizabeth scrambled out of the back seat, surprising the girl even more.

"Who are you?" the girl demanded. She was a pretty little thing, if a bit young, and someone gave her a large allowance for clothes. She'd spent it well.

"I'm Elizabeth Miles. I saw you with Max at the Fourth of July picnic. Were you looking for him?"

"I . . . uh . . . yes. But I guess he's not here." She glanced doubtfully at Jake who had climbed out as well.

"I don't suppose you've heard the news then," Elizabeth said.

"What news is that?"

"I'm very sorry to tell you, but Max is . . . well, he's dead."

The girl's face went white and she swayed. Jake caught her before she fell, and they took her to a nearby bench. When she wanted to know what had happened, Elizabeth told her. Jake, of course, was no help at all.

"Shot? Why would someone shoot him? He was just your father's chauffeur," she protested.

"We think it might have something to do with you," Jake said.

Elizabeth wanted to smack him, but she hastily added, "We thought someone might've been jealous of you and Max. Or maybe your family didn't approve of him."

"My family? They don't know I'm seeing Max."

"Are you sure?" Jake asked. "Could your father have found out and gone to New York to hire the motorcar and ask for Max to drive it?"

"Hire the motorcar?" the girl echoed stupidly. "I thought it belonged to your father," she added to Elizabeth.

"No, it's hired, and Max worked for Dandy Dan's Garage."

"Dandy Dan's? That's where I sent the letter."

"What letter?"

The color rushed back to the girl's cheeks. "I—I sent him a love letter."

"To the garage?" Elizabeth asked with a growing sense of dread.

"I know it was forward of me, but I wanted him to know how I felt. I was afraid he'd get back to the city and forget all about me. He told me you kept your motor at Dandy Dan's Garage and he had a nice little apartment above it. He said we could live there together if I came back to the city with him. So I wrote to tell him I wanted to be with him."

"And you sent it to Dandy Dan's Garage," Elizabeth repeated, ignoring Jake's puzzled frown.

"Yes, I found the address at the library. They have a New York City directory. But that couldn't have anything to do with Max getting shot. I told you, my family doesn't know anything about him, and my father doesn't even own a gun."

"Maybe he got one to shoot your lover," Jake snarled, trying to sound like a tough guy.

"Shut up, Jake," Elizabeth said. "Of course your father isn't involved. I'm sorry about Max. You better go along home now, before someone wonders what you're doing here."

The girl started crying, but Elizabeth sent her on her way.

"Why'd you let her go?" Jake asked.

"Because I know who killed Max now, and why."

***

"I never meant for them to arrest you," Dandy Dan explained to the Old Man when he and Elizabeth met him in the visitor's room in the New York City jail, known as the Tombs.

"I'm glad to hear it," the Old Man said with only a trace of sarcasm. "It was clever of you to go to the Plaza and hire one of your own motorcars, though."

"I figured they'd be looking for some fellow named Smith, and they never would've suspected me of hiring my own motor."

"What did Max say when he realized it was you?" Elizabeth asked.

Dan frowned at the memory. "He laughed at first. Thought I was pulling a prank, but I told him you'd asked me to meet him out on Long Island and pretend to be some kind of business associate. He believed that."

"Did you tell him the truth before you shot him?" the Old Man asked.

"Yes. I told him about the letter that girl sent. I knew what it was the minute it arrived. The handwriting gave it away, and she'd even put perfume on it. I didn't want to read it, but I had to. Can you believe it? He'd told her they'd live together over the garage. That's where he lives with my daughter! I knew what I had to do then. I couldn't let him treat my girl that way."

"Did your daughter know?" Elizabeth asked.

"About the girl or that I killed Max?"

"Both."

"Not until the cops came to arrest me. I had to tell her then and I had to tell her why I did it. She's pretty upset, but at least she's not missing Max as much as she was."

"I'm sorry we had to give you up," the Old Man said. "But the cops weren't going to leave me alone unless we solved the case for them. Don't worry, though. I've hired Pendleton to represent you. He says all they have is the operator and the doorman at the Plaza, who already identified the wrong man once, so now they don't want to identify anybody."

"What about the girl? Won't she testify about the letter?"

The Old Man nodded to Elizabeth who said, "I persuaded her parents that she should go to Newport to visit friends until this whole thing blows over. They were only too happy to get her far away from the scandal."

***

"Are you going to be able to finish the Killing Game with Vandermere?" Elizabeth asked as they made their way out of the Tombs.

"I think so. He's more eager than ever. He's invited me to spend the weekend with him, so we can proceed with the plan. He won't be able to resist betting on the fixed race after I get the telegram."

"How much do you think he's good for?" she asked.

"Ten thousand. He'll have it in cash. We'll stop for a drink on the way to the track. I usually pretend we're late and I have to run to the track to get the bet in on time. I give the mark my coat to hold and take the money. He's sure I'll be back because he has my coat and my motorcar is still there. When he finally goes looking for me, my driver, Jake, will slip away as well."

"I could be your coat," she said.

"What?"

"Vandermere knows I'm your daughter. You can leave me behind with him when you go to place the bet. After a while, I'll get worried and urge him to go look for you."

"Good idea! And when he's gone, Jake will take you away in the motor. And of course the mark can't go to the police because he lost his money trying to bet on a fixed race."

"Exactly, but . . . Well, Max got killed. What if something else goes wrong?"

The Old Man shook his head at such foolishness. "Don't worry, Lizzie. Nobody really gets killed in the Killing Game."

She didn't think that would be much comfort to Max.

THE TREDEGAR MURDERS

by Vivian Lawry

During the Civil War, prostitute Clara is hired to initiate four young soldiers from the nearby ironworks into the mysteries of sex. These youngsters have a big secret but clients' secrets are always safe with Clara. When two of them turn up dead, Clara has to stop the murders.

"Clara! Claaar–ah! I know ya'll hear me. Get your sweet ass down here!"

Beau's clarion call rang above the rumble of the train. Monday's my day of rest, but Beau's been a right good customer, brings me a heap of business. And his uncle set me up with the Butterfly League, so I try to accommodate him whenever he comes by. Luckily, I'd finished sewing coins into the hems of my petticoats and washing my French letters for the week ahead.

I donned a blue wrapper, shook out my blonde curls, and sashayed downstairs.

Beau's party crowded the front parlor of The Blue Moon. He and five cronies circled four boys, so young their Confederate grays hung loose from shoulders and hips. I'd seen boys in uniform as young as twelve, and these didn't look much older. I'd swear they'd never shaved. "Clara, darlin', you're a sight for sore eyes! I ain't seen you since Stonewall Jackson drove the Yanks back across the Potomac! Come give me some sugar."

I kissed Beau long, to the catcalls of his companions, and stepped back. "Down, boys—especially you, Beau!" More catcalls. "What can I do for ya'll this fine day?" I cocked one eyebrow. "If all ten of you expect a ride, you better be ready to set a spell."

"Naw, nothin' so strenuous." Beau dropped his arm across my shoulders. "We just want you to make men of these here boys." He nodded toward the four young soldiers, huddled together. "It's a cryin' shame but not a one of 'em's ever been with a woman! So we all chipped in. Now, I know as how your regular rate is four dollars a go, but we're willin' to give you twenty even, seein' as it's a Monday and they need some education." Beau shook a little leather pouch and the silver sang to me.

I took the pouch.

One soldier leered and pinched the nearest boy's rosy cheek. "I could use a piece of this myself! How about a double ride?"

Beau punched his companion's shoulder. "Now, Jake, you wait your turn like anybody else! Next thing you know, you'll be hagglin' to get three for the price of two!"

Another soldier sidled closer and whispered loud enough for all to hear, "How much if I just wanna watch?" The others laughed and one said, "Me, too!"

By now all the boys were pink as peonies. "Nobody's gonna watch anything, so you'd best run along to the racetrack or the saloon." I edged Beau toward the door.

"We'll pick 'em up in an hour."

"You want your money's worth, don't you? Make it two." I grinned and turned to the boys. "C'mon up to my room. We'll talk a bit and decide how to spend the afternoon."

The boys shuffled, looking at their feet. Finally one mumbled, "Sure. Let's get on with it."

The speaker led the way, drooping up the stairs, silent. They all looked like men heading to the gallows. I followed, chirping directions, feeling their tension.

In my room, I perched on the chair by my dressing table—knees crossed, leaning forward, giving them a view. They sat on the bed like birds on a wire, hats in their laps. "So, let's get acquainted. My name is Clara—as you must've heard. Who are ya'll?"

The one who spoke downstairs said, "My name's Silas Blalock." Silas's plain, sunburned face was square, his cropped blue-black hair tucked behind big ears.

The next boy shifted. "I'm Frank Clayton." Frank's face wore signs of battering—crooked nose, square chin a little off-center. Brown hair curled down his neck.

"I'm Private James Redmond." He dipped his chin, obscuring his long horse face but showing a high forehead ending in straight auburn hair.

"Martin Rosetta. I only been in a month." Thick eyelashes, apple cheeks, and curly brown hair made him look especially young and girlish.

In my business, names are money. Applying my memory trick comes natural. Blalock, a square block. Clayton, like a battered slab of clay. Redmond, red hair. Rosetta, rosy cheeks. First names aren't so important. Everyone could be "Soldier."

"So how do you men want to spend your time?"

Blalock straightened. "Just speakin' plain, if we had our

druthers, we wouldn't be spendin' time here a-tall."

"Ahhh. So why're you here then?"

"We're guards at the Tredegar Iron Works. Beau Levereaux—Capt. Levereaux—he's our commander. He says come, we come." The other three seemed comfortable with Blalock as spokesperson.

Not at all inclined to return the purse to Beau, I looked to Blalock. "Well, no one wants to rile the captain. I'm accommodating. Surely we can agree on something."

The four boys exchanged looks. Clayton and Redmond slumped.

Rosetta flushed rosier than ever. At a nod from Blalock, he said, "C'n you keep a secret?"

I laughed. "Why, secrets are my bread 'n butter! Have you ever heard of the Butterfly League?"

"The Butterflies? You mean that New Jersey battalion of cavalry that wears blue and yellow?" All four of them stared, looking horrified.

"What would I have to do with Yankee cavalry, whatever colors they wear? No, my Butterfly League are men who have . . . unusual . . . preferences in their pleasures. That's my specialty. I've pleasured men under pianos and in Hollywood Cemetery. One man likes to make love in a casket, suspended from his rafters by chains. One likes to cover me in jewels and pat them all night. One wants me to paint him head-to-toe in chocolate and then eat it off. I don't do whips or chains, no bonds rougher'n silk or velvet." I looked from one to the other. "I'll tell anyone what I do—but I'd never name names." I caught the gaze of each. "There's no shame in being virgins. So what's your worry?"

Blalock's laugh sounded grim. "I'm so far from bein' a virgin, I've done buried two babes and a husband!"

My jaw dropped, and Rosetta giggled. "You waitin' for a chicken to fly in?"

I snapped my mouth shut.

Clayton leaned forward. "That's our worry. We're all women."

I gasped. "Oh. My. Sweet. Jesus! You could go to prison just for wearing men's clothes—let alone a uniform!"

Rosetta's flush deepened to raspberry. "That's why you need to keep our secret."

"So how much will silence cost us?" Blalock jutted his—her—chin and squinted.

I dimpled. "You pay for my time, you've paid for my silence. But why'd you do it?"

Suddenly everyone talked at once. Blalock said, "I joined with my husband. The babes bein' dead, I'd no reason to stay to home.

He was killed when that gun down at the Iron Works burst." I'd read about that in the *Dispatch*. "I stayed on to finish what we started."

Clayton paced. "Home was hell. Pa beat me and Ma, and my brothers took up where he left off. I figured war wouldn't be worse." She shrugged.

Redmond flushed to his—her—red hairline. "My kin're all dead. I've no skills that'd pay a living wage. And unlike you—," her eyes raked me head to toe, "—I'm too homely to prostitute. Might as well soldier."

Rosetta cleared her throat. "I joined for the Cause. Why should only men stand with Virginia?"

"Well, your secret's as safe as for all my other customers." I cocked my head. "But how do you manage it?"

"Not all that hard. Just give a name and sign up. No one hasta see your privates unless you get wounded."

"Bind your breasts and wear loose clothes."

"Lower and gruffen up your voice. Slouch a little. Keep to yourself."

"That's how we came together—keepin' to ourselves." Rosetta grinned. "I went down to bathe in the river and there stood Clayton, naked as a babe, white in the moonlight."

Clayton tilted her head. "I knew Redmond here from before the war. We joined together."

"We watch each other's backs," Redmond said.

"I see." My admiration mounted. "Well, here's hoping none of you gets wounded. Now, let's get down to work. Those men're gonna grill ya'll something fierce. We need to decide on your stories."

I served sherry and walnuts while we spun possibilities. Eventually we agreed that Blalock-the-block liked plain sex, and all the others would chide him about it. Redmond would be into peacock feathers, applied liberally. Clayton would claim to get off on barking and nipping at me, and vice versa. And Rosetta would claim a hair fetish, with reciprocal plaiting—of *all* hair. We laughed a lot.

I told them how I came to be a soiled dove, orphaned at twelve, left with nothing but my body. I explained about French letters, those barriers to pregnancy and disease—and my insurance to live past age twenty-five. "And I tell you, the best thing that ever happened to me was Colonel Levereaux—Beau's uncle— introducing me to men with peculiar sexual pleasures. I had a *carte de visit*é made. Here—for comrades who might appreciate me." I gave cards to each of them—a picture of me naked, facing a brick wall drawing a butterfly, on my right buttock a tattoo of a heart pierced by an arrow. "I give those to my special clients, and they give them to others of good character. After a time, they started calling themselves the Butterfly League because of that drawing. Men with such particular desires pay well for pleasures *and* discretion. Your secret is safe with me."

***

Sheriff Coltrain sent an officer to haul me in. We rode the train from Ashland to Richmond. I'd had a late night, and was none too pleased to be dragged out with barely enough time to don lady clothes and grab a parasol. But I smothered my aggravation, batted my lashes, and produced a full-dimpled smile. "Eli—I mean, Sheriff—why ever would you want t' see little ol' me?"

"Don't try goin' all sugar and cream on me, Clara. I have a body from down at the Tredegar Iron Works—a woman in a Confederate uniform, head bashed in."

I didn't have to fake shock. "Really!" Dread left me light-headed.

Coltrain smirked "Really. And she had one of your cards."

I managed to say, "Well, you know how my cards get around."

"Yeah, well, you gotta take a look. Maybe you'll recognize her."

"Dead bodies give me the shakes!"

"Just look at her face—that's fine." He hauled me to my feet and pulled me down the hall. The woman on the table was Redmond—red-haired Redmond—who joined the army because she was too homely to prostitute.

Back in the office, I perched on my chair. No good ever came of getting involved with the sheriff.

"So, what do you know?"

"Not a blessed thing! I never met that woman."

"Is that so?" The sheriff leaned back, fingers laced over his flat stomach. "And your card?"

I shrugged and smiled, showing both dimples. "Now, Eli, you have my card. If something happened to you—heaven forbid—that wouldn't mean I had anything to do with it! Why, I hear tell that some men trade my cards, or sell them—for the art, you know."

The sheriff looked down his nose at me. I could almost see his thoughts churning. "So maybe she's one of them women what likes women. You ain't above that, are you? You sure she ain't one of your clients?"

"I think I would've noticed!" I looked straight into his eyes. "I swear on my mother's grave, I never shared pleasures with that woman."

"Hmmmph." He waved toward the door. "You get on about your business. But if you come across anything about her, you tell me, you hear?"

I paused at the door. "I hear, Sheriff."

I got back to The Blue Moon near supper time. Most of my business is of an evening. I was feeling like a cat with cream, having escaped the sheriff without losing much custom. And it just felt good to have hoodwinked Eli!

***

Elias Coltrain swept into the parlor like a high wind, grabbed my arm, and hustled me up to my room. He shoved me onto the bed and threw three of my cards down beside me. Clearly he'd come on his business, not mine.

He loomed over me, fists clenching and unclenching. "One week! One week ago today you looked me in the eye and lied through your teeth. Swore on your mother's grave you never saw that woman before!"

"Actually, what I swore was that I'd never had pleasures with her—and that's the God's honest truth! I hadn't ever met that *woman*. When we met, I thought she was a boy!"

He backhanded me so fast I had no time to duck. "Don't give me none of your sass!" His voice dropped. "And none of this splittin' a frog hair four ways to tell the truth without tellin' me what I'm askin'! I'll have it and I'll have it now."

"It, what?" I ducked as he raised his hand. "I mean, what's happened? Where did you get my cards?"

He glared. I flinched but didn't look away. "Off another dead woman dressed like a man. Can't be coincidence. What do you know?"

How little can I tell him? Toying with Eli was a dangerous game. But if I exposed those women, they'd be mustered out at least, probably worse.

"I don't know much. Awhile back, soldiers from the Tredegar Iron Works Battalion brought me four boys—virgins, they said—and paid me to make men of them. So we went to my room. The one who died last week said his name was Redmond and not much else—except that he reckoned he'd just watch. Then they all got shy, red as ripe tomatoes, shuffling their feet. In the end none of them wanted to ride. Easy money for me. Before they left, I gave each of them three of my cards."

"*None* of them? Why not?"

"Maybe afraid they couldn't—especially Redmond!" I shrugged and forced a grin. "I didn't ask."

"So who were the others? And the soldiers who brought 'em here."

I shook my head. "I only remember Redmond's name. What's happened?"

Coltrain propped his elbows on my dressing table, his hulking body dwarfing the dainty furniture. "I reckon I can say. This James Redmond—nobody knew her by any other name —worked at the Tredegar, a guard for the munitions. Body was at the end of the bridge over the Haxall Canal, half naked, clubbed on the head." Coltrain puffed out his cheeks. "Today another woman soldier, going by the name Frank Clayton, turned up dead in the Tredegar warehouse grain elevator. She was a guard, too, half-naked and strangled."

I gasped. In my mind's eye I saw Frank Clayton's crooked nose and jaw, broken by her father and brothers too many times. She deserved a better death. "Were they raped?"

"No sign of it." He pinched his lower lip. "The hell of it is, the Tredegar's shut up tighter'n a widder-woman's twat. Nobody'll talk to me for fear of the scandal, bein' as they're havin' trouble gettin' supplies and workers anyway. But there's a lot nobody's sayin'." He leaned forward. "*Maybe* you're tellin' me all you know, but it sure ain't all you can find out." He pinned me with a granite glare. "Here's what you're gonna do. You're gonna go down to the Tredegar and get the names of those soldiers and the boys they brought here."

"How am I supposed to do that? Hundreds of men work at the Tredegar!"

"Over 800 all told—and I gotta say it's a cryin' shame that a slave's hired out at $30 a month, while a private in our own glorious army's paid little more than a third of that! But my point is, half are slaves or free men of color, and not all the whites are soldiers, so don't make out it's a bigger job than it is."

I wailed, "What if they won't talk to me?"

"You have your ways with men! Use 'em. Coax. Dimple. Bat your eyelashes." The sheriff sneered. "Hell, I don't care if you give it away on the docks!" He stood. "But get those names to me within the week, and anything else you can find out. You don't want me coming all the way out to Ashland again." He left, the air heavy with his threat.

Eli Coltrain could make sure I never worked around Richmond again if he took a mind to. So directly after he left, I started planning.

***

Everyone I asked for directions smirked and pointed toward the river. Eventually I found Beau in his quarters. "You've just gotta help me!" I squeezed his arm and pressed my ample bosom against it. "I didn't tell the sheriff your name, or any of the others, but if I don't give him something, he'll nail my hide to the wall."

"That'd surely be a waste of a mighty pretty hide. But what do you think I can do?"

Beau's a sweet boy who tends to think with his stones. I drew breath and spelled it out. "You're in charge of the guards. Two murdered guards've turned out to be women passing as men! So what *can* you tell me?"

He hitched up his trousers and scratched himself. "Well, I was that surprised when Redmond and Clayton turned out to be girls. You could've knocked me over with a wet ribbon. That's what I told Brigadier General Anderson, and that's what I told the sheriff: 'You could've knocked me over with a wet ribbon.' No one asked about The Blue Moon, though, and I saw no reason to mention it." He grinned. "You scratch my back, I scratch yours."

"Yes, love, but what else?"

"They was good soldiers, both of 'em. Kept to theirselves. Never complained about more'n the food and shoes—same as everybody." Beau ran a thumbnail across his chin, looking slit-eyed at me. "Was all them boys women?"

I looked at him, wide eyed, trusting he'd been too drunk to remember what I told him the first time. "Don't you think I'd've told ya'll a thing like that? Redmond and Clayton said they just wanted to watch. The other two took a little coaxing, but I made men of them alright! I think they ended up right proud of themselves." I smiled and snuggled against his arm. "I really need to find those boys."

"They ain't on duty till sunset, so they're likely down to the river, cooling their feet." I turned to go, but Beau caught my hand. "Hey. Ya'll don't like them boys better'n me, do you?"

"Not for a minute. But I've got to get *something* for Coltrain!"

***

Rosetta and Blalock sat on the bank of the James, trousers rolled up to their knees, feet in the water. Rosetta saw me first and panic flashed across her face. "What're you doin' here?"

Blalock blanched under her tan. "We don't want nothin' to do with you."

"What'd I do?"

"Four of us talked to you and two of us're dead," Blalock snapped.

I felt punched. "That's nothing to do with me."

Rosetta's eyebrows leapt up. "Who'd you tell about us?"

"Nobody! Not even the sheriff." They exchanged skeptical looks. "I had to tell him Redmond'd been with me. But I gave him no other names. And now he's pressing me to get them for him." I sat down on the bank. "And I lied outright to Beau—Captain Levereaux. Said as how you two are men. But if we're gonna keep ya'll safe, you've gotta help me. Do you think they were killed for being women?"

Blalock blinked once. "Nah. A man found me out once, tried to rape me. I shot him in the face. Nobody since."

"But Redmond and Clayton weren't raped. So, tell me about them—anything."

Rosetta's brows puckered. "Well, being low-ranking, we got night patrol. Days're mostly sleeping, mending, and such. Some of the men play cards or dice, but we stayed away from that."

I dipped my chin. "Some of my clients are high up in the army. I hear the Tredegar's the only place in the South that can turn out munitions and heavy ordinance." I tapped my hand with my fan. "So it's guarded as closely as President Davis's house. I assume that means no Yankee spies could've done it."

Blalock scowled. "I take your point. It's likely to've been someone here."

"If it wasn't rape, and it wasn't *because* they were women, what's left? Were there other victims?"

Rosetta ran both hands through her curls. "Two slaves went missing—two handsome young striplings. One about two months ago, the other three weeks or so later. Everybody thought they'd run away north, advertised rewards for their return in the *Dispatch* and all. But what if they didn't run?"

"And what about that free black? His year in Virginia was about up, so we thought he'd left the state before he could be taken up." Blalock pursed her lips. "But he'd no cause to leave so sudden, or to sneak off."

I peeled off my stockings and slippers, dabbling my feet in the river as I considered the possibility of more victims. "Anyone else? Any white boys?"

"I know of one." Blalock scratched her chin. "That was about three months back. He was maybe twelve, apprentice to a millwright and pattern maker. He was found down by the dock—naked, stabbed, and his tongue cut out—but still alive. Havin' no letters, he couldn't write out what happened. He died a week later." She swallowed hard. "I heard he was treated pretty rough."

My stomach clenched and I grabbed my shoes and stockings. "I'm takin' a walk. I need to think."

***

I meandered along the water, thoughts roiling. *The naked apprentice and the women half-exposed, that's gotta have something to do with sex. The attacks are getting closer together. Both of the women patrolled at night; the coloreds went missing in the night. Is night especially dangerous? I've gotta find out when the apprentice was attacked, and all his injuries.*

I circled the boiler shop, the blacksmith, and the brass foundry and headed back. *What else do I know? Guards're everywhere. Since Virginia seceded last April, the Tredegar's had trouble getting raw materials. More river traffic than ever. Were all the attacks near the river? I'd wager all one attacker. Can I find him before another one? If I come up with something, can I count on Rosetta and Blalock?*

I rejoined the women, watching supplies being off-loaded into the warehouse. A stevedore swaggering along the dock called, "Why ain't you boys workin'? Leave the likes of her till the sun goes down!"

Blalock called back, "By sundown we'll be patrolling. Gotta take pleasures when we can!"

"You boys don't look grown enough to be out after dark, let alone ridin' a whore. Maybe we oughta take care of her for you!" He nudged the man smiling beside him and started forward.

Who knows what might've happened save the foreman stepped in. "Them barrels ain't gonna roll themselves into the warehouse. Get your sorry asses back to work!"

I tapped Rosetta's shoulder. "Let's go. We need a plan." While we walked, I explained my thinking. "So, given that the other suspected victims were young boys, maybe Redmond and Clayton were attacked because that's what they looked like. Which means you're in danger, too." We'd passed many soldiers with women on their arms. "Do many women come here?"

"Dozens."

Blalock snorted. "And everyone of 'em has round heels!"

"Hmmm. So there's plenty of sex to be had. He just likes boys." I squeezed Rosetta's arm. "You two mustn't go out alone, especially at night."

A sneer twisted Blalock's lips. "And how're night patrols supposed to make that happen?"

"I don't know yet. But keep your guard up and your weapons handy."

***

I sought out Annie Brennon, formerly of The Blue Moon. Annie'd "joined the army" right after Fort Sumter, employed as a private friend and companion to high-ranking officers. I should've thought of her sooner. She lived near the officers' quarters, wearing fine grays and a major's stripes—an open secret, not really passing as a male.

"Why, Clara, you're looking mighty fine!" She rose from a stool in front of her tent and squeezed both my hands.

After exchanging compliments, cheek-kisses, and news of Blue Moon doings, I got down to business. "I've heard tell of boys killed or going missing from here. I know a couple of boys among the guards and I'm right worried about them."

Annie cocked her head. "Customers at The Blue Moon?"

I shrugged prettily. "They visited me once."

She leaned in, speaking quietly. "It's all very hush-hush, but the last two boys killed was really women soldiers!"

I acted shocked, swore secrecy, and said, "Last two? I heard about an apprentice to the millwright—or pattern maker. Were there others?"

"I wouldn't tell this to just anybody—but I owe you a heap, Clara—for givin' me the general. Look where I am now!" She gestured toward the tent and all. "So, yes, there've been three: a cook's apprentice knocked on the head, and a drummer disappeared, leaving his drum behind—and a slave was found dead in the canal, though I hear he didn't drown."

I questioned closely, but Annie had no details.

She shook her head. "Hon, we got more'n twenty buildings here, spread over five acres. Hundreds live and work here, hundreds more pass through every day. The hunt's been on for weeks—but quiet, like, 'cause we can't afford to scare workers off. It's like lookin' for a grain of salt on a sand beach."

***

Blalock and Rosetta lived through the night. I found them, haggard and twitchy, near the jetty. "I wish I had good news, boys, but the brass's already done everything they can—or are willing to. So it seems we're on our own."

"I ain't surprised." Rosetta sounded resigned.

Blalock puffed her cheeks. "I guess we'd best keep weapons to hand—and pray a lot."

"And just wait to be attacked? We've gotta take action!" Exasperation sharpened my tone.

"We? Where do you come into it?"

"I *care* about ya'll. Also, I need to save my own tail from Coltrain. He gave me one week. I can either hand ya'll over, or we can catch this fiend. I'd druther it be the latter." I blew a wisp of hair off my forehead. "Here's my plan. One of ya'll—say

Blalock—goes on sick roll, not serious enough for hospital. When Rosetta goes on patrol, Blalock and I'll follow." I turned to Rosetta. "Meander along the waterfront, seeming careless. If you're attacked, Blalock and I'll be there." I swished my crinolines. "I'll need me some soldier clothes, though."

***

Rosetta strolled along the canal, stopped to take off her hat, ruffle her curls, and spit into the water. This was her fifth time around, Blalock and me following, hiding in the bushes or behind buildings. A full moon glimmered on the water. I suffered mosquito bites and stifled a sneeze, tension knotting my shoulders. Leaves rustled and Blalock stiffened, but it was only the wind. My calves cramped with crouching.

About four hours into the watch, a broad-shouldered silhouette jumped Rosetta and rolled toward the canal.

Blalock growled. "I cain't get a goddammed clear shot!"

I ran. The attacker's hands closed on Rosetta's throat. I grabbed his shirt and heaved. He grunted and fell sideways, taking Rosetta with him. I stomped just under his ribs and heaved again, pulling the knife from my belt. He turned, yanked me off my feet, and rolled over me. My blade slid off his ribs. He punched my face; I kneed him. Blalock clubbed him over the head with her pistol.

The three of us managed to bind his hands and feet while he waffled between making calf-eyes at Rosetta—calling her "the prettiest boy I ever seen"—and cursing Blalock and me six ways to Sunday. It was Jake, the soldier who'd wanted a double ride at The Blue Moon!

***

"Now, Sheriff, it isn't my fault that the army kept him. Murders at the Tredegar, by a soldier . . ." I shifted, trying to ease my bruised back. "But I'm here—as ordered—within the week." I smiled, showing dimples, hiding irritation.

"You look like hell. You know that?"

"Eli! What an ungentlemanly thing to say!"

"Hmmmph. But true. I hope you aren't scarred." He rubbed his chin. "The army's buttoned up tighter than a virgin's bodice. And I *really* want to know all about it."

"And what will telling ya'll do for me?"

"It'll get me off your back and you can go on plying your trade."

I sighed, but chose the path of wisdom. "Well, there was a soldier—one of the guards, who always volunteered for night patrol. He had a taste for boys. He'd see some boy who took his fancy, find him, and . . ." I shrugged and winced. "There were at least three white boys and three coloreds missing or found dead—plus the lad with his tongue cut out and the two women who looked like boys. He knew not to leave anyone able to accuse him."

"So what about those boy virgins, and the soldiers who brought 'em to you?"

"Oh, well, none of that turned out to be important." I smiled and fluttered my fan.

"Hmmmph. So you say." He scowled at me. "But then, you lie like a no-legged dog!"

"Why, Eli, you say the sweetest things!" I kissed the top of his head and left smiling.

SUMMONS FOR A DEAD GIRL

by K. B. Owen

*Madame Cartier, medium, is asked by a distraught
mother to contact her daughter, killed in the shirtwaist
factory fire of 1911. A skeptical reporter dares Mme.
Cartier to contact the girl—and this medium is up for
the challenge.*

I don't set much store by omens. Ironic, given the business I'm in.
But I keep that to myself. As a spirit medium, I'd lose clients in
droves. If I had that many.

So I didn't give much thought to the Labor Day Parade on
September fourth, in the year of our Lord nineteen-hundred and
eleven. Frankly, if I were our Lord, I'd have a mind to give the
year back, for it was a dreadful stretch, the worst being the
shirtwaist factory fire in March. One hundred and forty-six workers
died horrible deaths. Today's parade, led by the Women's Trade
Union League, was to honor the dead and push to make conditions
better for the living.

For me, news of the parade was a notice in the paper with a set
of streets to avoid. The day seemed the perfect opportunity to fit in
a few consultations and practice some of my—well, I call them
enhancements. I had no inkling the factory tragedy was about to
affect me personally.

Boris had just ushered out my last client of the day. I was in
front of the parlor mirror pinning gray-blond strands back in
place—the turban smashes my *chignon* dreadfully—when the bell
rang once again. I grimaced at my reflection.

Boris chuckled. "Poor Maddy. You're a victim of your own
success." He has always been a rather cocksure servant, but I found
the familiarity oddly comforting. Now that I was on the nearer side
of fifty, there was hardly anyone left to call me by my childhood
name.

I rubbed my temples. "I'm too tired for callers. Take care of it,
will you?"

After a long interval, he returned. In his most somber tones he
announced, "Mr. Bristow and Mrs. Haberstein." Dropping his
voice, he added, "Trust me, you'll want to hear this."

I gave Boris a glare. Blast the man. "You know I detest Bristow. I don't care who he's with—" I broke off as the two visitors stepped into the room. I nudged the turban out of sight behind the settee as Boris closed the door behind him.

Frank Bristow was the last soul on earth I wanted in my parlor. Yet there he was, a scrawny little man, derby pushed back on his head, twitching his pointed nose in my direction as I halfheartedly waved them into chairs. He undeniably looked the part of the nosy newspaper reporter.

In the months since I moved to New York City and set up practice, he'd made it his personal mission to learn my secrets. I banned him from my séances. He came in disguise. I showed him the door. He offered a bribe. I refused. He wrote skeptical articles about my "parlor tricks." I wrote editorial letters in reply. He harassed my clients, peppering them with questions about my techniques. Only after the large, solidly built Boris threatened the man with bodily harm did he leave my clients alone.

Now he had returned. With a fair number of spiritualists in this metropolis, several of them more successful and flamboyant than I, why was he so single-minded about *me*?

I focused my attention on the woman sitting beside Bristow. She was dressed in a serviceable navy walking suit that had seen much wear, as had her gloves and her heels. Obviously, Bristow was not bringing me a wealthy client.

Her deep gray eyes were her most noteworthy feature. They were haunted eyes. Believe me, in my line of work I know haunted eyes. Sickness, strain, anxiety, and deep sorrow were etched upon this woman's soul.

"Welcome, Madame Haberstein," I said soothingly, dropping the *h* and stretching the *stein* into two syllables. Clients respond well to my guise of expatriate Frenchwoman. A hint of the exotic never hurts. "I am Madame Cartiére. What may I do for you?"

The lady gulped down a sob.

Bristow leaned forward. "Mrs. Haberstein lost her only daughter in the Triangle fire—"

"*Désolée*. My condolences, madame," I interrupted. "You wish a séance, then, to attempt to speak with her?"

Mrs. Haberstein sniffed and shook her head. "Another medium—a gypsy, at the fair that came through town last week—told me it was impossible. She said that Lizzie is . . . *still alive*." She whispered the last words.

I sat back. "I—I beg your pardon?"

Bristow barely suppressed a grin as he looked in my direction. "A pretty little problem, isn't it? Mrs. Haberstein paid me a visit today, looking for more information about the fire, wanting the names of people she could talk to who might have seen her daughter."

I ignored the reporter. "Madame Haberstein, you have believed all the while that Lizzie perished in the fire. I assume her body was recovered and you identified it, *oui*? How can you believe *now* that she is alive, based upon the word of one psychic? Some of us are not entirely . . . trustworthy."

Bristow snorted.

Mrs. Haberstein's lower lip trembled in an attempt to maintain her composure. "I was too ill to identify Lizzie's body at the time. It was my husband who went down to the pier." She rummaged in her pocketbook and pulled out a filigreed silver ring, set with a single aquamarine. She held it out to me. "The body was too . . . charred to know it was her." She swallowed. "But he saw this on the finger. It was my grandmother's. I had given it to Lizzie on her eighteenth birthday."

As I took the ring, my stomach lurched in protest. Sensations of malice, terror, pain, and death prickled along my spine. I shuddered. I don't often feel psychic vibrations from objects anymore, unless the wearer experienced strong emotions. I tried to pass it back, but she shook her head.

"I have no money to pay you. Keep it. It is a sad reminder to me."

The last thing I wanted was a dead girl's ring, especially one that elicited feelings of horror. Letting the matter rest for now, I tucked it in a drawer. "The ring is too unique to be anyone's but hers. Your gypsy has been selling you a bill of goods, madame."

Mrs. Haberstein's lips thinned in a stubborn line. "Perhaps Lizzie lost the ring and another girl found it. . . ." Her voice trailed away.

"But if Lizzie had survived, she would have returned home, *n'est-ce pas?*"

She shrugged. "I cannot account for it."

One need not have the gift of second sight to know she was lying. I glanced at Bristow, who wore an amused expression. No help there.

"We have the names of several girls Lizzie worked with on the ninth floor," Mrs. Haberstein continued.

"Then why come to me? Monsieur Bristow would have more success interviewing them than I."

"I doubt that," Bristow retorted. "They're dead."

"I want you to summon them," Mrs. Haberstein said, as if they were a telephone call away. "They can tell me what really happened to my Lizzie. I understand that the spirits have greater clarity in such matters."

I grimaced. That sounded like one of my lines. Under less tragic circumstances, Mrs. Haberstein's perfect faith would have made her an ideal client.

Bristow's smirk wasn't visible to the lady. "I knew if anyone could help Mrs. Haberstein, it would be *you*, Madame Cartiére."

I could see his trap. He couldn't get into my séances or query my clients, so he had brought his own, who was sure to insist that he attend the proceedings.

I gritted my teeth. "I am much obliged to you, Monsieur Bristow."

My papa, rest his soul, hadn't raised any dimwitted children. We all knew how to run the game. I pulled out my calendar. Would a week be long enough to prepare? I hoped so. "*Voyons voir*, I have an opening . . . next Tuesday. What is your address, madame? For my records, you understand." I copied it down.

Bristow held out a slip of paper. "Here's the list. Why must we wait a week? Can't we have the séance *now*?"

"I am greatly fatigued," I snapped. "To summon spirits requires strength. I have no openings before next week." I quickly closed the nearly blank pages of my engagement calendar. "It is a wonder I can accommodate you as soon as that." I gave Bristow a frosty look. "May I speak with you privately, monsieur? Excuse us, Madame Haberstein. We'll be back *momentanément*."

Out in the hallway, Bristow hooked his thumbs in his vest. "Something wrong?" He rocked back and forth on his heels, whether from complacency or a futile attempt to appear taller, I didn't know.

"Would it not be more helpful to provide the woman with a list of *survivors*, rather than the names of dead girls?" I hissed.

"You are a summoner, aren't you? I thought you would be grateful for the opportunity to prove you can summon spirits from the *vasty deep*."

"You are a vile creature, taking advantage of this woman's pain."

He shrugged. "I offered her the names and addresses of survivors, but when I mentioned I knew a spirit medium, she jumped at the chance. You heard her: *the spirits have a greater clarity*."

Though I was wide awake to the risk, I had to admit the puzzle intrigued me. "*D'accord*, I will go through with the séance—"

"And allow me to attend," he interrupted.

I gave a reluctant nod. "One condition: I require a list of the names and addresses of survivors, specifically those who worked on the ninth floor." I must learn more about Lizzie.

He frowned. "Why should I? You'll only use it to manipulate the proceedings."

I rolled my eyes. "I am allowing you to attend, *oui*? You can decide for yourself."

He sighed. "I'll send it tomorrow."

***

Boris and I pored over the list. He pointed. "Gaspar Mortillalo, one of the elevator operators. He may know if Lizzie got out."

I glanced at a news clipping Bristow had included. "It says here, Mortillalo was only able to make three elevator trips before the rails buckled from the heat, yet saved one hundred and fifty people. I'll certainly talk to him. But I think I'll start with—" I squinted at the paper "—Sarah Rosen and Gertie O'Brien. They live at the same boardinghouse. That should save time."

"I say we divide up the names. We only have a week."

I shook my head. "I want you to watch the Haberstein house, learn the routine, find out if there's a chance for me to talk to the husband without Mrs. Haberstein present."

He frowned. "Why are we spying on our own client?"

"I don't want her to know I'm collecting information. It destroys the illusion." The longer I kept skepticism at bay, the more successful the séance. I was determined not to give Bristow the satisfaction of watching me fall on my face.

Boris cocked his head. "*And*?"

"And she's keeping something from me. I'll wager the husband knows."

"Knows what?"

"Knows why Lizzie would not have returned home if she survived the fire."

He pursed his lips. "Maybe she got hit on the head and has amnesia."

I laughed. "You're still reading those dime novels, aren't you?"

He muttered something I pretended not to hear. Boris obviously remembered a number of Russian expletives from his youth.

***

I had carefully considered the type of persona I wished to present. I pulled out my only business suit, left over from a short stint as a typist. The most boring two weeks of my life, I might add. I smoothed my hair into a no-nonsense bun and pinned on a stylish straw hat. Between my attire and the press pass I'd crafted, I looked the part of a lady reporter, the kind who works on "human interest" stories for the women's magazines.

The pretense unlocked the tongues of Gertie and Sarah. Though understandably fatigued from their twelve-hour shift at Max Roth's shirtwaist factory where they were newly employed, they were eager to be part of a story featured in *Harper's*. Yes, *Harper's Bazaar*. When I create a role, I don't go about it halfheartedly. It is neck or nothing.

"Lizzie was at another table. We didn't know her well," Sarah said. "We weren't allowed to talk much on the floor. Mostly you got to know the girls sitting next to you and maybe across."

Gertie nodded. "She seemed nice enough, though. Once I lost my needle in the rag bin. She got down on her hands and knees and helped me hunt for it."

"I remember that." Sarah sighed. "She got in trouble for stopping to help. I just wanted to slap Rachel."

"Rachel?"

The girls looked at each other.

"I don't like to speak ill of the dead." Gertie crossed herself. "But everyone knew Rachel was a snitcher. Lately she'd been picking on Lizzie. Even when the poor girl had the flu."

I frowned. "Lizzie was sick and still came to work?"

Sarah shrugged. "Most of us did. Something was going around in February. Poor Lizzie had it the worst, and the longest. But you don't get paid if you don't work."

"Is there anyone who survived the fire who might have known Lizzie better?"

Sarah clenched her hands until the knuckles were white. "There weren't a lot of us from the ninth floor who made it out alive." Her voice quavered. "The fire escape collapsed almost right away. The hall door was locked. The stairwell was crammed with girls. Screaming. It was a fight . . . a fight to get on the last elevator." She closed her eyes with a shudder.

I swallowed, keeping a tight rein on my imagination.

Gertie put a comforting arm around her friend's shoulders. "The tenth floor was luckier. You heard that story, Mrs. Carter?"

I nodded, remembering Bristow's clipping. The bookkeeper on the eighth floor had called up to the tenth—where the owners worked—and alerted them. They were able to escape to the next building from the roof. The bookkeeper said he'd also tried calling the ninth floor but couldn't get through. They'd had no warning at all.

Gertie brought me back from my dark thoughts. "Maybe you should talk to Katya."

I glanced at my list. "You mean Katya Marenko? She was a friend of Lizzie's?"

"I don't know, but they had stations right next to each other. They seemed to get along, as far as I could tell."

I stood. "You've been quite helpful. Thank you."

"When will the article come out?" Gertie asked.

"That's up to my editor. I'll send you a copy." I should be ashamed of how easily I can utter a falsehood. Ah well, one must go with one's strengths.

***

An elderly man answered the door of the Marenko flat the next day. Placing the man's heavy accent, I switched to Russian.

His eyes lit up and he responded in the same language. "Yes, Katya is home. Please, be comfortable." He gestured to a well-worn rocker that held pride of place beside the hearth.

Shortly, a brown-haired girl of perhaps sixteen with a candy-box prettiness appeared in the doorway. "*Babu* says you wish to see me?"

"Yes, dear. My name is Mrs. Carter. I'm writing an article for *Harper's* about some of the girls who worked at Triangle Shirtwaist."

She winced.

"I do not require details of the fire itself," I added hastily. "I'm sure you're tired of recounting them."

Her shoulders relaxed. "What do you want to know?"

"Did you form any friendships there?"

Katya shrugged. "As the foreman was always reminding us, we weren't there to make friends. We were there to work."

"Surely, spending twelve-hour days in cramped quarters, you must have made *some* friends."

She hesitated. "One. A girl named Lizzie. But she—" Her voice broke. "She died in the fire. I looked for her, before I squeezed onto the last elevator. But the smoke . . ." Her eyes welled with tears. "I had to leave without her."

"You mustn't blame yourself." I passed her a handkerchief. "What was she like?"

"She was very kind." Katya sniffed. "She worked extra to help me meet my quota when I was still learning the machine. Smiled, made jokes—not easy to do some days."

"Because of how rigorous the work was?"

She dabbed at her nose. "That didn't bother Lizzie. Even the petty girls didn't bother her."

"What petty girls?"

"Well, Rachel Krantz was the worst. She was always trying to get Lizzie in trouble."

"In trouble? How?"

"By reporting her, even for the littlest things. Billy wanted to help—" She put her hands to her mouth.

"Billy?"

Katya flushed a deep red. "I guess it doesn't matter. They're all dead now. Billy was Lizzie's . . . beau."

Ah, now we were getting somewhere. I leaned closer. "Tell me about it."

Eventually the story came out, of Rachel Krantz's interest in Billy Gantry, one of the cutters who worked on the ninth floor. When that gentleman did not return the feeling but instead only had eyes for Lizzie, Rachel looked for every opportunity to sabotage her rival.

I felt a surge of excitement. If Rachel had succeeded in getting Lizzie fired that last day, Lizzie might have been long gone before the fire broke out. "Did Rachel try to get Lizzie in trouble the day of the fire?"

Katya grimaced. "Rachel saw Lizzie and Billy sneak out to talk in the elevator corridor. She threatened to tell."

"And did she?"

Katya frowned. "No, I don't think she did. I don't know why, though."

I set aside my disappointment and tried another tack. "Did Lizzie's parents know about Billy?"

Katya shook her head vigorously. "They would never have approved. They wanted her to marry someone else."

That was interesting. "Marry who?"

"Lizzie never said his name, but I know she didn't love him. She and her parents argued about it a lot."

That would be reason enough not to come home, if given a chance. But where would Lizzie go? "Did she mention any relatives or friends in the city?"

"As far as I know, Lizzie only had her parents and a little brother."

I tucked away my notepad and checked my watch. Time to meet Mortillalo. "I must go, but thank you for your help, Miss Marenko."

***

Boris returned that night to find me stretched out on the settee, too tired to move.

"Bad day?"

I shook my head. "Exhausting. My feet hurt, and my purse is empty. After seeing Katya, I met Mortillalo at Wanamaker's for lunch. It's no cheap five-cent lunch counter, I can tell you." I gave him a pointed look. "What I do from here depends on you." It rarely took Boris more than four days to accomplish any task I set for him. He must have made progress by now.

He nodded. "I have news, but let me get some supper. I'm famished."

He returned with a heavily laden tray for both of us. Giving him time to eat, I recounted the story of Lizzie's secret beau. I also told him what I learned from the elevator operator.

"Mortillalo has no idea if Lizzie was on the elevator during his trips. All of the screaming and shoving made it impossible for him to recall individual girls. He focused on keeping the elevator moving. Not an easy task, given the fire and the overloaded car."

Boris grunted as he finished his third muffin.

"But there's a chance Lizzie made it out," I went on. My neck tingled with renewed excitement. "Shortly before the alarm was given, Mortillalo took her up to the tenth floor to deliver the day's inventory report. He doesn't remember bringing her back down. According to the newspaper account, most of the tenth floor workers escaped. If she was with them . . ." My voice trailed off. How many tenth-floor survivors would I have to interview before finding one who remembered Lizzie? We had only a few days left.

Boris blotted his lips. "Are you all right?"

I changed the subject. "Now that you've had a chance to fill your stomach, tell me about the Habersteins. Any chance of seeing the husband alone?"

Boris grinned. "I should get a raise for this. It turns out Mrs. Haberstein takes in ironing. The last three nights after supper, she left and returned about thirty minutes later with a bundle of shirts. The husband delivers them the next morning on his way to work."

"What about the first night? She didn't go out then?"

He shrugged. "That's why I waited until now, to be sure her routine is consistent. I can't account for the first night."

Thirty minutes . . . It left little time for subtlety, but I wasn't complaining. "Give yourself a raise, Boris. Any loose pocket change you find in the chaise cushions is yours."

He chuckled and said goodnight.

I remained in the parlor, pacing. I'd already wasted time interviewing people who had no idea whether Lizzie had survived. Should I change tactics? Assume Lizzie had been on the tenth floor, escaped, and was in hiding from her family? If she were alive, I needed time to search. Three days remained.

But the ring—the ring still bothered me. What corpse had been wearing the ring, if not hers? It made no sense.

I dearly hoped she was alive, despite the odds. I'd become rather attached to Lizzie. By all accounts, she'd been a kind-hearted soul. I'd originally assumed otherwise.

I stopped pacing. Why had I first assumed *that*?

Then it hit me. The ring again. I had distinctly felt . . . malice.

I hesitated, then opened the drawer. The clear blue stone winked in the light. I held it gingerly, bracing myself, allowing death and horror to swell and break beyond me like an ocean wave. What was beneath? Yes, dark emotions lingered from the most recent wearer. Bitterness. Jealousy. I allowed them to take shape. Then I was sure.

This was not the girl I sought. Another girl had died with Lizzie's ring on her finger. I knew who it was.

Rachel Krantz.

I didn't know why no one had reported her missing. Perhaps she had no family in the area. Bristow could look into that later. *If* he believed me. In the meantime, my best chance of finding Lizzie was to talk to her father.

***

The next evening I waited in the shadows of a narrow alley across from Broome Street, on the Lower East Side.

There it was—Boris's signal. Mrs. Haberstein had left on her errand. I hurried down the street and used the knocker.

After a long interval of no response, I tried the doorknob. Unlocked. I stuck my head inside, tentatively calling. Heart thudding in my chest, I crept down the hall to the kitchen.

A boy of about eight stood on a stool with his back to me, washing dishes. I cleared my throat. No reaction. "Hello?"

The boy stopped, cocked his head, didn't turn.

I tried again, louder. "Hello?"

He gave a quick, startled look over his shoulder, dried his hands, and hopped down. "Mama and Papa aren't home, miss." His voice had a faint lisp.

"I'm sorry to come in uninvited, but no one answered the door."

The boy tapped his ears. "I don' hear so good, since I got sick last year."

Ah. "Scarlet fever?"

With a nod, he gestured to a chair. "You wanna sit down? Papa's away, but Mama'll be back soon." He was already heading back to the sink to finish his task.

I bit back my disappointment. How had Boris missed Mr. Haberstein's departure? I had a mind to take back that raise I'd given him.

Perhaps the boy could be of help. "What's your name?"

"Sammy."

"Sammy, do you like magic tricks?" I waved him closer.

His face lit up. Dishes forgotten, he came over and sat at the table.

"I'm sorry about your sister. You must miss her a lot."

The boy nodded and sighed. "Mama is very sad."

"I'm sure she is. Now, watch carefully." I palmed the coin, then made it pass through my hand. "Was Lizzie very close to your mama?"

He shrugged. "I dunno. They fought a lot."

"Oh. What did they fight about?" I walked the coin over each knuckle.

Sammy kept his eyes on it, mesmerized. "She wanted Lizzie to marry Ronald. Lizzie said no. They were yelling so loud, even I could hear them."

"Who's Ronald? A family friend?"

"Hmm-mmm. He's older, like Papa."

"Do you remember exactly what you heard?" I produced a penny from behind his ear, then handed it to him.

He clasped it tightly. "I heard some of the words. Lizzie kept saying *no!* Mama kept saying *maybe*, and *marry*, and *Ronald*." He sighed. "It was the same fight, every day."

"Including the day Lizzie died?"

He nodded. "They yelled the loudest that morning."

I heard a quick, sharp whistle below the kitchen window.

"Thanks, Sammy. I have to go."

The boy smiled. "I like you. 'Bye."

I slipped out and joined Boris in the alley.

"Success?" he asked.

I gave him a wide smile. Things were beginning to make sense. "Let's go home. We have much to do."

***

I conduct my séances in the disused dining room, and all was ready when Mrs. Haberstein and Bristow arrived on Tuesday: the drawn shades, the incense, the flickering candles, the folding screen placed in front of the door that led to the kitchen. Boris ushered in the guests through the parlor end of the room.

I had dressed carefully for the occasion in my deep-sleeved blue velvet wrap and black silk turban, the cheap paste ruby in the center more flattering by candlelight.

"Welcome. Be seated, *s'il vous plaît*." I put a finger to my lips as Bristow looked ready to launch a barrage of questions. "Quietly. Frivolous chatter can discourage the spirits."

Bristow raised a skeptical brow and helped Mrs. Haberstein into a chair. Her expression was a mixture of hope and dread.

I was determined to give them a good show. I brought out my best tricks: the ghostly luminescent vapors, the sharp raps, the vibrating table, and my booming spirit guide voice, which caused even Bristow to jump in his chair. Fascination had replaced his air of disbelief by this point, and in spite of himself, he was caught up in the atmosphere I had created.

The séance concluded with the final question, my dramatic dénouement: "Where is Lizzie?" I demanded. "Show us, o spirits!"

Nothing.

I stifled a sigh, and raised my voice. "SHOW us!"

Quietly, Lizzie Haberstein stepped from behind the screen, pale, shaking, and very, very pregnant.

With a tiny squeak of astonishment, Mrs. Haberstein slumped in her chair.

***

Bristow picked up his teacup. "You have a flair for the dramatic, madame."

I suppressed a smile at the slight tremor that still rattled his cup in its saucer. "*Naturellement*, Monsieur Bristow." I nodded toward Lizzie and her revived mother, heads together on the settee in murmured conversation. Mrs. Haberstein had not let go of her daughter's hand all the while.

"How did you do it? And don't tell me you summoned her from thin air."

I had decided on an account that was sure to drum up future business, should Bristow publish it. "I was guided by the spirits of the dead girls. They pointed me to the settlement house on Henry Street, only two miles from the factory. Lizzie has been there the entire time. She wanted to be reconciled with her mother, but was afraid. I persuaded her to come."

"Right under our noses," he muttered, glancing at mother and daughter. "She didn't return because she was in the family way?"

I shook my head. "Not exactly. Madame Haberstein already knew her daughter was with child."

I remembered the girl's "flu" in February. Morning sickness. I'd also realized the word *maybe* that Sammy thought he heard was more likely *baby*. Who would be yelling *maybe marry* at the top of her lungs? *Maybe* implied choice. Mrs. Haberstein was having none of that.

Once I realized Lizzie was pregnant, I knew the best refuge for someone in her condition was the Henry Street Settlement. She confirmed the sorry tale when I found her.

"Her mother wanted to marry her off to a family friend," I explained to Bristow, "before the pregnancy became known. A man twice her age. She did not love him."

"Who's the father?"

"A co-worker, Billy Gantry. He died in the fire. Lizzie was on the tenth floor when the alarm sounded, and escaped from the roof. When she learned Billy had perished, she went to the settlement house under an assumed name. They didn't know she was a Triangle fire survivor."

"So which girl died wearing her ring?"

"Rachel Krantz. She caught Lizzie and Billy that day, threatened to tell the foreman. Lizzie bribed her silence with the ring. You'll want to check into that, of course. It could be quite a scoop for you."

Bristow raised an appreciative eyebrow. "Indeed."

That reminded me. I pulled the aquamarine ring out of the drawer and handed it to Lizzie. "This is yours, *mademoiselle*."

The girl's cheeks were streaked with tears. "Thank you for everything. I feared I could never go home."

"What will you do about the baby?" I asked.

Mrs. Haberstein smoothed her daughter's hair. "We will say that Lizzie was privately married to Billy Gantry at Christmastime and is now widowed."

Lizzie wiped her eyes. "Billy *was* going to marry me. Our talk in the corridor that day was about when we could elope."

Boris, who had come in to refresh the sandwich plate, spoke up. "If you need any . . . documentation, I have a friend who specializes in marriage licenses."

Bristow's nose quivered with indignation. "That's illegal."

I smiled. "But it is the *spirit* of the law that counts rather than the letter, *mais oui*?"

THE VELVET SLIPPERS

by Keenan Powell

*Mildred Munz, long-time maid—and mistress—to an
elderly employer, is playing a waiting game. But his
nephew Edmund and the pretty hired nurse, Katie
O'Brien, have their parts to play in the unspooling plot.*

Autumn, 1895
North Adams, Massachusetts

In the grayness before dawn, Mildred Munz carefully lifted the
bedcovers and placed one foot, then another, on floorboards so cold
they burned her feet. The fire in the hearth had long since died out.
Only dark cinders and white ash remained.

Her rustling hadn't wakened him. He wheezed and bubbled,
jerked and flinched as he had done in his sleep all night long and
for many nights prior. With each exhalation, the tang of vomit and
the iron smell of blood seeped from his body. She had grown
accustomed to the odor.

She straightened her nightcap and stood, more slowly than she
had in years gone by. She searched the shadows with her toes,
seeking the velvet slippers, though they were little defense against
the chill. But she wore them every night just the same. It pleased
him.

She gathered her dressing gown from the foot of the bed and
tied it around her thickened middle. Before leaving, she looked
upon him once more. He was as before, unconscious and contorted,
clutching his stomach.

When she opened the heavy oak door, its creaking roused him.

"What?" he choked out, his voice thick with phlegm.

"Just fetching your porridge," she whispered.

He cleared his throat. "No porridge, just tea. Sweet tea." He
pulled the blanket over his shoulder and rolled away from her.

"As you wish." She softly pulled the door closed.

On the landing, she nearly crashed into young Edmund.

"Well, now," he said.

Twenty-two years of age, his fair hair greasy with sweat, frock
coat draped upon his arm, shoes in hand and top hat askew upon
his head, Edmund was sneaking up the broad stairway yet again, a

habit he'd acquired since his return from Cambridge. He gave her a wicked grin and tipped his hat. "Top of the morning to you, Mrs. Munz." Then he sauntered by, the stink of whiskey and cigars trailing in his wake.

Were she to ask, he'd claim he was playing Whist with some Irish louts at the Hibernian Club. But she suspected he'd spent the night losing his uncle's money and what was left of his own shame at a brothel where snaggle-tooth girls sold their wares and men of all ages and callings contracted unspeakable diseases.

She didn't ask. She would not give him the satisfaction.

In the kitchen, she stoked the cooker's fire and added milk to the oats that had been soaking all night. As the porridge simmered, she walked down the dark hallway to the servants' quarters, no longer occupied by anyone but herself.

Mildred changed out of her nightclothes and into her maid's uniform, a black dress and white apron. She sat on her cot and pulled off the slippers that the master had given her years before.

***

He had caught her admiring the blue velvet slippers following an afternoon of lovemaking. As he rested upright in his bed, he lit a cigar and ordered her about the bedroom, find this, straighten that, insisting that she do so unclothed so he could admire her form.

"Fetch my dressing gown, Millie." He had taken his eyes from her to follow a veil of ghostly smoke pouring lazily from his mouth.

When she opened the wardrobe door, those blue velvet slippers stunned her. A flower motif adorned them, the rich velvet and sparkly beads so exquisite, for a moment she imagined they were a hidden fairy treasure.

"Like them?" he asked. His voice was rich and resonant, but teasing, daring Mildred to covet something that was well above her station. The slippers had belonged to his late wife, the mistress, who'd died many years earlier when she was still young and beautiful.

Mildred held her breath. Her long dark hair had tumbled around her face when she'd bent over to look at them. She stood and peeked around the curtain of hair at him, hiding her face lest her expression offend him.

She was nothing but a maid in the master's bedroom. But there had been moments during his ardor when she believed he truly had feelings for her. And, at times, when a golden afterglow warmed her, when she watched him sleep sweetly as a babe in its cradle, she had felt love. If she felt love, he must have felt it, too, she told herself.

As she stood in front of that wardrobe with her hair falling all around her, he flicked the air with one hand. In reply, she brushed the mane over her shoulders, baring herself to him.

He had smiled. "You may have those pretty little slippers."

Dinner had been served late that evening.

***

Now Mildred sat on the thin mattress of her cot, the cold iron frame jabbing her thighs, examining the slippers in her hands. The soles had been scuffed when he'd given them to her and some of the velvet was bald near the edges, the mistress having well-worn them. Now the material was so thin in places she could see through it. Beads were missing and stitches were breaking. Soon, the slippers would fall apart.

She slid the slippers under her bed and pulled out her ugly, sturdy, black boots.

Back in the kitchen, Mildred put the kettle on for tea, added a measure of arsenic to the porridge, and gave it a stir.

Later that morning after tending to her chores, Mildred returned to the master's bedroom for the breakfast tray. He'd eaten a fair amount of the porridge, despite his complaints, as she'd doctored it with a shot of whiskey. There was a knock on the door.

"Enter," the master commanded, his voice cracked.

The door opened and Edmund slipped inside, hair combed, freshly shaved and wearing a clean suit. He paused, his nose wrinkling at the stench. Mildred stepped backward, awaiting dismissal.

Edmund wore an especially nasty smile as his eyes grazed over her as if she were another piece of furniture. The message was clear. He would pretend that he hadn't caught her sneaking out of the master's bedroom before dawn in her night clothes; she was to pretend that he hadn't caught her. And the master could go on thinking that he was the only keeper of secrets in this house.

"Come," the master beckoned with one hand, unable to pull himself to a sit. "What is it you're about?"

"Uncle, you are looking worse today," he said.

It was true. The master's face was gray and hung on his skull like an empty burlap sack. Bits of dried blood were caked in the corners of his mouth. His eyes were rheumy and his white hair had thinned to a few long strands. Mildred had seen better looking corpses. Yet, he hung on.

"I despair for your health," Edmund said. "Dr. Kravitz has promised to come see you. He'll be along this afternoon."

"No doctors," the master said.

No doctors, Mildred prayed.

"Uncle, please humor me. You're the only kin I've left and I, yours. Would you abandon me to the world now? I am helpless without your patronage, without your guidance."

And without your money, Mildred thought.

Edmund had his way, as usual. Just after lunchtime, Mildred showed Dr. Kravitz to the master's bedroom. When the door closed, she pressed her ear to the wood but all she heard was garbled speech. She stood in the hallway for several minutes until Edmund's bedroom door slammed from behind, startling her. She turned to find him with that same evil grin, taking her in as if she were a stain on the wallpaper.

"I have cared for him all of my life," Mildred said.

"And your good service has not gone unnoticed," Edmund replied. He strode to the door, forcing her to move. He knocked loudly and called, "Uncle, it's me." He pulled the door slightly ajar and listened. When the master bade him enter, Edmund pulled the door wide so forcefully that Mildred's nose would have been broken had she not quickly stepped aside. After he entered the room, he closed the door soundly behind him.

She pressed her ear to the door again. Edmund's high-toned greeting cut through the oak, but his voice suddenly dropped, and then the voices faded.

Nearly an hour later, Dr. Kravitz appeared in the kitchen while Mildred peeled potatoes for the evening meal, the lamb already roasting in the cooker.

"It is typhoid fever and your master is gravely ill. I am sending a nurse who will stay at his bedside around the clock. You shall make up a room for her near his own. And I shall visit daily. Meanwhile, no rich foods, certainly not that lamb I smell. He is to have nothing but weak tea and broth." He pointed a finger at her. "And no whiskey. I know you've been slipping it to him, it's on his breath."

No whiskey meant no way to cover up the taste of arsenic.

"Yes, sir," Mildred said. "As you say."

The nurse, Katie O'Brien, a young redhead with milky skin and a trim waist, arrived just before dinner. She left her leather travel bag in the bedroom Mildred had made up for her across the hall from Edmund's, then followed Mildred to the kitchen. Miss O'Brien ladled out a bowl of clear broth and poured a cup of weak tea for the master. Mildred offered to take the tray up for her but she refused.

***

As the weeks wore on, Mildred was allowed into the sick room only to change the linens and tend the fire. Katie prepared and served all the master's meals, and Dr. Kravitz checked on him daily. Edmund visited his uncle's room the first thing in the morning and then again upon his return in the evening, otherwise absenting himself from the mansion all day long. Mildred knew not where he went; but whatever he was doing, she reckoned he was up to no good.

The master recovered his strength and soon was well enough to take air in the garden on warmer days. At first, Edmund carried him down the stairs but as the master's health improved, he was able to walk without assistance. Bundled in blankets, the master dozed as Edmund read to him and Katie served tea. One or both were always by his side.

Mildred hadn't been fooled. Not long after Katie had come to stay, the upstairs doors and floorboards creaked late at night as one visited the bedroom of the other. *Careful, girl*, Mildred thought. *You may regret the choices you make.*

In the garden, Mildred had witnessed Edmund and Katie making cow eyes at each other. Once when the master was soundly asleep, Edmund grasped Katie's fingers and pulled her close, stealing a kiss. She cooed and rested her head upon his shoulder.

In the rare moments when Edmund and the nurse were distracted, Mildred had tried to catch the master's eye. When she did so, he had looked away.

Mildred had found herself looking away as well.

Katie took her meals in the kitchen and it was during these times Mildred and she kindled a friendship. Katie O'Brien was from the south part of town, her family mill workers, as had been Mildred's. They had saved their money to send Katie, their little gem, to nursing school. When Mildred told Katie that all of her family had died, Katie patted her hand.

One day, Katie appeared in the kitchen with a small locket on a delicate gold chain around her neck. When Mildred asked about it, Katie blushed, then opened the locket, exposing a tiny photograph of Edmund.

"We are to wed," Katie whispered.

"Why are you whispering?" Mildred asked.

"It's a secret. Edmund wishes to wait until his uncle is fully recovered before he tells him. Then we shall plan a grand wedding, and this house will be full of light and laughter and joy."

Mildred took Katie by both hands. "I am so pleased for you," she said. "But you are young. You have a future. What about your family?"

"Oh, it will all be fine. Edmund says he will buy a house for my family, a lovely house with a garden close to the mansion so I can visit my mother every day."

It would be a cruelty to destroy this girl's dreams, a cruelty better left to someone else.

"More tea, dear?" Mildred asked.

Eventually the master was healthy enough that he no longer needed a nurse. Katie was dismissed and life returned to normal, almost. The master no longer desired Mildred in his bed. His eyes no longer twinkled when she bent across him to adjust his covers. Instead, he pulled away, his head turned aside.

It was as if she were nothing but a servant and had never been anything but a servant. When they were alone, she searched his eyes for a clue. All she saw was regret, quickly replaced by arrogance.

Edmund must have chastised his uncle for the indiscretion.

That was well and good since the master would die soon anyway. And Mildred knew where his will was kept.

***

A couple of years after he'd given her the slippers, he had made a new will and bestowed upon her half of his estate.

At the time, he said he didn't care what Edmund, his only heir, thought. The boy was lazy and foolish. What's more, Edmund, blonde and fair, in contrast to the Fairweather family's dark features, in no manner resembled the master's late brother. The master resented leaving his fortune to some bastard waif the boy's mother had begat like a common whore, while his idiot brother pretended not to notice.

That afternoon in the master's bedroom, Mildred had sat on his lap as he showed her the will, pointing to the words, Mildred Munz. She recognized her own name but was unable to read the rest, having never learned to make sense of written words. He folded the document into its sheepskin cover, tied it with a leather string and slipped it into his desk drawer before pulling loose the ties of her apron.

Soon she realized that nothing had changed. She was not the mistress of the manor. She merely walked in the dead mistress' cast-off slippers and then only at night. During the day, she was the housekeeper, Mrs. Mildred Munz. She'd never married, but everyone addressed her as missus, as was the custom.

Never married and, of course, never a mother. A respectable servant's only possession was her reputation. So when she got with child, the master sent her to Boston to see a doctor. After she came back, she continued to sleep beside him at night, and he continued to satisfy his needs with her body. But, for Mildred, there was no more golden afterglow.

No marriage, no children, not even a locket like Katie O'Brien's, and then it was too late for all of that. All the master had given her were those second-hand slippers. Day by day, the shame had shredded her soul as ground glass shredded one's stomach. But glass shards were too obvious.

Arsenic had been the solution.

***

After Katie O'Brien moved out, the master's health declined rapidly and Dr. Kravitz was summoned again. After his examination, he stood outside the master's door and muttered to Edmund, their speech quieting as Mildred passed by. But nothing more was done.

It would not be long now before Mildred would be free of this man and his house.

One Monday morning, Edmund had a great row with the master. Mildred could not help but overhear, standing outside the bedroom, a broom in her hand. Edmund must have learned of the will and her inheritance.

Edmund shouted. "What will people think?"

"People be damned!"

It satisfied Mildred to know that even though the master and she had grown apart, he had kept his word and half the estate would be hers. She didn't care if he was giving her the money out of affection for her or out of spite against Edmund.

"But our family honor!" Edmund howled.

The master's barked laugh started a coughing fit. When he recovered, he shouted, "Get out of my sight!"

The door flew open and a red-faced Edmund rushed out of the room with such fury, Mildred was afraid he would strike her.

***

The next day, Mildred walked to the druggist to purchase medicine for her skin rash. It had been her first afternoon out of the house in weeks, and the change in seasons surprised her. Time had moved more quickly than she'd noticed.

A few bright autumn leaves twisted on bare limbs, gnarled as an old woman's hands, then dropped into gray-green slime on the sidewalks. Tiny ice crystals floated in the air. Mildred pulled her thin wool coat tighter around her.

When she entered the shop, Mildred found her path blocked by a plump woman of her own age who looked vaguely familiar.

The woman stared curiously at her. "Millie?"

Circles of red on her cheeks looked as if they'd been drawn by a child, and made her pale skin appear blue. Her once-red hair had dulled and was streaked with white. She cocked her head a particular way and that was when Mildred remembered.

"Patty?"

A small boy tugged on the woman's hand, his face covered in a sugary crust. "Granma!"

"Hush, now, Michael," Patty said. "Granma's talking to an old friend." On her left hand, she wore a gold wedding band that was so tight it cut into her fat finger. Mildred now remembered hearing that Patty had married a tradesman, quit the mill, and grown a family.

Patty said, "Are you still at the big house? What a lucky girl you were, always luckier than the rest of us."

Mildred smiled. "Housekeeper, now."

"Housekeeper, you say! Fair play to you!"

"Granma!"

Patty leaned in conspiratorially. "He needs to pee. Come to my house for tea sometime, send word. Promise, now."

"I promise," Mildred said as she watched little Michael drag Patty from the store. But she knew, and Patty should have known, that Mildred wouldn't send word. The invitation and acceptance were just a nice way of saying goodbye.

"Let's see those hands," the druggist said.

Mildred held them aloft, the backs red, cracked, and scaly.

"Are you using the medicine I gave you?" he asked.

"I ran out several weeks ago. The master has been ill and I couldn't leave the house to purchase more."

He handed her the bottle. "Mind the dosage. There's arsenic in it. Too much will make you sick."

"I know," Mildred said, then paid him for her purchase.

Mildred took the long way home, walking through a small park. In the gazebo, a young man and woman stood at a distance, too far apart for stolen kisses. As Mildred drew closer, she saw it was Edmund and Katie O'Brien.

Katie reached up, jerked the chain from her throat and threw the locket at Edmund. It bounced off his chest and landed at his feet. Edmund, with an air of indignation, strode away. Katie fell to the gazebo floor, sobbing.

Mildred looked around, saw that no one was watching and hurried to the gazebo. She grasped Katie's elbow. "Get up," she murmured.

"I'm ruined."

"You're not ruined yet, but you will be if you keep up this nonsense."

Katie allowed herself to be pulled to her feet and guided to a bench.

"Wipe your face. Quickly now," Mildred said as she handed Katie a handkerchief.

"He promised. He promised to marry me but now he refuses. And I need a husband. He says his fussy old uncle is sending him back to Cambridge where there is no place for a wife and a child."

Edmund was lying. If there had been any discussion of Cambridge, Mildred would have heard the row.

"Will you have the child?" Mildred asked.

Katie drew herself up. She was Irish and a Catholic. Abortion was a sin but Mildred knew that there were many Irish Catholic sinners. "This is my child, too," Katie said.

"Then you must do what girls in your position have done for centuries. You will move to another town, pretend that your husband has died, and raise the child on your own. You're lucky, Katie girl, you have a profession."

"And how am I to do that?" Katie scoffed. "I have no money."

"Pack your bag and meet me at the train station tomorrow morning. Six-thirty sharp."

Mildred swept the broken locket from the floor, dropped it into her pocket, and marched back to the mansion. When she arrived home, she went straight to her room. She pulled the dusty slippers out from under her bed, took them to the kitchen and tossed them into the cooker's fire.

***

The next morning, Mildred hid in the kitchen's darkness, waiting for the sound of Edmund bumping up the stairs. Afterwards she allowed thirty minutes to pass, then crept upstairs and listened at the door to his snores. She entered quietly, found his clothes on the floor, and searched his pockets. She was in luck. There was plenty of money. Edmund must've had a good night gambling.

Just in case Edmund had come home penniless, she'd slipped laudanum in the master's tea the night before. She dropped Edmund's clothes back on the floor and let herself into the master's bedroom. In his desk drawer, she found several more bills hidden beneath the will. She was about to open it to see her name again when the master rolled over, his eyelids partially open. He registered her presence with a confused frown.

She went to his bedside. "Porridge this morning?"

"Just sweet tea," he muttered before he slipped back into fitful sleep.

Mildred hurried to the train station. She arrived a few minutes early and found Katie standing on the platform with the same leather bag at her feet that she'd dropped on the bed when she'd first come to the mansion. Mildred stuffed the bills she'd found into Katie's hands.

Katie looked down at her fist. "There must be five hundred dollars here!"

"Never you mind, girl. Put it away somewhere safe and, mind you, don't let some sweet-talking man take it. This is for you and your child."

Katie stashed the money in her bag and pulled it between her feet.

"And take this." Mildred handed Katie the broken locket.

"I don't want that."

"You may not now, but someday you may regret losing it. Besides, Katie girl, it's your proof. The man who did you wrong is set to receive a great inheritance."

"I don't want his inheritance."

Mildred smiled to herself. "You may not want it for yourself, but someday you may need it for your child. For his education."

Katie's eyes narrowed with suspicion. "Where did you get this money?"

"I've been saving up for this all my life."

Katie appeared satisfied with the response. "I'll never be able to repay you, Mrs. Munz. I don't know how to thank you."

"Cherish that child. That will be enough thanks for me."

Mildred returned to the mansion and prepared the master's sweet tea and porridge. She considered serving Edmund the special porridge as well, speeding up the unborn child's inheritance, but that would look suspicious if both the men died of the same condition at the same time. Besides, Edmund never took breakfast, always leaving soon after his daily visit to his uncle.

Like every other morning, Mildred opened the door to the master's room. When she stepped inside, the breakfast tray dropped from her hands. Clots of porridge were flung onto the silken bed cover. Tea splattered the oriental carpet.

A large knife was buried in the master's chest.

Edmund rushed in behind her. "What have you done?"

***

On Friday, Mildred, in heavy iron handcuffs and shackles, was hauled before a judge.

"What are the charges?" the judge asked.

"Murder, Your Honor. On Wednesday last, Mrs. Mildred Munz stabbed her employer, Lawrence Fairweather, to death," the prosecutor said. "If Mrs. Munz pleads guilty, we will accept a life sentence."

"You heard the prosecutor, Mrs. Munz," the judge said. "If you plead guilty, your life will be spared. If not, there will be a trial. And if you are convicted, you will hang. How do you plead?"

She had not done it. She could not have done it. She was at the train station with Katie O'Brien when the master was murdered. But she could not admit to that. As far as that black-robed shyster would be concerned, a thief who was a liar was a murderer.

"Not guilty," Mildred said. "I did not kill him."

"The evidence is damning," the prosecutor said. "The knife was from her kitchen. And the defendant . . . enjoyed . . . carnal relations with her master until he recently spurned her. Hell hath no fury like a woman scorned, Your Honor. She shall surely hang."

"I am entitled to a trial, am I not? Where is this evidence? I want an attorney."

The judge took in the porridge-crusted, tea-stained dress and apron Mildred had worn ever since her arrest. "Do you have the means to pay for an attorney?"

"My inheritance," Mildred said. "Master Fairweather left me half his estate. It's in his will, in the desk, in his bedroom. He showed it to me."

The judge's eyebrows rose. In that instant, Mildred realized she had confessed to a motive.

"Madam, I must inform you that you will never receive a penny. My law clerk and I were looking at this very question just this past Monday. Bring forward that volume." The judge beckoned to someone in the back of the courtroom.

Mildred turned to see Edmund walking up the aisle with a book in his hand. He stepped behind the bench, placed it in front of the judge, and opened it to a marked page. So this was how he had occupied himself during the day, learning the law from a judge.

"Here now," the judge said as stabbed a page with his forefinger. "It is well settled that a slayer cannot take under a will. All of the money which he, or she, would have received goes to the remaining heirs. In this case, that is Edmund Fairweather, your master's nephew and my law clerk. He promises to make a fine attorney one day."

Edmund wore that wicked smile of his as he pulled the sheepskin-wrapped document from his frock coat and handed it to the judge.

The judge examined it. "I now have the will before me. You are indeed named as an heir to the estate. You were to receive one pair of velvet slippers.

"I ask you one last time, Mrs. Munz, how do you choose: life in prison or the gallows?"

THE TRAGIC DEATH OF MRS. EDNA FOGG

by Edith Maxwell

Cycling home after a delivery, midwife Rose Carroll discovers the body of suffragist Edna Fogg. Clearly, she was murdered—but why? An abundance of motives and suspects confound the case, but Rose is on the job.

As I cycled home in the November dawn after safely delivering a baby, I hadn't expected to encounter a dead body. It was the red shoe sticking out from where no shoe should be that caught my eye, its color echoing the frost-burnished leaves of the lilac bush above it.

I let my bicycle fall to the side and hurried to the shrub. Pulling back the branches, my heart a-thud, I gasped when I saw that the shoe was on the black-stockinged foot of Edna Fogg. I pulled off my glove and knelt to touch the neck of the well-known women's suffragist, a lady in her thirties. Her skin was cold and yellow, and not from the chilly fall air, either.

Poor Edna. I didn't know her well, but I'd always admired her fortitude in speaking out for a woman's right to vote, much as my own mother did. Edna wasn't a Quaker like we were, but she embodied our values of equality and integrity. I sniffed, picking up a scent other than dried leaves and wood smoke, but I couldn't identify it. Perhaps it was a perfume Edna used.

How had she died? Surely it wasn't from natural causes, not with her ending up under a bush. I ran my gaze over her body. I saw no bullet hole or stab wound. I wanted to investigate further—perhaps she had an injury on her back or her head—but I knew from my encounters with him that Detective Kevin Donovan of the Amesbury Police Department would need to see her *in situ*. My eyes widened as I glimpsed a slip of paper tucked into Edna's hand.

I perked my ears at the sound of an approaching horse clopping along the cobblestones. It pulled an open buggy, and I stepped into the street, signaling the driver to stop.

"Excuse me, but a lady has died," I said to the driver. "Can thee please hurry to the police station and ask for Detective Donovan to come?"

"And why not the funeral parlor, miss?" The gentleman was about fifty. "If she's dead, as you say."

How much to tell him? "Please, I believe the police are needed in this case." I clasped my hands in front of me. Despite being half his age, I used my most authoritative voice and stood tall into my five feet eight inches.

He shrugged. "Very well." He clucked to the dark horse and clattered away.

I returned to Edna's side and closed my eyes, holding her released spirit in the Light of God. I also held my own, still very much of this world. I am a midwife, not a detective, and am accustomed on occasion to witnessing the unavoidable death of one of my mothers or newborns. But why did I keep encountering cases of violent death?

***

An hour later I sat in Bertie Winslow's cheery kitchen. I sipped the coffee she'd poured, inhaled the cinnamon-laden air, and continued to tell her the events of the morning. We'd worked together on several murder cases in the past, strictly as amateurs, of course, and I'd found I had something of a gift for investigation. I knew my good friend, the unconventional postmistress of our bustling mill town, would be willing to discuss this death with me.

"Kevin appeared with several other officers," I said. "As usual he looked askance at me, but thanked me for raising the alarm. And for pointing out the paper in Edna's hand."

"And then kindly told you to absent yourself, I assume?" A wry grin pulled at Bertie's mouth.

"Indeed. Although not before I witnessed him raising Edna's head and discovering a great bloody wound on the back of it."

"Poor Edna." Her eyes went wide. "So somebody whacked her to death."

"It appears so, although Kevin did caution me against mentioning the method, so thee'll have to keep that information under thy hat." I frowned. "Bertie, I know thee must get along soon to open the post office. But I was much disturbed by finding Edna Fogg's body, and I thought thee might have known her better than I."

Bertie cocked her head of curly blond hair. "I've always admired Edna's suffrage work." She peered into a mirror on the wall, her expression somber, and pinned on one of her fanciful hats at her usual rakish angle. She turned back to face me. "Did you hear she recently left her husband of many years?"

"No. I know nothing of her personal life. Does thee know why she left Mr. Fogg? Was he cruel to her, or—"

Bertie held up her hand. "I'm not sure why she left. I do know she went to live with Frannie Murphy, another suffragist. I'll have to ask Sophie what the nature of their friendship is, since she and Edna are both lawyers." Sophie and Bertie lived together in what would have been called a marriage if one of them had been a man. "I daresay Hiram Fogg wasn't a bit happy about the move," she added.

"I would imagine not. Does she have children?"

"I don't believe so."

"And what is his chosen profession? Is he also in the law?"

"No." She pursed her lips. "I believe he's a physician."

"I wonder what the paper I saw was. Surely not a suicide note. Perhaps it was a warning of some kind." I glanced at the clock as I finished my coffee. "Thee needs to go. And I must rest before my afternoon appointments. I didn't sleep more than dozing during the early stages of my client's labor last evening."

We walked out together and she mounted her horse, Grover. She'd named him after our president, an act completely in character with Bertie's irreverent nature. I waved goodbye and mounted my steel steed for the short ride home. Had Edna been equally as unconventional as Bertie and entered into a loving relationship with another woman? Perhaps Hiram Fogg had felt an irrational rage at being abandoned, especially for a woman, and had killed his wife. I'd have to see what I could learn, with the sole intent of assisting Kevin in his investigation, naturally.

***

Before my first pregnant client of the afternoon, I took a moment to pen a note to my mother. I jotted down pleasantries, inquired if she knew Edna Fogg from their mutual suffrage work, and told her about the death. I asked if she knew anything that might help in the investigation. Mother supported my talents in tracking down murderers. I sealed the envelope and set it out for the postman.

After my last client left at three o'clock, I sat and thought. Where could I learn more about both Hiram Fogg and Frannie Murphy, not to mention Edna? Bertie had said Edna was a lawyer, but I didn't know where she practiced. I snapped my fingers. I had a home visit scheduled later today. And Nan Pollard's husband was a lawyer.

Twenty minutes later Nan, cradling her eight-month-pregnant belly under sprigged fabric that strained at her full bosom, ushered me into an airy and spacious bedroom on Hillside Avenue.

"Will this do, Rose?" she asked, waving her arm to encompass the space. A four-poster bed draped with creamy brocade curtains held a position of honor. Two upholstered armchairs nestled near the east-facing window and a marble-faced fireplace was tucked into the opposite wall. Nan smoothed chestnut-colored hair off her brow, with a faint whiff of violet.

"It will do quite nicely, Nan." I made home visits to every client, whether the wife of a mill owner or the young mill worker herself. I thought it passing odd Nan had even asked, since she'd given birth here twice before.

"My maid will bring you whatever you need," Nan said with a calm smile. "Mr. Pollard says to summon the carriage should we need a doctor in attendance."

I'd assisted at her prior births as an apprentice, but I was confident to be the lead midwife this time around. "I doubt we'll need a physician, Nan. Thy previous births were quite easy, as I recall."

Her brows knit together. "Mr. Pollard is very much in favor of having a male doctor attend me. But I don't agree, and I've put my foot down. The birthing chamber is the realm of women, is it not?"

I smiled and stroked her arm. "I believe it is, Nan. And I will take good care of thee." It was an honest answer. But how was I going to raise the issue of what George Pollard might know about Edna Fogg? As it happened, I didn't need to.

"Rose," Nan lowered her voice. "I heard Mrs. Fogg was killed. And that you found her body this morning. Is it true?" Her eyes were wide.

"Let's sit for a moment." I led her to the chairs by the window. Talk of murder wasn't exactly the calming topic one would wish for a near-term mother-to-be. After we sat, I went on. "I did find her, sadly. I was returning at dawn from a birth."

"Mr. Pollard said she was bashed in the back of the head. What a terrible death." She brought her hands to cover her mouth.

"Any violent death is a terrible one. I believe Edna was a lawyer, like thy husband. Was George acquainted with her?"

Nan's nostrils flared. "Acquainted? Why, she stole his job!" Nan suddenly looked neither surprised nor saddened about Edna's death.

That was quite the accusation. "How so?" I kept my expression even, despite my keen interest to learn more about this story.

"They're both employed by Bixby & Batchelder, or were. When my George was up for promotion, they chose that woman instead." She nearly spat the word 'woman.' "And sacked Mr. Pollard." The anger slid off her face and sorrow crept into her voice. "Just like what happened to my Papa when I was a girl. He was a wrecked man after that."

"I'm so sorry, Nan. I trust George will find a new position soon."

"Maybe, if people about town stop laughing behind his back. And then Mrs. Fogg ups and leaves her own husband high and dry. There's just no decency in this world, Rose. What have we come to?"

***

At a few minutes before seven that evening, Bertie and I walked briskly toward the Free Will Baptist Church on Friend Street. She'd stopped by after supper and convinced me to attend a suffrage meeting with her.

"They're planning to start with tributes to Edna Fogg," Bertie said, tucking her arm through mine. "I thought you'd be interested."

"I wonder what her suffragist friends will say. One of my clients, Nan Pollard, told me her husband was passed over for a promotion in favor of Edna, and that the firm let him go. Nan seemed quite incensed about it."

Bertie snorted. "Sophie always says Pollard isn't exactly a Philadelphia lawyer."

I raised my eyebrows at the phrase. As a Quaker, I might interpret Philadelphia lawyer as one who embodied Friends' values rather than one with a keen intellect.

"Edna was smarter than him," Bertie went on. "I'm glad Mr. Batchelder recognized that."

"It's still quite rare for a woman to push ahead of a man like that." I glanced at Bertie as we arrived at the door. "Well, except for thee, of course." Bertie'd had quite a struggle to be appointed to her position as postmistress.

Inside, the hall was full of women, many seated, some conferring in small groups standing around the edges.

Bertie nudged me and made a small gesture toward a woman near us. "That's Frannie Murphy," she murmured. She hailed Frannie, who walked over.

Frannie was tall, not much older than I. She wore a mannish jacket over her black dress, with her auburn hair pulled back severely into a coiled braid.

"Frannie, I'm awfully sorry about Edna," Bertie said. "Rose here is a bit of a detective, you know."

"Rose Carroll." Frannie stared at me. "I heard you found my dear Edna. Was it a terrible sight? Do you think she suffered?"

I took her hand in both of mine. "I'm afraid I cannot say. But the detective told me she suffered a grievous wound, so perhaps she lost consciousness immediately." I hoped that would console her.

"Who would harm such a graceful and brilliant person?" she whispered. "Such a loving soul?"

Bertie looked sympathetic. "I heard she was living with you."

Frannie took a deep breath in and let it out. "Yes. She couldn't tolerate that husband of hers any longer. Hiram is an ogre, and I invited her to share my flat." She looked intently at Bertie. "Edna wanted only a platonic friendship with me, and even that was so rich, so full. Yet she spoke of moving on again . . . " She pressed her lips together and shook her head rapidly. "I mustn't dwell on it any longer. The suffrage movement needs me. And I have my memories."

Two women edged past us trailing a cloud of lavender. Frannie gave a low, sad laugh. "Edna would have been sneezing her head off at that smell. She had the worse reaction to scents."

An older lady walked to the front of the room and clapped several times. "The meeting of the Amesbury chapter of the Woman Suffrage Association will now come to order." She rapped a gavel on the table as Bertie and I made our way to two seats.

So Hiram Fogg was an ogre, at least according to Frannie, who had possibly been in love with Edna. And Edna had talked about moving on. I had much to consider.

***

"Kevin, I'm assuming Edna Fogg's death was murder, since a blow to the back of the head couldn't be suicide," I said the next morning. I stood in front of the detective's desk in the police station, where the smell of stale cigar smoke mixed with the aroma of old wood and the coconut scent of the Macassar oil Kevin used on his hair. "And the death could hardly be accidental, with her lying under a lilac bush. I've obtained information thee might find useful in thy investigation."

"Now, Miss Rose. I hope you haven't been trying to play private detective again." He cocked his head and gave a scolding look.

I bristled inwardly at his choice of verbs, but kept my annoyance to myself. "I've merely collected some facts which could shed light on Edna's life and motivations. I'll leave, naturally, if thee has already made an arrest in the case."

He let out a noisy breath. "Surely you know I haven't, although I have located a possible witness to the crime."

"Excellent. What was on that piece of paper she held?"

"It was a handwritten note, asking her to meet at that spot."

"Not signed?" I asked.

"Sadly, no." He gestured at the chair. "Sit down, then, and tell me what you have."

"First, Edna had left her husband. She was living with the suffragist Frannie Murphy."

"Mr. Fogg told us she'd moved out, but not where." Kevin frowned. "That Murphy woman is a rabble-rouser of the highest order. What was a lovely lady like Mrs. Fogg doing with the likes of her?"

"I believe they were friends and shared a passion for a woman's right to vote." I watched him. "As does my mother, and I, myself."

"Regardless, I'm going to be looking hard at this Miss Murphy." He sighed. "Go on, please."

I ticked off the items on my fingers. "Second, last night Frannie told us—"

"Who's us?"

"Bertie Winslow took me to the suffrage meeting. Frannie told us Edna was talking about moving on again. She didn't say where. Frannie herself seemed quite broken up about Edna's death. I believe Edna might have disappointed Frannie in the, uh, scope of their friendship."

He looked up, shocked. "You mean . . .? Oh, never mind." He grabbed a stub of a pencil and scribbled on a piece of paper.

"Third, yesterday I was with a pregnant client of mine, Nan Pollard. She said the law firm of Bixby & Batchelder recently promoted Edna over Nan's husband, George. They let George go from the firm. Nan was quite incensed about that, and about Edna's leaving Hiram."

"As well she might be," Kevin murmured, staring at his notes.

At my exclamation, he glanced up and cringed. "Sorry, I was thinking out loud. Of course there's nothing wrong with a lady lawyer earning her keep, Miss Rose. But marriage vows—well, don't you think they should mean something?"

***

I had several prenatal appointments after I returned home, but the whole time my mind was half occupied by thoughts of Edna's murder. The afternoon post arrived at two, with a return note from Mother. After greetings and bits of news about the Lawrence farm—Daddy's business, not hers—she wrote:

I met Edna Fogg at the April meeting where we founded the International Council of Women. She spoke even then about leaving her husband. He wanted them to raise a family, and that was not her chosen path. She dreamed of becoming a famous lawyer and planned to pursue that passion. Thee knows, my dear Rose, we women are not all suited for the life of wife and mother, despite thy calling to assist women in achieving exactly that.

So that was why Edna had left Hiram. Even though I hoped for children of my own one day, I agreed with Mother: not all women wanted to bear children, for various reasons. If they didn't, their choice was the difficult one of ceasing intimate relations with their husbands.

And perhaps the pressure of Frannie's feelings for her was the reason Edna had mentioned moving on again. Last night Frannie had seemed sincere in her grief for Edna—but Frannie could have killed her because Edna had spurned the younger woman's love. Frannie might simply be a good actress. She was tall, young, and strong enough to strike a fatal blow to Edna's head. It was well that Kevin said he'd be looking into Frannie.

I finished reading and refolded the missive, thinking all the while. What about Hiram? I needed to learn more about Edna's husband. Bertie'd said he was a physician. I could pay my beau, David, a visit at his office at the hospital. I shook my head. No, I couldn't—he was away at a medical convention.

Or the killer could have been George Pollard, furious at losing his job to a woman. I had time to call at the law firm where George had worked. Someone might be willing to talk to me about him. Yes, I'd walk downtown to Bixby & Batchelder—

My thinking was interrupted by a loud rapping on the front door. A driver handed me a note. It read, in a flowing, educated hand: *Please come quickly. My pains have begun. Nan Pollard.*

Good heavens. I made a quick calculation. She still had a month before the baby was due. I prayed the infant would be mature enough to sustain its passage out into the world and survive.

"I'm to take you to the Pollard home, miss," the driver said.

I checked the sky, cloudless and not too cold, with the sun still hanging above the horizon. "Thank thee, but I'll come along in a few minutes on my bicycle. I need to get my things together. Please have the maid put a large pot of water on to boil."

He tipped his hat and hurried back to the carriage.

I grabbed a piece of bread and a wedge of cheese and munched on them as I checked my birthing satchel. Labors were so unpredictable in length and intensity, I'd learned to snatch sustenance when I could. Cloaked, bonneted, and gloved, with my satchel strapped to the platform on the back of my cycle, I mounted and rolled down the hill.

Whether it was from the movement of the wheels or the intensity of the past two days I wasn't sure, but the last piece of the Edna puzzle fell into place in my brain as I rode. My eyes wide, I detoured to the police station, pedaling like a madwoman, my eyeglasses sliding down the bridge of my nose.

I dashed up the steps of the station only to learn that Kevin wasn't in. I slapped the scarred wooden surface of the front desk in frustration.

"There's no need for that, miss," the young officer said.

"I apologize. I need to leave the detective a note, then. And thee must see that he gets it with all due dispatch." I stood tall and fixed my gaze on him. "It regards the recent murder."

He stared at me, but recovered enough to say, "Yes, miss."

***

The distraught young maid pulled open the door to the Pollard home. "Oh, Miss Carroll, I'm glad you've come. She's up there a-screaming."

"Don't worry thyself. It's what women do. I'll attend to her shortly. Are the children about?"

"No. Mrs. Pollard told Nursey to take them to their grandmother's."

"Good. I have a question for thee before I go up." I conferred with her until a cry of pain drifted down from upstairs. "Please put that item aside for me. And bring up hot water as soon as possible." I ran up the stairs.

"Where have you been, Rose?" Nan wailed from her bed as soon as I walked in. Her face was flushed and the hair around her forehead curly and damp.

"I'm here now, Nan." I cleaned my hands at the washstand and set out my birthing supplies. "When did the pains begin, and how far apart are they?"

"A couple of hours ago. They're getting closer and closer." As a contraction set in, Nan cried out again.

"Now, now," I said. "Blow out thy breath gently. If thee becomes tense, thy body will have more difficulty letting the baby come out." This was her third labor. She should have learned how to give birth by now, but perhaps she was afraid of bringing another baby into a family suddenly without a breadwinner.

***

Three hours later, as I was settling Nan and her tiny but healthy baby girl onto fresh pillows, I heard a commotion and shouting downstairs. Nan and I exchanged a look. The voices quieted and a moment later there was a rapping at the bedroom door.

I pulled it open to see a red-faced George Pollard, with Kevin right behind him.

"I've got to talk with Mrs. Pollard," her husband said. "She'll tell this fool I was right here the whole time!"

Kevin, still behind him, shook his head ever so slightly at me.

Nan called out, "Mr. Pollard, come see your daughter."

"A daughter? Our first girl?" He rushed toward the bed. He knelt to stroke the tiny newborn's head, and then his wife's cheek.

Kevin cleared his throat. "This is all very nice. But I'm afraid I'm here on official police business, as Mr. Pollard well knows." He turned to me and murmured, "May I speak with the newly delivered mother?"

"I think thee'd better." I raised my eyebrows.

"Please step away from the bed, Mr. Pollard," Kevin said.

George glared at him but obliged.

"Rose, will you fetch me my wrapper?" Nan pointed to the armoire.

I hurried over. When I opened the door, the scent of violet flooded my nostrils. I sniffed as I narrowed my eyes and stared at the hanging dresses without seeing them.

"Please, Rose?" Nan called. "I need to be decent with this policeman in the room."

I grabbed the wrapper and shut the door. Nan handed the baby to George before donning the garment. Kevin approached the couple.

"Mrs. Pollard," Kevin began. "Where was your husband Sunday night between dusk and approximately five o'clock in the morning?"

"Why, he was right here with me, Officer. Weren't you, dear?"

George kept his eyes on the baby in his arms and nodded.

"Nan, on Monday thee told me Edna had been bashed in the head," I said. "Thee had no way of knowing that. Right, Kevin?"

"That is correct. You, Miss Rose, were the only person outside of the police to see that. And we made quite sure not to let that fact slip out to the newspapers."

"Why, I heard it somewhere," Nan scoffed, tossing her head. "The news must have gotten around town. I think the maid told me."

"I don't believe so. In fact, on Second Day thee said George told thee about the bashing." I turned to Kevin. "The maid is downstairs, and she's holding a shirt of George's that has bloodstains on it."

"Cut myself with the razor, that's all it was." George turned his scowl in my direction. A tic beat near his lip and sweat popped out on his forehead like nervous pearls.

"Nan, it pains me to say this," I said, "but thee helped kill Edna, didn't thee?"

"How dare you!" His nostrils flaring, George took a step toward me.

"Hand me the baby." I held out my arms. "She's very small and will not tolerate thy anger." To my surprise he obliged.

"Mrs. Pollard had nothing to do with it," George blustered. "She was home the whole night!"

"No, she wasn't," I continued. "Nan, I smelled the scent of violet when I found Edna's body. That's thy perfume."

"I'm not the only lady who wears violet!" She made as if to climb out of bed, but George put his hand on her shoulder. "Edna must have fancied the same aroma."

I smiled sadly. "Frannie Murphy said Edna had a severe sneezing reaction to scents. No, that was thee, luring her to that house with the note, pushing George to kill her. Thee couldn't stand that she was given his job."

"Well, it was neither fair nor right. And you don't have any proof of anything. Now give me my baby." She extended her arms.

I shook my head. With my unoccupied hand I drew the note the driver had brought me out of my pocket. "Kevin, I think if thee compares the handwriting on this note with the one found at the body, they will be identical."

"Officers?" Kevin called out as he took the note and thanked me with his eyes. Two policemen hurried in.

"We interviewed a witness who places you both, Mr. and Mrs. Pollard, at the scene of the crime Sunday evening at seven o'clock." Kevin laid a hand on George's arm, a move I'd learned was required by the police at the time of an arrest. "George Pollard, you are under arrest for the murder of Mrs. Edna Fogg." The men moved toward George. He cast an anguished look at his wife but didn't struggle as an officer ushered him out.

Kevin reached down and lightly touched Nan's shoulder. She twisted away. "Nanette Pollard, you are under arrest as an accessory to the murder of Mrs. Edna Fogg. I'll call for a police matron to stay with you until you are recovered enough to be transported to the jail."

"You can't do that!" She gazed at her baby with stricken eyes, as if only now realizing the impact of her crime. She brought her hand to her mouth as tears seeped from her eyes.

"Indeed I can." He instructed the other officer to fetch the matron. Kevin turned to me. "Thank you," he whispered.

I acknowledged his appreciation with a frown. I was getting better at detecting, true. I gazed at the sweet warm bundle in my arms. She and her brothers would now be no different than orphans due to the desperate, foolish actions of their parents. I'd helped justice to be served, but at a tragic cost. Perhaps I should stick to midwifery from now on.

CRIM CON

by Nancy Herriman

A San Francisco party in 1867 is interrupted by the murder of the hostess. Who killed Fanny? Her husband, his mistress, her rumored former lover? Suspects abound, but guest Celia Davies is an accomplished detective.

San Francisco, 1867

"What a dreadful man," said Jane Hutchinson, lowering her voice.

Celia Davies stood with her friend in a parlor belonging to that 'dreadful man.' Henry Shaw—tall, broad-shouldered, distinguished-looking—mingled with his guests, who'd gathered to celebrate his wife's thirtieth birthday. The atmosphere in the room, however, was about as festive as a wake's. Jane might not be alone in her opinion of Mr. Shaw.

"You could have refused the invitation," said Celia.

"But I *had* to support Fanny, and I'm thankful you agreed to accompany me." Jane selected a glass of lemon-and-sherry punch from the serving tray being brought around by a maid. "The brass to invite *her* here, though. Right under Fanny's nose, when everybody knows what's going on between them."

"Who?" asked Celia, scanning the group of people assembled among the potted plants, velvet cushions, and rosewood furnishings that crowded the Shaws' sun-drenched parlor. There were only two men—Henry and his younger brother, Marcus—and a few women besides Jane and Celia. Mrs. Frances Shaw and her sister, Lucinda Hayes, sat side-by-side on the silk-covered settee placed before the parlor window. Frances, who sadly looked older than her thirty years, was handsome nonetheless, her dark hair decorated with artificial flowers that emphasized the heart shape of her face. She noticed Celia staring and lifted a hand to her throat, her fingers splayed across her high lace collar.

Across from the sisters, a family friend, Edith Calvert, craned her long neck to peek at Henry and Marcus Shaw. She was so preoccupied with the two men—or perhaps only the one—that she nearly tipped her punch onto the wool mosaic carpet beneath her feet.

"Do you mean Miss Calvert?" asked Celia.

"Oh, goodness, no. *Her.*" Jane's nod was subtle.

Ah, yes. The striking Mrs. Marcus Shaw—Abigail—ensconced in a high-backed chair near to where her husband and brother-in-law stood talking. She was flaxen-haired and slim, her pink silk gown lending the right amount of color to her cheeks. Abigail oozed confidence, unlike the restrained Frances Shaw.

Jane raised her glass to her lips. "And for Henry to have suggested Fanny was involved in crim con . . . He's such a hypocrite," she murmured behind the cut crystal.

Now *there* was a phrase Celia hadn't heard since she'd left her village in England. A place where gossip, lubricated by the singular boredom of country life and the heady consumption of black Bohea tea, flowed freely. Criminal conversation. The accusation that a man was having an affair with a married woman.

Celia turned her back to the Shaws. "Such gossip, Jane. It's not like you."

"This party is simply an elaborate ruse." Jane pulled her attention off Henry Shaw. "He'd like to cast himself as the doting, forgiving husband, when he's made Fanny's life a—"

"Mrs. Hutchinson. Mrs. Davies."

Henry Shaw's voice boomed from immediately behind Celia, making her jump. She spun to face him. "Mr. Shaw. A most enjoyable party."

"What are you two ladies whispering about in this corner?"

"A bit of silliness," said Celia, feeling her face warm as she cast about for a believable story. "I was commenting, with reprehensible envy, to Mrs. Hutchinson on the loveliness of your home and its location. Where I live along Telegraph Hill can be so dirty and noisy. It would be a pleasure to live out here, in the fresh air and quiet, south of the city."

Henry Shaw's sharp gaze examined her, taking in her drab black gown. Celia was still adjusting to the news that the husband who'd deserted her had died, and she was now a widow. The mourning she wore was nearly as uncomfortable as Mr. Shaw's scrutiny. "You run a women's clinic there, Fanny tells me."

"I do. It is most rewarding work."

"I suppose it would be." His gaze flicked to Jane, standing stock still, before returning to Celia. "Wasn't there some story about your participation in a murder investigation a while back? A dead Chinese girl? I heard you helped the police solve the crime."

"My role was insignificant, Mr. Shaw. You know how gossip embellishes the truth at times."

"Well, that's how gossip works, doesn't it? Ladies." He

inclined his head and strolled off to join his wife and her sister, Edith having vacated her seat at some point.

"Do you think he overheard us?" Jane whispered.

"I pray not," said Celia, observing how Abigail's eyes tracked Henry's every movement. Did her husband notice? For Frances certainly did, turning ashen.

Edith reappeared at the parlor doorway. "Fanny, your cook says dinner will be ready in an hour," she said, which explained where she'd been.

"Oh." Frances jumped up, one hasty motion of skittish energy. The hand holding her glass bumped against Lucinda, who reached out to stop the contents from spilling everywhere. Her efforts came too late, and punch splattered Henry's trousers.

"Henry, I'm so sorry," stammered Frances. "I'm just—"

"Clumsy," spat her husband, angrily brushing at the stain. "You've gotten so clumsy, Fanny."

"Because you make me that way. I'm going up to my bedroom to change." Some of the punch had sprayed across her maize muslin gown. She slid a glance at Abigail. "Maybe I should stay there."

"Fanny, don't be ridiculous," said Henry.

"Do you need my help?" offered Edith.

"I can manage. Lucy, entertain my guests, will you?" Frances asked her sister, and swept out of the parlor.

An embarrassed silence fell over the room.

Gad.

"I'm sorry, everyone," said Henry. "Fanny hasn't been herself lately."

"If she's unwell, I may be able to assist," said Celia.

"Fanny will be fine, Mrs. Davies," said Edith. "She just needs a few minutes alone. That's all."

"I could use some fresh air before dinner," said Lucinda. She gestured toward the dining room and the doors, visible beyond the linen-covered table, that opened out onto the garden. "I think I'll go for a walk, if anyone would like to join me."

"That sounds excellent," said Edith, looking ready to sprint from the house.

"A good idea, Lucy. Thanks for suggesting it." Henry Shaw seemed genuinely grateful to her. "I need to go upstairs myself to find a change of clothes. If you'll excuse me."

He strolled off.

"I'll stay behind while you all go for your walk." Abigail fanned her face with her long-fingered hand. "This excitement has exhausted me."

"Are you sure, Abigail?" asked her husband.

"Yes, I'm sure. I might sit on the front porch where there's a nice breeze. You go with the others."

He bent to kiss her cheek. Celia was surprised she didn't recoil.

Jane set down her punch glass. "I'll fetch our hats, Celia."

Hats retrieved, Celia and Jane set out with the others. Given the location of the Shaws' house—far from the city and out among rolling sandy hills where cattle browsed in the distance and seabirds swirled overhead—the grounds were expansive. Eucalyptus, apple, and almond trees dotted the lawn. Brightly colored dahlias nodded their heads alongside beds of pink and red roses.

"I was not dishonest to tell Henry Shaw that I envied his property," said Celia, sighing over the contrast between the beauty spread before her and the pitiful state of her own garden.

"What a sad group of people." Jane watched Lucinda and Edith as they strolled among the flower beds, Marcus Shaw off to one side. He looked to all the world as if he were intensely interested in an evergreen bush tucked against the far fence. Celia might have been fooled, if not for how frequently he stole glances at the house. "Two unhappy marriages."

"Who is Frances reportedly involved with?" Celia asked.

"One of the Shaws' business partners." A gust of wind blew down from the hills, and Jane gripped the brim of her hat to keep it from tearing off her head. "I saw them at a charity event once. I never would've suspected they were romantically involved, the stiff way they spoke to each other. But some people are good actors."

"At least the partner is not here to add to the tension."

"You feel it, too?" asked Jane. "It's not just Fanny upset about Abigail. It's everybody, including me. But maybe not you, Celia. You're always calm."

"What about that time a murder suspect shoved me over a wall at Cliff House and I nearly plunged to my death?"

"Even then you kept calm, Celia. No, you did! Don't shake your head at me. And the murders you've so coolly helped solve . . ." Jane shuddered. "I don't know how you do it."

"Some people *are* good actors, Jane." *And others are not,* thought Celia, as Marcus Shaw gave up the pretense of enjoying the garden's plantings and returned to the house.

"You could never fool me," Jane insisted, taking Celia's arm. "Not for a moment."

They walked in companionable silence for some time, until Lucinda and Edith grew tired of the scenery and of each other's company.

"Let's go back," Lucinda called out. Not waiting for anyone's response, she charged ahead of Edith, who scurried to keep up with her friend's sister.

"Now I wish the carriage was coming for us this evening instead of tomorrow morning," said Jane.

"It wouldn't be safe to drive back to town with darkness falling."

"I wonder if it'll be safe to stay *here*, what with everybody's sour moods. Who knows what's next? Blows? Pistols at twenty paces?"

Lucinda had reached the doors to the dining room where she was met by Henry. He spoke urgently to her, grabbing her hand.

"Something is amiss, Jane," said Celia, increasing her pace.

"What?" Jane rushed after her. "What?"

"I don't know."

Just then, Lucinda shrieked and ran into the house. Henry turned to follow. Edith, her mouth agape, stared after them.

"Miss Calvert, what is it?" asked Celia.

"Fanny!" she cried. "It's Fanny! She's dead!"

* * *

The uproar had drawn the occupants of the house to huddle outside the doorway to Frances's bedchamber. Abigail clung to her husband's arm. Edith stood nearby, sobbing loudly. Even Celia's Scottish housekeeper, who'd accompanied Celia and Jane to serve as a maid, had joined the crush. Lucinda and Henry were not among the others, but the sound of two voices from inside the room indicated where they'd be found.

Addie tutted when she caught sight of her mistress striding down the hallway. "Weel. Another death, ma'am. We're cursed, we are."

"Thank you, Addie," said Celia. She inclined her head toward the Shaws' cook and their domestic, the both of them with their aprons pressed to their mouths and their eyes wide. "Perhaps you can take the Shaws' staff elsewhere. Until I learn what has happened."

"She's dead, she is. *That's* what's happened, ma'am," Addie commented, but did as Celia requested, bustling off the servants.

"Oh, dear," said Jane, hesitating. "I don't want to see this."

"Stay out here with the others." Celia bent close to her ear. "And let me know what you think of their reactions."

Jane blinked. "Was Fanny murdered?"

"There are plenty here with reason, are there not?"

Edith had finished sobbing. "She told me Henry wanted to get rid of her. And now she's dead!"

"Shut up, Edith," said Abigail, recovered enough from the shock to have released her grip on Marcus's arm. "It was an accident. She was always taking this or that for her various ills. She must have made a mistake."

Edith sucked in a breath, her nostrils flaring. "You!" She stepped up to Abigail. "You encouraged him! Or maybe you killed Fanny yourself!"

"That's enough, Miss Calvert," said Marcus.

Abigail had the audacity to laugh. "Edith, you always are imagining things."

"Come on, Abigail," said Marcus, leading his wife away.

Edith and Jane withdrew as well, and Celia entered the bedchamber. It was outfitted in yellows and blues, lace and fringe, delicate furniture, and a window overlooking the hills. Frances's four-poster bed was canopied in netting, and her dressing table groaned beneath bottles and combs and hair ribbons. A deeply cushioned chair sat by the window, an empty water glass upon the three-legged mahogany table at its side. As for Frances herself, her prone form sprawled across the room's sapphire-and-ivory carpet. Lucinda had collapsed next to her sister, the skirts of her muslin gown pooling about her. She wiped Frances's soiled mouth with a handkerchief.

As best as she could in a crinoline and corset, Celia knelt next to the body to examine it. Frances was still warm. How rapidly death had overtaken her.

"Why, Fanny?" Henry stared down at his wife. He held a torn paper sleeve, the sort used by apothecaries, in his fingers. "Why?"

"She was so unhappy." Lucinda stared at her filthy handkerchief. She crushed it into a ball. "Poor creature."

"What do you have there, Mr. Shaw?" Celia asked.

"What? This?" He held out the paper sleeve. "I found it on the floor."

"May I?" Celia held out her hand, and he deposited the sleeve in her palm. The powder it had contained was gone, but a fine residue remained. A cautious sniff detected no odor. She licked the tip of one finger and swiped the interior.

"Mrs. Davies, what are you doing?" Henry asked, sounding mortified.

"Don't tell Jane." She placed her finger on her tongue. Bitter. "Has your wife been in the habit of taking Epsom salts of late, Mr. Shaw?"

"Epsom salts wouldn't have killed Fanny."

"But oxalic acid would. It is commonly mistaken for Epsom salts." Although the acidic taste should have alerted Frances to her fatal error. Unless she intended harm, or was too distraught to notice in time.

"She'd been taking a medication made with Epsom salts because she was suffering from digestive problems, Mrs. Davies," said Lucinda. She shot Henry an accusatory glance. "As if she wasn't miserable enough."

"What are you implying, Lucinda? Between you and Edith—"

"You know what I'm suggesting." Lucinda stood, the handkerchief still clutched in her hand. "You drove her to it. Inviting that woman."

"*That* woman is my brother's wife. Of course I'd invite her to Fanny's party."

Lucinda's eyes narrowed. "*Of course* you would," she mocked. "You only ever think of yourself, Henry. Never the consequences."

With a sob, she dashed from the room.

Henry helped Celia to her feet. "You should send for the coroner, Mr. Shaw," she said.

"Yes, I suppose I should." His gaze lingered on his wife's body. "I had nothing to do with this, Mrs. Davies. Fanny was a hysterical sort. It's not my fault."

"Are you certain?"

Henry scowled and stalked off.

Addie stood in the doorway, one eyebrow lifted. "Weel?"

"Oxalic acid poisoning, I believe. The Shaws' maid dresses in black. I expect there is a supply in the house to remove dye stains from her skin." Ever since Celia had taken up mourning, she'd occasionally resorted to using a concoction made with the acid to do likewise.

Addie peered at Frances. "What a way to kill yourself. Why not simply take a strong dose of the laudanum she has there on her table?"

Celia scanned the bottles and tins scattered across Frances's dressing table. "Why not, indeed?"

***

"I'm not much of a detective, Celia." Jane frowned over her cup of tea. They'd found a spot in the house's dining room, away from the others. The evening shadows stretched across the lawn beyond the windows, reaching toward the road where a buckboard wheeled past, spinning up dust. "I'm no use. I didn't notice anything out of the ordinary. Everybody was dazed. That's all. Even Abigail, who has to be happy her obstacle is out of the way."

"She remains wed to her husband, Jane. Not all obstacles have been removed."

"Edith is broken up. She asked the maid for sleeping powders and has gone to her room." Jane sipped her tea. "Edith and Fanny were as close as sisters. She's always felt protective of Fanny, who was frail as a child, and continued to be. She's got to feel awful that she didn't stop this . . . this . . ." Jane's brow furrowed. "What is it, exactly? An accident? Suicide? Murder?"

"Lucinda blames Henry for causing Frances to kill herself. Edith, on the other hand, has implied both Abigail and Henry committed murder. But why publicly accuse Frances of an affair and then poison her? Why not simply demand a divorce?" asked Celia.

From somewhere within the house came the sound of anxious voices and muffled crying. Outside, a bank of clouds had dimmed the sunlight, erasing the shadows on the grass.

"Luckily for Fanny, Henry didn't demand one because her lover moved to New York, abandoning her," said Jane. "Since she and Henry continued to live together as husband and wife, the law won't permit a divorce."

"See, Jane? You are of use."

"The bits of trivia you learn at parties can be worthwhile, I guess," she said.

Celia tapped a fingernail against the rim of her porcelain teacup. "Maybe one of them did poison Frances."

"Would Henry or Abigail plan to kill Fanny at her birthday party, with so many witnesses? They'd be the first ones everybody would suspect."

"Perhaps they thought the sheer audacity of it would provide the perfect alibi."

Jane set down her tea. "It's so ironic that Marcus introduced Fanny to Henry. Actually, he first introduced Lucinda to Henry, but that relationship never blossomed."

"More trivia learned at parties?"

"They've got to be good for something," she replied. "Fanny and Lucinda's father is a banker, by the way. The banker the Shaws use for their business."

"I do wonder how long that arrangement will last, now that Frances has died suspiciously." Celia considered her friend. "What about Lucinda?"

"Her own sister?" Jane asked. "What a gruesome idea."

"It does happen," said Celia. "Concerning Henry, Addie has spoken with the staff. Both of the women state that he usually collected Frances's medications from the apothecary and would then deliver them to her room."

"So he could've easily put the poison in that packet."

"The maid also said she saw one envelope on Mrs. Shaw's side table this morning. She is quite certain of that quantity," Celia added. "She noted the amount because it reminded her she needed to tell Mr. Shaw that it was time to purchase more of his wife's medicines."

"And I saw the packet, too, when I peeked inside the room . . ." Jane paused. "But I couldn't have. Because Fanny had taken the powders."

"Which implies someone did indeed bring an additional packet to her room," said Celia.

"Have we ruled out Fanny poisoning herself, though?"

"Not precisely," admitted Celia. "However, as Addie suggested to me, a strong dose of laudanum would've been a preferable method. Oxalic acid is very harsh."

"Then my money is on Abigail. She stayed behind while the rest of us walked in the garden."

"As did Henry," pointed out Celia. "And Marcus left us, as well."

"What could *his* motive possibly be?"

Celia gave a slight shrug. "That wasn't all that was of interest in Frances's bedchamber, though."

"It wasn't?"

A rustling at the doorway interrupted them. It was Edith. "Do you have a moment, Mrs. Davies? I've heard about your activities with the police, and I want to show you the note Fanny sent me. The one that begged me to come today."

Did the entirety of San Francisco know about Celia's 'activities with the police?' "I thought you were resting, Miss Calvert."

"I know I should wait until the police get here . . ." She pressed a hand to her waist. In the other she held a crumpled piece of cream-colored paper. "Fanny was scared."

"Of what?" asked Jane.

"Here. Here's the note she sent me." She held it out. "Fanny claimed that if I didn't come to the party to protect her, she was afraid of what would happen."

Celia studied the message. *He wants to get rid of me.* "Who is the 'he' she refers to?"

Edith looked confused. "Henry. Who else?"

"How awful," said Jane.

Upstairs, a commotion erupted, startling Edith. "What now?"

Voices shouted along the corridor, and footsteps pounded down the staircase. Marcus burst into the morning room. "Here you are, Mrs. Davies. We need your medical help. It's Abigail. Somebody's poisoned her, too."

***

"A not so convincing attempt on your own life, Mrs. Shaw," said Celia.

Seated on the room's lone chair, she folded her hands upon her lap and regarded Abigail with interest. The woman had recovered—a quick administration of carbonate of magnesia had resulted in a thorough purging of her stomach—and now rested upon the thick bolster propped against the bed's headboard. She seemed utterly without remorse.

Abigail returned Celia's stare. "I've heard about you, Mrs. Davies. You think you're very smart, don't you? Well, you're wrong this time. I didn't try to kill myself."

"I did not say you did. The amount of oxalic acid you consumed was insufficient to cause serious harm." Aside from the harm she'd endured by having a purgative poured down her throat with its attendant consequences, Celia thought.

"I'm not responsible for Frances's death, either. You should question Lucinda." The light from the table-side kerosene lamp accentuated every angle, every line in her skin. The shadows cast were not flattering. "She could've killed Frances. She was jealous of them. Always had been. How convenient she contrived to spill punch on Henry so he was in the house with Frances when she died."

"As were you, Mrs. Shaw."

She momentarily pinched her lower lip between her teeth. "I wanted to speak with Henry. To tell him we were finished."

"Did *you* concoct the rumor that Frances was having an affair, expecting Henry to divorce his wife?" asked Celia. Abigail's expression did not alter. "But that tactic failed. And now Frances is dead and you lie here, ill, pretending to be a second victim."

"I didn't concoct any rumor. She *was* having an affair."

"I don't know whether to trust you, Mrs. Shaw," said Celia, "but I will say that whoever killed Frances needn't have bothered. She was already dying."

"What?"

"Of syphilis. There is a tin of blue pills on her dressing table. Mercury, to treat the disease." It all made sense. The flowers Frances wore to conceal the thinning of her hair. The very high necklines, even on a warm day, to hide the residual blemishes from skin ulcerations. Her weak constitution.

Abigail sat up. "Henry's not at fault. He and Fanny . . . they hadn't been together in months. Years."

Celia exhaled a sigh. "Mrs. Shaw, it is time for the truth."

"I am telling the truth," she insisted. "As I said, Fanny had been having an affair. With one of Henry's associates. I saw them once, at the Willows, when Henry was away from San Francisco on business. She and Henry were so miserable together."

"Which you were not helping."

Tears trembled in her eyes. "I only carried on with Henry to make Marcus jealous."

Gad.

"I have another question. Who brought you the powders you took?"

"Frances's maid." From the bedside table, Abigail picked up a handkerchief to dab her eyes. "I spotted her outside of Edith's room and asked her for a soporific to help me sleep. She handed me the packet she'd brought up for Edith."

Celia tucked her brows together. "She'd brought it for Edith?"

Knuckles rapped upon the doorframe. "Sorry, ma'am," said Addie. "But you need to come quick. Miss Hayes means to shoot Miss Calvert out on the front lawn!"

Abigail gasped, and Celia hastened to her feet. Hiking her skirts, she thundered along the hallway and down the stairs. She halted outside the open front door. In the middle of the yard, Lucinda leveled a pistol at Edith.

"You killed her! You killed Fanny!" Lucinda screeched.

Henry pushed Celia aside and charged onto the lawn. "What are you doing with my army revolver, Lucy? For God's sake, put it down before you shoot someone."

"Mr. Shaw!" Celia shouted, chasing after him. "Don't! It's too dangerous!"

He stopped a few feet from the women. His coat was off, and the white of his shirt glowed like a beacon in the twilight. "Lucy, hand it over."

The revolver shook in her hand. "But she killed her, Henry. She poisoned Fanny. I saw her this morning. In the pantry, mixing up something. It took me so long to realize what she'd done, because I was positive Fanny had killed herself."

"You're saying Edith poisoned Fanny? Abigail, too?" he asked, slowly inching forward. "You're upset over Fanny's death and not thinking clearly."

"I'm thinking very clearly." Lucinda drew back the hammer. "Fanny never sent you a note, did she, Edith? The one I overheard you telling Mrs. Davies about. The one claiming Fanny was afraid of Henry. I found it in your room. It wasn't Fanny's handwriting."

"Don't forget, this is Edith we're talking about, Lucy," said Henry. "She'd rather put a spider out of the house than kill it. She's incapable of murder."

Rage darkened Edith's face. "I'm no coward, Henry, and I

cared about Fanny more than you ever did. Fanny was dying. Because of what you'd done to her, you wretch."

Edith launched herself at Henry just as Lucinda discharged the revolver. The shot went wide, missing them both. Addie, standing on the porch, screamed.

Lucinda raised her hand to fire again, and Celia leaped forward, knocking the gun from her hand. She grabbed the woman's arm. "That's quite enough, Miss Hayes."

"No." She struggled to break free. "Edith . . . she killed Fanny."

Celia was strong from lifting and moving patients and easily subdued her. "What do you say we leave Miss Calvert to the police?"

Lucinda glared at Edith, pinned to the ground by Henry. Marcus sprinted from the house to assist him. "Fanny's dearest friend. How could she?"

"There is no good answer. There never is." Celia slid her hand down to meet Lucinda's, cold and quivering. "Let us go back inside, Miss Hayes. We've nothing left to do out here."

***

"Once again, Mrs. Davies, I find you at the center of a murder." Detective Nicholas Greaves attempted to look stern, but Celia wasn't fooled by the expression. His spaniel-brown eyes always betrayed him.

"Think of all the time I have saved you, Mr. Greaves, by solving the crime already," she quipped, amused by the smile tugging the corner of his mouth.

"Guess I should thank you, then." Out on the darkening road, Edith was being helped into a carriage by his assistant, Officer Taylor. "Poison. A mighty rough way to kill somebody."

"But silent, compared to a gunshot, and quick, in this case."

"Why'd she do it?"

"She'd discovered Frances was dying from syphilis and reasoned this end was better than the lengthy agony Frances faced. Since she blamed Henry for infecting Frances—erroneously, if Abigail is to be believed—Edith tried to implicate him in his wife's death. Two birds, one stone." The evening breeze chilled Celia through the shawl wrapped around her shoulders, and she tugged it closer. "I should have suspected Edith earlier. This afternoon, she pretended to have been in the kitchen speaking with the cook, when actually she'd gone up to Frances's bedchamber with a medicine packet. One that contained oxalic acid, which she'd prepared this morning in the pantry."

The detective waved the carriage driver to depart. "I don't understand why Miss Calvert poisoned Abigail Shaw, though."

"She did not mean to," Celia explained. "The soporific was intended for Edith all along. She'd instructed the maid to bring the medicine from the pantry, where Edith had intentionally left it. She must have imagined that by poisoning herself—with a weaker mixture, since she did not plan to die—she would deflect suspicion. Unexpectedly, the maid gave the preparation to Abigail instead."

"You're too clever for me, Mrs. Davies," he said.

She tucked her hand into the crook of his elbow. "I shall remind you often that you said so, Mr. Greaves."

"I'm sure you will," he said, chuckling.

He escorted her into the house, where the flickering parlor lamplight beckoned, ready to envelope them in its warm and soothing glow.

STRONG ENOUGH

by Georgia Ruth

*Hannah Robinson is suffering following the
disappearance of her husband Doyle, but neighbor
Samson is quick to help her with the farm chores.
Maybe too quick. Does he know where Doyle is? She's
afraid he might.*

*McDowell County, North Carolina
Autumn of 1918*

From the porch, I could see my neighbor coming up the hill, big
boots takin' big strides. I thought about warming up the coffee. It
seemed the natural thing to do. But I couldn't make myself move
from the rocker. I was give out.

Samson crossed the clearing to the molasses vat, where he'd
worked only a week ago when he come at daylight to help my
husband with our sorghum cane crop. Doyle had already harnessed
the mule to rotate the crusher. I had started the fire. Can't do
nothin' without a really hot fire.

Last year my job was to skim the bubbles off the top. This year
I wasn't up to it.

I caught sight of the mule and couldn't remember when I last
fed the animals. I needed to check on their water. But still I set.

Samson swiped the bottom of the metal with a finger he put to
his mouth and then rubbed on his overalls. Doyle had said it was
the best molasses crop in a while 'cause it'd been a dry year. First
run was fifteen gallons and the second one thirteen. Yeah, he was
real proud of all his doin's: the new linoleum floors in his
granddaddy's house, the solid white oak barn filled with hay from
the fields he plowed, the tobacco crop he sold the first of the month
for spending money, and on and on.

I watched Samson walk along the chute that had taken the
green juice down the hill through a coupla strainers to the holding
tank. Eight gallons of juice to make one gallon of molasses. I don't
deny it was hard work. The fire was out now, but the heat had been
fierce, like the flames of hell.

Samson headed my way. "Halloo the house!" He crossed in front of the ailing rose bush that Doyle's first wife planted a year before she died. Samson come to the bottom of the steps and stood with fists on hips, looking at me silently rocking.

"Mornin', Mrs. Robinson. Ya heard from Doyle yet?"

"Not a word since Thursday." And that was the truth.

"Can I help with the firewood? You're gonna need some soon. Woolly worms are mostly black this year."

"That would be neighborly of you. I'm not up to swingin' that axe yet." That was a lie.

He walked behind the house to the stack of logs Doyle had aimed to split. Soon I heard the familiar whack of blade hitting wood. My stomach flipped over. Best to get up and make biscuits. Still I set. I noticed a few drops of blood I missed when I scrubbed the porch and burned the swing. Flashes of memory attacked me. As soon as one image appeared, I closed it off, but another would come back just as fast. Like I was warring with a spirit.

I heard the kitchen door open in back, and the heavy footfalls and an armload of kindling filling the box beside the hearth. I'd heard that clunk nigh on to twenty years, especially when that was my chore at the orphanage. Knew it like the sound of songbirds, like the rustle of leaves on a rainy night. All normal sounds of time moving on, time that can't be stopped by no man.

The kitchen screen door squeaked again and popped back. Granny Parker would expect me to show my gratitude. I moved my left leg and pain raged upwards. A fierce burning inside my core. A reminder of my sins, Daddy would say. But he had no use for a half-breed so he didn't keep me long after Mama died. That was alright with me. After that beating he gave me, it seemed better to live with my granny than stay with him. Seemed like life was always about choices. But how could you choose if you didn't know what was out there? Or how much strength you might need and how much you had?

I heard water sloshing into the horse trough. Samson come back around to the porch.

"I threw a little corn out to the chickens, and fed and watered ol' Blue. Didn't see your milk cow." He put one foot on the bottom step and leaned against the rail.

"Doyle slaughtered it when the baby died. Said it was too much trouble."

"Where's the dog?"

"Gone with Doyle."

Samson stood quiet for a bit. "Hannah, can I get you some help? One of the church ladies will come to see about your needs."

"Thank ya kindly. I think I just have a tetch of that flu my little one had."

"Could be. It's been a bad year for it. Paper said thousands are dead."

I nodded.

"Could be that's why Doyle ain't come home."

"Could be."

"Well now, I have to be getting' to my own chores. I'll look in tomorrow, if that's awright."

"Suit yourself. I'll be here."

And he did suit himself. He come over to help every day for two weeks. Rain or shine. The fourth day, I made him some biscuits. Seemed proper. Even opened a jar of peach preserves I put up last summer, more like a lifetime ago.

He wasn't the only visitor. Other farmers nosed around for awhile. And the law. They asked if I'd heard from Doyle, but I hadn't. Weather-worn faces showed pity on me. The preacher come by to set a spell and talk my ear off. Leastways, he brought me a jar of honey.

And Miz Bradley brought her world-famous chicken soup. I was recovering my appetite. She invited me to stay over with her and Teddy. "Just till you get your strength. You look mighty peaked. It's hard, sure enough. My sister lost two of her young-uns to that flu bug. No doubt poor Doyle just couldn't handle losin' his only child. He'll come back. Some men have to hide their sorrow."

I didn't think I could listen to hours of her chatter, so I politely declined her invitation. What made me feel better was to set in hot water in the new claw tub out in the bathhouse Doyle bragged on. I even washed my hair. After awhile I was healing outside. Inside was a different story.

Samson took to settin' with me on the porch every afternoon. It felt right. Soon it would be cold, and I'd be stuck in the house.

"Church homecoming dinner is next week," said Samson. "Have ya heard?"

"I thought it was last week."

"That was a barn dance at the McFadden's for the boys goin' to war."

"Reckon I missed a few things."

Samson chuckled. "Reckon I did, too."

Long silences between us mostly seemed natural, but I knew it wouldn't last.

"Doyle ain't coming back, Hannah."

"No, I reckon he ain't."

"I saw you upta the cemetery the other night." He was rolling a cigarette as he spoke.

I didn't answer or quit rocking.

"I wondered who was buried there."

I didn't answer.

"A fresh grave. No marker. Was it your baby?"

My eyes filled with tears. The awful recollection come back full force.

"Did she die of the flu, Hannah?"

I could hardly breathe. I felt slick with my own sweat.

Samson took the jar of tea from my fingers and placed it on a stool by the door.

"Y'know, I remember when I was here helpin' Doyle with the molasses. He seemed differnt, mad at every little thing. What happened that Wednesday night, Hannah?" He put his big hand on mine. It was warm and powerful.

I jerked away.

"I unnerstand, really I do." He reached forward to touch the faded purple and yellow bruise on my face. "Where is he, Hannah?"

"Just cause you've been nice to me, Samson Crawford, don't mean you can take over." I stood up and escaped to the front room. He followed.

"I think we need to talk," he said.

I crossed to the kitchen sink in the corner and pumped water into a glass. Refreshing cool well water that didn't for one second make me feel better. He come up behind me and placed his rough hands on my shoulders. Beneath their weight, I trembled.

"Tell me."

I looked out the window at the trees wearing their autumn dress. Winter was a-comin'. What would I do by myself? I was almost healed now, and I could walk better. Could I get through the winter and plant a garden and a tobacco crop on my own? Was I that strong?

And here come Doyle's best friend pretending to like me. What would he think if he knew my husband would rather be dead than live with a crazy girl. That was the kinda talk I'd heard at school.

"The baby had a fever." I breathed it aloud. "And Doyle got angry."

"At the little one?"

"No," I said. I had to say it straight out 'cause I knew where this was going. "I had a hard delivery, and I wasn't healin' as fast as he wanted. But he was swelled up with attitude, mad at me for holding his daughter 'stead of him. He thought I should be more . . . more accommodatin'. For him." I didn't tell how Doyle took the baby from me and put her on the porch swing, her tiny arms beatin' the air, mewing like a kitten, hot to the touch.

Samson stepped up closer behind me, ran his hands down my back and placed them on my hips. His smoky breath was heavy on my neck. I twisted away to face him. But I still could hear my baby crying. I still could see her, in my every waking moment and often in my dreams.

"I think you need to leave, Samson Crawford." I folded my arms across my breasts.

"I'll be back. You're a beautiful woman, Hannah." He gently pushed a black strand of hair from my forehead. "But I know what ya did."

He pressed me up against the sink. I was trapped. His arms closed around me and drew me up tight. I watched his pale eyes as he slowly leaned over, lips parted to kiss my cheek, my neck. The smell of hay and animals and man enveloped me. I felt as though I was drowning.

"Don't worry. I'll take care of you," he crooned, dark whiskers tickling my ear.

He turned me loose and was gone out the door.

***

I went to church yesterday. I smiled at every woman, bowed my bonnet to every man. They pelted me with fancy sayin's about how I'd overcome and this too would pass. I hoped so. Somebody proclaimed, "God heps him who heps hisself." Maybe. Maybe not.

My feelings were empty, like last year's oil jar. Granny Parker would say I needed to reach out to Jesus to get filled up again. But it didn't happen. Granny taught me to love the Lord, and I prayed that all things would work together for good. But I don't think He loved me back. Not after what I did. I couldn't make no sense of it, only that some live long and some don't. She was a saint, but she got sick and died. I miss her so.

Preacher fussed at us all morning and the wood bench was hurtin' my bottom. He talked about our neighbors sacrificed to a faraway war. "Brother George Russell went down last month, may God have mercy on his soul." Sounds of sobbing rose out of a pew in the middle, and from my perch near the back, I could see Brother Zebulon's shoulders shaking. He had returned from France without his leg. His wife was on the ladies' side of the congregation, plumb wore out but settin' straight and making her two little ones behave. How could any woman be so strong? A man behind Zebulon put a large hand on his shoulder. I recognized those hairy knuckles. They belonged to Samson. From here, that hand looked comforting. Maybe I had him all wrong. Maybe I had no right to judge him.

I couldn't stop a sudden flashback. In my head, I could hear the baby wailing while Doyle had me in bed. Her cries were my cries. I couldn't get to her without making Doyle crazy mad. I thought to get his business over fast and get back to her. My baby screamed for me one last time as the dog's teeth dug into her throat. Then she was silent. My husband was layin' back, proud of hisself when that evil hound of hell trotted into the bedroom with a bloody muzzle. I couldn't move for the pain. Doyle shouted and ran to the porch swing. "No! No!" But it was too late. All I could do was cry until I had no feeling left. He said he buried the poor thing up in the cemetery. I checked later to make sure.

My insides ached with the memory. I had to think on something else. I bunched up my skirt with both hands and held on tight 'til the black swirling in my head passed.

The singing did lift me up some, but then the preacher told us we was goin' to hell if we didn't fall on our knees and confess our sins. Somebody in the congregation cried out for mercy. The end times could come any minute like the flood, he said. We had to prepare. Somebody else jumped to their feet and praised God for a healing. Then there were shouts, and folks headed down front to the altar for prayer. Seemed everyone had their own version of hell to run from. No doubt about it, I thought, taking stock of my neighbors, I'd have some company in that fiery pit. I scooted out the door.

It was a sunny day, and I enjoyed a slow walk on the red clay roadbed. When I heard a wagon coming behind me, I slipped into the woods. It was cooler in the shadows. Last week's snow still clung to faded ferns, and I was alone. And likely to stay that way. Granny Parker would say, "Me and my God." But no, I was alone.

Coming on to the ruts that led to my house, I stopped. Beyond the barren trees, the little cabin looked deserted. My last five chickens were milling around. The mule stood at the barbwire fence, ears pointed toward me.

"I know I fed you, silly ol' thing."

I figured he was glad Doyle wasn't around to crack a whip on his behind. Our only horse, my horse now, was stretched out on the ground soaking up the sunshine. As I walked the road, he raised his head and kinda sat up, like I was the queen passin' by. I giggled. I noted it was my first inside smile in a long time.

"Hello, Mr. Blue." I spoke to the big roan that put out his long front legs and shoved with strong back legs to stand up and shake the dust from his winter coat. He ambled toward me, seemed like his ears pricked for words of wisdom. I reached out to his soft nose, his warm snort. "I'll do better, old boy. We're gonna make it." Tears filled my eyes, but I didn't let them fall. I turned toward the house, one foot in front of the other, head down, my thoughts on eggs and my low supply of chicken feed. I didn't see him 'til he stood up from the rocker. My breath stuck in my throat.

"Didn't mean to scare ya," said Samson.

"How did you get here so fast?"

"Guess my legs are longer and stronger." He grinned. "And I come through the Bradley's pasture."

"You're lucky you didn't get shot. They must be at church."

I went inside the cabin, trying to gather my thoughts. I placed my bonnet on Granny's breakfront. I'd put it in the bedroom chifforobe later, when he was gone. I knew without looking that the shotgun was in its corner by the door.

"You want some eggs?" I took my apron off the handle of the icebox to cover my Sunday best. "Got some cornbread, too."

"Yeah, sounds good. Then I gotta get on home."

I busied myself making a fire in the woodstove to heat up my skillet.

"There's gonna be a hog killin' this week. I'll bring you some bacon," he said.

"I sure could use it. And I gotta taste for liver mush."

He watched from a chair while I laid out forks and plates. "I'll see what I can do."

We ate our supper without much conversation, and he left like he said. The next day he come again. Then his visits got longer. We never talked about the past until one day he asked why I never used molasses.

"Too sweet for me."

He studied my face. "Maybe it's time to move on. What about I take the jars to Marion and sell them for ya?"

I held his steady gaze. I nodded.

"You can come with me if ya want."

I didn't have a mind to go to town. Last time was two years before, on my wedding night. Doyle was a widower needing a healthy girl my age, I needed a home, and the Elhanan Bible Institute and Orphanage needed a donation. Seemed like the choice was clear. Heavy rains hit that night. Didn't bother my new husband none that we stayed in bed the whole time, but I wearied of it. I slept only when Doyle went downstairs to try a hand of poker and drink with his friend Charlie. We took our meals at the hotel restaurant and heard tell of the flood and all those folks gettin' drowned or crushed further up the mountain. Railroad tracks washed away and trains stalled in Marion. Hundreds of travelers stranded.

When the rain slowed to a drizzle after a couple days, Doyle hitched our wagon and carried me along ribbons of red mud to my new home. He said he was taking care of me, but he was truly frettin' about his place. I reckon he was thinking how Charlie lost everything and had to find a town job. We had our own trouble crossing creeks that had turned into tumbling rivers. It took a full day of struggle to finally reach his homeplace. The cabin stood. But the crops were flattened by the storm and he nearly had to start over. Looking back, it seemed like a bad omen for our marriage. Doomed to struggle and fail. Kinda like Charlie. He got drafted and killed.

No, married life didn't appeal to me thus far. That was one choice, and it appeared a narrow path to travel. The other choice was living by myself, but I didn't think I could do all the chores. No way I could hire help.

I looked forward to getting old and just settin' on the porch.

In late November, Samson sold several cases of molasses, enough to cover winter supplies. As I counted the money he brought me, and pushed a little toward him for his trouble, he watched me.

"Wonder what Doyle took besides his dog?"

"Didn't take nothin'. Musta not planned to be gone. Musta had an accident, and he couldn't get back to the house." That was my story. It sounded smooth since I'd practiced it for so long.

"I don't believe he left Cove Creek. This is where his kinfolk are buried. Strange that no body was found."

"Packs of coyotes in the area coulda found him first. Didn't you tell me you lost a couple of calves last spring?"

"Maybe." He nodded his head. "Guess you're right." He stared hard at me. "Did he take his gun?"

"Probably. Never you mind. I have one of my own." I still had the tobacco money, too, but I didn't tell Samson.

One night he stayed later than usual. The sun set at five thirty, and it was comin' dark when he laid aside the paper he read.

"Woman, it's time to decide."

I put down his shirt I was mending. My hands quivered. The comfortable silence between us shattered. Like I always knew it would. I didn't deserve peace. God gave me a baby after all my begging, and I didn't take care of her. I'd regret that to my dying day.

"To my mind, we need to get married." He said it out plain.

My stomach pitched. "It's too soon for all that."

"What's there to wait on? Folks already know I'm comin' over every day, doin' your outside work. No doubt gossipin' about the rest."

"Just seems that we should respect the dead."

"And how do you know he's dead, Hannah?" he whispered, his glittering eyes fixed on mine.

"'Cause he didn't come back."

I rose from my chair to take our coffee cups to the sink. Samson's footsteps followed me. I wasn't getting trapped again in the corner of the kitchen. I moved toward the door, snatched my shawl from the peg and stepped out into brisk night air.

"Ya planning to run?" He stood at the door, the lamplight spilling out on the porch.

I was quiet. He come up beside me. "Look at me." When I didn't, he put his thick fingers on my cheek and turned my face toward him. "Make no mistake, I know what happened. I know how hot that fire was. I was watchin'."

I stayed silent, afraid I'd say something he could use against me.

"Did he hurt the baby? That's all I can think, Hannah. Is that why ya killed him?"

Tears pricked my eyelids. I wanted to scream out that Doyle was dead when I found him. He had killed hisself. But my story was that he'd taken off. He'd left me. Because he did. When he died, I was left alone to care for myself. All alone in the world.

"I unnerstand. He had a quick temper. You deserve better than Doyle. He just wanted a brood mare."

That was true. He wanted a son, a passel of them to help on the farm. But it took me forever to have just one baby, a sickly little girl. How he hated her crying all the time. I got used to it, but it twisted Doyle's nerves. Even made his dog jittery. Seemed like it brought out the wild in both of them.

The law would think just like Samson, that I killed Doyle because he hurt the baby. They would never believe I didn't shoot him. The legend of Frankie Silver was too strong in this county. I had to hide the body so I wasn't put in jail like her.

There was nothing I could do for Doyle. He was already dead. His face was gone. I couldn't lift him, I couldn't drag him to the cemetery. I couldn't bury him in our hard clay or in the woods amongst the tree roots. I for sure couldn't tell nobody. Besides that, I couldn't even get near him. His killer dog stood over him, snarling at me like I was the enemy. It was then I went stark ravin' mad. Bitter memories of all the times I was mistreated rushed over me. Why me? I craved the power to hurt and punish. I snatched up the gun and shot that dog dead.

Didn't do myself no good 'cause then I had another bloody mess on my hands. And I was bleeding too. My insides were burning strong. The fire under the molasses vat come to mind, a hot fire just like the one ole Frankie Silver made a hundred years ago.

When I found Doyle's body with his head shot off and the gun at his side, I thought it was my fault 'cause of the baby. He always said I couldn't do nuthin' right. "Dumb Injun." Cruel words started by the kids at the orphanage. This time I didn't make no mistake. I put Doyle and his dog in that fire piece by piece.

I stared down Samson, this man who thought he knew so much. But he never heard the sizzle of flesh like I had. "I did what I had to do."

He took a short charred stick from his pocket.

"I found this in the ashes. Looks like a bone to me. What do ya think the law will say? You know what they did to Frankie Silver." He lowered his voice. "Hanged her."

I nodded slightly and bit my lip to keep from crying out. He'd trapped me again. He come sliding over here, pretending to be friendly, but he was sneakin' around gathering evidence. Not for his friend Doyle. For his own gain, to ease me into his bed. To get my farm. I could see it now. How foolish I was to think that this man was differnt, that he was nicer than Doyle. Surely all the honorable men on earth had perished from war and disease.

"C'mon in the house, Hannah. It's cold out here."

What could I do? Everyone would believe his tale. And it was winter. Where could I go? It was time to stand up for myself.

"You're wrong, Samson. You can't prove I killed Doyle. The ashes are gone, scattered in the woods."

"I know. I saw you. I watched while you tore down the molasses chute. While you hitched up the mule to move the crusher and the vat to the barn."

"You spied on me?"

He pulled me close to his growing need.

"You're a beautiful woman, Hannah. I like to watch you."

My heart hammered now.

He traced my jawbone with his thumb. "I won't tell, y'know. I'd protect my wife."

"I ain't your wife."

"Think on it, sweet, sweet Hannah." His heavy palm covered my breast while his other one held me in place. "I'll promise to honor you when you promise to obey."

I knew then. Doyle hadn't killed hisself. Truth was as clear as a streak of lightning in a black sky.

"You wasn't watchin' me or you'd know I shot the dog, not Doyle. You killed him, didn't ya!"

"Like you said. I did what I had to do." Samson's eyes blinked fast. "He was a mean cuss, Hannah, and he was talkin' about how you killed your baby, like you was crazy."

"I didn't kill her." A sob escaped from my throat. "I loved my baby."

"Then he told me how he was gonna take you again that very night. Said you owed him a young 'un. Called it a contract." He put his big hands on my arms and rattled me. "I swear to you, Hannah, I thought he was goin' to hurt ya, and I couldn't let it happen. Girl, I love you, always have. Even while he was here. That's why I kept comin' around, just to get a glimpse of you."

I didn't believe his flattery. The look in his eye was probably liken to that of the savage that took my mama, when my life started in evil. I killed her when I was born. Granny Parker said Mama had already wished herself dead but some things aren't for us to choose. We get what we get. Like my baby girl did.

I was chilled clean down to my bones. I wished my granny was here to tell me what to do.

Samson's forehead furrowed, his gaze at me hardened. His breathing was heavy as he pulled me into the cabin with one strong hand. The other hand shut the door. I glanced at my gun, but it seemed like the choice was clear 'cause I needed a good provider.

For now, I'd stick to my story that I didn't know where Doyle went. Granny Parker would say that was true. But if this new contract didn't work out, well, I'd already cleaned up a bigger mess than Samson Crawford could make.

I was strong enough to handle whatever come my way.

AUTHOR
BIOGRAPHIES

AUTHORS

JOHN GREGORY BETANCOURT is the publisher of Wildside Press, as well as a best-selling author. He lives in Maryland with his wife, Kim, and an assortment of cats, dogs, and children.

Born and raised in Philadelphia, **SUSANNA CALKINS** lives in Highland Park, Illinois, with her husband and two sons, and works at Northwestern University. Holding a Ph.D. in history, Susanna writes a historical mystery series featuring Lucy Campion, a 17th-century chambermaid-turned-printer's apprentice, for St. Martin's/Minotaur Books. Her books have been nominated for the Bruce Alexander Historical Mystery Award, the Mary Higgins Clark Award, and the Agatha for best historical mystery. Her third novel, *The Masque of a Murderer,* was also awarded the Sue Feder Historical Mystery (Macavity) Award. Her fourth in the series, *A Death Along the River Fleet*, was released in 2016. "The Trial of Madame Pelletier" was inspired by a real poisoning trial that she researched when taking a graduate class in modern French history.

CARLA COUPE fell into writing short stories almost without noticing. Two of her short stories—"Rear View Murder" in *Chesapeake Crimes II* and "Dangerous Crossing" in *Chesapeake Crimes 3*—were nominated for Agatha Awards. She has written a number of Sherlock Holmes pastiches, which have appeared in *Sherlock Holmes Mystery Magazine, Sherlock's Home: The Empty House, Irene's Cabinet,* and other anthologies. Her story "The Book of Tobit" was included in *The Best American Mystery Stories of 2012.*

In her youth, **SUSAN DALY** wanted to be Trixie Belden, the thinking girl's Nancy Drew. When she got a taste for blood with her first crime short story in 2014, she found ridding the world of deserving victims so enjoyable she has developed a morbid and permanent partiality for it. Her stories have appeared in anthologies from the Canadian Sisters in Crime, *The Whole She-Bang 2 & 3* and the Guppies' *Fish Out of Water.* Susan is a member of Sisters in Crime (both the Toronto chapter and the Mother Ship) and the Guppies. She lives in Toronto, Ontario, a short commute from her superlative grandkids. She can be found at www.susandaly.com.

MICHAEL PAUL DELL is a mystery writer, hockey blogger, and independent researcher who is obsessed with hidden truths. The son of a police detective, Michael grew up in Western Pennsylvania wanting to fight crime, but thin bones and a general dislike for the sight of his own blood made it far safer to stay home and memorize *Columbo* episodes. In 2014, he earned an MFA in Writing Popular Fiction from Seton Hill University. When not chronicling the adventures of Honest John Churchfield, he enjoys recording fake radio shows, reading old comic books, and watching ridiculous amounts of professional wrestling. He currently works as a freelance fiction editor (EditOneNine.com) and hopes to one day find a box of money.

P. A. De VOE is an anthropologist and Asian specialist who writes historical mysteries and crime stories immersed in the life and times of Ancient China. She's published short stories, *From Judge Lu's Ming Dynasty Case Files*, in anthologies and online. *Warned*, second in her Chinese YA trilogy (*Hidden, Warned*, and *Trapped*) received a 2016 Silver Falchion award in the Best International category. *Trapped* has been nominated for a 2017 Agatha Award. For more information and to get a *free* short story go to padevoe.com.

CAROLE NELSON DOUGLAS's hard-boiled feline sleuth, Midnight Louie, finished his 28-book alphabetic mystery trek through Las Vegas (1992-2016), but in 1990, Carole reinvented Irene Adler as the diva-detective of her own adventures, becoming the first woman writer to create a Sherlockian spin-off series and the first author to make a woman from the stories a protagonist. *Good Night, Mr. Holmes* was a *New York Times* Notable Book of the Year. An Agatha nominee, Carole was an award-winning newspaper reporter on women's issues. She likes strong female protagonists like noir urban fantasy action heroine Delilah Street, swashbuckling 17th-century Miranda Hathaway, and Jane Doe (the inspiration for the one in *Blindspot*). As for Irene and Louie, they will be back! And Jane Doe, too!

MARTIN EDWARDS' eighteen novels include the Lake District Mysteries and the Harry Devlin series. *The Coffin Trail* was shortlisted for the Theakston's Prize for Crime Novel of the Year, while *All the Lonely People* was nominated for the John Creasey Memorial Dagger for best first crime novel. His genre study *The Golden Age of Murder* has won the Edgar®, Agatha, H.R.F. Keating and Macavity awards. He has edited thirty crime anthologies, has won the CWA Short Story Dagger, the CWA Margery Allingham Prize, and the Red Herring award, and is series consultant for the British Library's very successful series of Crime Classics. In 2015, he was elected eighth President of the Detection Club, and he is currently also Chair of the Crime Writers' Association.

KATHY LYNN EMERSON (*aka* Kaitlyn Dunnett) is the author of fifty-six (so far) traditionally published books written under several names. She won the Agatha for *How to Write Killer Historical Mysteries*. Currently she writes the Liss MacCrimmon Mysteries (*Kilt at the Highland Games*) as Kaitlyn and the Mistress Jaffrey Mysteries (*Murder in a Cornish Alehouse*) as Kathy. As for short stories, check out the collections, *Murders and Other Confusions* and *Different Times, Different Crimes*. She lives in Maine.

CHARLAINE HARRIS is a true daughter of the South. She was born in Mississippi and has lived in Tennessee, South Carolina, Arkansas, and Texas. After years of dabbling with poetry and plays and essays, her career as a novelist began when her husband told her to stay home and write. Her first book, *Sweet and Deadly*, appeared in 1981. When Charlaine's career as a mystery writer began to falter, she decided to write a cross-genre book that would appeal to fans of mystery, science fiction, romance, and suspense. She could not have anticipated the huge surge of reader interest in the adventures of a barmaid in Louisiana, or the fact that Alan Ball would come knocking at her door. Charlaine is a voracious reader. She has one husband, three children, two grandchilden, and two rescue dogs. She leads a busy life.

PETER W. J. HAYES is a former marketing executive, ad copywriter, journalist, bartender, truck driver, eel hatchery worker, security guard, and Christmas tree salesman. His mysteries and crime writing have appeared in *Shotgun Honey, Yellow Mama, Out of the Gutter,* and *The Literary Hatchet* (Issue 14). Peter's work has also won the Pennwriters' short story and novel beginnings contests and been shortlisted for the Crime Writers' Association (CWA) Debut Dagger award. He is a member of Pennwriters and the Pittsburgh Chapter of Sisters in Crime.

NANCY HERRIMAN retired from an engineering career to take up the pen. She hasn't looked back. Her work has won the RWA Daphne du Maurier award, and *Library Journal* has said that her 'A Mystery of Old San Francisco' series is "just the ticket for anyone who misses Dianne Day's 'Fremont Jones' series as well as readers of Rhys Bowen's 'Molly Murphy' historicals." Her latest release is *No Pity for the Dead*. When not writing, she enjoys singing, gabbing about writing, and eating dark chocolate. She currently lives in Central Ohio. Find more at: www.nancyherriman.com

KB INGLEE writes historic mysteries set from the early colonial period through the 19th century. She works as an interpreter at Newlin Grist Mill, a 1704 water-powered mill in Pennsylvania. Her collection of Emily stories, *The Case Book of Emily Lawrence*, is available from Wildside Press or on Amazon. kbinglee.weebly.com

Obsessed with books, dogs, and creepy old houses, **SU KOPIL** writes short fiction about peculiar people. Her stories have appeared in *Woman's World* magazine and anthologies including *Murder Most Conventional, Flash and Bang, Destination Mystery*, and *Fish or Cut Bait*. She is the owner and founder of EarthlyCharms.com, a graphic design company that has been working with authors since 2000. Visit sukopil.com or follow @INKspillers.

VIVIAN LAWRY, a founding member and two-term president of Sisters in Crime–Central Virginia, has won the Sandra Brown prize for short fiction and was a 2015 finalist in the *James River Writers/Richmond Magazine* best unpublished novel contest. Her work appears in more than fifty literary journals and anthologies, from *The Alembic* to *Xavier Review*, including both volumes of *Virginia Is For Mysteries*. She coauthored two Chesapeake Bay Mysteries, *Dark Harbor* and *Tiger Heart*. Her most recent book is *Different Drummer*, a collection of offbeat fiction. She also writes historical fiction, magical realism, and memoir. This is her first story in a Malice Domestic anthology. Learn more at www.vivianlawry.com and visit her on Facebook or Twitter.

National best-selling author **EDITH MAXWELL** is the author of the Agatha-nominated 2016 Best Historical Mystery, *Delivering the Truth,* as well as the Agatha-nominated 2016 Best Short Story, "The Mayor and the Midwife," which features the same protagonist and 1888 setting. She writes the Quaker Midwife Mysteries and the Local Foods Mysteries; blogs at WickedCozyAuthors.com, at Killer Characters, and with the Midnight Ink authors. Find her on Facebook, twitter, Pinterest, Instagram, and at www.edithmaxwell.com.

CATRIONA McPHERSON was born in Scotland and lived there until immigrating to California in 2010. She is a former academic linguist, now a full-time writer. Her bestselling 1930s detective novels, most lately *The Reek of Red Herrings*, have won Agatha, Lefty, and Macavity awards and been shortlisted for a U.K. Dagger. The series is currently in development for television, at STV in Scotland. Writing short stories about the members of detective Dandy Gilver's household is Catriona's newest passion. She also writes modern standalone suspense novels. These have won two Anthony awards and been on the Edgar® and Mary Higgins Clark shortlists. *The Child Garden* was an Agatha finalist. Catriona is a past president of Sisters in Crime and a proud member of the Malice tribe.

LIZ MILLIRON has been making up stories, and creating her own endings for other people's stories, for as long as she can remember. She's worked for fifteen years in the corporate world, but finds making things up is far more satisfying than writing software manuals. A lifelong mystery fan, her short fiction has been published in online magazines *Uppagus* and *Mysterical-e*. She has also had stories included in *Lucky Charms: 12 Crime Tales*, *Blood on the Bayou* (the 2016 Bouchercon anthology), and *Fish Out of Water*. She is a past president of the Pittsburgh chapter of Sisters in Crime. Visit her at lizmilliron.com, find her on Facebook at facebook.com/LizMilliron, or follow her on Twitter (@LizMilliron).

KATHRYN O'SULLIVAN is delighted to have her short story, *He Done Her Wrong*, published in *Malice Domestic 12: Mystery Most Historical*. Set in 1930s Hollywood, the story features sassy stage and screen icon Mae West and is a sneak peek at Kathryn's new book. She also writes the Colleen McCabe series (*Foal Play*, *Murder on the Hoof*, *Neighing with Fire*) and is a Malice Domestic Best First Traditional Mystery Novel winner, Pacific Book Awards Finalist, published playwright, Telly Award-winning Web series creator/writer/costumer (*Thurston*), and professor at Northern Virginia Community College. www.kathrynosullivan.com Twitter: KthrynOSullivan

K.B. OWEN writes the Concordia Wells Mysteries, set at a fictitious 1890s New England women's college and featuring a young lady professor turned amateur sleuth. The first book of the series, *Dangerous and Unseemly*, was the winner of *Library*

Journal's "Best Mystery of 2015: SELF-e." The fifth and most recent novel, *Beloved and Unseemly*, was released November 2016. K.B. also writes the "Chronicles of a Lady Detective" series, set in the late nineteenth century and featuring the adventures of a female Pinkerton operative. Both series are published through Misterio Press. K.B. Owen is a former college instructor with a Ph.D. in 19th century literature, a background she now uses to create all sorts of unseemly predicaments for her characters. KBOwenMysteries.com/books.

VALERIE O. PATTERSON's first novel for young readers, *The Other Side of Blue* (2009), published by Clarion, an imprint of Houghton Mifflin Harcourt, was nominated for an Agatha Award. Her second, *Operation Oleander* (Clarion 2013), was selected as a Junior Library Guild selection. Her short stories have appeared in *Defying Gravity: Fiction by D.C. Area Women* (2014) and *Chesapeake Crimes II* (2006). She has had articles published in *The Writer*, the *Washington Independent Book Review*, and the *North Carolina Literary Review*. She is a member of Mystery Writers of America and Sisters in Crime, as well as the Society of Children's Book Writers and Illustrators. Valerie has an MFA from Hollins University and currently lives in Virginia where she writes and practices law.

KEENAN POWELL'S first publications were illustrations in *Dungeons and Dragons*, 1st edition, when still in high school. Art was an impractical pursuit (not an heiress, didn't have disposition to marry well, hated teaching), so she went to law school instead. The day after graduation, she moved to Alaska. Early in her career, she defended criminal cases, including murder, for several years. She still practices law in Anchorage, Alaska. During the summer of 2009, there was a string of homeless deaths which the Medical Examiner had ruled were the result of "natural causes". While attending a seminar, she learned of a little-known law that permits the ME to rule natural causes without autopsy. These deaths and this loophole were the inspiration of her first book.

Like most people, **MINDY QUIGLEY** was born. Despite being so blonde she lacked visible eyebrows, she passed an average childhood in the suburbs of Chicago. Her thirst for knowledge and sweet tea led her south to the University of North Carolina, where she met her British husband, Paul. An adventurous few years in Edinburgh, Scotland followed. When Paul's job took them back to the U.S. in 2013, Mindy turned her hand to fiction writing, publishing a number of short stories and the Mount Moriah mystery series, which is based in part on her time working in the Pastoral Services Department of Duke University Medical Center. She now lives contentedly, eyebrows and all, in Virginia.

VERENA ROSE's story, *Death on the Dueling Grounds,* was born after lunch at the Old Ebbit Grill in Washington, D.C. An avid reader of history, Verena started researching the Old Ebbit and pre-Civil War Washington City. She is currently working on an idea for a novel featuring Zeke Wallace, Horace Kingsley, and Noah Hackett. In addition to this new venture of writing, Verena works full-time as a tax accountant, and is the long-time Chair of Malice Domestic, an Editor of the Malice Anthologies, and an Editor and Co-publisher at Level Best Books. She lives in the Maryland suburbs with her four cats and loves spending time, whenever possible, with her teenaged grandchildren.

GEORGIA RUTH lives in the storied gold mining foothills of North Carolina where she records and shares the folklore of neighbors, many of whom can trace their roots back to Wales and Ireland. Although she recently published a biography, *The Bear Hunter's Son, A True Story*, her former careers in family restaurant management and retail sales inspire endless plots with fictional characters and conflicts. Her short story, "The Mountain Top", is included in *Best American Mystery Stories 2016*. A list of her other stories is on her website: georgiaruthwrites.us

SHAWN REILLY SIMMONS is the author of the Red Carpet Catering Mysteries starring Penelope Sutherland, a chef who works behind the scenes on movie sets (Henery Press), and of several short stories appearing in different crime fiction anthologies. Shawn's first published short story, "A Gathering of Great Detectives," appeared in *Malice Domestic 11: Murder Most Conventional*. She is a member of Sisters in Crime, Mystery Writers of America, the Crime Writers' Association, and the Dames of Detection. Shawn is an editor at Level Best Books, and has been on the Board of Directors of Malice Domestic since 2003. When she's not writing and editing, Shawn enjoys cooking, running, reading, and drinking great wine. She lives in Frederick, Maryland, with her husband, son, and English bulldog.

MARCIA TALLEY is the author of *Footprints to Murder* and fourteen previous novels featuring Maryland sleuth, Hannah Ives. A winner of the Malice Domestic grant and an Agatha Award nominee for Best First Novel, Ms. Talley won an Agatha and an Anthony Award for her short story "Too Many Cooks" and an Agatha Award for her short story "Driven to Distraction." She is the editor of two mystery collaborations, and her short stories have been published in more than a dozen magazines and anthologies. She divides her time between Annapolis, Maryland, and a quaint cottage in the Bahamas.

MARK THIELMAN writes fiction and serves as a magistrate judge for Tarrant County, Texas. Mark began his legal career as an assistant district attorney for Dallas County, Texas prosecuting misdemeanor and felony cases. Among other positions, he served as Chief of the Child Abuse Unit. In 1997, Mark moved to the Tarrant County District Attorney's Office in Fort Worth where he remained until 2014. There he continued prosecuting felony offenses, including child abuse and capital murder. Born and raised in Sioux Falls, South Dakota, Mark moved to Texas to attend college. He graduated from Texas Christian University with a BA degree and the University of Texas School of Law. Mark is married to Betty Arvin, an attorney in Fort Worth. They have two teenage sons. He can be found at markthielman.com.

VICTORIA THOMPSON writes the Edgar® and Agatha Award-nominated Gaslight Mystery Series, set in turn-of-the-century New York City and featuring midwife Sarah Brandt and detective Frank Malloy. Her latest is *Murder in the Bowery*, May 2017. The characters in "The Killing Game" will be featured in the debut novel of her new Counterfeit Lady series, *City of Lies* (November 2017). She also contributed to the award-winning writing textbook, *Many Genres/One Craft*. Victoria has taught at Penn State University and currently teaches in the Seton Hill University master's program in creative writing. www.victoriathompson.com

CHARLES TODD (actually **CAROLINE** and **CHARLES**) is the author of the best-selling Inspector Ian Rutledge Mysteries, set in England's Scotland Yard just after the Great War, and the Bess Crawford Mysteries, set during the Great War; two stand alones, and the short story collection, *Tales*. Publisher: Wm. Morrow. Their short stories can be found in many anthologies as well as *Strand Magazine* and *Alfred Hitchcock's Mystery Magazine*. They have been Guest of Honor at Malice and own an Agatha, among other honors. They live on the East Coast. www.charlestodd.com and Twitter.

Best-selling mystery writer **ELAINE VIETS** has written 30 mysteries in four series. In *Brain Storm*, the first Angela Richman Death Investigator mystery, she returns to her hardboiled roots. To research the series, Elaine passed the Medicolegal Death Investigators Course for forensic professionals. *Fire and Ashes*, her second death investigator mystery, will be published in July 2017. She's written short stories for *Alfred Hitchcock's Mystery Magazine* and for anthologies edited by Charlaine Harris and Lawrence Block. *The Art of Murder,* featuring South Florida PIs Helen Hawthorne and Phil Sagemont, is her 15th Dead-End Job mystery. She's won the Anthony, Agatha, and Lefty Awards. Elaine is a former national director-at-large of the Mystery Writers of America and has served on the board of Sisters in Crime. www.elaineviets.com

62904051R00230

Made in the USA
Lexington, KY
22 April 2017